MW00352106

A Small Hotel

Hotel

A Novel

Suanne Laqueur

Copyright 2021 by Suanne Laqueur

All rights reserved. No part of this publication may be reproduced, distributed or transmitted in any form or by any means, including photocopying, recording or other electronic or mechanical methods, without the prior written permission of the author, except in the case of brief quotations embodied in reviews and certain other non-commercial uses permitted by copyright law.

Suanne Laqueur/Cathedral Rock Press
Somers, New York
www.suannelaqueurwrites.com

This is a work of fiction. Any characters, businesses, places, events, and incidents are either the products of the author's imagination or used in a fictitious manner. Any resemblance to actual persons, living or dead, or actual events is purely coincidental.

Book Design by Ampersand Bookery
Cover Design by Tracy Kopsachilis

A Small Hotel / Suanne Laqueur. – 1st ed.

ISBN 978-1-7372649-5-8 (paperback)
ISBN: 978-1-7372649-9-6 (hardcover)
ISBN 978-1-7372649-6-5 (ebook)

For my mother, Carol,
also known as Goldee because she is *bra som guld.*
Good as gold.

And for my dad, Bernie,
research assistant, bottomless font of trivia,
and recaller of necessary historical details.

And for Amy Burke Mastin,
whose loved ones met her at the station far too early.

Family Tree

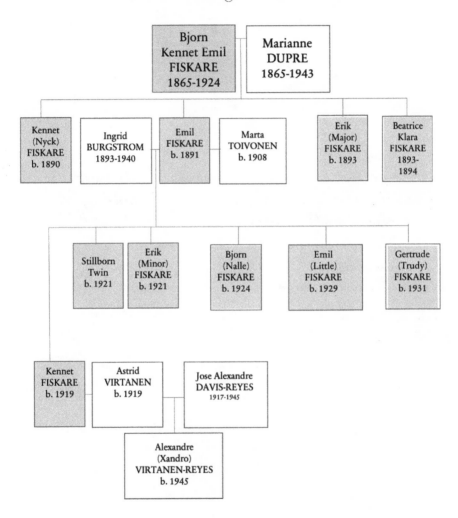

Bjorn Kennet Emil FISKARE 1865-1924 — Marianne DUPRE 1865-1943

Kennet (Nyck) FISKARE b. 1890

Ingrid BURGSTROM 1893-1940

Emil FISKARE b. 1891

Marta TOIVONEN b. 1908

Erik (Major) FISKARE b. 1893

Beatrice Klara FISKARE 1893-1894

Stillborn Twin b. 1921

Erik (Minor) FISKARE b. 1921

Bjorn (Nalle) FISKARE b. 1924

Emil (Little) FISKARE b. 1929

Gertrude (Trudy) FISKARE b. 1931

Kennet FISKARE b. 1919

Astrid VIRTANEN b. 1919

Jose Alexandre DAVIS-REYES 1917-1945

Alexandre (Xandro) VIRTANEN-REYES b. 1945

"O boating on the rivers,
The voyage down the St. Lawrence, the superb scenery, the steamers,
The ships sailing, the Thousand Islands, the occasional timber-raft
and the raftsmen with long-reaching sweep-oars,
The little huts on the rafts, and the stream of smoke when they cook
supper at evening."

—WALT WHITMAN,
"A Song of Joys," from *Leaves of Grass*

PART ONE:
The Fisherman in Love

"There's a small hotel
With a wishing well
I wish that we were there together."

—RODGERS & HART

JULY
1941

To Look at Her
with Intention

Long ago, on the shores of the St. Lawrence River, there was a small hotel.

It was built at the turn of the century and named for the family who owned and ran it: the Fiskares. *Fisk* is the Swedish word for fish. *Fiskar* is the plural. One fisk. Two fiskar. Add an E to a school of fish and you make a profession: *fiskare* means fisherman.

The river folk had no trouble pronouncing Fiskare, yet they couldn't seem to attach the surname to the new inn on Clayton's waterfront. From the start, the locals called it the Fisher Hotel. Rather than correct their neighbors, the Fiskares simply repainted the sign:

THE FISHER HOTEL

Clayton, New York

EST. 1895

Built in the shape of an L, the hotel's short end, with its double veranda, faced the river. Over the wide front steps, a large wooden fish was suspended by two chains.

"The fish was carved from wood salvaged from a shipwreck," the guests were told. "Legend says a gold coin is in the fish's belly, and Swedish tradition says wishes made on gold always come true. So touch the tail and make a wish."

Over the years, both the fish tail and the fish tale grew smooth, the varnish worn away from countless wishes and countless tellings.

On a July day in 1941, the school of Fiskares went together to meet the train from Watertown. This simply meant crossing the street, for the Fisher Hotel was situated kitty-corner to the Clayton station.

Gathered on the platform, they made a handsome clan. The patriarch, the widowed Emil Fiskare, stood with his brother, Major. Neither man was tall, but each stood straight with arms crossed, chins jutting a bit and gazes squinted over the river. When still, they seemed immutable as two pillars, but when walking, each man limped. Major had been stricken in the polio outbreak of 1894, while Emil's lame leg carried a load of shrapnel from the French front.

Emil's children clustered in three distinct groups. The youngsters, Little and Trudy, stood close to the tracks, craning their necks down the line. They had put copper pennies on the iron rails, and checked frequently on their placement.

The eldest sons, Kennet and Minor, stood together, as they always did. Kennet was twenty-two that summer, Minor two years younger, yet they were alike as twins—trim, blond and amiable with blue eyes and suntanned skin. They were not tall men either, and from their father and uncle they'd learned how to arrange their posture and demeanor so they appeared bigger than they were.

Nalle, the middle fish, sat alone on a bench. He'd always stood apart from his siblings in looks: dark-haired among their blond heads, brown-eyed against their blue gazes. It was as if every gene of the Fiskares' French-Canadian ancestors saw in Nalle a chance to survive, and swarmed his cells like ants on a melon rind.

When it came to character, the family regarded Nalle as their superlative: the smartest, the kindest, sweetest and finest. That day at the depot, he was also the saddest. He'd had a hard time of it since his mother's death, six months prior. He'd been Ingrid's favorite, and her loss shattered him. Even now he retained the air of one rebuilding from the ruins and wanting to be let alone as he did.

Standing in the middle of the Fiskares was Marta Toivonen. Not a Fiskare by blood—she'd come to them in 1931 as a cook and housekeeper, but then became so essential, she was considered family. When she told Little and Trudy to step far back from the tracks now, they obeyed instantly.

The train the Fiskares waited for was bringing Marta's cousin, Astrid, for an extended visit. This distant relative had come a long way: steamship from Rio de Janeiro to Florida, then another ship to New York City, and finally the train journey to Clayton.

Trudy came by Kennet and took his hand, dancing lightly from foot to foot. "Will she speak English?"

"Only a little," Kennet said. "But she speaks Swedish. She'll fit right in."

All the Fiskares spoke English in the world, Swedish at home, and French if they had to.

Unable to get Kennet to dance, Trudy next tried Marta, who wanted none of it. Marta was dressed in her best, quivering in both anxiety and anticipation. Excited to meet her longtime pen-pal in the flesh and eager to make a good impression.

"You'll see to the baggage?" she said to Kennet and Minor.

"Of course," Kennet said cheerfully, as if she hadn't asked four times already.

"Don't forget to tip the porter."

"Marta, we've been meeting trains since we could walk," Minor said. "We know how it's done."

"I know, but—"

"You want everything to be just right," Kennet said. "And it will be."

He kept his voice calm, though his heart kicked up a few beats when he heard the muted blare of the train's horn in the distance.

Astrid was coming.

It was ridiculous how Kennet's nerves crackled at her imminent arrival. After all, she was nobody to him. They'd never met. She lived on the other side of the earth. What he knew was from stories Marta told, bits Marta read from Astrid's regular letters, and two photographs displayed in the sitting room. For ten years, Kennet had been walking past those photographs, often for no other reason than to note how Astrid's eyes followed him.

One picture was Astrid at age twelve, sitting in a chair, composed and serene, a faint smile touching one corner of her closed lips as her gaze broke the fourth wall of the frame. The other photograph showed Astrid, dazzling at eighteen, turned almost entirely away from the camera and looking back over her shoulder. A wide, toothy smile this time. Infectious, anticipatory joy in her eyes, as if the picture were taken moments before she entered a ballroom. Like her younger image, her gaze broke through the flat plane of the picture frame and laid a hand on the viewer.

I know you, she seemed to say.

Sometimes Kennet came to look at her with intentions. When he was befuddled with a problem, smarting with rejected affection, feeling like a chump or raw with the grief of missing his mother, he stood before young Astrid and stared into her calm, compassionate gaze until he felt better. When he successfully sorted a problem, or his ardor was reciprocated and he felt accomplished, confident and pleased with himself, he took his deeds to the young woman and basked in her praise. Sometimes, if his mood was especially proud, and he was sure no one could see, he put his back to the picture, then looked over his shoulder, mirroring Astrid's pose.

He'd ask silently: *And what do you think of that?*

He liked to imagine that Astrid's eyes crinkled just the tiniest bit, along with her nose.

I knew you could do it, she said to him. *I know you.*

It was silly, but he rather liked knowing that wherever he went, whatever he did and however he felt, Astrid was watching. Astrid's back was against his and every now and then they'd look over shoulders at each other, smiling with a shared secret.

Now, after ten years of such covert and stupid games, Astrid was coming. She was an actual, honest-to-God *person* and she was actually, honest-to-God coming to Clayton. Kennet was finally going to meet her. See her. Talk to her.

He felt exhilarated, as if standing on a precipice with a panoramic view of the world. His life lay spread out before him, but one step toward it could result in a screaming spiral down to death.

Minor yawned, which Kennet took personally. He knew he was being a boring romantic, or a romantic bore. He didn't need his smart-aleck brother's clairvoyant confirmation right now, thank you very much. He'd gone far out of his way to keep his little infatuation with Astrid a strictly guarded secret. It was the kind of thing Minor loved to pounce on and tease to shreds. He was always exposing Kennet's musings for the maudlin crap they were, but never more so than when Kennet was musing about a girl. In that regard, the devilishly handsome Minor was a curse. He only had to glance in a girl's direction to win her besotted attention. If Minor detected a mere whiff of feminine intrigue coming off

Kennet right now, with Astrid mere yards away, he'd open the throttle on his irresistible charm and ruin everything, the bastard.

The whistle of the train, closer this time, made Kennet's stomach coil. He had no idea why he felt this absurd way, any more then he knew how he could look at Astrid's photograph and feel like he *knew* her. But he did. And when she arrived, he might discover it was all a bunch of hooey and Astrid didn't know him from a pebble on the sidewalk, nor would she even want to.

And might *is being mighty generous about it, fat-head.*

It wouldn't be the end of the world, he thought. But when a fellow carried a little story in his fat head for ten years, crafting and embellishing and, on occasion, comforting himself with it, you couldn't blame him for being reluctant to see it end. Kennet knew he'd probably built Astrid into something akin to a movie star: both knowable and untouchable at the same time. She played a role he himself had scripted, always saying and doing the right thing, acting according to his direction. On the silver screen, today would end like *Sleeping Beauty,* with Kennet kissing the dream into reality.

It won't be anything of the kind, he told himself. *You're going to shake hands and help with the baggage. And if the past is any indication, she'll fall in love with Minor and pine for him the whole visit.*

Bastard.

"Why are you looking at me like that?" Minor said, raising his voice above the approach of the train.

Kennet blinked. "Like what?"

"Like I owe you money."

"I'm just mad at you for something you haven't done yet."

"You and everyone else."

The train was pulling in. Time seemed to slow down for Kennet Fiskare, whose feet inched a little closer to the edge, the book of his life opened below, a licked fingertip poised to turn a page.

The story either begins today or ends today, he thought.

Like a dragon, the train hissed out a cloud of steam. The station agent set out his little step. Marta moved forward, peering along the windows of the passenger cars. Emil and Major Fiskare followed, hats in hand, each favoring a leg.

Trudy waved at everyone and no one. Little stuck his hands in his pockets and moved closer to Nalle, which he did when he was feeling shy. Nalle ruffled Little's head and smiled a sad smile.

"Ready?" Minor said, dropping his cigarette and stepping on the butt.

Have at me, Kennet thought, regarding the hulking, snorting train.

Time, already slowed, began to pull apart in places, stick together in others, as if Kennet were trying to simultaneously participate up close and observe at a distance. A girl began to descend the steps, reaching gloved fingers to the station agent's proffered hand.

It's her.

Astrid, slender as a church spire in a pale blue dress. Laughing as she hugged Marta. The wind off the river blew the skirt of her dress into swirls. She held the crown of her hat down with one palm as she turned to shake hands with Emil, then with Major. She bent from the waist to extend a hand to Trudy, rose a bit to shake with Little, then straightened all the way up to be greeted by the tall Nalle. Nalle tucked a hand under her elbow and led her toward Kennet and Minor.

Children of hotel proprietors are trained from birth to welcome strangers and put them at ease. Kennet had an array of polite conversation at his disposal, but as Astrid Virtanen came nearer, he felt all of it dissolve and drain away. He had no script. The pages of his book were blank.

"This is my brother, Minor," Nalle said.

Minor sighed. "I have a first name, you know." He put out a hand. "I'm Erik Fiskare. So nice to meet you."

Kennet seethed behind a smile. Minor rarely, practically *never* introduced himself by his proper name. Not unless the person was special. It was happening already. Minor's undefeatable good looks and charisma would win the day. They always did. It was over, and Kennet was about to slam the book of his life shut when Astrid turned to him, looking up from beneath the brim of her hat, which she still held by the crown.

The curls waving around her ears were blonde, but Kennet knew that already, from her picture. Under smooth, arched brows, her eyes were grey. He hadn't known that.

Something—perhaps his mother's exasperated spirit from beyond the grave—made him put out a hand and say politely, "I'm Kennet Fiskare."

Her gloved hand went into his and the pretty smile she'd given Minor turned into something to rival the sun.

"I know," she said, looking him full in the face.

They went on shaking hands, and while Kennet had no immediate plans to move from this spot, he knew if he did, Astrid's silvery gaze would follow, just as her photograph's eyes tracked him from a frame.

She was here.

She saw him.

And she knew him.

Kennet turned a page in his heart, stepped from the edge and began the fall into love.

A Swell Dame

Kennet's mother, Ingrid Fiskare, had never been a beautiful woman. Nothing was displeasing about her appearance, but nothing about it was memorable. She was tall and angular, more function than form. Hair of no particular color, not quite blonde, not quite brown (she herself used the word *råttfärgat*: rat-colored). Her eyes were a rather uninteresting, pale shade of blue, with no variation or depth, and framed by thin, almost unnoticeable lashes. Her mouth had the unfortunate habit of resting naturally in a downward curve. When she smiled, it was a tall smile that showed more gums than teeth. Handsome was the most generous term one could use for Ingrid Fiskare and even Kennet, who was a stickler for picking the right words and considered *handsome* to be a masculine term, had to agree.

Kennet observed all the mothers he knew, analyzed, compared and contrasted, and got a few things straightened away in his head. Ingrid was smart, shrewd, practical, frugal, industrious, generous and a host of other admirable adjectives that made her a pillar of the community and made the Fisher Hotel the heart of Clayton. Ingrid was not, however, outwardly affectionate, and her expression seemed completely devoid of any spontaneity or humor. She didn't romp with her children or tease them, didn't kiss and hug Emil, at least not in Kennet's sight. Ingrid didn't even joke around with other adults. Her laughter always seemed carefully measured out, as if she had only so many chuckles allotted per day.

Kennet loved her. But he often wished she were *softer*.

"Your mother's a swell dame," Major Fiskare said, one day in 1928 when Kennet was nine and Minor was seven. "When it comes to marriage, looks don't mean bushwa."

"How do you know?" Minor asked. "You're not even married."

Major snorted. "I don't have to be hitched to know when a chick is berries."

Much to their mother's despair, Kennet's and Minor's vocabulary was peppered with words they'd learned from Major, who called wonderful things darb, swell, hotsy-totsy, jakes, the cat's pajamas, or—Kennet's particular favorite—berries.

Everything Major did was berries. How he looked, how he dressed, how he lit a cigarette. How the rolled-up sleeves of his shirt showed his ropy forearms and their down of golden hairs. How he nonchalantly turned his hand to check the time on his silver wristwatch. (Wristwatches were a piece of men's fashion that became popular after the war, but people said, "That Fiskare swell was wearing one before the Armistice was signed.")

Most berries of all was how Major talked.

When he wanted a kiss, he said, "Give me some cash."

"You're pulling my leg," he said, when he didn't believe something.

"Tell it to Sweeney," he said, when he thought someone was pulling his leg.

He said, "I'm going to iron my shoelaces," instead of saying he going to the bathroom.

"Bullshit," he'd say in masculine company. "Bushwa," if ladies were present. He referred to ladies he liked as chicks, dames and dishes. Men he liked were eggs and birds and cats. If Major *really* admired a man, he said, "That fellow knows his onions."

If Kennet and Minor were good, Major called them pals. But if annoyed with his little nephews, Major would call them punks. Kennet tried to know his onions and not be a punk. While he loved his father with the unquestioning faith of water being wet and sugar being sweet, Kennet secretly believed the sun rose and set on his handsome and wild uncle.

"Major, why don't you get married?" Minor asked. "You're always surrounded by a bushel of tomatoes, why don't you pick one?"

Major grinned. "I'm too busy. Besides, I'm like the Lone Ranger. Apart from my drinking, smoking and colorful language. Anyway, we're talking about your mother, who's a fine lady. A little severe, maybe, but… Well, look at her face when she's around Nalle. You can see her whole heart in her eyes."

This was true. Whenever a crack formed in Ingrid's stern, Scandinavian facade, letting a bubble of spontaneous joy escape, it was usually for four-year-old Nalle. He was her favorite. Everyone knew it and no one begrudged it. After the difficult, dangerous birth of Minor and his stillborn twin, every doctor in Clayton, Alexandria Bay and Watertown told Ingrid she was done having children. Nalle proved them wrong.

"She brought that boy home like he was an Olympic gold medal," Major said. "I'll never forget the day because it was the first and only time I heard Ingrid swear."

Kennet and Minor nearly fell over. "You heard her *what?*" They crowded the arms of Major's chair like two news reporters after a scoop. "She said a swear? What? What did she say? What?"

Major blew smoke at the rafters of the porch. "Oh, I never tell tales out of school, my little fish."

The nephews begged, cajoled, wheedled their uncle and finally bribed him with their stash of penny candy. By his own admission, Major was a sucker for a sucker.

"Now tell us," the boys demanded.

"Well," Major said, carefully unwrapping a Tootsie roll. "She was sitting on the porch with Nalle. And I sat down by her and lit a cigarette, gave her a smile and said, 'Well, my dear, Doc Jensen's eating a big dish of crow tonight.' Jensen was the one who couldn't shut up about how she'd never have another baby. Anyway, Ingrid didn't blink an eye or turn a hair as she said, 'That quack can kiss my ass.'"

"Tell it to *Sweeney*," Minor cried. "She did not."

"I don't believe you," Kennet said, trying to shape his mother's voice around the words. It was like trying to put a coat on a snake.

"Sure as I'm sitting here," Major said around the bulge of chocolate in his teeth. "Swearing *and* slang in one sentence. Telling you, pals, I laughed so hard, I fell off the porch." He jabbed the two fingers holding his cigarette at the boys. "Marry a dame like that, hear me? One who doesn't take bushwa from anyone. A dame who surprises you when you least expect it."

Ingrid thumbed her nose at the doctors and easily had another baby in 1929, a boy they named Emil, whom everyone called Little. Then came the Crash, and life got very different in Clayton. Not right away. The Crash happened in October (an event young Nalle took literally, spending weeks looking for pieces of whatever thing had *crashed*), after the Thousand Islands' season had ended and the hotels and summer homes closed up. Nothing seemed terribly amiss that winter and spring. But then summer came and the closed hotels on the islands didn't open again. People didn't return to their cottages. Kennet, who was eleven in 1930, became aware of a growing sense of unease among the adults in his world. His parents looked grim as they went over their ledgers and papers. No amount of candy could get the worry out of Major's face. In the Fisher Hotel, more and more rooms stood empty and idle, and there was less mail for Kennet to sort into pigeonholes. Trains rolled through Clayton and only a few travelers stepped from the passenger cars, but dozens of rumpled, disheveled men hopped furtively from the freight cars and gathered around the depot, looking for work, for food, for anything.

But the seriousness of the Crash didn't truly sink in until 1931, when Ingrid revealed she was having another baby. Kennet distinctly remembered being told when both his youngest brothers were on the way, and the air of celebration and happiness. Now, Ingrid's voice was dull as she shared the news. As if announcing it would rain horse manure for the next year and a half and there was nothing anyone could do about it. Emil just leaned an elbow on the table with his mouth shut up in a palm.

"Maybe it'll be a girl," Minor ventured.

Nobody said anything.

"Or twins."

Emil's whole face disappeared into his palm and Ingrid whispered, "Minor, *please,*" her voice cracking around the edges.

"There's an art to keeping your mouth shut, punk," Major said testily to his nephew, and Minor's eyes filled with tears.

Nalle got up from his chair and went around the table to Ingrid. His finger pushed at the deep furrow between her eyebrows. "Don't do that," he said, a little desperately. "Ma, stop. I don't like when you wrinkle…"

That got Ingrid to smile, but only a little. The wrinkle smoothed out, but then it reappeared. The warm, pleasant kitchen suddenly felt cold and oppressive and Kennet found it hard to breathe. Something was wrong. If a baby on the way wasn't joyful… If Emil was hiding his face, and Major was snapping at Minor, and not even Nalle could cheer Ingrid up, then something was very, *very* wrong in the world.

Ingrid's fifth pregnancy nearly killed her. At long last, she had the daughter she always wanted, but at a price. Her body took long to recover. Her spirit even longer. She couldn't nurse Trudy, and was both mortified and terrorized by the thought of feeding her infant an unnatural, suspicious and expensive substance called *formula*. Every other week she was sure Trudy was developing scurvy or rickets, or otherwise suffering needlessly due to her failure of a mother. The added financial stress and anxiety chiseled away what little strength she had. All up and down the St. Lawrence, the hotel business was dying. Times were terrible, money was tight, but something had to be done. Ingrid could no longer manage alone.

And so Marta Toivonen came to the Fisher Hotel in 1931, inquiring within about the sign in the window reading *Help Wanted: Cook/Housekeeper.*

The hotel desk clerk sent Marta to Major Fiskare in the bar. Major sent Marta to the marina to talk to Emil Fiskare, who directed the woman to his house behind the hotel, where Marta should talk to Mrs. Fiskare.

"Just rap on the kitchen screen door," Emil said. "Follow the sound of the shrieking."

Indeed, the scene in the kitchen that day was one of utter con-fusion. Kennet, now twelve, had his hands over his ears and an eye on his mother, who stood by the sink with the baby. She just stood there. Doing nothing. She ought to have been blowing her stack. Instead, she looked like she'd given up. And if Ingrid had given up, little hope was left in the world.

Kennet spied the woman at the screen door just before she raised a fist and gave three quick raps. She held his eyes through the mesh and called, "Hello?"

His hands holding his head together, Kennet only stared.

The woman's gaze narrowed, then she came in, plump and neat in a print dress and straw hat, a handbag beneath her elbow. "Mrs. Fiskare?" she said.

"That's me," Ingrid said, as if she wished she were anybody else.

"I've come about the job," the woman said. "I'm Marta Toi-vonen."

Her speech was tight and precise, as if all the words were packed into the front part of her mouth.

A little curiosity came into Ingrid's face and her chin tilted. "Toi-vonen is a Finnish name."

"Yes, ma'am. Born in Finland, lived a bit in Sweden."

"But your accent sounds British."

"I spent most my life in England." As Marta took in the kitchen's chaos, her face betrayed no emotion. Kennet still had his fingers dug in his hair. Minor had a bloody nose. Nalle had a hacking cough. Little had wet his pants. And the baby, Trudy, wailed with the red-cheeked pain of new teeth.

"I haven't started lunch," Ingrid said faintly.

"I see," Marta said, and put down her handbag. She assessed the damage and went for Minor. "Let's sort this first. Sit down, ma'am, you look fit to topple." She pinched the boy's nose and tilted his head back, then addressed Kennet. "What's your name?"

He told her.

"You look like a smart young man. I bet you know where ice is."

Kennet got her some and followed her direction to wrap it in a clean dish towel.

"And who are you?" Marta asked her patient.

"Edik," Minor said through his pinched nose.

"Erik," Kennet said, puzzled. Minor rarely, almost never introduced himself by his proper name.

"We call him Minor," Nalle said between coughs, "because we have an Uncle Erik, too."

"Cover your mouth, dear."

"We call our uncle Major," Minor said thickly.

"Is that right?" Marta said. "I spoke to a Major Fiskare in the hotel, but I thought it was his rank."

"He's Erik Major. I'm Erik Minor."

"Keep your chin up, dear. Now hold the ice like that and pinch with your other fingers. No, like this. There's the way. Now then…" Her efficient gaze settled on the unfortunate Little. "And what's your name?"

"Emil," he said, just as Kennet, Nalle and Minor answered, "Little."

"See, our father is Emil, too," Nalle said.

"And we can't have another Minor," Minor said, puffing out his blood-spattered chest. "So we call him Little Emil. Or just Little."

"I see," Marta said.

"My real name is Björn," Nalle said. "But our grandfather was Björn. It means bear. Nalle means little bear."

"Then why don't we call *him* Little," Little complained.

"Because I'm bigger."

Marta smiled at Little. "No matter your name, it's no fun sitting in your spent pennies, now is it?" She took him by the hand and asked the table, "Is there a bathroom downstairs?"

Kennet pointed.

"Now be a gentleman and fetch us a dry pair of trousers? Underpants and socks, too, please."

Kennet ran into the hall and hit the stairs, scrambling with hands and feet, not wanting a miss a minute of the action. When he returned, Ingrid was washing up Little in the bathroom and Marta had Trudy perched on her wide hip, stirring something hot in a mug. She put the steaming cup in front of Nalle.

"Drink that down, now. It'll feel good on your throat. Give me those wet clothes, ma'am, and sit down. Catch your breath." Still holding Trudy with one arm, Marta put a cup of coffee in front of Ingrid. "Milk and sugar, hope that's all right." She took the clean clothes from Kennet. "Thank you, dear. Here, Little, straight back in the loo with you. Ma'am, not to be disrespectful, but do you keep a bit of whiskey for cooking?"

The two women regarded each other and Kennet, who was old enough to know Clayton was dry, tasted the unspoken words and the complicit understanding.

"Top shelf of that cabinet," Ingrid said, pointing. "Way in the back. The bottle says vinegar, but it's Kentucky Tavern. Kennet, go get her the stepladder."

Kennet held the baby while Marta retrieved the whiskey. He went on watching, fascinated, as Marta confidently opened drawers and cupboards and found what she wanted on the first try.

"How did you know where the cups and glasses were?" Nalle asked.

"Why, they were right where you'd expect. Most women organize their kitchens the same way. We can walk right in and help each other. Isn't that right, ma'am?"

"Yes," Ingrid said. Her expression was a little more composed, but her whole upper body still seemed clenched.

Marta poured some whiskey into a glass, dipped a finger and rubbed it on the baby's gums. Then she dumped the rest of the booze into Ingrid's coffee cup. "Waste not, want not."

All at once, everyone and everything could breathe again. Ingrid's shoulders came down from her ears. Trudy didn't stop crying, but the volume of her lament was halved. Nalle stopped coughing. Minor stopped dripping. Little stopped complaining. Kennet pulled his school books toward him and picked up his pencil again.

"There we are," Marta said, giving the baby back to Ingrid. "We can hear ourselves think. Now for lunch. I saw the vegetable gardens out back. Are they for hotel use or family?"

"Both. And you're hired."

"For the afternoon," Marta said. "We'll discuss it more when we've had a bite."

The Harvey Girls

"…And this is my room," Trudy said, leading Astrid by the hand around the upstairs hall. "It has two beds because my friend Kirsten stays over a lot."

"Kirsten's practically our sister, too," Little said. "Her mother died and her dad's a fisherman, so he's always away. Her only other relatives are in Syracuse, so she just stays here."

"I see," Astrid said. "I love your collection dolls, Trudy."

"Little and Nalle share this room across the hall. It's the biggest, but they can't see the river from their windows. Here's our bathroom."

"We just had it fixed up," Little said. "We had to get a whole new tub. The old one had a crack."

"Look, it has a shower head attached to the wall," Trudy said. "You can take a regular tub bath, or you can stand up and wash. Now over here, Kennet and Minor are in this room. They're oldest, so they have the best view."

Minor turned around from his dresser mirror where he'd been combing his hair. "We do?"

"Apparently," Kennet said. He was leaning on the doorframe, watching the guided tour.

Astrid smiled at him, her arms stretched out long as the youngsters pulled her toward the other side of the landing.

"Paps sleeps in here," Little said, opening the master bedroom door and quickly closing it again. "But it's private. And along this way is our guest room."

"We wanted you to stay in here," Trudy said. "But Marta said it was more proper for you to stay in a room at the hotel. Because you're a lady."

Astrid was standing in the doorway of the guest room, a hand on the jamb. She looked back over her shoulder at Kennet. A perfect embodiment of her photograph, right down to the shared joke in her eyes. But in vivid, gorgeous color. Blue dress, blonde hair, grey eyes and red lips.

Kennet smiled back and died a little.

"Well," Astrid said. "I'll have to tell Marta that *this* lady would rather be in a home than a hotel."

Which seemed to Kennet both an exciting and horrifying prospect. Astrid living in this family space for the next month, doing intimate bedroom-y and bathroom-y things right alongside him. A sudden vision of her in the bathtub, wet head rising above a souffle of bubbles. He swallowed hard and ducked back into his bedroom to hide the blush in his face, before remembering Minor was in there and Minor never missed a thing. He went back into the hall, standing stiff and awkward like a coat rack, ridiculously resentful of the immediate claim his youngest siblings had staked on Astrid's attention. They were leading her toward the attic stairs, up toward Marta's room.

I need to talk to you, he thought, eyeing the seams of Astrid's stockings as she began to climb the stairs. She looked back at him a moment.

I know, her gaze said. No joke in her eyes now. Just a promise.

"Come on, Astrid," Trudy called. "You have to *see.*"

Watching the high-heeled shoes disappear up the stairwell, Kennet wondered if Astrid would see Marta's bedroom and somehow know it was the place where it all began.

But of course she would know.

She had to know.

"Marta's going to *live* with us?" Kennet said.

"Yes, at a reduced salary in return for room and board. Now take these towels up to her, please."

Ingrid had a way of saying *please* that indicated all discussion was over. Kennet took the stack of towels and climbed the stairs to the house's third floor. Half of it was a dusty clutter of stored junk, but the other half was a large, airy bedroom with gable windows overlooking the river. It had a small adjoining bathroom that all the Fiskares made use of. It was a cozy place to iron your shoe-laces, as Major would say. If you were laid low with a stomach ailment of some kind, you could upchuck in peace and privacy. (*Upchuck* was another of Major's expressions, and Kennet appreciated its terse accuracy.)

Now this attic space, which Kennet associated with storage, solitude or sickness, would be occupied by Marta Toivonen. What would she make of it? He paused in the open bedroom doorway and softly knocked on the jamb.

"These are for you," he said, holding out the towels.

"Oh, clever boy," Marta said. "Thank you. Just put them down anywhere."

Kennet set the stack of towels on the corner of the bed. Marta had put an orange scarf over the lampshade, which made all the room's corners and edges soft and dreamy. A portable gramophone on a chair played the Andrews Sisters. A cigarette burned in an ashtray by the open window. Marta was dressed in what looked like men's pajamas, with another scarf tied around her pin-curled hair and knotted in the center of her forehead. She was tacking a large map to the wall between the windows, and paused to smile at him over her shoulder.

"You can have a look around," she said. "We'll be seeing much of each other, and nothing like a peek in someone's room to get to know them."

Kennet kept his hands politely behind his back as he peeked. Marta had pulled a second chair close to the bed, and on it was a small Bakelite radio, an even smaller clock, magazines, and a mysterious black leather box with rounded corners.

"What's this?" he asked.

Marta tucked her cigarette in the corner of her mouth, came over and fiddled with the box. It popped open like a surprise, revealing itself to be a camera.

"My prize possession."

"Holy smokes," Kennet said.

"It's a VPK Series Three. Bought it used. Still, I had to give up ice cream, film magazines and going to the pictures for a month to save enough." She raised the camera to her eye and pointed the lens at Kennet. "May I?"

He nodded, yet stepped back involuntarily, as if the machine were poised to take his soul.

"Don't be shy," she said. "Lean against the wall with your shoulder. Right there. And put your hands in your pockets. Now don't look at me, gaze over toward the window, like you're thinking deep thoughts. That's how singers and movie stars do it. Lovely. You look just like Bing Crosby. Hold still…"

A whirring click.

"Now look at me."

Another click and the camera came down, Marta smiling broadly behind it. "There now. When you're famous, I'll be able to tell everyone I took your picture."

The cigarette was still clamped between her lips and sporting an inch of ash. She wasn't a pretty woman, but Kennet was already half besotted with her accent and her brisk speech.

"Cripes, I'm about to spill on the rug and your Mum will have a fit." Marta handed him the camera and got to the ashtray just in time. Then she picked up a small box of thumbtacks and rifled through their colored tops as she went back to her map.

"What are you doing?" Kennet asked.

"Marking the places I've lived." She crunched one tack into Finland. "I was born here, but the Russians took over when I was still a baby. So my Pa moved us to Sweden." She pushed another tack into the map.

"Do you speak Finnish or Swedish?" Kennet asked.

"A little of both, and neither very well." Her fingers pinched another tack out of the box and hopped westward from Sweden, over to England. "From the time I was four, I lived here. In Cheshire."

"What did you do?"

"Do? Grow up and work my fingers to the bone on my Pa's dairy farm." She shuddered. "That's a miserable existence. Never cared much for beasts and I'm not all that keen on cheese. And running a dairy business means being so relentlessly hygienic, you may as well be a surgeon." She lit another cigarette. "It got better when I learned to cook for forty farmhands. I'd rather do that all day than muck out cowsheds."

"Did you go to school?"

"Of course. Wasn't much good at it. Never managed any levels or a leaving certificate. Then Pa had real bad luck when foot-and-mouth came through in nineteen twenty-three."

"What's foot-and-mouth?"

"Bloody nasty disease for livestock. Gives them blisters in their mouths and on their feet. Some of them go lame. The farm started to fail, so my sister and I figured we'd try to find a better wage." She took another red pin and skimmed it across the Atlantic Ocean, back into the familiar territory of New York State, finally pressing just off the shore of Lake Erie.

"You know Jamestown?" she asked.

"Farfar lived there when he first came to America."

They smiled at each other, as if discovering they were long-lost cousins, and in that moment, Kennet thought Marta was *berries*.

"Lots of Swedes in Jamestown," she said. "We had some relations there, and they gave us a base. I worked at a hotel for a bit, but in housekeeping, not cooking." She sniffed, as if recalling a bad smell. "But then guess where I went?"

Kennet couldn't imagine. His few trips to Canada and his one sighting of Niagara Falls paled in comparison to Marta's journeys. Her life was a transcontinental adventure while he'd been nowhere and done *nothing*. His eyes jumped to the other side of the country, looking for the most absurd, improbable place, and he poked a finger in the skinny panhandle of Idaho.

"Oh, get away," she said, laughing. She pressed a pin into Texas, kitty-corner to where the state's outline made a sharp right angle. "Slaton, Texas."

"Why'd you go there?"

"I answered an ad in the paper. The Fred Harvey Company was advertising for young women to be waitresses in Mr. Harvey's restaurants. He built eating houses all along the Santa Fe railroad and he wanted nice girls to wait on the customers. It was just my ticket: work in a restaurant and see a bit of the country."

She fetched a small scrapbook off her dresser and turned its thick pages. "Here we are. Rattle of drums, fanfare of horns. Ladies and gentlemen, the Harvey Girls."

Kennet peered at the photograph of seven women, posed in the arched entryway of a flat-topped building. All dressed in identical black dresses with white aprons, all standing sideways with a hand tucked into the apron's pocket. Marta was at the center of the line, her smile the widest and most welcoming. Her shoulder thrust a hair forward. Her chin lifted a tad more.

"It was strict as boarding school," Marta said. "Your skirt couldn't be more than eight inches off the floor. Black stockings at all times, even in the roasting summer. No chewing gum. No cigarettes. No makeup. Hair in a net. Yes sir, no sir, the customer is always right, sir. Lights out at ten-thirty."

"Did you like it?"

Marta stubbed out her cigarette. "I liked that I wasn't afraid to try. I liked eighteen dollars and fifty cents a month, plus room and board. That was a bloody fortune, and I sent a lot of it home to Mum. I liked the other girls. I liked some of the regulars—railroad men and salesmen we got to know by name. And I liked Texas for a while, until I realized Texas wasn't for me at all."

She told him about the glaring sun and the incessant wind. How it blew your thoughts into a scramble. How it shortened your fuse, tried your patience and occasionally made you feel sad when you had no reason to be.

"How long did you stay?" Kennet asked.

"A year. You had to sign a contract to stay on the job a year. You forfeited half your pay if you broke the terms. So I stuck it out, got another red pin in the map and headed back to New York." Her fingers rattled in the box, then pushed a red tack into the middle of New York, where the Great Lakes scratched across the topography. "Ithaca was a treat. There's a lovely Finnish community in the Great Lakes. I worked as a cook on a farm for a year. Chickens this time, not cows. And finally..." She picked out one last red pin and pushed it along the northern border of New York, where Lake Ontario narrowed into a thin blue line and became the St. Lawrence River. "I ended up in Clayton."

Kennet lifted the VPK Series III to his eye and gazed at Marta though the viewfinder. "Why'd you come here?" He hoped it didn't sound rude. He was all at once unspeakably glad she'd come.

One of Marta's hands touched the scarf bound around her hair and the other clutched at the lapels of her pajamas. "Young man, don't you dare click that shutter."

"I won't."

"Never take a picture of a lady without her permission."

"I won't. I promise."

"I came here on holiday. I had some money saved and my chum Carole said it was a lovely place. Neither of us had a vacation in years, so we went all-in. Took the train from Syracuse, booked a room at the Fisher Hotel. I saw the sign saying 'help wanted' in the window. I told myself if it was a nice stay and a nice town, and if the sign was still in the window at the end of the trip, I'd inquire within. I spoke to your Pa—he's ever such a nice man—and he sent me over to the house to talk to your Mum."

Kennet had still been gazing at her through the camera. He'd always enjoyed his status as the eldest child, but now wondered if having a smart, worldly, slightly bossy older sister wouldn't have been such a bad thing. He lowered the camera and smiled deep into his cheeks.

"And here you are."

"Here I am."

He carefully pressed the camera back down into its case and handed it to Marta. "I haven't been anywhere really. Except Canada."

"That's somewhere."

"I know, but it's right...*there.*" He gestured vaguely toward the windows and the river. "I can get in a boat and go there any time I want. I haven't taken a trip like you. I haven't been on a journey."

"You will." Marta held up the box of tacks. "Tell you what, all the green tacks in here? Those are for you. When you grow up and start making trips and journeys, you'll send me postcards and I'll put the pins in the map."

"What if you don't work here anymore?"

"We'll be pen-pals. I love writing letters. I write regular to all my girlfriends from the Harvey House, and my Mum and my sister. And my little cousin, Astrid. You wait—your Pa will have to paint your mailbox red when all my correspondence starts coming in. So what do you say? We'll be pen-pals. Deal?"

"Deal."

They shook on it, then Marta looked at her wristwatch. "Am I keeping you from chores or homework or bedtime?"

"One of those," he said sheepishly.

"Then vamoose." She grinned. "I learned that word out West."

The visit had been satisfying as a piece of cake. On the way out the door, Kennet stopped dead, his attention seized by a picture on the dresser. A photograph of a girl. Not just a girl but a... *girl.* She was perched on a high-backed chair, feet neatly together, hands folded in her lap. Rendered in black and white, her blonde beauty was dazzling as the sun on the river. Sharp and keen, like the blade of a sword.

Kennet took two steps sideways and the girl's eyes followed him. He backtracked and her gaze followed.

It's you, he thought, not knowing what he meant. He leaned out of the picture's periphery and she kept looking at him.

I know you, said the faint smile around her lips.

"Who's she?" Kennet said. He didn't touch the picture. He didn't dare even point at it, lest the girl's sharp looks cut him.

"That's my little cousin," Marta said. "Astrid. She's about your age."

The look Kennet gave Marta was bewildered, hovering on the edge of accusatory. How could she have been chatting away about trips and journeys, about hair nets and Texas and cows, all the while this picture, this *girl* was in the room with them? Marta crossed her arms and her chin tilted, as if she understood.

Kennet swallowed hard and looked once more at the photograph. Why didn't Marta say so? Why didn't she *tell* him?

"Tomorrow, pet," Marta said. "I have lots of stories and we have lots of time."

A Match to the Side

During lunch on the afternoon of Astrid's arrival, Minor followed Kennet's gaze across the table to Astrid and back again. Then he smiled, but not a teasing smile. A *wily* smile, accompanied by a deliberate wink. That night, when he and Kennet were dressing for dinner, Minor opened his closet and pulled out a blue collared shirt.

"Here."

"What's this?"

Minor hooked the hanger on Kennet's finger. "It's called a shirt. Wear it."

Kennet frowned. Minor had a natty wardrobe, but he shared it with the same reluctance with which he shared his first name. "This is your favorite."

"I know. Don't spill anything on it or I'll kill you. Are those the best shoes you got?"

"You know they are."

"Go shave, for crying out loud. You look like the wild man of Borneo."

"What are you up to, Minor mine?"

Minor cast his eyes to the ceiling and shook his head. "I'm helping you. Go. Scrub your fingernails."

"Yes, mother."

He felt sleek and fine with Minor's best shirt on his back. Not that it mattered, because he barely got a word with Astrid during that first dinner.

The Fiskare children knew two kinds of evening meals: grand dinner or nursery supper. The latter simply meant eating in the kitchen, while grand dinner was on a level with Thanksgiving or Christmas or other momentous occasions. Like the company of a beautiful, thrilling cousin from Brazil.

The dining-room table was set with the best china, roses from the garden and even candles. Johnny MacIntyre had come—he was Major's oldest and closest friend and long considered one of the family. Scotch-Irish to the bone, he was a tall, powerfully built man, save for his left arm, which was withered and lame. He'd been crippled in the same polio outbreak that struck Major. Their friendship had taken root in sickness, blossomed in recovery, and flourished in a shared determination to shatter expectations. Now in their late forties, they were a pair of twined oak trees, each man's strengths compensating for the other's weaknesses.

"Now tell us, my dear," Major said. "How does *en skandinav* end up in Brazil?"

Kennet smiled, recalling his own skepticism. When Marta first took a blue thumbtack and pressed it into the map in her bedroom, just beneath the eastward bulge of South America, Kennet was sure Marta was pulling his leg. Brazil evoked images of tropical birds and palm trees, and that didn't fit at all with his idealized narrative of Astrid as a winter princess, dressed in a fur-lined hood, riding in a sledge drawn by a white bear.

No boy likes his idealized narratives about girls altered.

"Were you born in Brazil?" Johnny MacIntyre asked. Growing up with Major had made him nearly fluent in Swedish.

"No, in Finland," Astrid said. "But we fled for Sweden when I was still a baby."

"Fled what?" Little asked. "The war?"

"You could say it was a little private war inside the great war. Finland had just gained independence from Russia, but the Finns couldn't agree how to run the government. So they were at odds with each other, then Russia came to fight on one side and Germany on the other."

"As if war and influenza weren't enough," Marta said. "Honest to goodness. Men and their wars. Put women in charge of the world and you won't have all this nonsense."

"Our queen hath spoken," Emil said.

"So you ran away to Brazil?" Trudy asked Astrid.

"Sweden first. I lived there until I was six. Then we moved to Brazil."

"It was nineteen twenty-four," Marta said. "I remember the year exactly for two reasons. First, because my parents talked of nothing else. How my uncle had fallen in with some crazy movement with the idea to make a utopia on the other side of the world."

"What's a utopia?" Little asked.

"A perfect society," Astrid says. "Like a paradise. Where everyone lives together and shares everything and all is equal peace and prosperity."

"Communism without the state suppression," Major said dryly.

Marta shrugged. "I don't understand it any more than I understand Bolshevism or socialism or any other 'isms.' My aunt and uncle made up their minds and they packed up, booked passage and went."

"Is that right?" Emil asked Astrid.

Astrid smiled and patted her cousin's arm. "Just as the queen hath spoken."

"Oh, get away," Marta said.

"What's the second reason you remember the year?" Emil asked.

"It was right around the time my sister and I were deciding to make a go of it in America," Marta said. "The idea of leaving home and being on our own across the Atlantic scared me stiff, but I thought to myself, *Well, if little Astrid can leave home and sail across the ocean to Brazil, I can do the same. Maybe she's scared stiff, too. I'll write her, and we can be brave together.*"

"Thus started the great correspondence." Astrid glanced at Kennet. He was living for those little looks she kept flicking his way. "Which outlasted the utopia."

"Trouble in paradise?" Johnny said.

"Almost immediately." Astrid told how coffee crops had depleted the soil of the land the Finns bought. They managed to craft and cultivate a network of small vegetable gardens, but nothing near what it would take to make the community self-sufficient.

"At which point, some Finns left," Astrid said.

"All the way back home?" Emil asked.

"Some did. Others went to Rio or São Paolo. My mother wanted to go back to Europe but my father had fallen in love with the land and was determined to make something of this little colony. I don't think she ever forgave him." She looked quickly around the table. "You mustn't tell her I said that."

"She's coming here?" Trudy asked.

"Yes. In three weeks. So no tattling."

"Fish never tell tales out of school, my dear," Major said.

"I can vouch," Johnny said. "You need a secret kept or a body buried, you call the Fiskares."

Astrid said the Finns who resettled in Rio and São Paolo told their story to locals. Brazilians became interested in Penedo—the little piece of Finland transported to South America. They started coming to see the colony on weekends.

"My father was the first to open a boarding house," Astrid said. "And of course he put in a sauna."

"What's a sauna?" Little asked.

"It's a little room, or sometimes an outbuilding. It gets heated up with hot rocks and steam and you sit in there. It's like taking a dry bath."

"You just sit in there and be hot?"

She nodded. "You sweat out all your troubles. Finns are mad for them. A Finnish house wouldn't have a sauna any more than it wouldn't have a roof. Anyway, turns out all the posh Brazilians were mad for them, too. Soon they were coming up to Penedo in droves, like it was a spa resort. They'd spend a weekend immersing themselves in Finnish culture and taking saunas."

"Gee whiz."

Astrid leaned toward Little with a conspiratorial air. "Everyone's mad for something. To the point where they'll pay for it. Oh, thank you," she said to Major, who was holding out his cigarette case.

She took one and Kennet reached for his lighter. Among so many useful things, Marta had taught him how to properly light a lady's cigarette. Whenever he struck a match or flicked his Zippo, he always heard a tiny echo of her brisk, instructive voice, admonishing him to hold the flame still while the lady leaned in. Never to blow out a match, but shake it to the side and wave the smoke away.

Kennet held the flame steady and still as Astrid leaned in. Her fingertip touched his wrist bone, just once, lightly, then she leaned back and exhaled. Her smile went around every chair.

"I'm so glad I came," she said.

"Well, we're delighted to have you," Emil said.

The rest of Astrid's first week in Clayton, Kennet barely got a minute with her.

I need to talk to you, his eyes begged.

I know, her gaze replied. *Soon.*

He tried to be patient, give everyone their chance. It was easy to be magnanimous about Marta monopolizing her cousin. He was truly happy about their reunion. It was everyone else elbowing their way in for a piece of Astrid's pie that irritated him. Major chatting her up in the bar as he made before-dinner drinks. Emil buttonholing her over dessert. Trudy and Little were completely besotted, and now Kirsten Lund had joined the junior fan club, dragging Astrid this way and that to show her the best Clayton had to offer. Even Nalle shook off his black armband of melancholy because he suddenly needed to pour his life story into Astrid's lap.

Astrid was enthusiastic, attentive and interested. Or one hell of an actress. Kennet hadn't decided because nobody was giving him a goddamn turn, only snatched minutes here and there. Still, they'd been memorable minutes. Like when he found Astrid in the sitting room, examining her own photographs on the little table by Marta's armchair.

"Isn't it funny," she said. "Finding yourself in a house you've never been to. I walked right past these pictures and stopped short. *Wait. That's me. Here I am.*"

"Here you are," he said.

She set the photograph back on the table. "Tell me. Who is this?" She pointed to the sepia photograph of Björn Fiskare on the mantel.

"My grandfather. People called him the Old Bear."

"Is he alive?"

"No, he died right after Nalle was born."

She stepped closer, arms crossed and head tilted a little. The Old Bear stared down at her, dignified and unsmiling. "Do you remember him?" she asked.

"My first memory is of him. Sitting in his lap, playing with the fish on his chain. See?"

The photograph of Björn was cropped beneath the vest of his suit, and Kennet's fingertip touched the chain arching from one vest button to the little pocket where Björn kept his watch. Off the chain hung one large fob shaped like a fish, and four smaller fobs, also fish.

"A jeweler made the big fish as a wedding present. And then each of these little fish when a child was born." Kennet's finger touched each one, naming them. "Uncle Kennet. He's oldest, and I'm named after him. Then my father, Emil. Then Major—his real name is Erik. And this last fish is Major's twin, Beatrice. But she died young."

"Oh dear," Astrid said faintly.

"I loved to sit in Farfar's lap and play with those fish. Especially the big one. It was made in sections and it could wiggle back and forth." He brought his pointing finger down from the mantel and looked at his palm. "I remember when I was done playing with it, my hand would smell…like gold, I guess. Just a funny metal smell lingering on my fingers. I liked it."

Now Astrid reached a finger and drew a little soft circle in Kennet's palm. She looked up at him and smiled. "Bra som guld."

Good as gold.

A shiver ran over Kennet's skin, and his toes curled tight in his socks.

"Dinner's ready," Marta called from the next room.

"Tell me more later?" Astrid said.

He nodded. He wanted to put his palm to his nose and inhale the scent of her touch. He put the hand in his pocket instead, and with the other, gestured toward the dining room.

Like a Gentleman

The Fisher Hotel's first touring boat was called the *Marianne*. Björn built her in 1905—a narrow, single-deck wooden craft with open seating. As the tourism industry boomed around the Thousand Islands and vacationers clamored to see the sights in both fair and poor weather, Björn converted the *Marianne* to a covered boat. He and Emil built her sister craft, the *Marianne II*, with an enclosed cabin, and business doubled. The crown jewel of the little fleet was launched in 1919: the *Marianne III*, with her closed, covered cabin, working glass windows and, luxury of luxuries, her built-in washroom.

Marianne was retired now, shut away on sawhorses on Grennell Island. The *II* and *III* docked at the hotel marina, along with the family's personal boats. The two Erik Fiskares always berthed their Gar-Woods side by side, the *E-Major* and the *E-Minor*. Nalle, the little bear, called his Chris-Craft *Melissa*, which meant honeybee.

Astrid looked around the marina, a hand shading her eyes. "Little doesn't have a boat yet?"

"Not until he's sixteen. It's the rule."

"Rule of the house, or rule of the river?"

He grinned down at her. "Both."

"And will Trudy get a boat?"

"Of course. She'll probably divide ownership with Kirsten. Those two share everything."

"I don't quite understand the situation with Kirsten." Astrid glanced down the street, at the rest of the family approaching the marina. "I don't want to put my foot in my mouth, so can you explain in thirty seconds?"

"Kirsten's mother died when she was four. Her father had made a mint smuggling booze from Canada, then lost it all. When his wife died, he lost his mind. Went on a crackerjack bender that..." He shook his head, a keen eye on the little girls, who were now running ahead of everyone. "That's better off unspoken," he said. "Long story short, my mother took Kirsten in until Charlie Lund pulled himself together. He found work fishing off the coast of Maine. He comes home every few months. Sends money in between. A letter if he can be bothered to put two words together. I don't know. I don't have much good to say about Charlie. Sometimes it seems Kirsten's just one of his bills to be paid."

"Or maybe he feels like he failed her," Astrid said. "And he's better off out of her life."

"Maybe."

"Where's your boat?"

He pointed to his Baby Gar. Across its stern, in black letters, read *Hildur*.

"Hildur?" Astrid said. "Like Hildur, the queen of the elves?"

"You know that story?"

"Of course. She's a queen, but she's cursed to live on earth. She can only return to the elven kingdom for one night a year, but at the cost of a human life. And the curse won't be broken until a human can prove who she is and where she's been."

"That's right."

She crossed her arms and looked at him sideways. "After what Major said about keeping secrets and burying bodies, I'm rather intrigued by you naming your boat for her."

There was no more time to discuss—Trudy and Kirsten came pounding down the dock, seized Astrid's hands and pulled her toward the *Marianne III.*

"We're not done talking about this," Astrid called over her shoulder, looking just like her photograph.

If you only knew, Kennet thought.

"She's a bit of an all right," Minor said. He sat up with Kennet at the wheel of the boat, while everyone else gathered with Astrid in the cabin, pointing in all directions at every passing item of interest along the river. A spirited, show-offy free-for-all, nothing like the smooth, practiced commentary that Kennet and Minor had been reciting to customers since they were sixteen and allowed to give tours.

Minor jostled Kennet's leg. "I said, she's a—"

"I heard you the first time. Yes. She is. Now be quiet."

Minor put two cigarettes in his mouth and curled away from the wind to light them. He passed one to Kennet, then settled back, relaxed and confident, the wind lifting his hair into yellow and gold waves.

Regarding his brother, Kennet's already tangled thoughts made a new snarl. Minor had come in late last night, waking Kennet out of a sound sleep. Tip-toeing into their shared room, shoes in hand, Minor slid out of his clothes without a sound—not a jingle of a belt buckle, not a soft thump of fabric on carpet. Like liquid he slid into his bed. No creak, no thump, no rustle. He was *assumed* into the bedclothes, disappearing into sleep, leaving Kennet wondering if he were having a lucid dream of some kind. Or worse, wondering if Minor weren't here at all. He was dead. This was his ghost laying himself to rest.

Kennet sat up on an elbow and whispered, "Mine?"

No sound.

"Erik?" The proper name was always foreign in his mouth. Like a word in Chinese or Hungarian. But it worked: the lump of sheets and blanket stirred.

"Shh," Minor said. "Go to sleep."

But Kennet lay awake, breathing the air between their beds and pressing it to the roof of his mouth. A strong scent was coming up off Minor's discarded clothes. Artificially fragrant, but too stringent and piney to be a woman's perfume.

This morning, the brothers were bashing around each other in the bathroom, elbowing and hipping at the sink as they washed and brushed and shaved.

"You using aftershave now?" Kennet asked casually.

"Nah. It stings my delicate face."

It was then Kennet noticed little bruises on his brother's upper arms. Small, delicate ovals lined up on Minor's biceps. A couple more clustered on his sides, above the towel wrapped around his waist.

"Who've you been wrestling with?" Kennet said.

Minor spit out a mouthful of toothpaste. "What?"

"Must've been a hell of a match. They left fingerprints."

Minor looked over his shoulder, twisted an elbow. Then shrugged. "The rich hold their money tight and their lovers tighter."

Kennet hitched one side of his butt onto the vanity and crossed his arms. "Who is she?"

Minor rinsed his foamy lips and tossed his toothbrush into the water tumbler. "Fish never tell tales out of school."

He wiped his mouth on the hem of Kennet's undershirt and sauntered out.

"You're looking at me like I owe you money again," Minor said, bringing Kennet's thoughts back to the boat and the present.

"I'm looking because you're a dish."

"Yeah, well…" Minor crossed one knee over the other and picked the knife-edge crease of his trouser leg into place. "I'll take the wheel if you want to head back and press your suit."

"In that crush? Forget it. I'll wait it out."

"Don't wait too long. I think Nalle is falling in love."

Kennet's head whipped around to scan the cabin. Minor laughed heartily, for of course, Nalle was sitting apart and alone, communing with the river.

"Made you look," Minor said.

"Son of a bitch."

"Don't talk about our mother that way."

"Who's your new girlfriend?" Kennet asked, thinking he could startle an answer out of his brother.

No such luck. Minor only smiled and drew pinched fingers across his lips. His reticence was admirable, considering he'd started out as a boy who talked first and considered the consequences later.

Major's story about Ingrid calling Doc Jensen a quack was a delicious thing. Kennet could go for *months* on a tale like that, sucking on it like a piece of penny candy, drawing out the flavor around the edges and making it last. He didn't need verification that it was true. Keeping it tucked in his jaw during the times when Ingrid was particularly stern or humorless was enough for him.

Minor, though, was a cat murdered by curiosity. He was hopeless at savoring things in the silence of his heart. The tale was irresistible. He couldn't stand it. He had to know. And on a morning when Major had joined the family for breakfast, Minor blurted: "Ma, did you really call Doc Jensen a quack and say he could kiss your ass?"

Emil spewed half his cup of coffee over Nalle in the high chair. Major went pale and stood up so fast, his chair went over backward. Fork in hand, a napkin still tucked into his collar, he ran for the kitchen door, narrowly missing the swat of Ingrid's hand as he passed her chair.

"You big-mouth fool," she cried after him. Then she collected herself and washed Minor's mouth out with soap. The whole while, Emil hid behind a newspaper, lips pressed together tight and little choked, wheezing noises sneaking out his nose, like stifled sneezes.

Over the racket at the kitchen sink, Kennet leaned close to his father and whispered, "Did she?"

Emil's red face went redder and he nodded, not meeting Kennet's gaze. "You make me laugh and I'll use you for bait."

Kennet thought the whole thing hilarious. Minor, not so much. A mouthful of Lifebuoy was the least of his problems.

"Major's really mad at me," he said to Kennet, kicking stones along the river.

"He'll come around," Kennet said comfortingly. "He always does."

"I don't know. I think I really stepped in it."

"Did you apologize?"

"I tried." Minor was a portrait in misery. "I brought him my whole box of candy. He didn't even look at it. Just yelled at me.

I mean he really *hollered*. Said there was an art to keeping your mouth shut and I was probably too stupid to ever learn it. Then he slammed the door."

Kennet winced. A door banged shut on both your apology and your candy seemed the worst thing that could happen to a fellow. Minor's whole face was clenched up. Kennet hadn't seen his little brother cry in a long time, but he was pretty close to tears, and it made Kennet feel desperate. Minor was always so devil-may-care when he got in trouble. Now he looked like a bleeding cut and the whole world was iodine. Kennet recognized the attitude—he felt that way whenever he displeased or disappointed Emil. But where Kennet seemed to learn lessons quickly and course-corrected for the next excursion, Minor just couldn't help sailing straight into bad weather.

Minor was always in trouble, either for the door of his mouth being loose on its hinges, or an utter disregard for rules and social niceties. Growing up, Kennet had watched Minor pull fabulous pranks at the hotel with a fascination equal parts horror and admiration. It was Minor who put baby Nalle in the dumbwaiter and hauled him up and down between floors. Minor who dropped toys down the laundry chute and when that got boring, tried dropping himself. (He took the plunge from the ground-floor linen closet, when the metal chute was an angled slide and not a death drop— Minor was a daredevil but he wasn't stupid.) Minor filched pairs of men's shoes left outside rooms at night, shined them himself and pocketed the tips. He turned *Do Not Disturb* signs to the *Maid Please Make Up Room* side. Tall for his age, with a flair for the dramatic, he dressed up as a waiter and delivered bottles of champagne (stolen from the bar) to rooms occupied by couples. Or he brought breakfast trays to rooms occupied by single ladies, hoping to catch them in their underwear.

Sometimes, he got away with it. Most often, he got caught, the penalty for which was *få sina fiskar varma*—getting your fish warm. And with the same mix of dread and appreciation, Kennet watched Minor get the business end of Ingrid's wooden spoon or, when they were older, be summoned to the pantry to be strapped by Emil.

Minor neither sulked over the hidings nor learned from them. He didn't pretend he didn't care—five whacks of Emil's old razor strop on your butt made you care deeply about your misdeeds. But Minor seemed to treat it all as a game, and what was more, so did Emil.

When Kennet was called on the carpet or bent over the sugar barrel to take his due, Emil always looked grim, sorrowful, as if the old adage were true and the punishment hurt him more than it hurt Kennet. A whipping on Kennet worked the way it was supposed to, as a deterrent. Minor negotiated such punishment ahead of time. He calculated risk against loss and settled on a fair price to pay for whatever deed he'd cooked up. If he pulled it off, he pocketed his prize or the thrill and went on to the next caper. If he got caught, he went over the barrel like a gentleman, took his deserved licks and hoped for better luck next time.

More than once, Kennet had seen Minor leave the pantry, hands rubbing the seat of his pants. And staring after him would be Emil, with a little smile at the corner of his mouth, his expression both exasperated and affectionate. As if he were well aware his second son was a fresh, incorrigible, irredeemable handful, and Emil would have it no other way.

Needle in the Water

The *Marianne III* chugged east, squeezing between Wellesley Island and Fishers Landing, slipping beneath the Thousand Islands Bridge. Professional habits died hard, and though he wasn't working, Kennet's mind quietly pattered his speech.

Folks, we're in the main American channel, which is about a half mile wide. It's three miles straight north to the Canadian mainland. Further along, the river is between eight and ten miles wide.

We're approaching Alexandria Bay. On one end of the waterfront is the Thousand Island house and at the other, the Crossman House. In between you'll see the Monticello, the Marsden Inn and the St. Lawrence Inn...

He thought the river especially beautiful tonight, sparkling under the last of the sun, starting to reflect back orange and pink. The houses looked trim and pretty, waving coquettishly. The hotels and resorts bowed, dignified and handsome. He knew them all by name. He felt strongly they knew him. Clayton was his home, but the river was his *place.* With the wheel of a boat in his hands and the roll of the water beneath his feet, Kennet felt at one with the world, strong and secure beneath the title of River Rat. It hadn't been handed to him: he wasn't entitled to the epithet because he was merely born here, and first put his hand on a tiller as a tyke of three. He had to prove himself. Show he was wise and proficient in swimming and sailing, that he knew his way around a boat, from stem to stern. That he could read the water and read the skies and pilot accordingly. Handle bad weather, broken engines and unhappy guests. Most of all, that he understood and obeyed the international rules of the waterway.

The rest was just rote memorization and geography.

Directly across from the bay, you'll see Heart Island and its beautiful castle, built by George C. Boldt, owner of the great Waldorf-Astoria Hotel...

"My goodness," Astrid said, materializing at Kennet's elbow. "Look at that. It's like something out of Europe. No, don't get up," she said to Minor, who was scrambling to his feet.

"That's Boldt Castle," Kennet said. "It's a replica of a castle along the Rhine river."

"Boldt poured a million dollars into it," Minor said. "But then his wife died and he abandoned the project."

"Just left it?" Astrid said. "It's not finished?"

"Nope. It just is." Minor did get up now, excused himself and moved toward the cabin.

"Enjoying the tour?" Kennet said, strangely shy, now that he was alone with her.

"The delivery was a little chaotic," she said. "I hope there won't be a test later."

"There will, but it's true-false. You'll do fine. Here, practice question: *precisely one thousand islands make up the Thousand Islands archipelago.* True or false?"

"False?"

"Correct. One thousand eight hundred and sixty-four is the official number."

"What makes an island officially an island?"

"It has to have one square foot of land above water, all year round. And it has to support two living trees."

She pretended to write it on her hand. "One foot. Twelve months. Two trees."

Trudy came up to the helm, making Kennet wonder if he'd ever get more than sixty seconds alone with Astrid, or if he'd have to start chloroforming his siblings.

"Here," Trudy said, putting a nail into Astrid's hand. "You have to drop it overboard for Old Nick."

"Is that so?"

"Tru," Minor called from the cabin. "Come back here."

Trudy scowled. "Why?"

"I think I just saw a mermaid."

She was gone in a flash, leaving Astrid laughing. "You are all delightful." She looked at the nail in her hand. "I know this tale. Whenever you cross a river, you drop a bit of steel and say, *Nick, Nick, needle in the water! Thou sink, I float!*"

Astrid weighed the nail in her palm a few times, then tossed it over. Beneath the river's undulating surface lived Old Nick, the Scandinavian maritime devil, king of the river.

"My father called him Fossegrim," Astrid said. "Same god, different name."

"Ah, but we Fiskares have our own versions of folklore. We think of Nick and Fossegrim as two different gods."

Fossegrim was the mischievous fiddler, playing enchanted songs on the violin, seducing men, women and children with his beautiful music. He'd joke around with your soul, but meant no real harm. He was too busy with his music. Old Nick was the unforgiving deity who demanded obeisance and tribute. Kennet never went on the water without throwing a bit of metal overboard.

"We used to throw pennies," he said, "but after nineteen twenty-nine, nobody in their right mind was throwing money away. Paps said there was already enough gold in the river and Old Nick would understand. In hard times, any metal would do."

"What do you mean enough gold?"

"Well, when Napoleon was exiled, his family smuggled all his wealth out of France and sailed with it to Canada. The ship sank in the St. Lawrence and the gold was never recovered."

"Really?"

Kennet smiled. "So the story goes. My grandmother's family was French Canadian. They talked all the time about Napoleon's gold. My father and Major elaborated the legend for us kids, mixing it up with other famous shipwrecks in the St. Lawrence, all of them supposedly sunk with a fabulous hoard. So I grew up thinking the river is full of golden treasure, all of it guarded by Old Nick." He shrugged. "It makes a good tale to tell tourists."

They stood quietly a while. The sinking sun was turning some of the smaller islands to shadow, silhouetted against indigo and lavender and apricot. The skirt of Astrid's dress blew about her knees. The occasional hearty gust made the fabric caress Kennet's leg.

"When my father said Old Nick lived in the river," he said slowly, "I used to think he meant my Uncle Kennet. Everyone called him Nyck."

"Tell me, are there any Fiskare men named George?"

He laughed. "Not a chance. Every boy is doomed to be some combination of Emil, Erik, Björn or Kennet. Plus a family nickname, to make it even more confusing."

"Where does your uncle live?"

"In Montreal."

"Are you close? The way Minor is with Major?"

"No." Kennet hesitated. "No, see, Uncle Nyck lives in a sanitarium."

"Oh. Goodness."

"He fought in the war and when he came back, he was…"

"Changed?"

"Yes. His body came home, but his mind was still in France. Still fighting."

"I'm so sorry."

"It bothered me. Being his namesake but having no relationship with him."

Kennet was an observant child, and he noticed how people shook their heads when they spoke of Uncle Nyck and the war. Voices dropped into mumbles, glances went sideways and downways, and deep sighs followed.

"Uncle Nyck lived far away to begin with," he said, "plus all this sad, secretive mystique surrounded him. So I guess it wasn't such a stretch to believe he was Old Nick and lived underneath the river. That way, when I dropped pennies and nails overboard, I wasn't bribing a god. I was just giving my uncle a present."

"That's both sensical and sweet," Astrid said.

"I like everything and everyone to have a place."

"Does anyone call you Nyck?"

"Not really. Minor and I have a little joke. I'll say, 'Minor mine, you are so fine.' And he'll say, 'It ain't no trick to love my Nyck.' But that's just between us. Nobody regularly calls me Nyck. Paps calls me *gullgosse*."

"Golden boy."

"In a manner of speaking."

"Well, I can't steal his endearment. And you're definitely not a Ken or a Kenny."

He laughed. "No."

59

"So now that we're friends, may I call you Nyck?"

He looked at her. Beneath his snagged gaze, he felt the smile widen his mouth. "I'd like that."

Now that we're friends.

Kennet wasn't sure if Minor dropped hints within the family circle, but as the halfway point of Astrid's visit approached, the social dynamic shifted. The Fiskares' competitive grip on their guest loosened. They drifted away to their work, their friends, their pastimes and puttering.

After much begging and cajoling from the youngsters, Marta conceded defeat and agreed Astrid could leave the hotel and stay with the family the rest of the visit. But she insisted Astrid take her attic room with its adjoining bath.

"Don't be silly," Astrid said. "No reason for you to move out. I'll just take the spare room."

Marta lifted a foot and put it down again. "My room. Take it or leave it, cousin."

Astrid laughed, kissed Marta and moved into the attic room. Soon she was incorporated into the family's daily life: in the kitchen, cooking and washing up, or out in the garden, tending and weeding. Sweeping the hotel veranda and greeting guests. Sorting mail into the pigeonholes behind the front desk.

Kennet was busy all day—ferrying guests, running tours, making repairs to boats, tending to hotel and home business. Gradually, unobtrusively, Astrid began to accompany him. First on his morning runs, delivering the mail sacks and the first load of passengers out to Wellesley Island. Soon, she was coming along on sightseeing jaunts, either standing by him at the wheel, or mingling with the guests in the cabin. Her English still wasn't proficient, but she quickly amassed a collection of polite, chatty phrases and had a knack for looking like she was following conversation, even if she wasn't. She was best with children, easily entertaining their short attention spans so parents could enjoy the tour.

At the marina, she helped Kennet dock the boat and if he had repairs to make, she handed him his tools, asking questions, curious about everything and everyone.

"Is Johnny MacIntyre another your mother took in?"

"My grandmother, rather. Major and Johnny have been friends since they were tykes. They both survived polio."

"I see."

"Being lame kept them from doing a lot of things, so they've always banded together to do as much as possible. Major has two good arms, Johnny has two good legs. As a team, they're a force of nature."

Although some might see their friendship as unnatural, he thought.

"What's it like here in the winter?"

"Quiet. Slow and sleepy. The river has a whole different look. Summer is a showy time of year. Fall is really beautiful, when the leaves change. But winter is stark and sparse. It's still painted in a hundred colors. You just have to look harder to see them."

He'd always found it hard to articulate his love for the river, how it never looked the same two days in a row. As if every day were a gold coin counted by Old Nick. Or a song composed by Fossegrim. Or, if he were in a morbid mood, a life claimed by Hildur. Every day the river rolled along in a different look, with an endless supply of stories and songs and lives.

Astrid was looking at him.

I want to kiss you, he thought, as his mouth saved him with a question. "What's winter like in Brazil?"

"It's winter right now," she said.

"Of course," he said quickly, though he'd completely forgotten the seasons were opposite on the other side of the equator. Which made him think how she'd be going home in a couple weeks, to another country on another continent in another hemisphere. He'd put so much emotional investment into her arrival, he'd forgotten to factor any into her leaving.

"What's the matter?" Astrid said softly.

He shook his head and wiped his hands off. "Nothing, I just remembered something. This is done now. Let's go see about lunch, before the next train comes in."

They ambled up the street toward the Fisher Hotel.

"Your grandfather built the hotel?"

"He built it, but it was really my grandmother's creation. She was a woman ahead of her time. See the wing of the dining room? It used to be a ladies' tea room. Back in the eighteen nineties, women couldn't go into bars or taverns. All the ladies getting off the train and waiting for a ferry, or getting off a ferry waiting for a train, they just had to wait at the depot. Barely a place to sit, let alone have something to eat or drink. So Marianne had my grandfather build a little annex off the hotel. It was only for women and children, and only women worked there. They served tea and sandwiches and ice cream, and it was a smash."

"Is your grandmother still alive?"

"Yes. She lives in Montreal now. She has a cottage out on Grennell Island and used to come for the whole summer. But I think after my grandfather died, it just wasn't the same for her. And she hasn't been in the best of health. She only came a few weeks this year. Major's been renting her cottage out. He has a little place on Grennell, too. I'll take you by and show it to you."

"I'd like that. I like…" She stopped and turned in a slow circle, taking in Clayton's waterfront and its little downtown. "I like everything about this place. It feels good here."

"It feels good to have you here," he said. Blurted, rather, and felt foolish. But she was still looking past him, her expression thoughtful.

"You know my last name is Virtanen."

"I know."

"*Virta* is Finnish for *river*."

"Well, no wonder this place feels good to you."

"But it is a wonder," she said, putting a hand on his arm. "Rio means *river* in Portuguese. So why doesn't it feel like this?"

He had no answer. He bit his tongue to keep from saying the fish in him wanted to swim in her river. She'd slap his face.

Or maybe she'd say to come on in. The water was fine.

They'd reached the hotel and were mounting the front steps. Astrid stretched up high and touched the tail of the carved wooden fish.

South American Way

That night, the temperature dropped and it rained fish hooks and hammer handles. Undeterred, the Fiskare kids built a fire in the sitting room and brought out a box of Campfire Marshmallows. Minor was in charge of the record player—he guarded his vinyl collection even more fiercely than his wardrobe. Nalle brought down his ukulele and played along by ear. Marta was roundly beating Emil at backgammon. Major and Johnny MacIntyre dropped by. "Just for a splash," they insisted, which meant they'd park in armchairs with whiskey lowballs and stay at least two hours.

"You speak such good Swedish," Astrid said to Johnny.

Johnny flipped a thumb toward Major. "He taught me everything he knows."

"Which is why I have so little left," Major said.

"Rubbish," Marta said. "You had enough to fix my Swedish good and proper."

Major waved a hand. "I merely polished your rough edges."

"Modesty, uncle?" Minor said wryly. "Are you perhaps running a fever?"

"Kennet, tell Astrid your poem," Trudy said.

"No thank you," Kennet said.

"What poem?" Astrid said.

"He wrote a poem about Swedish when he was in school. He won a prize."

Astrid raised her eyebrows. "Was this in college?"

Kennet laughed. "In second grade."

"Recite, brother," Minor said, taking Kennet's toasting stick. "Sing for your supper."

"You all have it memorized," Kennet said, grabbing it back. "One of you recite."

"It should come from the master."

"Don't make him," Astrid said. "Poetry should be spoken voluntarily or not at all."

"Hear, hear," Major said.

Nalle, quiet all this time, put down his ukulele and stood up. He put a dramatic hand on the mantel and cleared his throat. "A Slöjd of Swedish," he said. "By our esteemed laureate, Kennet Fiskare."

"Cripes," Kennet muttered.

Swedish slurps and slurs (Nalle said)
Slip-slop up and down the slopes of speaking.
Sentences that slalom.
Or slingshot.
Slow like a sloop, then slap happy like a slipstream.
Slender. Sluggish.
Släkt.

Applause around the room and Nalle bowed before extending a hand toward Kennet. "Our poet, ladies and gentlemen."

"What a masterpiece of alliteration," Astrid said. "Have you written others?"

"No," Kennet said. "I retired at age seven and rested on my laurel."

During the recitation he'd been patiently turning his long stick over the embers until the marshmallow was a perfect golden brown. He slid it carefully off the point and gave it to Astrid. Her eyes widened as she took a bite, hand coming up to catch the bubbling white drops of melted sugar. "Oh my goodness," she murmured around the decadent mouthful.

"They taste better toasted outside," Nalle, the purist said. He still stood by the mantel, with the photo portrait of Björn Fiskare just over his shoulder.

Astrid made a frame of her sticky fingers and smiled. "Den gamla björnen och nallebjörnen."

The Old Bear and the teddy bear.

Good naturedly, Nalle shifted his pose and expression into the same formal stance as the old man.

"Start working on some mutton chops," Major said. "You'll be a dead ringer for Pappa in about twenty years."

"I was admiring the watch chain," Astrid said to Emil. "Kennet told me some jewelers in the family made the little fish especially for your father?"

"Trudy, run upstairs," Emil said. "The middle drawer of your mother's jewelry case has a small black box. You know the one. Bring it down."

It truly was amazing, Kennet thought, how easily and innocently Astrid coaxed stories and secrets from everyone in the family. She made you want to tell and show her everything.

Emil opened the box and held up one of the little gold fish from the photograph. "My brother Nyck has another of these small ones, along with the watch chain itself and the large fob at the end."

"Because he's eldest?" Astrid said, holding the fish up to the light.

"Well that, and because he married into the deWrenne family, who are the jewelers. His descendants will be good stewards of the heirlooms and appreciate their worth."

"And Nyck deserves them," Major said quietly, addressing his drink more than anyone else.

"Where's your fish?" Astrid asked him.

"Put away safe. And my mother has the fourth fish." Major reached to tug one of Trudy's braids. "This rascal will inherit it someday. Our sole surviving daughter in two generations."

"And well worth the wait," Emil said. He tipped another little charm out of the box and showed it to Astrid. "My father left this to me. Not sure why, but it's pretty. As far as heirlooms go."

It was a square saint's medal, also wrought in gold.

"It's Saint Birgitta," Astrid said. She turned it around and over, and read the engraving on the back. "B.K.E.F, 1865."

"Probably a christening present," Major said.

"Commemorating the last time a Fiskare stepped into a church," Johnny said.

"Quiet, you."

Astrid handed the charms back to Emil and thanked him for showing her, then accepted another toasted marshmallow from Kennet.

"Asta, where did you go to school?" Kirsten asked.

"In Penedo, until I was thirteen. Then I went to a wonderful boarding school in São Paolo. And a really terrible one in Rio."

"Why terrible?" Kennet asked. He touched his chin discreetly, signaling Astrid had a bit of melted marshmallow on her own. (*Be a gentleman if a lady needs to powder her nose,* schooled the memory of Marta's voice. *Don't make fun, don't make a fuss. Just quietly make it known.*)

Astrid smudged her chin and smiled her thanks. "It was Catholic and strict and snobby. Good education, but you learned by fear. Miss one answer and you got rapped on the knuckles. Make one of the nuns mad and you knelt in the corner for an hour, holding all your books. Everyone was so nervous all the time, and nervous people can be mean people. I came home on my first holiday looking like this...." She held up her pinky finger. "All bones and exhaustion. My mother was horrified."

Trudy, sitting on Emil's lap, turned wide, solemn eyes to her father. "I don't ever want to go to boarding school."

Emil squeezed her. "I would never send you."

"How did you stand it?" Kirsten asked.

"The library," Astrid said. "I hated where I was, so I ran away to books. I did have one literature teacher who was lovely. And I made friends after a time. You learn to adjust. Still, fear is no way to make a child learn. If I become a teacher, I'll..." She trailed off abruptly, as if an unseen hand covered her mouth.

"You want to be a teacher?" Marta asked.

"Yes," Astrid said slowly. "But my mother has other ideas."

She looked at Kennet and in her direct gaze he sensed a painful subject being avoided. He asked, "What's Rio like?"

"Tell us about Carnival," Minor said.

Major looked at his nephew. "How do you know about Carnival?"

Johnny MacIntyre smacked Major's arm. "How do *you* know about Carnival?"

"What's Carnival?" Kirsten asked.

"It's the season right before Lent begins," Astrid said. "You have it here, don't you? Mardi Gras? Fat Tuesday?"

"It's more common in the South," Major said. "In states with French and Spanish colonial roots. Not so much here up north, in the land of puritanical protestant prudes."

"Pardon your alliteration," Kennet said.

"What's a prude?" Little asked.

"Someone who worries someone else is enjoying themselves," Major said.

Astrid laughed.

"What happens during Carnival?" Marta asked.

"Parties, parades, endless celebration. Lent is the penitential season—you fast, you sacrifice, you go without, you give something up. So in the days leading up to Lent, people go a little crazy. Fazendo tudo."

"What's that mean?"

"Doing everything. Everyone packs in as much fun and food and drink as possible. Celebrating to excess, because everyone is in disguise and masked. There's a saying: *por trás da máscara de carnaval, tudo pode acontecer*. Behind the mask of carnival, anything can happen."

"Like what?" Little, Trudy and Kirsten asked in one voice.

Emil gave a few pointed coughs behind his fist. "Minor, what happened to the music?"

"Coming up." Minor gave a record a spin in his fingers and laid it on the turntable. "Astrid, you know this one. Nalle, you too."

A crunchy scratch as the needle lowered, then Carmen Miranda's hit, "South American Way" came out of the little speaker. Minor turned it up and began to samba. Astrid got up and joined him, singing the Portuguese lyrics:

> *Ai, ai, ai, ai*
> *É o canto do pregoneiro*
> *Que com sua harmonia*
> *Traz alegria*
> *In South American Way*

Marta ran and got two bath towels. She and Astrid wrapped them around their heads in Miranda-style turbans. Not to be outdone, Minor joined them with a towel turban and his shirt stuffed with enough socks to make an impressive bust. He put the needle at the beginning and sandwiched himself between the women. Hips swinging, fake maracas shaking, the trio belted out another verse:

Ai, ai, ai, ai
E o que traz no seu tabuleiro
Vende pra ioiô
Vende pra iaiá
In South American Way

"Souse," Astrid said. "*Souse* American way."

"Souse," Minor repeated.

"Rounder. Sing around it, not through it. *Souse*."

Minor honked and pulled at the word while Trudy and Kirsten ran to wrap up their heads and cram their arms with bangles.

"Help me, I want big bazooms, too," Trudy said, handing Astrid some socks.

"Ah, no, there will be no bazooms," Emil called. "Big or otherwise."

"Spoilsport," Marta said.

"Ingrid will strike the house with lightning and she'll aim for you first."

Astrid tossed the socks away. "Are we ready?"

"Take it from the top, Nycky," Minor called. Kennet backed the needle up again and leaned cross-armed against the wall, a little envious as he watched the show. He had no desire to join, but he wished he could carry a tune like Astrid. Or play the ukulele like Nalle. Or dance a tenth as well as Minor.

Astrid was facing the mantel between verses. All at once she looked back over her shoulder at Kennet. A little wicked smile made her nose crinkle, making Kennet grin back and slide a hand under the lapel of his shirt, miming a pounding heart through the fabric. Astrid laughed, tossed her head back and sang:

> *No tabuleiro tem de tudo que convém*
> *Mas só lhe falta, ai, ai berenguendéns*
> *Ai, ai, ai, ai*
> *É o canto do pregoneiro*
> *Que com sua harmonia*
> *Traz alegria*
> *In* Souse *American Way*

Illegal in Summertime

Whistling "South American Way," Kennet walked into the kitchen, desperate for lunch and a cold drink. He was shocked to find Marta and Astrid at the table. Well, that wasn't the shock. What threw him was Astrid was crying, her head on Marta's shoulder, a wadded-up handkerchief in her fist. Marta had both arms around her cousin, a cheek against Astrid's fair head.

"It'll all sort out," she said. "You'll see." She looked back and saw Kennet frozen in the doorway. "What are you, the butler?"

"I'm sorry, I'll just—"

"Oh, sit down," Marta said, nudging a chair out with her foot.

"I don't want to interrupt."

"You're not," Astrid said, picking up her head.

"When two biddies have a heart-to-heart over a cup of tea, it gets emotional sometimes," Marta said. "Sit and be a biddy with us."

She lifted the lid of the teapot and frowned at the contents. "Now it's stewed." She poured some of the ink-black tea into a cup and pushed it toward Kennet. "This one," she said to Astrid, "he likes tea you can stand a spoon up in. I'll fling the rest down the sink and wet another pot."

"Don't go to any trouble," Astrid said, blowing her nose. Crying didn't agree with her. Her voice sounded thick. Her cheeks were mottled, eyes damp and puffy.

She was lovely.

And upset.

Do something, you damn fool. Say something encouraging.

Caught in the awkward zone where compassion locked horns with minding one's business, Kennet stirred a little sugar into his cup while considering and rejecting a half million overtures. Astrid squared her shoulders and gave him a wan smile.

"Homesick?" Kennet asked gently.

"Oh…" Astrid waved a hand. "I'm many things right now."

He looked back at Marta. "I think our friend needs a little Christmas."

"Brilliant," Marta said. "Just the thing."

Kennet got the stepladder and went climbing for a candy tin Marta kept in a high cabinet. Dutch blue with white lettering: *Betty Anne Creamy Mints.* Inside were cookies.

"But these are pepparkakor," Astrid said. "Christmas cookies."

"Illegal in summertime," Kennet said.

"But just the thing for the dog days," Marta said. "Especially if you're feeling down. I always make a dozen and squirrel them away. When any of us are in a pickle and there's nothing for it, we'll say, 'Well, have a little Christmas.'"

They all took one of the round, crispy cookies. Astrid held hers to her nose a moment, inhaling. Marta used Ingrid Fiskare's recipe, heavy with all the spices evoking holiday time—cinnamon, ginger, clove and orange peel.

"Now make a wish," Kennet said.

They put the cookies in the palms of their hands. This was tradition. You made a wish and pressed on the center of your cookie. If it broke into three clean pieces, your wish came true. If not, you still had a cookie.

I wish there was something I could do, Kennet thought, and pressed down. His cookie broke in half.

Across the table, Astrid looked up at him, then held out her palm, where three pieces of pepparkakor lay.

"See now," Marta said. "It will all sort out by Christmas." She checked her watch. "I've got my errands to run. Kennet, I know a cookie won't hold you, so there's cold ham if you want a sandwich."

Kennet expected Astrid to leave the kitchen as well, but she stayed, lingering over her tea.

"You could say I'm homesick," she finally said. "Being here has made me realize how sick of home I am. And sick at heart at the thought of my mother coming here."

He'd forgotten her mother was coming for the last week of the visit. After exercising such patience waiting for his siblings to get the hell out of the way, he bristled at the thought of another intruder. But aloud he only drawled a long, "Ah," as if the mysteries of the universe were solved.

He took great pains with his sandwich making, stretching out the simple task to let her talk freely behind his back. She told him that when her father died, the hotel in Penedo was doing poorly. Under Liisa's ownership, it utterly failed. Liisa sold the property, and the proceeds were enough to keep Astrid and the boarding school in Rio.

Kennet set down plates on the table. "What's your mother like?"

"She's a passionate Finn. The only thing truly Finnish about my father was his surname. He was a Swede at heart, but my mother loved her country and her culture. I don't think she was ever the same after they fled to Sweden. And when my father moved us to South America, something in Mor died. Or rather, something in her was defeated. She personified defeat and forever passed herself off as a weak and victimized woman."

Kennet wasn't surprised Astrid used *mor,* mother, not Mamma or Ma.

Liisa Virtanen suffered asthma as a child, which worsened after Astrid's birth. In between episodes of genuine suffering, Liisa used the ailment to her advantage.

"Conveniently her worst episodes occur when she's not getting her way," Astrid said. "Playing the romantic consumptive when she was in the rudest of health."

She blushed a little and shook her head apologetically. Kennet could sense how it made her feel disloyal to speak honestly of her mother.

"It's such a brutal end to your childhood idealism," he said slowly, "when you realize you love your parent because not loving them isn't an option, but you also discover things about your parent that aren't lovable."

"The stress about money is really making her sick now. But there's nobody she can placate. Her poor health won't make money appear out of thin air."

Currently, Liisa was resting in Florida before she'd make the train journey to join Astrid in New York.

"Why Florida?" Kennet asked.

Astrid paused. "We have friends who offered to host her."

This didn't add up. "Wasn't it expensive to travel all the way from Rio to Florida?"

Again Astrid's demeanor went tense and distracted. She wanted to tell more, but something had a hold on her.

There's a secret here, Kennet thought. "I'm sorry," he said. "I'm being rude and nosy."

"No, no," she said. "You're easy to talk to, but it's hard to find the words when you've never felt free to talk of such things."

"You must worry about your mother."

"I promised my father I'd take care of her." A wistful smile. "Did you promise your mother, too?"

"In a way. She was more worried about Nalle than Paps."

"Did you get to say goodbye? Or did she die when you were away?"

"I had some last moments. I sat on the floor so my head was right on a level with hers. And she told me things…" He ran fingertips over his brow. "The whole while, she was doing this. She wasn't a cuddly, petting person. Usually she only touched my forehead if she thought I had a fever. So the memory of her caressing me that way is strong."

Emotion pressed him on all sides as he remembered the gentle touch and Ingrid's serene, unblinking gaze. She was doped to hell on morphine at the end, and her words fell soft and measured, like dripping water from a loose tap. As she stroked Kennet's eyebrows, she said she was leaving him her engagement ring in her will, for him to give to his fiancée. He'd be head of the family someday, and Ingrid always knew he'd do a fine job. Her hand smoothed his hair, and she asked him to take special care of Trudy and Kirsten, and to let Marta stay as long as she wished. She closed her eyes and said she worried about Minor, because the world could be cruel toward things it didn't understand. Then she gave a tiny, loopy chuckle and tapped the end of Kennet's nose, declaring that Little was going to surprise everyone someday. Just watch.

But when she got to Nalle, tears gathered along Ingrid's sparse lashes and she couldn't go on. Now it was Kennet who reached soft fingers and touched his mother in a way he never had before. Tracing her damp eyelids, her cheekbones, the straight line of her nose and the sharp ridge of her brow.

"Kind lady," he murmured.

"Pardon?" Astrid said.

"Nothing, I was just remembering. Did you get to say goodbye to your father?"

"No, I was at school." She drew a deep breath. "I was also in a bit of a disgrace. I did something stupid."

"Oh."

"It's unpleasant to get into. The point is my father died disappointed in me. I didn't get a chance to put it right. Make it right. Which gives the promise to take care of Mor a little more weight. Do you know what I mean?"

"I'd say it gives a lot more weight." Kennet wiped his mouth with his napkin, then held out cupped palms to Astrid across the table. "Here. Let me hold it."

She smiled, laughing a little.

"I mean it," he said, wiggling fingers. "You've got lots of time before she gets here and no reason to stagger under your troubles. Give them over. I'll hold them and you enjoy yourself. And who knows—maybe when I hand them back, you won't recognize them."

She gazed at him, then reached and put her hands in his. "All right then."

Their fingers twined and squeezed as the worries changed ownership, then Astrid sat back with a long exhale and another laugh. "You know? I actually do feel a little lighter now."

"Good." He gestured toward her plate. "When you're done, you want to go for a drive with me?"

Aix-les-Bains

"I hope you don't think it weird I brought you here," Kennet said. "We kids take turns coming to tidy things up once a month. It's my month."

"Not at all," Astrid said. Hands on hips, she looked around the quiet rows of Clayton Village Cemetery. A gravel path wended around and among the rows of headstones and markers. A meadow ran along one side, waving grasses dotted with black-eyed Susans and tansy aster. Busy with dragonflies and bees.

A tall, white marble obelisk marked Björn Fiskare's resting place. At its base, a smaller white stone snugged close:

BEATRICE KLARA
Beloved Daughter
1893-1894

"She was Major's twin," Kennet said. "They both had polio in the outbreak of ninety-four."

"My God," Astrid said, touching the dates beneath the little girl's name. "Just a year old. This was your grandparents' only daughter?"

"Yes."

"I can't imagine." Her hands cupped opposite elbows, hugging herself. "Losing a child. It must just…change you. Change everything you are and everything you do."

"From what I understand, they were never the same after. It's impossible to be the same."

"I wonder how it changed Major. I mean, change who he might have been if his twin had lived. How it affected him to have half his soul taken away…"

"I'd tell you if I knew. He doesn't talk about it. Sometimes, if he's flummoxed or exasperated or just plumb tired, he'll mutter to himself, 'Oh, Bea, what are we going to do?' But that's all I've ever heard him say."

"The things a body can stand." She sighed. "I'll pick some flowers."

Kennet unpacked his shears and trimmed the grass around the stones, while Astrid made little bouquets.

"Major said your grandmother has Beatrice's gold fish?"

"Yes, but it's silver," Kennet said. "Marianne asked the deWrenne jewelers to make it so. She said silver was for a girl."

"Do you agree?"

He ran a forearm along his sweaty brow. "I wouldn't call it a universal law, but I was the kind of kid who loved to sort and label and classify things. Maybe to a fault."

"But it's such an endearing fault."

"All my life, I've thought of the most important women as silver, and the most important men as gold. For a while, I even believed my father was made of gold."

From hip to knee, Emil Fiskare's left leg was a constellation of shrapnel scars, bits of metal blown there in the Somme Offensive. As a child, Kennet was particularly fascinated with the divot in his father's thigh where, if you pressed, you could *feel* something under the skin. Something hard and tantalizing and unobtainable.

"That's a Hun's gold tooth," Emil said, straight-faced and earnest. "He blew himself up trying to blow me up. His head exploded in a hundred pieces, and his gold tooth went into my leg. So deep, the doctors couldn't get it out. Now it's mine. Finders keepers, right?"

Kennet took such a tale at face value when he was five. Later he'd cast his doubts on the story's veracity. The lump was probably another piece of metal. Still, he liked the idea that his father had a bit of gold inside. It gave bravado to his limp and lent an air of romance to his short stature, thinning hair and quiet, almost abstracted demeanor. Until Kennet could believe the gold tooth was slowly dissolving, sending its noble atoms and particles through Emil's veins.

"Which means, possibly, that I have a little gold in my veins," Kennet said. He laughed at his sneakers. "I've never told that to anyone."

Astrid sat on the grass, stretching out her legs and leaning back on her hands. "Tell me something else."

"After Beatrice died," Kennet said, "my grandmother wore the silver fish pinned inside her blouse. It made a lump over her heart and it would dig into my cheek when I hugged her."

"Like a piece of shrapnel she carried on the outside," Astrid said.

"Yes," Kennet said. "Exactly. So I decided war hurts men on the inside, and it hurts women on the outside."

"What a thoughtful little boy you were."

Kennet lay back in the grass, with his mother's gravestone casting a shadow across his face. Surely this was an odd, even macabre place to pass the time of day with a lady. Yet it was peaceful. He imagined Ingrid would enjoy the company and conversation. And Astrid, braiding her extra flowers into a chain, seemed in no hurry to leave. Still, Minor would have Kennet for *breakfast* if he found out Kennet took a girl on a date to a cemetery.

"Minor's a twin, too," he heard himself say.

"What?" Astrid looked up from her work and twisted this way and that, looking around the family plot.

"She doesn't have a stone," Kennet said. "No stone, no grave, no name. She barely had a body, so there was nothing to bury."

She stared at him, open-mouthed. "But... What *happened*?"

"I don't know really. I was only two, I have no memory of it. And like my grandparents were changed, well... You can imagine how my parents rarely talked about it."

"Does Minor?"

"Not to me. I imagine he talks about it with Major, but I couldn't swear an oath on that."

"Unbelievable," Astrid said. "Two boys named Erik, each missing a twin."

"It's said we Fiskares repeat our names and repeat our tragedies."

"Did you ever notice how Minor's profile looks different, depending on what side you stand on?"

Kennet looked at her, hands laced beneath his head, frozen in half a sit-up. He'd never *not* noticed the duality in his brother's face. When Minor turned one way, his profile was fresh, wide-eyed, interested and friendly. When he faced the other, the outline of brow, nose, lips and jaw was tentative, cautious and brooding. When Minor turned dead-on and you looked him full in the face, why, right *there* was his missing sister. You couldn't miss her in the asymmetrical, slightly diagonal arrangement of Minor's features and their mercurial shift between guarded and open.

And yet, everyone Kennet knew seemed to miss it.

Astrid saw it.

"Seems like Minor fights a war that hurts him both inside and out," she said.

I'm falling in love with you, Kennet thought.

"Nyck?"

"Hm?"

"If America goes to war, will you fight?"

"I suppose so. Minor said he'd join the Navy. Nalle wanted to join up the day Hitler invaded Poland. He was all of fifteen."

Astrid shook her head. "Nalle is so good, it makes you wonder what war he has going on inside."

"That's easy. His war is missing Ma."

"He makes me think of a word we have in Portuguese. *Saudade.*"

"Sawdust?"

"Saudade. It doesn't have a direct translation. It's an intense longing. An emotional state of melancholy and desire for things you've lost. Sometimes things you never had in the first place, but your heart believes they were yours."

"Like when people long for the good old days which really weren't all that good?"

"Yes. Or longing for a truly golden time that you know is over and will never come again. That's Nalle's saudade."

"Mm."

She rubbed her fingers along her cheekbones. "All the fellows at home talk war nonstop. They're convinced the Nazis already have a psychological foothold in Argentina and could easily make a—"

"Hey," he said, dropping a hand on her calf. "I'm a little weighed down now with a good friend's troubles. I don't have an extra arm to hold onto worries about Nazis and war. So..." He smiled and motioned toward the meadow. "Just dump them over there. They'll keep."

"You're right, it's too nice a day." She got up and draped her chain of flowers over the top of Ingrid's stone. "Is this disrespectful?"

"She'd like it. She loved flowers."

Astrid stepped back, surveying her decoration. "This will sound strange, but I like that she has her own stone. One half of my father's grave is blank, waiting for Mor. It's so morbid and…mocking, in a way. And it makes such a disgusting assumption about the rest of my mother's life. What if she wanted to get married again?" She shivered. "If I die before my husband, give me my own stone and let him go on living. If he finds love again, I won't haunt him."

Kennet pretended to write the direction on his hand. "I'll contact your lawyer immediately."

"Smart alice," she said in English.

He laughed. "Smart *aleck*."

"How did your parents meet?"

"In the war."

"What do you mean?"

"Paps was fighting and Ma was running a canteen for soldiers."

"Where?"

"She ran them all over France for the YMCA. Paris. Cherbourg. In nineteen eighteen she was stationed in Bordeaux. See, General Pershing decided he didn't want to grant soldiers leave to the big cities anymore. So he picked one place in the southeast of France, near the Italian Alps, and everyone went there on their eight-day pass. The canteen was an old casino in a town called Aix-les-Bains."

"What was there?"

"The way Paps tells it, everything was there. A theater room for entertainment acts. Another big room for movies. They put pool tables in the old gambling rooms. The ballroom was set up with booths selling candy and cigarettes, and the bar was turned into the canteen. Ma said four hundred and fifty men came into the casino every day. Three thousand men a week."

"She went to Europe alone? On her own she just…*went* and did all this work?"

"Pretty much."

"Oh, Nyck." Astrid's hands dropped to her sides. "I'm so sorry she's gone. I would've loved to hear this story from her. I would've had a thousand questions."

"You know, I didn't truly appreciate the story until Marta came to live with us. She was fascinated with how my parents met and she peppered them with questions I never thought to ask. I knew a lot of my father's war anecdotes, but I really had no idea of how important my mother's work was until she told Marta about it…"

The YMCA girls tried to think of everything and anything an exhausted, anxious and homesick soldier could want. They made a reading room in the glassed-in conservatory, pulling easy chairs into the puddles of sunshine, making sure writing paper, pens and envelopes were always at the ready. A man from Huyler's, the New York City candy and restaurant chain, came out to install a soda fountain, and soon the girls were making hundreds of ice cream sundaes, milkshakes, phosphates, egg creams and sodas. When they weren't filling the soldiers' bellies with treats, the girls were organizing dances, games, entertainment, trips into the mountains, sightseeing. If a soldier wanted diversion, he got it. If he wanted a chair in the sun and a book, he got it. If he wanted to sleep the day away, nobody disturbed him, other than to bring up a tray with a sandwich.

"And your father was one of them," Astrid said. "They met and fell in love?"

"They met in March of nineteen eighteen," Kennet said slowly. "Then Paps went back to the front and they wrote letters. Each thinking they'd never see the other again because a fellow's chance of survival was slim to non-existent. But Paps lived to see another eight-day pass, and he went back to Aix-les-Bains in June. It was springtime in the Alps. My mother was there. And she remembered him."

"It's like something you'd read in a novel," she said. "Or see at the pictures. And— What are you giggling about?"

"The surprise ending," Kennet said.

"What do you mean?"

"I was conceived in that old casino in Aix-les-Bains." He looked up at her. "I always thought it would make a great opening line for a novel. Or my autobiography."

"Well, well, well," Astrid said. "C'est la guerre, indeed."

"Yes, along with learning to appreciate my mother's war work, I also learned to count on my fingers. And I don't think Ma and Paps knew that I knew she was pregnant when they... I'm sorry, is this a crass topic?"

She laughed long and hard. "Oh my goodness, look at you. You're blushing."

He rolled on his stomach to hide his heated face. "I seem to have run out of polite conversation."

"Nyck, this is truly the best story I've ever heard in my life."

"Ma would spank me for telling her tale out of school."

"I wish I could've met her."

Cheek on his forearms, Kennet looked up at her, wishing he had another pepparkaka to wish on. "She was a kind lady," he said.

Kind Lady Lives Here

Sometime in 1933, Kennet began to notice strange, chalked marks on the sidewalks of Clayton, starting with a picture of a cat outside his own house on Hugunin Street. He and Minor and Nalle walked around their town and discovered similar marks at other houses. Like the top hat outside Dr. Tomlinson's, next to a plus sign with a circle in its upper-right quadrant. A box with an upside-down comb at the Pullmans' place. A capital T with many crossbars outside Police Chief Crouch's house.

Armed with paper and pencil, the boys hunted down the marks, carefully noting what symbol lay outside what establishment. Then they went to the one person they were sure would know what the strange signs meant.

"Ah," Major Fiskare said, regarding his nephews' detective work with an extremely serious air, which was why his nephews revered him. "These are the marks left by hoboes, as a warning to other vagrants."

"How do you know?" Minor said.

Major ruffled his namesake's head. "I asked around."

"A warning against what?" Kennet said.

Major pointed to the weird, many-times-crossed T at the Crouch home. "This means an officer of the law lives within. Best move on."

His finger tapped the box with the upside-down comb at the Pullman residence. "This means a vicious dog lives here, and correctly so."

The three boys nodded in fearful agreement, for they'd always given a wide berth to the Pullmans' nasty mongrel.

The top hat and the plus sign outside Doc Tomlinson's house meant a gentleman lived there, and a vagabond wouldn't be charged for medical care.

"And this?" Nalle asked, pointing to the cat outside their own home.

Major smiled down at his little school of fish. "What do you think?"

"Beware of mice?" Minor ventured.

"Something to do with milk?" Kennet said.

Nalle had no guess.

Major, enjoying the moment, blew a smoke ring. "It means 'kind lady lives here.'"

Kennet and his brothers walked home in contemplative silence, pausing briefly to inspect each hobo symbol chalked on the sidewalk or carved in a tree. They stopped as one before their home, gazing from the white cat up to the house and back again.

Kind lady lives here.

"Gee whiz," Minor said softly.

Times were hard. Times were frightening. People were broke and struggling. Strangers came through Clayton. Down and out, hungry, jobless, homeless. Skirting the officers of the law, avoiding the vicious dogs, they came to the Fiskares', where they were given a bit of charity by the lady of the house. A doughnut. A cup of coffee. A scrap of respect. They thanked her and moved on, but not before chalking a cat on the sidewalk outside her house, as a message to everyone who came after:

Kind lady lives here.

The Fiskare boys exchanged glances. Ingrid was famous. Ingrid was known. Ingrid was a legend. If the symbol had meant, "Royal duchess abides within," the boys couldn't have been more impressed.

An awed wonder squeezed Kennet's chest as he went inside and heeled off his shoes in the hall, looking around his home as if seeing it for the first time, with the newfound knowledge that *kind lady lives here.*

He stood in the kitchen door, watching Ingrid wash dishes at the sink, her back to him. Little sat at the table with crayons and paper. Trudy sat in a blanket-lined orange crate, cozy and contained, sucking on a Zwieback and banging a set of tin measuring cups. Every now and then, Ingrid made an O of her fingers and blew soap bubbles at her daughter, who laughed when they stuck to her hair.

A warm, golden scent emanated from the oven. The big soup pot bubbled on the stove, along with the coffee pot which was always filled. Next to the stove lay two rows of upside-down cups, and a plate of doughnuts, covered with a clean dish towel.

Kennet was a gangly fourteen, walking the line between boy and man and always falling onto the wrong side of things. He hadn't been a demonstrative child, and became even less so as he entered his teens. But now he came up behind his mother, slid clumsy arms around her waist and set his brow against her shoulder. He breathed in her lemon scent, reveled in her famed reputation, and loved her terribly.

She made a little laugh in her chest. "Nalle-bear, where have you been?"

"No, it's me," Kennet said.

He felt the surprise in her body as she turned abruptly, breaking the belt of his arms. "Goodness," she said. "What's the matter? Do you feel all right?"

"I'm fine," he said.

Her damp hand brushed his brow anyway. "What is it?"

"Nothing."

He was sad that she thought he'd only come to her this way if he were ill or in despair. Sadder that it was his own doing. "I just wanted to hug you," he said, wishing he could explain better. Wishing he could tell her how proud he was to be her son. How humbled he was by her fame. How important her coffee pot, cups and plate of doughnuts were at a time when jobs were scarce, money was tight, brows were constantly wrinkled with worry, and strange men knocked on doors looking for anything to get them through.

Kind lady lives here.

Kennet stood on the sidewalk outside his house, looking down at the white cat.

Astrid took his hand. "Do you still have those troubles of mine?"

With his free hand, he patted his pocket. "Safe here."

"I'd like to tell you about them." She squeezed his fingers. "But I'm afraid you might not like me afterward."

"Why, did you murder someone?"

"No."

"Burglary? Embezzlement? Espionage?"

"Nothing as clever as that."

"Then you're stuck with me liking you."

She didn't answer, only went on looking at him with her silvery eyes, moving him to put his hand on her face and stroke her cheek.

"I do like you, Asta," he said softly.

I think I might love you.

She turned her head and kissed the heel of his hand.

"So," he said, "is this a walking conversation, a driving conversation, or a boat conversation?"

"It's a bar conversation."

The World Wasn't
Enough

For the first fourteen years of Kennet's life, the bar at the Fisher Hotel was closed in compliance with Prohibition. When the ban on booze was lifted in 1933, Kennet still wasn't allowed in the bar without permission—Ingrid's ruling superseded the Constitution—which of course made it a tantalizing and irresistible place. Dark and masculine with mahogany wood, the high stools with the spinning seats, the long mirror reflecting the lines of liquor bottles. Low, deep murmurs of conversation punctuated by boisterous laughter. Sometimes the radio turned to a ball game or a boxing match. Cigarette smoke and beer. And holding court behind the bar, Kennet's beloved uncle.

No doubt Ingrid understood the allure, for she kept her kitchen dry and when she needed bourbon for a pecan pie, or sherry for a sauce, she dispatched a well-behaved son into the inner sanctum.

"Well, look who's come to have a drink with us," Major would call. "Kennet, we thought you'd never get here."

Caught between shyness and the desire to be one of the gang, Kennet would shove his hands in his pockets and keep eyes on Major as he approached. "Ma needs a little whiskey for cooking."

"Sure she does," Major said with a wink. He'd fill a shot glass, then take one of the bar's square napkins and fill it with maraschino cherries, twisting the ends together. "Share those with your posse. And here's for you, sourpuss." And he'd hand Kennet a wedge of lime. Like Kennet, Major preferred sour to sweet, and if Kennet had been able to linger, Major would've poured him a little bubbling glass of quinine water to go with the lime.

When Kennet turned eighteen, Major brought him into the bar for some serious lessons on consumption and etiquette. Kennet learned the subtleties of distilled liquor and how to properly pull a draught of beer. How to order drinks for himself, for a lady, for a group of friends.

"Nobody likes a sloppy drunk," Major said. "Fiskare men have no heads for booze, so know your limit and stay within it. If your date is getting soused, all the more reason for you to keep a clear head. Nothing funny about a drunk woman, and a fellow who takes advantage or worse, leaves her to fend for herself, is a fellow who doesn't know his onions."

Major mixed a plethora of cocktails that might appeal to his nephew's sour palate, and a gin rickey with two limes ended up being Kennet's preferred splash. He now brought two of them over to the little table tucked into a window alcove, where Astrid sat. When she reached for a cigarette, he had a match at the ready. He held the flame still, then shook it to the side and waved the smoke away.

"Skål," she said, raising her glass.

"Skål." They clinked and drank.

"I don't want my mother to come to Clayton," Astrid says. "I'm terrible, I know."

"You are berries."

"I want this place to myself. I want this to be my memory alone." She leaned to looked out the window. "If I lived here, I'd never want to leave."

"Could you?" he asked. "Stay, I mean. If not here, then somewhere else?"

She shook her head.

"If I can be blunt, is your family broke?"

She nodded.

"What's going to happen when you go home? If the financial situation is as bad as you say, how will you and your mother survive?"

"Marry rich," she said quietly. "It's an old trope. But effective."

Kennet's stomach tightened but said nothing, only gave a curt nod and lit his own cigarette, thinking he should've known the past couple weeks were too good to be true.

"When Mor gets here," Astrid said, "she's going to speak as if I'm engaged to be married. I am not. At least, not officially."

Now Kennet's chest caved into his shoes. He wanted to slam the rest of his drink in one go, but managed to sip slowly with another cool nod.

"Why don't you buy another round?" she said quietly. So he did, and brought back a little bowl of salted nuts to go with the liquid courage.

"You look so troubled, I can't stand it," he said, sitting down. He put out his cupped palms to her. "Tell me everything. I'll hold what I can."

"I told you when my father died, I was…" Her hand turned over in the air. "What's the English slang for being disgraced?"

"You were in the doghouse."

She exhaled a plume of smoke. "Well, whatever the expression, long story short, I did something stupid. My father pulled me out of the boarding school I loved in São Paolo, and sent me to that miserable Catholic school in Rio, where I could mend the error of my ways and find a suitable husband. Then my father died, so I was expected to find a rich, suitable husband." She squeezed her eyes shut. "It's such a cliché. Honestly."

"Tell me about him. What's his name?"

"Jose Alexandre Davis-Reyes. We call him Zé." Her eyes were bright and she took a fortifying swallow of her drink. "I can't paint him as the villain in the story. We've been close a long time. He was the first friend I made in Rio. He helped turn things around for me. Helped me lift my head up and look in the mirror again. He was there when I got the news my father died."

Kennet passed her his handkerchief. He felt similar to the way he felt when Astrid's train pulled into Clayton—like he was standing on the precipice of his entire life. Except this time, it was her life as well, spread out before him like the open pages of a book.

You have a stake in this story, he thought. *Cliché or not, take what's written here seriously. Take what she puts in your hands and hold it carefully.*

He pushed emotions to the side, lit more cigarettes, and listened.

Zé Davis-Reyes was born in Washington, DC, the son of a Brazilian diplomat and an American mother. His father had been personal secretary to Joaquin Nabuco, the first ambassador from Brazil to the United States.

Zé's mother was a Davis, of the Philadelphia and St. Petersburg Davises. Her uncle, the publisher F.A. Davis, founded the city of Pinellas Park on the Gulf Coast of Florida.

"So those are the 'friends' in Florida," Kennet said. "Where your mother is staying right now."

Astrid nodded. "Zé's family has a house on Snell Isle. They divide their time between Brazil and the States."

"Is Zé in publishing, too?"

"He works for Assis Chateaubriand at Rádio Tupi."

The names meant nothing to Kennet, but radio, damn, that was something. Radio was the soundtrack of Kennet's life. Not just music but news, stories and sports. Nothing was anything until you heard it on the radio.

He almost envied the guy.

"You want another drink?" he asked.

"No, I'll fall out of my shoes. Just something soft."

She went to powder her nose, and Kennet asked Major for two quinines.

"Everything all right?" Major said, garnishing the drinks with lemon and lime. "You two look like you're plotting murder."

"We are," Kennet said.

"Excellent. Can I assist?"

"We have it under control, but we may need some bodies buried later."

"You know where to find me."

Astrid came back, and it was as if intermission had ended and the curtain went up on a new act.

"So your mother considers you officially engaged," Kennet said. "You do not. What does Zé officially consider you?"

"He wants to marry me," Astrid said. "His family wants it, too. But Zé isn't stupid. He knows my mother's motivations. He hasn't officially proposed and he won't until…"

"Until?"

She explained it was Zé who insisted Astrid take this trip, before they entertained the idea of getting engaged.

"I've never been anywhere," she said. "Sailing from Sweden to South America was the most momentous journey of my life and I don't even remember it. Before this summer, I'd been from Penedo

95

to São Paolo to Rio and back. Every other journey I took was in a book. I wanted to see something of the world."

"I know the feeling," Kennet said, envisioning Marta's great map of the world and her little box of tacks, all the green ones waiting for him. All the places he hadn't been yet.

Zé arranged Liisa's sojourn in Florida so Astrid could travel alone a month.

"You asked if it was expensive," she said. "I don't know. Zé paid for this trip." She put up a cautionary finger. "And *not* as a bribe. He made it clear. This wasn't, 'I'll give you this chance to see the world if you marry me.' He said, 'I'll give you this chance to see the world *and,* then, see if you want to marry me.'"

She sighed. "Even with it made clear, I didn't like the idea, but Nyck, it was my only chance. Not just to leave Brazil but to go across the equator to another continent. See America. And see Marta, because she's always epitomized my idea of an independent, traveled woman. A woman who made her destiny instead of waiting for things to happen to her."

"Marta wasn't saddled with a manipulative mother," Kennet said without thinking. "Cripes, that was rude. I'm sorry."

"It was accurate."

"You deserve more than a marriage of convenience."

"I wish it were that easy."

"It is. You're not a pawn. You're not a piece of property."

"Nyck, please."

"You're a person, not a term of negotiation."

Her hands went to fists on the tabletop. "I *know*, but..."

And all at once, all the pages in the book of her life were laid out before him. He could read the story as easily as his own. As if it were his own.

"You promised your father," he heard himself say. "And you're a lady of your word. Your father meant the world to you. He loved books and poetry. He loved being a host and giving travelers a haven. He made sure you were educated and could learn all you wanted to know. He gave you everything, and in the end, in your heart, you feel like you let him down."

The words coming out of his mouth didn't seem to quite belong to him. Some higher understanding spoke *through* him, and he knew what he said was true by the way tears slid down Astrid's cheeks, the way her chin faintly nodded.

"When he was dying, you made a promise. You gave him your word you'd always take care of your mother. And when he died, you still felt like you hadn't made it right in his eyes. Hadn't earned his forgiveness. And that promise took on more meaning." He held up his cupped hands. "And more weight. It's the heaviest thing you've ever carried."

She pressed his balled-up handkerchief into the corner of her eye and nodded harder.

"I understand. Asta, listen, I let my father down once. I did something really stupid. Not just stupid and disobedient, but stupid and dangerous."

"What?"

"I'll tell you another time. I just need you to know this: the look on my father's face made me want to die. It was the one and only time in my life I literally wished I were dead. It was crushing. I got the worst hiding of my life, and it didn't do shit to make me feel I'd atoned, pardon my French. Even when Paps forgave me, when he said to my face I was forgiven, it took a long time to believe. I carried his disappointment around for months. It shaped everything I did ever since."

He took the handkerchief away from her, refolded it into something more robust, and wiped her face himself. "I know," he said. "I understand how heavy it is. I know it wasn't a promise you made lightly."

"I'm sorry."

"Bushwa," he said. "Being a lady of your word is nothing to be sorry about. But tell me, has seeing this bit of the world helped make a decision about marrying him?"

"It did. Until I got here." A smile broke through her trembling lips and she gave her head a little toss. "Everything was fine and I thought I'd be satisfied with what I'd seen, until I got to Clayton. Until I stepped off the train and a young man put out his hand and said, 'I'm Kennet Fiskare.' And all at once, the world wasn't enough."

"Why, that lousy punk. He ruined everything."

She put her palm on his cheek. Stroked it once. "Everything."

Pass the Salt

Her troubles safe in his pocket, Kennet went on offering Astrid a host of entertaining activities, but mostly she wanted to go out on the boat.

"Just her and him on the *Hildur*," she said. "Unhurried hearts harkening to the…"

"Hushed history of…"

"Helping hands holding hard to happiness."

"Holy hell."

As he sped them along the southeast side of Grindstone, Astrid quizzed him on every island name, consulting her trusty Thousand Island guide to keep him honest.

"What's that," she said, pointing.

"Whiskey Island. So named because it was one of the main drop-and-load points during Prohibition."

"Your first job?"

He laughed. "I was a kid. But Major and Johnny made quite a decent, if unrespectable living running booze across the river."

"Did your father have a piece of the action?"

She laughed as he made a show of looking everywhere but at her.

"I'll take that as a yes," she said, then held up a palm. "Don't tell me how many bodies were buried."

"No bodies," Kennet said. "Just booze. The one time I remember my mother raising her voice to Paps, I mean really hollering at him, was when she discovered he was stashing booze in the hotel basement. Making it a pick-up site. She told him to get all of it out. And not because she was a temperance advocate. She just didn't want that racket anywhere near the house or business."

"Was it dangerous?"

"Risky, for sure. Paps and Major had the best boats and knew every square inch of the river from here to Alex Bay, but still, the feds watched this place day and night and plenty of rumrunners got arrested."

"*This place* meaning the entire river? Or just this part of it?"

"Where we are now. The eastern end of Grindstone. The US-Canadian border hugs it real tight here." He pointed ahead. "See that little island, just due north? It's called Watch Island and has the best view of the entire channel. When my folks did runs, Johnny would be stationed there, keeping an eye out for the feds. When the coast was clear, he'd signal Paps and Major, who were waiting on Whiskey Island. Then they'd head toward Clayton with the goods."

"Clearly Johnny was the brains of the operation."

"He came up with all kinds of tricks. He painted the boats white on one side, black on the other. Cruising back and forth, the feds thought they were seeing two different boats."

Kennet told how Johnny would strap sacks of sugar to the wooden cases of liquor. If Emil or Major had to ditch the haul in the river, the weight of the sugar quickly dragged the crates to the bottom. Hours later, when the sugar dissolved, up bobbed the cases again and the Fiskares plucked them from the water and finished the run.

"So the St. Lawrence is filled with gold *and* sugar," Astrid said. "What a thought."

"Johnny's family farm was at the head of Grindstone Island," Kennet said. "Every day the island boat came to pick up the ten-gallon milk cans. Sometimes Johnny would put liquor bottles in the cans, then turn the screw to make the cream go all thick. It padded the bottles so well, you couldn't even hear a clink. One time, the feds themselves helped Mrs. MacIntyre load the cream cans on the boat, every one hiding illegal booze. Johnny crowed about that conquest for years."

"Who were they delivering to," Astrid asked. "I mean, were trucks waiting in Clayton to move the cases to other cities?"

"No, it was mostly a local, word-of-mouth operation. They had clients—so to speak, from St. Vincent to Ogdensburg. But most of the business was between Clayton and Alex Bay, among people they could trust to keep quiet. With one notable exception..." He grinned down at her. "Paps, Major and Johnny once delivered a case of whiskey to Irving Berlin."

"The composer?"

"He had a place up here and word got to Johnny, 'Mr. Berlin wants a case of Canadian whiskey.' So the Fiskare boys delivered it, and got invited inside. And who do you think was visiting Berlin at the time?"

"Carmen Miranda?"

"Bing Crosby."

Her mouth fell open. "Get away."

"Irving Berlin opened a bottle right there and then, poured everyone a shot and Bing Crosby made a toast. Apparently Major was struck speechless."

"It was Bing *Crosby*. Can you blame him?"

"He denies it to this day, but Paps and Johnny insist Major couldn't say a word. Not there. Not back on the boat. He actually kept the shot glass. Berlin went to offer them each a cash tip, but Major shook his head and just wanted the glass. He still has it. Johnny teases that Major keeps his teeth in it."

"You tell the best stories."

"There's the *E-Minor*," Kennet said.

"Where?" Astrid shaded her eyes and scanned the river.

"Up ahead."

Astrid had both hands piled on her forehead now. "How do you know from so far away?"

He shrugged. "Same way I know the names of the islands, I guess. Here, take the binoculars."

She lifted the eyepieces and turned the tubes, focusing. Kennet whistled "South American Way" through his teeth, ever so slightly smug.

"You're right," she said. "Stop gloating."

"I'm not gloating."

She swiveled her mechanical gaze on him. "Tell it to Sweeney," she said in English.

He laughed and bent to set his eyes against the lenses. Her hands turned the tubes again. Beneath them, her breath drew in and exhaled warm.

"I see you," she said softly.

"You're far away."

"You're so close."

A shiver spread across his shoulder blades. He held still, looking through brass and glass, wanting to see Astrid seeing him. He could have stayed there forever, but the boat wobbled under his inattentive hand on the wheel, reminding him he was slacking off on the job.

Astrid looked toward Buck Bay again. "Is that Nalle with Minor?"

"Doubt it. Nalle's working." Kennet held a hand out for the binoculars. "Take the wheel a second. Just hold her steady."

"Aye, Captain," she said, a little archly. He shot her a *why I oughta* look before pressing the tubes to his eyes.

The doubled, blurry *E-Minor* swam into singular focus. Minor at the wheel, shirtless, blond and magnificent. A young man on the seat beside him. Dark-haired like Nalle. But not Nalle.

"Who is it?" Astrid asked.

The stranger had an arm slung across the seat back, his hand touching Minor's neck.

"I don't know." Kennet focused tighter, as if looking for little fingerprints on Minor's nape.

Astrid's hand fell on his, pushing the binoculars down. "It's just a friend."

"Sure."

She smiled, the wind blowing her hair in her face. Her fingers were still in his. He squeezed them, then slowly guided their joined fist back to the wheel. "Both hands on the helm, skipper."

"Where to?" she said, not letting go.

"I'll take you to Grennell Island. Show you my grandmother's place."

"Help me drive."

He put his arm around her and she slid close. "You don't drive a boat," he said by her ear. "You pilot it."

She dug her head back against his shoulder. "Oh, desculpa aí, capitão."

His nose pressed against the sunny crown of her head a moment. *I had no idea,* he thought. *I didn't know it could ever be like this.*

Over the wind and spray and hum of the engine, Astrid sang "South American Way."

Ostensibly, lord only knew how many thousands of years ago, the Fiskares' land had been one hook-shaped peninsula on the south side of Grennell Island. Tide, time and erosion had shaped it into a bulge on the mainland, and two small islands connected by bridges.

"When he died, Farfar left the main part of the property to Uncle Nyck," Kennet said. "Major got the island just offshore. The island off that belongs to Marianne until she dies."

"Nothing for your father?" Astrid said.

"He got the house and the hotel."

"I see."

"Uncle Nyck's family sold their share, so only these two little islands are left in the family."

Kennet tied off at the long dock on Major's island. At its far end, a path forked: one way meandering down along the shoreline, the other leading to the house. Along the latter was a signpost reading:

Tre Fiskar

Three Fishes

Private Property

"Is Tre Fiskar the name of the house or the name of the island?" Astrid asked.

"Both. Marianne's property is called Tre Önskningar. Three Wishes. But practically nobody can pronounce önskningar, so most of the locals just refer to it as Tre-O."

He'd walked a few paces down the shoreline path before realizing Astrid hadn't followed. He looked back. She was still gazing at the signpost, then at him, expression puzzled.

"Will we go say hello to Major?"

"Not sure he's home," Kennet said, although he'd seen the *E-Major* tied at the shorter dock and Astrid probably had, too. She missed nothing.

He held out his hand. "Come on, I'll show you around."

His hand stayed out hopefully as she came along. Her eyes and nose crinkled as their palms slid together and fingers entwined and folded down.

As they rounded a bend in the path, the house's front facade came into view between the trees. Major and Johnny sat on the front porch.

"See, he's home," Astrid said, and waved.

The men waved back but didn't call out or beckon. Kennet kept walking.

"You don't want to go up?" Astrid asked, her arm pulling out long now.

"No," Kennet said, more abruptly than he intended.

Her hand slid from his. "Is something wrong?"

"No. Just…it's sort of an unwritten family rule. If Major and Johnny are together and alone, we leave them alone."

"Oh." She looked back at the two men on the porch a moment. "Are they lovers?"

"What?" His voice was raised and perhaps his demeanor was menacing, for Astrid stepped back from him, expression horrified and fingertips touching her mouth.

"Oh my God, Nyck, what a tactless thing to say. I'm sorry."

"How in the hell—"

"I offended you. I'm so sorry. It was thoughtless."

She kept moving back and he kept advancing. But a rock caught the edge of his sneaker and he tripped. He almost went sprawling flat on his face, but recovered enough to get a knee and a hand down in the gravel. And then he was laughing.

"What?" she cried. "Don't make me stand here with my foot in my mouth."

"I'm sorry," he gasped. "I'm laughing at the stupidity."

She crossed her arms. "My stupidity?"

"No, mine. Holy *mackerel*…"

Her toe tapped the path several times. "Well, if you don't mind, I will now take the boat and leave you here to laugh yourself to death."

"I have the keys."

"Oh, get up, you fat-head."

Kennet staggered up, still wheezing. "Yes, they're lovers. And yes, everyone knows it. We know everyone knows and we just pretend nobody knows and we all talk around the subject. You're the first person who ever looked at them and said, 'Oh, they're lovers? Interesting. Pass the salt, please.'" He started chuckling helplessly again.

"Honest to God, Nyck," she said, fists on her hips now. Indignant, but smiling. "First you blush telling me about your parents' shotgun wedding. Now you're shocked I know about queer men. I'm a little concerned by how sheltered a life you think I've lived."

"I honestly didn't contemplate what you'd know. I'm so conditioned to dance around the subject, even my thoughts do the Charleston."

She shrugged. "What's to think about? Your uncle is queer and you love him anyway. Pass the salt."

His laughter died. "I don't fool myself that everyone feels the same."

"No. You're loyal but you're not naive and…" She bit her lip. "And I'm about to say something tactless again."

"Pass the pepper?"

"You're loyal, but you're not naive, and you know what Johnny and Major have is the exception, not the rule. Which makes you worry about what kind of life Minor's going to have."

He stared, dumbfounded again, then nodded slowly. "I think we both know whoever was on the *E-Minor* wasn't just a friend."

"You did say the Fiskares repeat their names and repeat their tragedies."

"I did."

"Plus, a woman knows when she's being charmed for the benefit of the charmer, and when she's being charmed for the benefit of others." She waved a dismissive hand. "Which is neither here nor there. The point I'm making is that with Minor, the not-talking-about-it isn't quite so funny."

"No," he said. "No, it isn't, and watching out for him is one of the things I promised my mother."

"Major is safely established behind the old bachelor narrative. Minor is young. He's smart as all get-out. He's ten steps ahead of everyone, cunning and wily. But he could trip one of these days. And you worry."

"I do." He kicked at the ground a little. "Either that he'll trip or someone will trip him. Ma said people aren't always kind toward what they don't understand."

"You're one of the kindest fellows I've ever known," Astrid said.

I'm so in love with you, he thought, as he said aloud, "I've never known anyone like you in my life. Well. No. That's not exactly true. You're a lot like Marta."

"I wanted to be like her when I grew up."

"You did. You are. But a thousand times more beautiful."

A flickering, melting moment.

"Thank you," she said softly.

He tapped his mouth, shaking his head. "You have the damnedest way of making people share their secrets."

"I feel I know so many of yours now. Maybe I should tell you one."

"Never tell a secret out of obligation."

"Did Major teach you that?"

"No, I just came up with it now."

"I have two secrets to tell you. One now. One later. Maybe. Take me someplace where we can sit down."

Fiskare

He took her to the little rocky beach on the west side of Tre-O.

"Someone's been camping," she said, pointing to a ring of stones and the charred remains of a fire within.

"Oh that's us," Kennet said. "My brothers and sisters, I mean. We come here to fish and swim and cook out." He sighed. "In fact, we were planning to bring you here tomorrow for a surprise *fika* and I just let the cat out of the bag. So don't let on you've seen it already. I'll be murdered."

She drew pinched fingers across her lips. "I've never had fika on an island. Will there be coffee and cake?"

Fika, the beloved Swedish ritual of taking a break with friends, wouldn't be fika without coffee and cake.

"This is a *fiskfika*," Kennet said. "A gathering of Fish. Slightly different. Same feeling, same purpose, but with a different menu. You'll see."

"It's so quiet and still," she said. "You wouldn't know anything or anyone else was on the island."

"The way my grandmother's house is built, you feel like you're in the middle of the sea. Her bedroom has big windows on three sides, and it's like sitting in the sky."

"Will you show it to me?"

"Her bedroom?"

They both blushed and looked away.

"Holy mackerel," Kennet muttered.

Astrid pressed hands to her cheeks. "I keep eating my foot. I meant her house."

"Her *house*. Yes. I will show you her house when the tenants leave."

She sat on one of the large pine logs by the fire and dug in her straw bag. "So," she said. "A secret."

He sat next to her. Forearms on knees, fingers laced and heart thumping.

Astrid handed him a book. It was the last thing he was expecting, and he laughed a little as he took it. It was an old tome, with thick cream pages. Hardcover, yet worn and soft at its corners. It was marked in several places by pieces of stiff paper. The front embossed in gold with a single word:

BYRON

Kennet felt his world contract just a bit as he stared at the name. As if time and place stopped what they were doing and took a step in, curious.

Byron.

The oddest feeling came over him. He knew nobody named Byron, yet the sound of it in his mind was like an old friend waving. Someone he hadn't seen in a too-long time.

Hello. I know you. Fancy meeting you here.

So strange. Was he thinking of Björn?

Of course. That must be it. Byron is an English version of Björn.

The feeling within shrugged and wrinkled its nose, unsatisfied.

"Do you know his work?" Astrid said.

A lightbulb went off then, and Kennet opened the cover to the first page:

Herre Byron: De Samlade Dikterna
The Collected Poems of Lord Byron

"I don't," he said, turning the soft pages. "Cripes, this looks well loved."

Well loved and well annotated. All through the poems, around, over and under every stanza were penciled notes in a fine hand. Some in Swedish. Others in Portuguese.

"It was my father's," Astrid said. "All those notes are his. Except for this one…"

She took the book and fanned the pages under her thumb. She put the bookmark in her lap and turned the tome back toward him. "Look at the first line."

Han varit fiskare i unga dagar
och med det yrket höll han stadigt i…

The word *fiskare* had been carefully circled in pencil.

"Huh," he said, touching the word. "Here I am."

"Yes."

"Like finding a picture of yourself in someone else's house."

Her hand came out of her lap then, holding two photographs, which had been marking the page. He stared.

He stared harder.

"Wait," he said. "That's me."

They were the pictures Marta took on a long-ago day in 1931, when she knocked on the Fiskares' kitchen door and brought order out of chaos. By sundown, she'd moved into the attic room and had unpacked all her wonderful things, including her camera. When Kennet brought her towels, he stayed to visit. She took his picture.

"Lean against the wall with your shoulder," she'd said. "And put your hands in your pockets. Now don't look at me, gaze over toward the window, like you're thinking deep thoughts."

Kennet stared at his twelve-year-old self, composed and contemplative. In the second photo, he looked right at the camera, as Marta had told him to.

"When you're famous, I'll be able to tell everyone I took your picture."

"I didn't know you had these," he said, barely able to breathe around the words. "How do you have these?"

"Marta sent them." Astrid held the second picture at arm's length and moved her head and shoulders side to side. "Your eyes follow. No matter where I stand."

He couldn't speak. Couldn't take in the incredible symmetry. All these years of looking at Astrid's photographs, feeling her gaze follow, feeling she knew him.

All this time, she was doing the same?

Without him even knowing?

Astrid was turning more pages now. *Stop*, part of Kennet thought. *No more.* Even as the other part of him begged, *More. Tell me more, show me more, don't ever stop.*

She was passing him another picture. An older Kennet in the boathouse. All his weight on one bent leg, the muscles in his arms taut as he wielded a plane above the hull of the *Hildur*. Looking at the camera, a cigarette held tight in the corner of his mouth. Through the haze of smoke, his expression was wary, as if he'd been startled out of his work.

He'd forgotten the day, but he remembered now. Marta calling him from the boathouse door. Looking up to see her behind the camera. The whirring click. And he laughed at her, chiding, "Never take a gentleman's picture without his permission."

"Marta sent me the others," Astrid said. "I asked for this one. I mean, I asked her to take a picture of you later in life. You were stuck at twelve in the pages of this book. I wanted to see you grown up."

"Why?"

"I don't know exactly." Her eyes closed as she shook her head slowly. "I just felt like I knew you."

"I'm not even smiling in this one."

"That's why I like it. You're working, but your expression says, 'Darling, what is it? You look troubled. Come here and tell me everything…' You'd stop working, put down your tools and listen to me. You'd do anything."

I would, he thought. *I'm in love with you and I would do anything…*

"But most of all," she said, "I like how these two pictures go with the two halves of the poem. Listen."

She held up the picture of young Kennet staring thoughtfully to the side, and read:

> *A fisherman he had been in his youth,*
> *And still a sort of fisherman was he;*
> *But other speculations were, in sooth,*
> *Added to his connexion with the sea,*

Now she held up the picture of Kennet in the boathouse:

> *Perhaps not so respectable, in truth:*
> *A little smuggling, and some piracy,*
> *Left him, at last, the sole of many masters*
> *Of an ill-gotten million of piastres.*

She put the photos into the spine and closed the book. "A fisherman," she said. "But also a bit of a pirate…"

She touched the tip of his nose. Her finger trailed down across his lips.

It was Kennet's first un-orchestrated kiss. He didn't think, didn't calculate, didn't ask. He simply leaned and slowly, quietly, kissed her mouth. Out the corner of his eye, he saw her eyes close, the fringe of lashes fluttering once above her cheekbones. His hand moved into her hair, curving around the back of her little head. Her palm slid along his neck, thumb drawing along his jaw. Then his other hand in her hair. And her other hand on his face. Then his mouth opened. Then hers.

At the first touch of her tongue, he fell off the log, but they didn't stop kissing. She fell with him, her body sweet and warm on top of his, but the kiss never faltered. She was rolling and his elbow knew to move just so and cradle her head in the soft, sandy dirt. Her arms were up around his neck and he knew just how to hold her. She sighed deep in her chest when he moved on top of her a little. Not too much. He knew precisely when it was just enough to let her feel his weight and his strength, but no more.

He *knew* how to love this woman.

It had been easier than falling off a log, but now the sun was mercilessly overhead and sharp rocks were digging into his hip and leg. This place was fine for fikas, but not for lovemaking.

"Come on," he said, getting up.

"Where are we going?"

"Someplace shadier. And softer." He drew her off the ground and they brushed off dust and pebbles and bits of this and that. Taking her by the hand, he led them back to the shore path and inland a bit, to a shady, grassy area dotted with wildflowers. There they lay beneath an oak tree and kissed. They kissed with eyes open and eyes closed. Kissed around words and through laughter and within silence. Then all at once they stopped kissing, both going limp as if the enormity of their combined feeling fell out of the sky and smashed them flat into the earth. Kennet's head dropped onto Astrid's breastbone, feeling the fist of her pounding heart. She had an arm thrown across her face, breathing hard.

Ten years, Kennet thought. *We've been reaching and running toward each other. Non-stop. And now we're here. Finally.*

Good lord, I'm so tired…

"Oh my God," Astrid said faintly. "I didn't think it would ever…"

"I know."

She laughed. "I'm exhausted."

"I know." He pressed into the beat of her heart, his one elbow still rocking her head, the other tight at her waist.

"Nyck."

"I know. I know…"

He was enormously, embarrassingly sleepy. Her fingers running through his hair weren't helping.

"Feels so good," he said.

"Cafune."

"Hm?"

"Cafune. Portuguese for… Well, it has no translation. It just means to do this." Her fingers ran furrows along his scalp.

"Like this?" He caressed her arms.

"No. Cafune is fingers in your hair, nothing else. English doesn't have a word like it."

"We need one," Kennet said.

"I love untranslatable words. Like *pålägg*. English doesn't have one word meaning 'anything you can put into a sandwich.'"

"Yes it does. 'Sandwich-stuff.'"

"That's two words."

"I hyphenated them."

"Clever boy."

"Tell me another."

"Korova. It's Russian. It's a buddy you bring along on a prison break so you can eat him."

He lifted his head off her heart and stared. "I'm not sure if I'm horrified there's a word for that, or if I'm horrified you know what it is."

"I don't even remember where I learned it."

He put his head back down again. "More cafune, please."

"More of it or more words like it?"

"Both."

In between kissing, they thought up words in all their languages that didn't translate to one word in English. Like *lagom,* which was Swedish for not too much, not too little, but just right.

"Your tongue when we kiss is lagom," Astrid murmured beneath his mouth.

Or *resfeber*—what the Swedes called the anxious and anticipatory race of the traveler's heart before a journey began.

"Like the resfeber when your train pulled in," Kennet said. "And I wasn't even the traveler."

"*Desenrascanco,*" she said. "It means slapping together a solution with no plan and with whatever's to hand. It's a very Fiskare word. You're all so resilient and resourceful."

Her hand played in his hair and her heart beat beneath his cheek. His hand slid from her waist, glided over her ribs to curve around a breast. Warm and lovely in his palm. She covered his hand with hers, not thwarting him, rather letting him know this was lagom: not too much and not too little. Just right. Just enough.

"Sleep with me," she whispered. "A little while."

So what did you and Astrid do when you realized you were in love? Kennet mused as he drifted away, interviewing his future self.

Why, what any normal couple does. We thought up some words, then took a nap.

He smiled beneath closed eyes. He must never, under any circumstances, let Minor find out.

Fiskfika

The day of the fiskfika dawned overcast, but by late morning the sun was breaking through, and the Fiskares loaded up the *Hildur* with rods and reels, provisions and cooking gear.

When Astrid came down to the dock in her two-piece bathing suit and straw hat, Minor let out a long wolf whistle. "And whose little girl are you?"

"Oh my God, is that your best line?" Astrid said, laughing.

"I worked a long time on that line. You don't like it?"

"You sound like a lecher."

Wide-eyed, Minor put a hand on his chest. "Gosh, really?"

It was a bit of a squash with all the Fiskare siblings, plus Astrid, plus Kirsten, plus the clobber, but they managed. The water looked a little sullen as they zipped out to Grennell Island, green-grey like a badly-erased chalkboard. Kennet thought the western sky was sulking as well, undecided as to what it would do with the day.

"Nick! Nick! Needle in the water!" Trudy and Kirsten cried from the seats, and everyone flung a nail overboard.

The greedy river god was appeased, and the weather held. Once set up at the little campsite on Tre Önskningar, they swam and fished. Late in the afternoon, they built up the fire and made their signature camp supper. First bacon was fried in their one battered pan. Then potatoes were fried in the bacon grease, followed by the fileted fish. Fresh greens were picked from whatever was growing wild—mostly rocket and dandelion. They added chunks of tomato, picked that morning from Marta's garden, and drizzled the salad with, what else, Thousand Island dressing.

"It's on the sweet side," Minor said to Astrid. "And we like how it cuts the bitterness of the wild greens. Except for old sourpuss over here, who likes them plain."

Kennet plucked an undressed dandelion leaf out of the salad and ate it.

"Yuck," Trudy said.

"I like things that are kind of bitter," Kennet said.

"Kind of?" Nalle said. "He can peel and eat a lime the way we'd eat an orange."

"He eats the *peel,*" Kirsten said.

"When we were young, all of us raided the bar for maraschino cherries," Minor said. "But Kennet stole lemons and limes."

"You should see how he drinks tea," Little said. "He steeps it so long, Marta says you can stand a spoon up in it."

"I don't brew tea," Kennet said, "I stew it."

"Gross," Little said. "And he barely adds any sugar."

"No worries if you burn the toast," Nalle said. "Just give it to Kennet."

"Are we done criticizing my palate?" Kennet said.

"Kennet has no fear of catching malaria," Minor said. "He has quinine water in his blood. *Now* I'm done."

As her eyes volleyed around the ribbing, Astrid nibbled on a plain dandelion leaf. Obviously trying to keep her expression placid, but a corner of one eye kept screwing up.

"It's an acquired taste," Kennet said, laughing.

Onto her fork Astrid pushed a bit of fish, a bit of bacon, one small wedge of potato and a few leaves of dressed salad. She chewed with her eyes closed, face up to the darkening sky. Then she looked around the circle, smiling happily. "This is the best lunch I've ever had."

"I wish you could live with us forever," Kirsten said.

Astrid leaned and kissed the girl's head. "I do, too."

"Holy smokes, it clouded over," Nalle said, looking up beneath the visor of his hand.

Everyone except Astrid stood or swiveled to gaze at the western skies.

"What are you looking for?" she asked.

"Not *for* but *at*," Minor said, pointing. "Wolfe Island."

"More specifically, the clouds over Wolfe Island," Kennet said. "See how they're gathering up? That's a storm. Now we have to watch them."

The Fiskares had been taught from the time they could tell west from east: if storm clouds divided over Wolfe Island, then the storm would divide. Part of it would move south to Oswego, the other north to Montreal, leaving the river a safety zone. If the clouds didn't divide over Wolfe Island, they had ten minutes to get off the river. If they were already off, they were to stay off.

"One time we didn't," Little said. "We were having a fika here and the clouds didn't divide. Kennet tried to beat the storm home."

"He lost," Nalle said.

"We got in *so* much trouble," Trudy said.

"We don't have to tell this fish tale," Kennet said.

"Oh but we do," Minor said.

"Every year I get older, the gravity of that night just sinks in a little more," Nalle said. "I mean, we could've been killed."

"What happened?" Astrid asked.

"I hit a shoal," Kennet said. "Engine died before we reached the marina and we foundered out there in the storm. Luckily someone spotted and picked us up."

"Not so luckily, Paps and Major were waiting for us on the dock," Nalle said. "And back at the house, we got our fish warm."

"Paps *fried* our fish," Little said. "Even Trudy."

"Deep-fried," Minor elaborated. "Twenty smacks each."

"Liar," Kennet said. "You all got twenty between you."

"Kennet got a million," Trudy said.

Astrid raised eyebrows. "That must've taken some time."

"Paps made us sit and wait in the kitchen, and we had to *listen*."

"And count," Nalle said quietly. "It was a bad night."

Kennet looked at him, then nudged a little into Nalle's side. "Worse than the night you ate the one rotten clam at the bake and upchucked until dawn?"

Nalle laughed. "Now *that* was bad."

But not as bad as the night Ma died, Kennet thought, nudging Nalle again and then holding still against his tall frame. *You cried until dawn and didn't speak for a good two weeks. Poor Paps, cut down on one side with grief, cut up on the other from worrying about you. Little bear-brother, you are the authority on bad nights...*

Astrid was looking at him. A shivering rash of goosebumps swept up his arms.

"When I was in primary school," she said, "a friend and I loosened the caps on all the inkwells in the classroom. The teacher made every single pupil kneel holding all their books, until the culprit confessed."

"Did you?" Nalle asked.

"Yes, and my friend, excuse me, my *former* friend played dumb. I got paddled in the principal's office. Then I had to scrub the classroom floor. *Then* I got walloped again when I got home."

Nalle patted her shoulder. "Bad night."

"Warm fish."

Now raindrops began to fall on Kennet's arms.

"Here she comes," Minor said, scrambling to his feet.

The fist of clouds over Wolfe Island had clenched tight, squeezing out a blanket of rain. They could see the curtain of it coming down the river. They stashed the gear beneath some pine trees and made a dash for the footbridge to Tre Fiskar, heading toward Major's house.

"Will he mind?" Astrid said, running alongside Kennet.

"Of course not." He took her hand. "Every rule has its exception."

As guarded as they were of their privacy, Major and Johnny were generous men. The young people were soon situated on the little front porch of Tre Fiskar, with thick towels and five-cent Cokes. There they weathered the storm, telling hilarious stories of not-so-finest moments.

Kennet and Astrid shared the porch swing, holding hands. Kennet was consumed with pure happiness, edged with another emotion that took some time to pin down. It was paternal. Or maybe dynastic. An abstract feeling, yet precise. His uncle's house unfolded into the concept of a home Kennet might own one day. Astrid morphed into a wife. His siblings chewed on the idea of children. And these would be the stories they'd tell together.

This, he thought, playing with Astrid's fingers. Playing with the future as he laughed and teased and reminisced about the past.

I want this.

I want this to be my life.

Just like this.

A Small Hotel

Later that night he was in the boathouse, making small repairs on the *Hildur*. The radio on, a litter of Tootsie Roll wrappers on the workbench. When he heard footfalls on the dock outside, he knew without looking around it was Astrid.

She slipped inside the door and leaned her back against it.

"And whose little girl are you?" Kennet said.

Her eyes crinkled. "You make a terrible lecher."

"I do, don't I?"

Her dress was green and white stripes. Her undressed hair parted in the middle and tucked behind her ears. Her cheeks a little sunburned. Her eyes silver.

"I'm so in love with you," Kennet said. Or tried to say. Half of it stuck in his throat.

On the radio came Rodgers & Hart:

There's a small hotel
With a wishing well
I wish that we were there together...

He held out his hand to her. "I dance better than I lech. But only a little."

They danced and kissed and disappeared in each other. Kennet tried to make up better words to the song:

There's a Hotel Fisher
With a wishing fish…er…
I wish fish were dished up for dinnnerrrrr….

"You compose worse than you lech," Astrid said.

"Don't marry Zé," Kennet whispered in her hair.

She leaned back to look at him, but he tucked her head back against his chest and kept going. "Don't marry him. Don't leave New York. Don't go home. Stay here forever. Stay with us."

"Stay with you."

"I'm part of here. Part of us. Stay."

She wound both her arms around his waist, forehead to his heart.

"Don't marry him," he said.

"I'm having a hard time seeing how I can."

"Then stay in Clayton."

"I don't see how I can do that either, but… I'll come back. I'll… I'll figure it out. I can work. I'm not afraid to work. I'm not afraid to be on my own."

"You'll be with us."

"Don't let's talk about it anymore. I came to tell you the fika is continuing in my room tonight. With cake."

He put his tools away and locked the boathouse door behind them. Holding hands, they were only a few steps along the dock when he stopped. "Right here," he said.

"What was right here?"

"Remember the other day, I told you I'd done a stupid thing and let my father down? Well, the story Minor told this afternoon was it. When I tried to beat the storm home. Paps sent the others back to the hotel with Major. He held me back. Right here on the dock, in the pouring rain…" He laughed a little. "We throw that expression around—oh my father's gonna *kill* me. But that night, I really thought he would. Actually, I hoped he would…"

"You damn *punk*," Major shouted in Kennet's face.

"Take them home," Emil said to his brother, indicating the four younger Fiskares. He put a palm in the center of Kennet's chest, holding him back. "You stay."

"Paps, I—"

"*Shut your mouth.*"

Kennet rolled his lips in, frightened in every bone of his body.

"Did you watch the clouds?" Emil asked when the others had gone.

Kennet stared at his sodden shoes.

"Look at me when I'm talking to you. Did you watch the clouds?"

Now Kennet looked through the rain, met his father's gaze and wished he were dead. "Yes, sir."

"Did the clouds divide?"

"No, sir."

The hand on Kennet's sternum drew back a few inches, then it shoved him, hard. Sneakers slipping and sliding on the wet dock, Kennet went sprawling. A yelp of surprised pain as his hip bone collided with wood. Another yelp, this one full of fear, as his father's feet planted on either side of him.

"You could've killed all your mother's children tonight," Emil shouted, tall and terrible. "You could have sheared this family tree down to the goddamn ground. You would've left it to *me* to tell your mother it was the end of the family. To tell my brothers it was the end of our name."

He may have had a lame leg, but the blood of the Old Bear bellowed in Emil's upper body. His hands reached, his fists curled around Kennet's wet clothes. He hauled the boy to his feet and shook him, as if trying to loosen teeth. "If any of them drowned and you lived, I'd make you sleep in the graveyard the rest of your days. I'd build a goddamn shed for you in the family plot and make you *live* among your dead siblings."

"I'm sorry," Kennet cried, wanting to throw himself overboard.

"My only *daughter,*" Emil roared above the rain. "This family's sole girl in two generations, you damn fool pathetic *excuse* of a..."

Kennet was drowning in shame now, reduced to worm food, to chum, to insignificant sand and pebbles beneath the tromp of his father's rage. To a miserable *punk* in the eyes of his adored uncle.

He wanted to die. Not just die, but be tied to the mast and beaten to death, then his shredded skin and broken bones tossed into the river for Fossegrim to devour. Within his father's fisted grip, he was buckling and sliding down to the dock boards, falling to his knees, doubling in half, wanting to disappear, disintegrate between the cracks. But then Emil was down beside him, on his knees, his hands open now and his arms crushing Kennet to his wide chest.

"You fool boy," he said hoarsely, one hand holding Kennet's head hard against his pounding heart. "You damn fool boy, don't you know what it would've done to me if you died?"

Kennet was sobbing now, braying like a wounded horse.

"Don't you know?" Emil said, rocking him. "You damn fool boy. If you die, I die."

"I'm sorry."

"Get up now. Come on." Emil put his good foot on the dock and levered the both of them up. "Come inside. Your mother needs to see your face and you need to answer for what you did."

"I can't."

Emil's fingers closed around Kennet's clothes again. They didn't squeeze or shake. They held him up, turned him to face his deeds, moved him forward. "You can. And you will."

"It was the last time I cried," Kennet said.

Astrid frowned. "You didn't cry when your mother died?"

"I did. But not the way I did that night on the dock. I was weeping in a way and feeling in a way that scared me. I felt loathsome. I'd never been so ashamed in my life. I sobbed like a... I'd say a baby but it doesn't even come close."

"Like a condemned man?"

"Something like that."

"Did your father tell you to stop?"

"Stop crying?"

"Mm."

"No."

She smiled. "I didn't think he would. I like your father. He lets his sadness show."

"What do you mean?"

"He misses your mother terribly. You can see it in his eyes, because he's not trying to hide it. In Brazil, see... Men are constantly in a competition to prove how manly they are. They can't stop thinking about their masculinity for five seconds. Displays of emotion, crying, sentimentality—this is all weakness to them. And you see it in the way fathers treat their sons. *Don't cry. Stop crying. Be a man. Don't be a sissy. If you're going to cry, go play with the girls.*"

"Well, to be fair, Scandinavians can be notoriously stoic."

"Only in public, though. Your father isn't rending his coat and weeping in the streets, but among family, he doesn't have a fake smile pasted on, for the sake of his sons. He's not making a hearty show of having *moved on*. He's in a sad place right now and he's not pretending otherwise. He's letting you and your brothers see that normal human emotion doesn't make a man weak"

Their eyes caught and her voice trailed away. The wind blew a single tendril of hair across one eye. Kennet reached and brushed it back.

"What was I saying?" she said.

"Not pretending you don't feel a certain way?"

"Right."

"When I'm with you, I feel really good."

"Because you are good."

"Then the herdsman declared Hildur was the murderer and he produced the golden ring as evidence," Astrid said, reading from the Fiskares' worn book of Scandinavian folk tales:

> *Then Hildur revealed to all that she was indeed the Queen of the Elves, but had been banished from her homeland by a curse. She could only return once a year at the cost of a man's life.*
>
> *By breaking down the barrier between the human world and the elvish world, and by surviving the trial, the herdsman also broke the cycle of murder. Hildur was freed; after telling her story, she vanished, never to be seen again. The herdsman stayed on*

at the farm, and eventually inherited it for his own, and lived
happily ever after.

"Everyone gets away with murder in fairy tales," Minor said.

"True," Kennet said, "but at least the hero got the farm."

"It makes a nice change from getting the princess," Astrid said.

The cake was devoured to crumbs. Marta and Emil had come up to the attic for a slice and a couple stories, but then said goodnight. Astrid, in pajamas, sat propped against stacked pillows, Trudy on one side, Kirsten on the other. Little lay cross-ways at their feet. Nalle lounged on the rug. Minor sat on the window sill, smoking. Kennet was everywhere between and completely in love.

The book passed around, everyone taking a turn with a favorite. Nail Broth. The Old Woman and the Fish. The Christmas Wasps. The Princess on the Glass Mountain. Old Nick and the Peddler.

Kennet was caught between wanting time to fossilize the evening in amber so they could stay here forever, and wanting everyone to just leave, leave, *leave* him alone with Astrid.

And then all at once, they did. Every one of his siblings said goodnight and left Kennet. Alone. In a bedroom. With a woman. In her pajamas.

This was lecherous.

And delicious.

Shaking all over, he took the book of Byron poems off her bedside table and put it in her lap. "Read mine again."

Trying to be a gentleman, he sat on the floor and laid his head on the mattress by her outstretched legs.

A fisherman he had been in his youth,
And still a sort of fisherman was he;
But other speculations were, in sooth,
Added to his connexion with the sea,

Her voice was gorgeous around the words. Her hand stroked his head while he held still, amazed at what he could feel. Astonished at what he could be. Until now, he'd always felt inept and clumsy and shy with girlfriends. Analyzing every single move and word before execution. Now, with Astrid, he just talked. He just touched. With Astrid, he just *was.*

She closed the book and jettisoned a few pillows, coming face to face with him. And he found kissing upside-down a wonderful thing.

"I should tell you my second secret," she said.

"Never tell a secret out of obliga—"

"I'm not a virgin."

Which, like the secret book of poetry, was the last thing he expected.

"Oh."

"Oh?"

He blinked, confused. "How did you think I would respond?"

"I wasn't sure." She smiled. "This is, after all, the land of puritanical protestant prudes. Major said so."

"What if I were appalled and outraged?"

She shrugged. "I'd think you were a judgmental prig not worthy of any more of my time or secrets."

"Good for you."

"Do you want to know who he was?"

"I only want to know you. Did you love him?"

"I liked him enough to sleep with him. But I soon found out he didn't feel the same."

"When?"

"After I slept with him."

"How dare you want what he wanted."

Her eyes lifted toward her forehead. "South American men…"

"He was the reason your parents sent you away to Rio?"

"Yes."

"So you're not a virgin." He slid his hand around the back of her head and drew it close. Whispered into her mouth: "Neither am I."

"You're a man. Nobody expects you to be inexperienced and untouched."

He started to speak, then stopped. "That is," he said slowly, "the sad, unjust, silly and stupid truth."

"Thank you for that." She smiled a slow, wicked smile. "Din slampa."

You hussy.

He laughed and whacked her with a pillow.

"Slyna," she said, whacking him back.

"I'm a fallen man."

"You're a pirate." She tossed her pillow away and wrapped arms around his neck. "And I love you awful."

His own pillow fell away and he gathered her close. "I love you," he said, pressing a ring of kisses around her mouth. "You're my treasure." His kiss sank deep and she opened to him, a high keen of pleasure in her throat, her fingers in his hair. "You are every bit of gold and silver I ever wanted."

"Nyck."

Her grip on his head tightened, pulling his chin up. Her lips ran across his throat. She licked the line of his jaw and he was so hard, he was dizzy. He ran trembling fingers down her white neck, lingering at the V where her pajama top buttoned. "God, I want to be alone with you. Really alone."

"I do too."

"I should go."

"Yes."

"I'm going now."

"All right."

They kissed some more instead. Her hand fisted around his shirt and pulled him toward her, toward the bed and her body. He was doing the same, but pulling her toward him, toward the floor and his hard lap and his arms. Teetering on the edge of *I don't care* and *I must care,* they pressed foreheads, breathing hard, trapped and frustrated and purely alive.

"Have you ever felt this way?" she whispered.

"Never. I didn't know. I knew, but I didn't."

"Nyck..."

"Stay here in Clayton. Stay forever." His fingers tightened in her hair. Not too much and not too little, but lagom. Enough to hold her in his gaze and speak his truth: "This can be your home and I can be your man."

She moved into his arms, crying softly. His eyes were dry, though. His mind made up.

"I'll help you. We all will. I'll talk to your mother. She can come live here, too. I bet she'll love it. And when she sees how happy you are..." He buried his face in her hair. "Don't cry, Asta. It will all work out. It already has."

What Are Uncles For?

Like so many other young, working men in the Thousand Islands, Kennet had been easily seduced by the rich female swells summering at the grand resorts. These women—mavens from New York and Philadelphia and Boston—wanted diversion and a thrill, while the local fellows wanted uncomplicated experience and, occasionally, a good word put in with an influential husband... Once he got back from his golf game.

It was a satisfactory arrangement, as long as no one got caught.

"Or knocked up," Major said. He'd given Kennet a box of Sheik condoms long before giving the lessons on drinking and bar etiquette. Naturally Kennet was mortified, but Major was having none of it.

"My brother, God love him but he has a prudish side. Over in France, he saw syphilis and gonorrhea take out as many soldiers as the Huns did. Still, he'd rather the birds and bees peck and sting him to death before he has a man-to-man with his boys about sex. So that leaves me to do the dirty work. Oh, sit still, this conversation won't kill you. You're a good egg but you're at a hot-blooded age and come summer, this town is crawling with dames looking for a lover. Nothing wrong with tom-catting around when you're young, but it's all fun and games until your paramour starts barfing her breakfast. Or worse, until it starts burning when you take a piss. You feel like explaining your cock problems to ol' Doc Jensen?"

"Jesus H, no."

"Then take those, use them, and when you run out, get more. If you're embarrassed, go get them in Ogdensburg where nobody knows you. Any of your friends scoff and say real men don't wear rubbers, scoff right along but take it from me, real men are smart."

The conversation was rather killing, mostly because of words Kennet wasn't used to being bandied about—*Sex! Lover! Cock! Rubbers!* But always wanting to prove he knew his onions, Kennet put the box in his pocket and thanked Major for the advice.

"What are uncles for?" Major exhaled heavily, muttering, "One down, three to go. Cheese on a cracker, Ingrid, did you *have* to have four boys?"

All the unspoken rules concerning Major's sexuality had Kennet's tongue in a practiced vise. So he didn't ask the obvious question and when he thought about it, the answer seemed obvious as well. Sometimes you didn't know what you wanted until you tried a bunch of things and eliminated what you *didn't* want. Just because Major preferred male company didn't mean he was completely ignorant of women. Hell, women *loved* him. No doubt he took a few spins before deciding the ride wasn't for him.

Then again, what the hell did Kennet know?

He had his first summer tumble at sixteen, and every summer since. The assignations took on a familiar pattern. Some heady flirtation on a boat tour or a daily ferry ride. A discreet signal. Sometimes a bold proposition. The passing of a hotel room key. A frantic, rigorous coupling. Sometimes a bit of chat afterward but nearly always, as soon as breath was caught, the key was given back and Kennet was shown the door.

No wonder he came to view summer as the time for sex, and sex as something you did fast and fervent.

What did he know?

Nothing, it turned out.

They went to Marianne's cottage. The tenants were gone, a lady had been in to clean. It was spotless, empty, locked and *theirs*. All theirs for the taking. All that magical afternoon they took and took. And took again.

He didn't know.

"I'm so happy," Astrid whispered, running a hand all over his chest. He caught it and kissed her fingers, then bent to kiss her mouth again. She tasted like him or maybe he tasted like her, but how was he to know lovemaking had a flavor, any more than he could knew how his name sounded when Astrid keened it against his shoulder. Or how her hair smelled when she was in a writhing, fevered sweat. Or how a lover's eyes staring back into yours when you came into pieces made you feel you knew everything there was to know.

The cottage's little Frigidaire was unplugged and empty, so they had brought along some sandwiches and a bottle of milk. And good thing, because Kennet discovered lovemaking made you ravenous. They ate in bed, gulping and munching, wiping mouths on forearms because they had no napkins, kissing around bites because they had no patience.

Kennet had never been so comfortable in his own skin. He went downstairs to get the radio, naked as a newborn. He brought it back up, walking starkers past Astrid, dragging a chair close to the bed, dealing with the plug, fiddling with the dial. Astrid never took her eyes off him and he never wanted her to.

"Come here, river rat," she said.

He dove back into bed. He felt superb. Lying on his side, propped on an elbow while the other hand drew long, soft vertical lines between Astrid's breasts. Her fingertips caressed his wrist. Dinah

Shore was singing "You'd Be So Nice to Come Home To," and the walls drew close and held them in soft arms.

Under stars chilled by the winter
Under an August moon burning above
You'd be so nice, you'd be paradise
To come home to and love

"All my life," Astrid murmured. "I will never get tired of looking at you."

She rolled on her side and kissed him. He ran his palm up her soft throat, his thumb under her chin. Then he slid it into her hair, winding it around his fingers and pulling her mouth deeper into his.

He was drunk on kissing. The summer mavens had rarely kissed him, and never like this. The sweetheart necking he'd done in high school was nothing like these long, slow, lingering kisses where the boundary of his mouth got lost with Astrid's. How she made little sounds, and her nipples rose up to meet his touch. He felt every inch the pirate within the fisherman. Her touch added more inches, and she gave a wicked little laugh and pulled him on top of her again. This was a new discovery, too: that you didn't do it, get dressed and go. You could do it and lie around, and then do it again, lie around some more, and then do it again. As much as you wanted. All afternoon, until you were limp and sated and wanting for nothing.

"I love you so much," he whispered as the light outside grew dimmer.

"I've never known anything like it." She smiled, cheek pillowed on her upper arm, blonde hair falling partly in her eyes. Her hand soft on his face now. "I didn't know falling in love would be like this."

"How did you think it would be?"

"Like an explosion. A slap in the face. A fever. But this...?"

"This?"

"This is like coming home. Like finding a new book that becomes your favorite book." She brushed his mouth with hers. "Like finding a picture of yourself in someone else's house."

"A picture with eyes that follow wherever you go."

"Eyes that say, 'Darling, you look so troubled. Tell me everything.'"

"Eyes that say, 'I know you...'"

"I love you."

"Asta, I—"

They both jumped in their skin, then froze up at the sound of the cottage's front door opening. A pause, then it closed.

"What the hell," Kennet said, starting to get up.

The wind must've blown it open. But I'm sure I locked it...

"Kennet?" Major called.

"Oh my God," Astrid whispered, moving closer to Kennet's body, turning her head into the pillow, looking for anywhere to hide. He flipped the blankets over their naked skin.

"Kennet?" Louder now, but not angry. An edge of urgent alarm in his uncle's voice.

"What'll we do?" Astrid said.

"It's all right," Kennet murmured, then called out, "Major?"

"Come out here, I need to talk to you. Hurry."

Kennet kissed Astrid. "Don't be afraid, it's all right." He pulled on trousers and his shirt, slipped out and closed the door, keeping himself between his uncle and the bedroom.

"Her mother's here," Major said. "Just arrived on the train. Unannounced."

The blood drained from Kennet's head so fast, he swayed back a step. "Oh shit."

"Minor telephoned and we fixed an alibi, but we need to move fast."

"*Shit.*"

"Stay calm. Here's what's going to happen. Have her get dressed and fix her face. Johnny and I will take her back to Clayton. Your story is you've been here, getting the place ready for the next renter and doing work for me."

"Got it."

"You haven't seen Astrid because she's been with me and Johnny, sightseeing. Sit tight for an hour after we leave with her. Or better, run around and get sweaty. Rub some dust and dirt on your clothes and hands, make it look like you've been working all day. Come home without a clue. Understand?"

"Understood."

The door opened behind him and Astrid emerged, miraculously transformed into a respectable lady. Dressed, combed, shod. Cool and calm as if stepping out of a shop instead of a bedroom.

"You heard all that?" Major said.

"I've been with you all day on the boat and I haven't seen him."

"Good girl."

She touched his arm. "Thank you."

"What are uncles for? Now give each other a kiss and let's start the subterfuge."

Kennet and Astrid kissed quickly. "Wait outside a minute?" he whispered in her hair. And when she was gone, he faced Major and looked him in the eye.

"Thank you."

Major snorted and shrugged a shoulder. "Thank your brother. He thinks fast. Had a plan in hand before the train even pulled out."

"He learned quick thinking from you. But really, I meant thank you for not embarrassing her."

Now Major looked directly at him. "Who am I to embarrass someone for loving who they love?"

Kennet nodded. "I'm grateful."

Major patted Kennet's jaw. "See you at home. Remember: sweat and dirt and you haven't seen her all day." He headed for the door in his lurching stride, then turned back. "Not to embarrass you, but you're a smart egg. You'll destroy all the incriminating evidence? Flush the rubbers. Check under the bed for the wrappers. Throw them away at home, not here."

"Right," Kennet said, and when the door closed, he squeezed his eyes tight. He opened them slowly, blinking through bursts of yellow and orange. Back in the bedroom, he stripped the sheets and rolled them into a bundle to take home and launder. He crouched down and collected the torn wrappers from the floor, checking under the bed for any incriminating scraps of evidence.

He wasn't such a smart egg the last time they made love. He fell asleep afterward, still tight inside Astrid's body. But sleep made him go loose and slack and when he awoke and rolled away, he left the rubber behind. Astrid pushed away his panicked, fumbling fingers and quickly got it out herself and flushed it. Calm and unfazed, she told him to find some vinegar in the cottage's pantry, which he did. She shooed him out of the bathroom, told him not to worry and get back in bed.

His heart thudded heavy in his chest as he sat on the edge of the bare mattress. He put a hand in the place where Astrid lay naked just a few minutes before, looking for the warmth from her body.

A Flair For the Dramatic

The flaw in the plan, which not even Minor saw coming, was the romantic idealism of two ten-year-old girls. That Trudy and Kirsten wouldn't entertain the idea of Astrid and Kennet's romance being a secret was so obvious, nobody thought of it. And in the space of time it took for Johnny and Major to squire Astrid back to Clayton, Liisa knew in gushing, swooning detail how her daughter had fallen in love with the son of the hotel proprietor.

By the time Kennet returned, dirty and sweaty, Astrid had been yanked out of the Fiskares' house and into a room at the hotel.

"Oh Nycky, this is not good," Minor said, not an ounce of teasing in his tone. He was pale. "It was an ugly scene. Astrid's mother...Mrs..."

"Virtanen."

"Whatever the hell her name is, she lit into Astrid like nobody's business. Marta tried to intervene, soothe things down, and Mrs. Virtanen slapped her."

"What?" Kennet's hands went to fists.

"Paps is furious."

But Kennet was already walking away, looking for Marta. He found her in the kitchen, chopping onions. No doubt using them as an excuse to explain her swollen eyes.

"Marta, are you all right?"

She didn't answer. He put his hand on her arm but she just shook her head, still chopping.

He took the knife away and turned her toward him, pulled her in and wrapped his arms around her trembling shoulders. He'd never done such a thing. But she shivered in the embrace and wept on his dirty shirt front.

"I'm sorry," he said, patting her back. "I'm sorry this happened. This is all my fault, but—"

"How can it be your fault?"

"—I'm going to fix everything."

"You've done nothing wrong."

"I'm going to take care of this."

"God, Kennet, please don't make a scene."

"This woman barges unannounced into your house, starts berating your cousin, who is *our* guest, and then she slaps you for no good goddamn reason and you're telling *me* not to make a scene? The scene's been made. This show is going on."

"I mean don't make a scene in front of the… You know what I mean."

"I promise, I will be a gentleman," Kennet said, letting go of her. "But hell if I'll be a doormat."

"You look like a doormat," Minor said, appearing in the kitchen. "Did you leave any dirt on the island?"

"It was part of the alibi, remember?"

"Well, you're not going into war looking like that. Upstairs. Move."

Kennet showered and shaved. He dressed in Minor's best clothes as if donning armor. He walked over to the hotel, went up to the second floor and knocked on the door of the second-best suite.

A woman with all Astrid's features but none of her silvery allure opened it.

"God kväll," Kennet said, smiling. "Jag—"

She slammed the door in his face.

"Mor, släpp in honom," Astrid cried faintly from the other side. *Let him in.*

Kennet counted five, then knocked again. "Mrs. Virtanen, I need to speak with you, please."

Raised voices within, but it was in Portuguese and he couldn't understand. He only knew a handful of words in that language. He could sing the lyrics to "South American Way," but that wouldn't do him much good right now. But he did know another word: *desenrascanco.* Slapping together a solution with no plan and with whatever was to hand.

"It's a very Fiskare word," Astrid had said. "You're all so resilient and resourceful."

Kennet went on knocking and calling politely. He was perfectly calm. When Liisa opened the door a crack, put out a single pointed finger and said he was to leave this *instant* or she would call the police, he went on smiling and speaking politely. Again, the door slammed on his nose, but he wasn't upset. He was resilient and resourceful and he'd find another solution.

He left the hotel and walked to the riverfront. He noticed a penny in the dust and smiled as he picked it up. He threw it as far as he could into the St. Lawrence.

"Mrs. Virtanen, I'm a fisherman and a pirate," he said quietly. "I was conceived in a casino in Aix-les-Bains. The gold in my veins is inherited from my father, who got it from a Hun's tooth. My namesake uncle is king of the river. I do not give up my treasure to the likes of you…"

By the next morning, Liisa had taken her daughter not only out of the hotel, but out of Clayton. When Kennet telephoned the

Riverview Inn in Alexandria Bay, he was told Miss Virtanen was accepting no calls.

Desenrascanco, Kennet thought. Next plan was to go to the inn in person. If that failed, he'd have to get creative. No worries. He had three brothers: two to hold the ladder, the third to drive the getaway car.

He went to Emil and asked for Ingrid's engagement ring.

"Gullgosse," Emil said softly. "Sit down and let's talk about this."

"Ma left me the ring in her will. To give to the girl I want to marry."

"I know, but—"

"I'm going to marry Astrid."

"This isn't how it works, son."

"It's how it worked with you and Ma."

"That was different. It was war."

And she was pregnant with me.

As if reading Kennet's mind, Emil's expression went slightly stern. "You and Asta haven't gone and done anything stupid now, have you?"

"Paps."

"Well?"

"*No,*" Kennet said, lying.

"It's been a beautiful summer for both of you. I know how you feel—"

"If you know, then—"

"—and I know it seems perfectly plain and simple."

"Because it is."

"You're wrong. Life is more complicated than one idyllic summer. Love is more complicated. Marriage is the most complicated of all, you don't just plunge into it because you've spent three romantic weeks in each other's company."

It's one week more than you and Ma spent, Kennet thought, biting his tongue and clenching his fists. Enraged that war made different sets of rules in different times and places. He was losing patience and temper. Losing his solutions. Now was the time to argue calmly, like an intelligent adult, but everything he could think of to say sounded whining and petulant and stupid.

"Sit down, Kennet."

"Thank you, I'll stand. It's about all I can do right now, short of setting the hotel on fire."

"Well, don't do that," Emil murmured. He offered Kennet his pack of cigarettes. "It's a hell of a pickle."

"She's being pushed to marry someone she doesn't love."

Emil lit their smokes and shook the match out. "People in dire financial straits will do dire things."

"You think marrying for money is a good idea?"

"No. I don't think marrying someone you've known for three weeks because it gets you out of another marriage is a good idea, either."

Kennet breathed smoke, seething, wanting to tear the world apart. "I'm just supposed to let her go? Paps, you don't understand."

"If it's meant to be, it will work out. Son, believe me, if you were ten, even five years older, established with a good job and security, this would be a different conversation. You'd be eloped to Canada yesterday, Major would be negotiating rings at deWrenne Atelier, and I would be playing dumb."

Despite himself, Kennet glanced at his father, eyebrows raised. "Really?"

"You're twenty-two. You've never been west of Niagara Falls or south of Syracuse. There's a whole world out there." Emil heaved a long sigh. "And possibly a whole war out there, too."

"Which is why I can't just let her leave," Kennet cried through his teeth. "It's not like she lives in California. She'll be on the other side of the equator. If we get into the war then who knows what… I'll never be able to… Oh god*dammit.*"

"If she wants to do this, if she defies her mother and wants to stay, she can stay. She's welcome in this house and I will stand by both of you. But…"

"But?"

"I've been talking to Marta. I know the situation. I assume you do as well."

He did. And it was suddenly, unbearably heavy how intimately he knew both the situation and Astrid.

She won't stay. She promised her father. She can't put that weight down.

Not even for me? Not even if I carry it for her?

He envisioned a giant scale. One pan held all the love he'd cultivated in three short weeks. On the other side was a lifetime. A father who died before amends could be made. Promises sworn. Unassuaged guilt and shame. Burdens that were hard enough to bear without someone else using them as weapons.

No matter how much weight Kennet took on, Liisa Virtanen had her finger on the scale and a different definition of "taking care." It was her way or nothing.

She'll make Astrid choose. It's Liisa or me.

But aren't I doing the same? It's Liisa or me?

Do I even have that right?

That's not love. It can't be love.

Major said don't tell secrets out of obligation. What is love but laying bare all your deepest secrets?

The scales tipped.

I'm going to lose her. She's leaving. It's over.

"I know you know I'm right," Emil was saying. "And I know you'll go to the station tomorrow and say goodbye like a gentleman. But you don't have to feel good about it. It's not easy doing the right thing when love is ripping your stomach open and making your teeth ache. It's one of the worst parts of growing up."

"Can't believe people fall in love on purpose," Kennet muttered.

"I'm sorry, Nyck."

"Don't call me Nyck. Please."

The name belonged to Astrid now. Nobody else.

Emil got up, crushed his smoke beneath his shoe. "She's a fine, lovely girl. I wish—"

"Paps, please, I don't want to talk about it anymore."

"All right. I don't blame you." His hand fell warm and strong on Kennet's head, then his kiss brushed Kennet's hair. "I don't blame you one bit, gullgosse. And I'm sorry."

"I know."

"Now please go talk to your sister. Both of them. They're convinced they're entirely to blame for all of this. Trudy's about to shave her head and dress in sackcloth to atone. Cripes, and I thought Major had a flair for the dramatic."

She was ripped out of him so fast and so thoroughly, Kennet was surprised he wasn't left with a gaping wound or a missing limb. Ten years he'd dreamed of her. He'd fallen in love in mere weeks.

She was gone in an afternoon.

He went to the station, but he and Astrid barely got a goodbye. He was desperate to give her something so she wouldn't forget him, but he had nothing meaningful. He wanted to offer her gold, but he just had dumb rocks and bits of junk he'd collected along the shore or retrieved from the river bottom. He hoped she'd give him some kind of memento—a lock of her hair, her book of Byron poems, something. Anything.

But nothing. In front of everyone, Liisa especially, they could only shake hands.

He'd never felt so useless and helpless and angry. Appalled that it kind of helped to be mad at Astrid, too.

He could cut her dead. Dismiss her as weak. Or cruel. A doormat. It would be easy to do.

Love is doing the hard thing. The right thing?

What's right—letting her go, letting her come back to me in her own way and her own time?

I can't make her stay.

It's no use carrying what she'll never let go of.

Asta, Asta....

He wanted to scream. But everyone was watching him.

Take her. Take her hand and run.

"Asta," he said under his breath.

She looked up at him beneath the brim of her traveling hat. Pale as milk. Silvery eyes liquid with ten thousand agonies. "Nyck."

Shocked, stunned, bewildered, he shook her hand and behaved like a gentleman.

"Don't marry him," he said through his best front desk smile. "If you love me and—"

"Nyck, I love you."

"If you love and want me then hang onto that and wait. Wait while I figure this out. I can do this. Desenrascanco. All right?"

"Astrid," Liisa said sharply from the step of the train.

"Hang *on*," Kennet whispered. "Drop all that other shit and just hang onto me. All right?"

She nodded. Short, curt and brisk. A dazzling smile as the wind caught the brim of her hat and she pressed it down with her gloved palm. She moved away from him. A wave of dizzy nausea as the reel of Kennet's life story began to reverse.

This was how it began and ended. A book opening, pages turning backward, the book closing. A train pulling in. A handshake. A train pulling out.

If resfeber was the nervous excitement before a journey began, what was its opposite? What happened when you turned resfeber upside-down?

Saudade, he realized. *Longing for things lost. A golden time that will never come again.*

A Better Man For It

Kennet numbed the pain of Astrid's absence with work. He got a second job. Then a third. Then ditched all of them for a more lucrative position down at Pine Camp, expanding the military training site. He boarded in Watertown and came home on weekends. He pinched his pennies until Abe Lincoln howled, socking everything away for the golden time he believed would come back.

He wrote to Astrid, posting the envelopes to both the address in Florida and the address in Rio. He telegrammed her ship, but no reply came. He imagined she was being watched like a hawk, and like him, she was quietly plotting and planning how to make this story turn around and read left-to-right again.

Then in late September, the telegram from Brazil came. Not for him, but for Marta.

Not with a plan, but with a punch.

"Astrid got married," Marta said, the yellow slip of paper quivering in her fingers. "She married that fellow. Last weekend."

"Jesus H," Minor said softly.

Trudy started crying.

Emil put his hand on Kennet's back, pressing down as if to hold Kennet to the earth.

Kennet felt his entire being cloud over. Like a storm gathering above Wolfe Island. He would not divide, and he had ten minutes to get away from his loved ones before the full power of his rage thundered down. He pushed back his chair and walked out of the house. Napkin still in hand, he hopped onto the *Hildur* and sailed out to Grennell Island. Tre-O was shut up tight for the season, but he knew how to get in without a key.

"Desenrascanco, darling," he mumbled.

He broke a few things. Punched and kicked the walls. Bellowed at the ceiling before toppling face-down on the bare mattress and wallowing in his misery. He ate his heart out good and proper. Then there was nothing more for it. He went home and went back to work. Changed now. As his grandparents had been changed after Beatrice died, and his parents were altered by their stillborn daughter. Kennet looked in the mirror, expecting his face would have an obvious duality now, just like Minor. A subtle rearrangement in his features would prove Astrid abided within him, occupying half his soul.

He gazed hard at his reflection.

She wasn't there.

The next letter came in December. Addressed to Marta from Liisa Virtanen. But it was Emil who handed it to Kennet and suggested they step outside.

"Is she dead?" Kennet said, his voice hollow inside his head.

Half of Emil's mouth managed a smile. "No, son, she's not dead."

They went onto the porch. The day was brisk, but the southwest sunshine made a little warm splash on the one wicker chair left out for winter. Kennet sat and unfolded the letter.

"The first part is small talk," Emil said. "Skip to the end."

We've had a terrible time of it this past month, as darling Astrid was hospitalized with acute peritonitis, after suffering a miscarriage. Such a shock for young newlyweds who I'm sure weren't expecting to be parents so soon after marrying. Of course Astrid is heartbroken, but Jose has been angelic. Such an honorable man, as well as a dear, devoted and understanding husband. There will be other children. I'm sure you agree that this one wasn't meant to be and everyone is better off.

Kennet looked up. "Is she saying what I think she's saying?"

Emil lit a cigarette. "I don't admire the woman but she does know how to get a point across."

Kennet crumpled the paper in his hand and walked to the far end of the porch, where he stared at the river, stunned. After a moment, Emil's limping tread scuffed up behind. He offered the cigarette but Kennet waved it off. One drag and he'd upchuck on his shoes. He pressed his teeth together and drew a long breath, remembering the magical afternoon in the cottage. The bouts of decadent, juicy lovemaking. How he'd dozed off after the last time, then rolled, still half-asleep, off Astrid's naked body, leaving the rubber behind.

Emil cleared his throat. "Do you think the baby she lost was yours?"

Kennet opened his mouth to speak. Then shut it.

"Don't rationalize, son. Just tell me what's in your heart. Do you think it was yours?"

"Yeah. I do."

"Right," Emil said quietly. "So do I. For what it's worth."

"I'm sorry."

"What about?"

Kennet shrugged.

"I'm not angry with you or ashamed of you. Right now I feel nothing but sad. Because married or not, here or there, alive or dead, that would've been my first grandchild."

All at once, the loss of Astrid seemed *total*. She was far away before, but still present, still connected. Now she was gone. Utterly and irrevocably severed from him. Any last reminders of their love gone. Disintegrated into a hundred silver pieces. Nothing to name or embody or bury.

Kennet's gaze blurred hot and wet. He turned his head against one of the porch uprights, squeezed his crossed arms tight, clenched fistfuls of his jacket. He locked his jaw tight, refusing to give into the saudade. He'd allow the tears to fall, but he would not help them along. His eyes could leak but *he* was having none of it.

Emil retreated back to the chair and sat. A long silent time passed while Kennet fought this all-consuming emotion.

He won.

Barely.

"So this is love," he said.

"So it is."

"Delightful. Can't wait to do it again."

He went to his father. This time he accepted a cigarette and was glad for the bracing bite in his throat and lungs, shoring up the rickety walls he'd built around the pain.

"I'll tell you something," Emil said. "Ingrid was pregnant with you when we got married."

"I know."

Emil chuckled. "Do you, now?"

Kennet's face was still numb, but he could feel the corners of his mouth lift. "I can count, Paps."

"Well, then..."

Kennet sat on the floor, back to the shingles, arms around his bent knees. "What else do you want to tell me?"

"I've been to war and I've seen fear that can't be put into words. But you don't know the true definition of fear until you look into the eyes of a young, unmarried woman who's discovered she's going to have a baby. A woman in that position doesn't have a lot of choices. In fact, she only has two: make herself not pregnant, or make herself not unmarried. Choosing will drive her to swift, sometimes desperate action. She's worrying more about what others will think and say, than worrying what's best for her."

Kennet raised a single index finger as he looked his father in the eye. "If I'd known Astrid was pregnant, I would've gone after her."

You should've gone anyway.

"I would've helped you."

"If she wasn't married, I'd still go after her."

You should still go. Go now. Go get her.

"I'd still help you."

Then help me now, Kennet wanted to scream. But didn't. He rubbed the heel of his hand across his sternum. "I feel fucking sick."

"I know you do."

"My whole chest feels caved in."

"For sure."

"I think my heart's broken."

"I don't doubt it, son. And I'm so damn sorry. But hear me through. Try if you can to put Astrid's shoes on. An unmarried woman discovering she's pregnant will do desperate things and think about the consequences later. Your mother had granite nerves and an iron stomach, but she was beside herself when she found out you were on the way. The war not over and my chances of living slim to none. Not to mention we'd known each other about as

long as you and Astrid. Maybe less when you add all the days up."
He rubbed his hands together and sighed. "I don't need to tell you
a woman's got other choices, but she takes an even worse gamble
with her life if she goes that way."

"Was it ever an option?"

Emil looked at him. "No. Come hell or Hildur, we were together.
Because when you know, you know."

"That's the trouble. I knew. But I didn't...know."

"All I mean to say is don't judge Astrid too harshly."

"I'm not. I just feel I should've fought harder. I should've done
more. God*dammit.*" Kennet chucked the cigarette, meaning to
lob it over the railing, but it bounced off a spindle and showered
sparks onto his legs. Everything in the world was laughing at him.
Mocking him. He was nothing but a chump. A damn fool of a
boy. A punk who didn't know his onions.

"Neither of us know this fellow she married," Emil said. "He
could be a fine, honorable and understanding man who did the
right thing for someone he cares for. So don't judge him too harshly,
either."

"Doesn't leave me anyone to be mad at."

Emil smiled. "I'm here. Be mad at me."

As he dropped his chin, bubbles of laughter escaped Kennet's
aching throat. He longed to be young again, young enough to
crawl into the haven of Emil's lap and be soothed. He scooted on
his butt to put his back against the leg of Emil's chair. Emil's hand
rubbed circles between his shoulder blades.

"You were wronged," Emil said. "Your heart's broken, and that
just has to hurt until it doesn't."

"I'll get over it."

"No, you won't. But you'll get next to it and learn how to take
it along."

"Shit," Kennet muttered.

The chair creaked as Emil leaned and kissed Kennet's head. "You are my eldest and finest. And I'd fight another war for you."

Kennet closed his eyes. Three words he'd always struggled to say naturally with his father now spilled out without thought: "I love you."

"You're the best thing that happened to your Ma and me. You're honorable and decent and kind. You don't deserve this, and I'd fix it all if I could. But you'll come out a better man for it."

The Bender

Kennet was home for the weekend, puttering at his workbench in the boathouse. The radio was on, and when "A Small Hotel" started playing, he nearly flicked it off. Then he stood still with his fingers on the dial. Remembering.

When the door opened, he whirled around, startled out of his daydream and positive it was Astrid come back to him.

And whose little girl are you?

But it was only Little.

"Hey, bud," Kennet said, trying to hide the disappointment.

"I wanted to give you something."

"Oh?"

Little came over to the workbench, hands stuffed in his pockets. "You might not want them. I don't want to hurt your feelings. You can say no and you won't hurt mine."

Kennet had to smile even as his brow furrowed. "Wow, I don't know whether to be curious or afraid."

Little brought a hand out of his pocket and revealed two flattened pennies, obvious victims of the train.

"This one is from the day Astrid came," he said. "This one is from the day she left."

Kennet's smile died. An invisible hand curled around his heart and squeezed hard enough to make his throat warm. He lifted a palm. With a tinkling clink, the thin strips of copper dropped into it.

"That's real swell of you," he said softly.

Little's shoulders went up, down and around. "I miss her."

"I do too, kid."

"Think she'll ever come back?"

"No," Kennet said. "No, she won't come back. But these will help me remember the best summer of my life." He hooked an arm around the boy's neck and kissed his head. "Thank you. I feel better."

"Marta says dinner's ready in half an hour." Little dug his crown into Kennet's side another beat, then headed for the door.

"Hey," Kennet called after. "You know what Ma said to me before she died?"

"What?"

"She said, 'One day, Little is going to surprise you. You watch.'" He jingled the loose fist with the pennies. "She was right."

Little grinned. "She was always right."

Dear Nyck,
Forgive me. Please, please forgive me…

The letter went on, written in Swedish in Astrid's beautiful hand. Passionate, ardent words. Tender, genuine apologies. Heartfelt pleas for forgiveness. And through it all, love. Between every line, love. In the ring above an Å or the dots over an Ö, love.

He read it several times. The words in his head sounded far away, as if from the other side of a long bridge.

He'd crossed such spans before. He thought about the night he tried to beat the storm home and lost. All the Fiskare siblings got their fish warm that night, each taking five licks from Emil's razor strop. But then Emil threw everyone but Kennet out of the pantry, made them wait in the kitchen while Kennet had to drop his trousers and take five for each brother and sister on his bare skin. Twenty in all. His fish not just warm but deep-fried.

Lying in his bed that painful, shameful night, Kennet felt lower than low. Disowned. Forsaken. Cast out. But then Emil came into his bedroom. He sat on the edge of the mattress. He kissed Kennet's head and talked to him. His voice was soft in the dark, as if he stood on the far side of a bridge.

A boy would lie there in sullen, martyred silence. A man now, and a captain, Kennet made the decision to cross over and he answered his father. When Emil asked if he understood and would remember, Kennet promised he would.

Emil said he was forgiven.

It took a long time for Kennet to believe it.

We all make promises, Asta. And they can be such heavy things.

It was time now to navigate the difficult ravine between a young man and an older, wiser one.

He could give Astrid silence and make her suffer. Or he could be honorable and decent and kind. If he loved her, he could ease this saudade. Help her not long so intensely for their golden time.

He went to find Minor.

"I need to go to Montreal."

"Business or pleasure?" Minor said.

"Both. I'll handle business. You're in charge of pleasure."

So they went. Kennet made an appointment with deWrenne Atelier. He spent a pleasant morning with his distant cousins, the descendants of Anton deWrenne, who'd carved the fish fobs for the Old Bear's watch chain. Kennet explained what he wanted, put down a deposit, and was told to return in two days.

Kennet then put himself in Minor's hands, embracing a weekend of debauchery. Minor steered Kennet clear of the worst of Montreal's underbelly, and kept the train from completely going off the tracks during the bacchanal of drinking, women and oblivion.

The bender was occasionally interrupted by moments of civility, such as a very nice dinner with Minor's friends, a married couple, Guy and Natalie, and Natalie's younger brother Pierre.

Guy and Natalie left after coffee and dessert, but Pierre lingered at the table for brandy and cigarettes. He sat quite close to Minor, and the air between them was thicker than smoke, but at last, a little sorrowfully, Pierre said goodnight and left the restaurant. A single backward glance over his shoulder and Minor raised a single index finger off his glass.

"You can go with him," Kennet said. "I know my way back to the hotel."

"Trying to get rid of me?"

"No. But I know you're queer and you don't have to dance around it."

Minor snorted. "Goodness me, are you just discovering this?"

"Nah. I've known a while. I've only recently discovered how to bring it up."

"Step one: get a few drinks in your belly."

"Exactly."

"Being pissed does oil the wheels of conversation."

"So?"

Minor leveled a gaze at him, unfazed. "So?"

"You want to go with Pierre or not?"

"Not. Thank you for asking. Now finish your drink."

"Yes, mother." He took a long swallow and shivered at the burn. "So."

"So?"

"Do you...have anybody?"

"I've had a lot of anybodies. But my Johnny MacIntyre hasn't come along, if that's what you're asking."

"Does Major know?"

"He was first to know. Cripes, are you really this dumb, or are you pretending to be dense to help the conversation along?"

"I'm really this dumb."

"Jesus." Minor jiggled the ice in his glass and downed what liquid was left. "So as Marta would say, when did the penny drop?"

"First one dropped when you crawled into bed at three in the morning, smelling like aftershave. Brushing our teeth the next day, I noticed you had little bruises all over you. Shaped just like fingerprints."

Minor laughed. "The rich hold their money tight and their lovers tighter. I remember."

"Couple days after that, Astrid and I saw you swing by on the *E-Minor*. You had a fellow with you."

Minor's face went far away. "Man, that guy... Laurence. He was something else."

"What happened to him?"

Minor flicked a shoulder. "Went home with his rich wife. Like I knew he would."

"He was married?"

"You cannot be this dumb *and* be related to me. I refuse. Can you divorce a sibling? Honest to God, I'm going to hire a lawyer tomorrow and find out."

"At the risk of sounding like a drunk chump, you're my favorite brother and my best friend and I care about what happens to you."

"I know," Minor said. "When I'm nervous I crack a lot of jokes. Make enough and they build up into a wall."

"You don't have to hide who you are from me. If I was disgusted or ashamed of you being queer, I wouldn't be sitting here asking you questions about it."

Minor cleared his throat and rubbed a circle on his chest. "Damn, my heart's pounding."

"Why?"

"Because you're my rock-dumb brother and I care about your opinion. Now buy another round and give me a second to calm down and put my thoughts in a line. Jesus H..."

Kennet signaled the waitress. Minor lit a cigarette and settled back in the booth, picking invisible lint off his sleeve. "Major taught me three things about being gay. And if you don't mind, it's the word I prefer over *queer*. I don't care what slang you use when my back is turned. To my face, use gay or nothing." He smiled. "Please."

"Noted."

"Three things he taught me. One is not to be ashamed of who I am. Which I'm successful at. Most of the time, anyway. The second thing is to be really fucking careful about who I let close to me. Which I mastered after getting beat up a few times."

"Beat up when?" Kennet said sharply. "By whom?"

Minor waved it off. "My problem, not yours. And lesson learned, so don't worry about it. The third thing Major taught me is to be realistic. Guys like me don't get somedays and someones. Not if we want to operate in nice society. We get discreet bachelorhood or a marriage of convenience with a secret-but-devoted piece on the side. If we're lucky. If we're really lucky, we get a Johnny Mac-Intyre and we get to be a town's worst-kept secret because our family's been here forever, we own a bunch of prime real estate and we proved ourselves men during Prohibition. Major's an exception, not a rule. I don't even hope to have my life turn out like his."

"What do you want your life to be?"

"Hell if I know."

"Come on, what's your dream?"

"You mean six two, dark hair, blue eyes, big bank account and nice ass?"

"Is that it?"

"Jesus, I don't know. If anything…" His gaze went away a moment, then he shook his head. "Never mind."

"Tell me."

"It's dumb."

"And I'm your dumb, drunk, jilted brother. Indulge me."

Minor laughed, eyes circling the ceiling. "I always figured I'd know a guy was the one by the way he said my name. My real name. My whole life, *Erik* never sounded like it belonged to me. It's a word on a piece of paper. I have no connection to it. I can't even connect it to me through Major. We both share this name that's…" Minor gestured to the smoky air around him. "Out *there* somewhere. When I get really dark and broody, I think the name Erik belongs to the part of me that died with my twin."

Kennet's hairline tightened as his brows flew up. "My whole life, I think I can count on one hand the number of times you've mentioned her."

"Yeah. Anyway, I was out at Major's place once, digging up stumps. I heard Johnny calling him from inside the house. Something mundane like, 'Erik, where's the bottle opener?' The hair on the back of my neck went up. Even though he wasn't calling to me, it was like I heard the sound of my own name for the first time. Or rather…how my name would sound if a lover called me, wondering where something was in the house. *Our* house. I could imagine a life like that. I'd still be Minor Fiskare, but at home, someone who knew me best would call me Erik.

"Ever since, I've had this notion that if I met a guy and one day he said something ordinary like, 'Erik, you got a match?' And it sounded good in my ears and made the hair on my arms and neck stand up... He'd be the one." Minor smiled. "But I've been taught to be realistic, so it's wiser to say he *could* be the one."

"Well, I hope someday he comes along."

"You're serenading me with Gershwin now? Please don't."

They had a last cigarette and finished their brandies.

"I'm really sorry about the baby," Minor said. "I mean it. I don't know why, but... Just made me so sad. Astrid was special. We all fell a little in love with her and I know it was only a few weeks, but I really thought she was your one."

"Whose little girl aren't you?"

"Jesus H, I'm sorry."

"Anyway, this little Canadian jaunt has been a tonic. And I'm grateful. I'll get over the heartbreak, but a world without you isn't survivable."

"Thank you," Minor said softly.

"For?"

"For being my brother and best friend. For standing by me. For being breathtakingly dumb, but kind and loyal and all those other sappy adjectives that mean the world."

Kennet raised his empty glass. "Minor mine, you are so fine."

Minor raised his. "It ain't no trick to love my Nyck."

They tottered out of the restaurant and almost immediately ran into Pierre.

"Well, good evening," Minor said.

"Again," Kennet said.

"I think I left my cigarette lighter on the table," Pierre said. "Did you see it?"

Minor glanced at Kennet before answering. "No, but I'm an expert finder of lost things. I'll help you look."

"And I'm an expert finder of ways back to the hotel," Kennet said. "Goodnight, boys."

Alcohol had never been a loyal friend to Kennet but tonight, it nestled him into dreamless, heavy sleep, tender as a lover. When he woke in the wee hours, the booze hadn't left any of its usual calling cards: sour stomach, pounding head, raging thirst, bone-deep regret. He felt light and fresh as he rolled over to the sound of the door quietly opening and closing. Minor moving on soft, socked feet, in and out of the john, undressing, sliding into the room's other twin bed.

"Have a good time?" Kennet yawned.

"Mm."

"Hair stand up on the back of your neck?"

Minor laughed softly. "No, but something else was standing up—" The laughter turned to a guffaw as he caught the pillow Kennet hurled at him.

"Keep that fish tale in school," Kennet muttered.

Minor threw the pillow back. "Don't drop a baited hook if you're—"

"Good*night*, Minor."

Kennet returned to deWrenne Atelier to collect his commission. His cousins had done a beautiful job. Nestled in the palm of his hand was a one-inch replica of the *Hildur*. It had a little loop at the bow so it could be threaded onto a chain.

"I'll need you to ship this," Kennet said. "It can't come from my address in the States."

His cousin smiled, delicately touching the rims of his glasses. "Certainly."

Kennet wrote the check, gave the address in Rio, then reached in his inside pocket for a small envelope. He held it tight a moment, hoping he'd said all the right things.

Dear Asta,

Forgiven. Please, please don't tear yourself apart. I have no regrets…other than I should've fought harder. Made more of a stand. Moved the earth.

For that, please forgive me.

You left Clayton with my entire heart in your hands. Believe me when I say you still have my heart. And now you have my boat.

Remember this, Asta. Just her and him on the Hildur. Unhurried hearts harkening to the hushed history of helping hands holding hard to happiness.

It was our golden time and I won't ever forget.

I still love you.

Nyck

He passed the envelope across the glass counter. "It's important you include this in the package. It's more important than the boat."

"You can depend on me."

"I appreciate it, thank you."

"Give my regards to your family. And if we don't speak before, Merry Christmas."

They shook hands and Kennet left the shop. Knowing he'd done all he could, but wishing he had something to show for it. Some visible proof of how doing what was best had changed him. Wasn't there a prize for winning a moral victory?

This kind of war hurts everyone on the inside, he thought.

Both he and Minor were quiet on the drive home, each occupied with their own deep thoughts.

"Feeling any better?" Minor said as they neared the border of New York.

"No. But thank you for asking."

Minor grinned and flicked on the car's radio. Ray Noble and his orchestra, with Snooky Lanson singing "By the Light of the Silvery Moon." The brothers sang Major's call-and-response version, which was the only version as far as they were concerned.

"By the light," Minor warbled.

Kennet strummed an imaginary ukulele and sang-spoke the punchline, "Not the dark but the light."

> *Of the silvery moon.*
> *(Not the sun but the moon.)*
> *I want to spoon*
> *(Not a fork but a spoon.)*
> *To my honey, I'll croon love's tune...*

They were crossing the Thousand Islands Bridge, back into the States. Far below, the waters of the St. Lawrence were chilblained and cut with small whitecaps. Where it iced up near the banks, the sun reflected back sharp, bouncing off the bare, fallow farmland. The grand hotels and resorts slept behind their shuttered windows. Leafless, skeleton tree trunks pointed up among the ruffled pines.

Allow us all the alliteration, Kennet thought, smiling over his beloved land and realizing while he didn't feel terrific, he felt a hell of a lot better than the week before.

> *Honeymoon*
> *(Not a brown sugar moon)*
> *Keep on shining in June*
> *(Not July but June)*

The song abruptly cut out in the middle of a verse. An odd beat of dead air, then the station announcer broke in, his voice pitched high and urgent:

"We interrupt this broadcast to bring you this important bulletin. Flash. Washington. The White House announces Japanese attack on Pearl Harbor…"

NOVEMBER
1944

A Damn to Give

The countryside of Jefferson County shivered under a pale, watery sunshine as the three oldest Fiskare sons bombed along Route 12 in the family Ford. Riding shotgun, Kennet blew on his hands and rubbed them vigorously. Even with wool socks and gloves, his fingers and toes had been complaining all day.

After Pearl Harbor, the work at Pine Camp, the military's training base, quadrupled and Kennet was kept on for the duration of the massive expansion. The Army purchased another 75,000 acres of land and took possession like a horde of Mongols, wiping five villages off the map and displacing over five hundred local families. The beefed-up workforce began constructing an entire city: hospitals, warehouses, barracks, mess halls, buildings for Army business and buildings for Army recreation. At the same time, one of the worst winters in recorded history was breathing down the neck of the North Country. Men fought frozen machinery, machinery fought the frozen ground, and nature fought the men with hypothermia, chilblains and frostbite. The numbing cold and constant tingling pain in fingers and toes could drive a man to drink.

As the hard winter turned to soft summer, the work at Pine Camp ended and Kennet was shipped out to Camp Polk, Louisiana, for basic training. Finally his poor, suffering extremities knew true relief, but even now, three years later, they bitched and moaned when winter came around again.

Nineteen forty-two had been a cold, dark, depressing time in Kennet's life, when he defined himself by the loss of Astrid. Emotionally speaking, the Army was the best thing that could have happened to him. The first thing the military did was strip your possessions and your personality away—happiness, heartbreak, handsomeness, even hair. As soon as the barber started running clippers over the top of Kennet's head, he felt a slight change within. He watched, mesmerized, as hunks of his blond hair started falling around his shoulders and tumbling to the floor, taking with them the sweet memory of cafune—Astrid's fingers running along his crown and temples. The fuzzy pile was swept up and unceremoniously pushed onto the bigger pile of shorn locks in the corner.

Well, that's that, Kennet thought. He fell into line, one of hundreds of men who now looked just like him. Within a single hellish week, he grasped that Uncle Sam had no interest in a fellow's hurt feelings, and boot camp simply didn't give a guy the time or energy to pine. His ass would be whipped into shape, come hell or Hildur. He could do it the hard way and bring his pissy attitude along, or he could chuck it over the side and embrace being worked into physical and mental oblivion. Even be grateful for it.

Training with the 21st Army Infantry Battalion took Kennet to four different bases in two years: from Camp Polk to Camp Barkeley in Texas. ("Not for me either," he wrote home to Marta, who was finally sticking his green pins in her world map.) Then Camp Ibis in Needles, California, and finally Camp Cooke in Lompoc.

The farther he moved from New York, the longer the supply lines of memory stretched, until the intense heartbreak could no longer be sustained. He'd never forget Astrid. He hadn't gotten over it. But just as Emil said, he learned to get next to it. Or, more accurately, to get in *front* of it and put Astrid where she used to be—over his shoulder. As the weeks and months passed, as his surroundings changed, he looked back at her less and less. He never stopped completely. He missed her, but it no longer hurt like an untreated toothache. He thought about her and wondered what she was doing, but it didn't turn his mind into a nest of angry red ants.

The thought rose: *I love her, I will always love her,* but it became as ordinary as the sky being blue and sugar being sweet. The ache of missing her became like his chilblained fingers—occasionally acting up when his mood turned cold and blue.

Sometimes more troubling thoughts came: *Does she still love me, does she miss me, does she wonder about me?* But even these were faced down with a newfound pragmatism: *You'll never know. Either you believe she does or you believe she doesn't. Decide which it is and get next to it.*

"Jesus H," Minor said, swatting Kennet's shoulder with the back of his hand. "What's a brother gotta do to get you to smile?"

"Just sit there and look beautiful," Kennet said, breaking out of his deep thoughts. "And try not to get yourself killed again."

Minor had gone straight into the Navy after Pearl Harbor. He was sent first to machinist school in Chicago, then posted to the carrier USS *Lexington* as a Machinist's Mate. He was the first Fiskare son to see action: in the Coral Sea, the *Lexington* was struck by two torpedoes and five bombs in the space of eleven minutes. The ruptured fuel lines released gasoline fumes, which were ignited by a generator, and the resulting explosion shook the carrier from bow to stern. Minor was blasted clear through the wall of a boiler room. Bleeding heavily from a gash across his forehead and temple, he lay unconscious in the rapidly rising water of the broken main and would have drowned if buddies hadn't found him and hauled him out. After a month's hospital stay, he was reposted to the cruiser USS *Indianapolis*.

"Quit staring at me," Minor said, shaking out a cigarette.

"Can't."

"Then stare and give me a light."

Kennet flicked his Zippo, studying his brother's scarred profile. Minor's right side was his brooding, cautious side, and even with half a grin and a cigarette poking jauntily from the corner, his face was set in a way Kennet had never seen before. Minor seemed smaller. Not diminished, but *condensed*. All the unnecessary and immature distractions of his personality shaved off or pinned firmly down. His devil-may-care attitude had found a damn to give. For the first time in his life, he appeared to measure his words before doling them out.

Nalle hitched forward and reached a hand over the front seat, looking for a drag. He ruffled first Minor's hair, then Kennet's, then stretched longer to turn up the radio dial, catching the tail end of the Merry Macs:

> *If the words sound queer and funny to your ear, a little bit*
>   *jumbled and jivey,*
> *Sing "Mares eat oats and does eat oats and little lambs eat ivy."*
> *Oh, mairzy doats and dozy doats and liddle lamzy divey.*
> *A kiddley divey too, wouldn't you?*

"Park it, junior," Minor said.

Nalle settled back in his seat with his head against the window, his feet in the opposite well. In three years, he'd packed two more inches and about twenty pounds onto his frame. The little bear was now a full-grown grizzly.

He had just turned seventeen when Pearl Harbor was bombed, irritated when he needed parental consent to enlist, furious when Emil wouldn't give it.

"Ma would do it," Nalle said.

Emil banged a fist on the table. "She would *not.* She'd want you to go to college. If you don't know what being accepted would've meant to her, then you didn't know her at all."

Nalle couldn't argue. With his acceptance to University of Vermont, he'd be the first Fiskare to ever attend college. He conceded the point, Emil smoothed his fist into a palm, and they brokered a deal: no enlisting until Nalle had a year of higher learning under his belt, at which point Emil could protest, but he couldn't forbid.

Nalle came into his own in Burlington and became captain of the university's cross-country ski club. And it was from this club that he was recruited by the 87th Infantry Regiment, the Army's first mountain unit to be trained specifically for winter combat. Out of deference to Emil, Nalle completed his sophomore year before heading to train at Camp Hale in Colorado.

On this late autumn day in 1944, all three Fiskare sons were home on leave, all three certain it would be the last time for a long time. They'd received no definitive orders, no word of a future mission, no hints at the master plan. As grunts, they were the last to know where they'd be going, and when, and what for. But each had a feeling the time was nigh and a reckoning was due. Emil must have felt it as well, for he'd done something Kennet thought extraordinary.

His first night home, Kennet sat down to a game of backgammon with his father and noticed a strange glint of gold along Emil's neck. Strange, because the men of Kennet's time were largely unadorned. Men's jewelry was understated to the point of invisibility: cufflinks, collar pins, tie pins, wristwatches, even a signet ring on the pinky—these were rare, but acceptable. Necklaces were far out of the ordinary. It took Kennet's nape a good few months to get used to the feel of the ball chain with his dog tags. Of course, now he felt odd when he took them off. Slightly naked without their weight at his neck and their tiny clinks and clanks against his chest. Still, it was military issue, not a fashion statement. What the heck was Emil wearing?

"Paps, what is this?" He reached across the little table and hooked a finger inside Emil's collar.

Emil's hand came up with a jerk as if to stop him, then he smiled sheepishly. "Oh, just something to soothe your worried old man."

Across the first joint of Kennet's finger ran a gold chain, but unlike any he'd seen. Its flat, gold links cunningly fit together like tiny cubes. Pulling it further from Emil's shirt, Kennet saw the Old Bear's Saint Birgitta medal suspended off the chain, along with two of the tiny gold fish that were once his watch fobs.

"Where'd you get this chain?"

"The deWrennes made it."

"Why?"

"Because… See, after Minor was wounded and Nalle joined up, I needed something more than just plain hope. I needed…magic, I guess. No, not magic. A charm. A talisman. Something real and tangible to symbolize all three of my boys, something to hold and touch and keep close to me. I told Major, and he went up to Montreal and had the chain made. Then he gave me his gold fish, so I'd have three things to hang on it. Tre fiskar. Tre önskningar."

Three fishes. Three wishes.

"Look at that," Kennet said, gathering the two fish and the medal together. They made a satisfying handful, warm and weighty, clinking together like his dog tags. "It's handsome on you. I like it."

"It's silly," Emil said, glancing down.

"No." Kennet let the little charms fall onto his father's heart and he put his palm over them. "No, it isn't. I like knowing you have us close to you this way. It's perfect. Really, Paps. I mean it."

"It helps," Emil said. "I put it on first thing in the morning. Take it off last thing at night. And I'm not a religious man, but in my own way I say a little prayer, and…" His voice got husky and he shrugged. "It helps."

"I like it," Kennet said again. He patted the charms one last time, then Emil tucked the chain back inside his shirt. And at that moment, if Emil had pulled him into his arms, Kennet couldn't have felt safer.

Emil's One

It was good to be home, and Kennet caught both himself and his brothers looking thoughtfully, often intensely around the house. Staring at walls and floors and objects and furniture. Taking slow, deliberate time to take detailed inventory and press it into their memories. As well, each of them was carving out time with every family member, making occasions and creating memories they could fold up small and take along in a pocket.

It was too cold for boat rides, and gas was rationed anyway, but Kennet puttered at the marina with Emil, just to be alone and talk. He bartended with Major, jawing away together between customers.

Conscious that the youngsters weren't so young anymore, Kennet made even more of an effort to cultivate his relationships with Little, Trudy and Kirsten. He'd always grouped them together as one entity, and while the girls were as inseparable as ever, Little had grown into his role of the only boy at home. At fifteen, he possessed a quiet confidence and a sunny disposition that made Emil trust him implicitly with the running of the hotel's front desk.

"That boy's got a natural head for hospitality," Emil said. "I'm a little ashamed to say I didn't see it coming."

"Ma said one day Little would surprise us," Kennet said.

Kennet took Little out alone, just the two of them, wanting to remember his brother as he was now, not a child. Another Sunday, he dressed in his nicest and took Trudy and Kirsten to lunch, where he listened more than he talked. These were no longer little girls to be teased, coddled and petted, but young women on the cusp. Capable at home, competent in the hotel, and well-entrenched in war work. For some inexplicably romantic reason, both girls had pledged not to cut their hair until the war was over. They shrugged in explanation, barely disturbing the thick bellpulls of their braids.

"I'll be home before you can sit on the ends," Kennet said.

"You better," Trudy said. She'd inherited Ingrid's plain looks but not Ingrid's severity. She had Emil's generous smile and the wicked twinkle in her pale grey eyes was pure Major.

"Promise you'll be careful?" Kirsten said.

"I promise." Kennet was a little alarmed at Kirsten's burgeoning beauty. She was lively, but cool and circumspect for a thirteen-year-old. You could make her laugh, but good luck pulling her leg.

The only relationship Kennet struggled with was Marta. She didn't seem herself and Kennet couldn't tell if it was worry about the war and the boys, or worry about something practical like money or the roof or rationing. When he tried to pin her down, she waved him off.

But finally, one evening, it was the two of them alone in the kitchen and Marta was making pepparkakor. Kennet had a big cup of stewed, black tea to go with his cookies, and was a good ways into W. Somerset Maugham's new book, *The Razor's Edge,* slowly realizing he didn't want to read about a soldier wounded and traumatized by the deaths of comrades in battle. The story was making his stomach hurt. He should go up to the attic and find his old, battered beloveds. *Jungle Tales of Tarzan* or *Dr. Dolittle.* Or even one of the *Winnie-the-Pooh* books, for crying out loud.

Marta closed the oven door and sank into a chair. "That's the last batch," she said, as if there would never again be any pepparkakor in the world.

Kennet closed the book and pushed it away. "Cheese on a cracker, are you going to tell me what's the matter? And don't say 'nothing.'"

"All right." She sighed, and then managed a wan smile. "Your Pa asked me to marry him."

Kennet knocked over his cup, then quickly righted it. "He did what?"

"Your Pa asked—"

"I heard you. I'm sorry. He..."

"Yes." She handed him a dish towel to mop up the tea.

"Oh."

"Nobody knows yet. Except Major." She picked up a cookie and broke it in half, but did nothing with the pieces..

"Major knows everything," Kennet said absently.

"I wanted to talk to you first. Before telling anyone else."

"Did you say yes?"

"I didn't say anything. Not until I talked to you."

"Why me?"

She swatted his upper arm. "Because you're like a bloody brother to me," she cried. Now she was herself, but in a distraught way. "What do you think? Oh Christ..."

"Well, when did this... I mean, how did... Holy *shit*, Marta."

She held up her hands and let them fall. "I never would have thought. Not in a million years."

"He's quite a bit older than you."

"I can count, thanks ever so much."

"Do you love him?"

She drew a long breath. "Try to understand, I loved your Mum awful. She was dear to me. We understood each other. We worked together like gears in a machine. I admired her so much and she was so devoted to your Pa, of course I came to feel the same way about him. It wasn't a chore, mind you. I always thought he was a lovely man. Not in a romantic way. A respectful, admiring way."

"I understand."

"I adored them both. And when your Mum was dying, she asked if I would stay on when she was gone. Not for your Pa's sake but for Little and Trudy and Kirsten. And I promised I would. You know this."

"Of course I do. I don't know what we would've done if you hadn't. Especially the girls."

"It was an easy decision. I love this town. I love the hotel. I love the river and the community. I love the girls and Little, Minor and Nalle…" She swatted his arm again, lightly this time. "And I love you, you big lump."

"But do you love my father?"

She nodded. "I do. I'm not settling, if that's what you mean."

"I don't object to another woman loving him. He's not a man to go through life alone. And neither are you."

"I'm thirty-six. Long ago I accepted I wasn't going to have a home and kids of my own. It was too late even before the war, and then the war blew any chance I had to bits. But I felt part of your family, and it was a good life. Trudy and Kirsten were so young and so attached to me, I could sometimes pretend they were my girls. And now…" She sniffed, but her face had gone soft, all lit up from within and lit up from without. "Here's your Pa. This lovely man. And maybe it's not too late after all. But I can't say yes to him unless it's all right with you. Minor and Nalle, too. But mostly you."

"Do I have to call you Mum?"

"I'll thump you if you do."

"Well, then let me be the first to say congratulations."

"We have your blessing?"

"You don't need my… Yes. If it means that much, yes."

She exhaled and gave a little laugh. "What a weight off my chest."

He took her hands and squeezed them, then playfully examined her bare fingers. "No ring? I'm going to have to take the old man to task."

"I don't need a ring."

"Oh, but you do."

"Well, I wouldn't have accepted one until we'd talked. And cripes, if I was nervous about telling you, your father was tied in a knot."

"Why?"

"Because he thinks the world of you, fat-head. Come off it, now. Everyone knows Nalle was your Mum's pet. Your uncle owns Minor, and as for the youngsters, well, they belong to everyone. But you're Emil's one. Not because you're his eldest but because you're so alike. He told me so once. He said, 'I just love being with that boy.'"

Kennet chewed on that, along with the sound of his father's first name in Marta's voice. He'd never once, ever, heard her say *Emil*.

"He needs to know you're all right with us getting married. Go find him tonight? Please?"

"Of course."

Horse's Neck

"Let's go have a drink," Kennet said.

Emil looked up from his paper. "Now?"

"Now. I need to talk to you."

"What about?"

"About who's going to pay for your wedding."

A beat as Emil stared at him. Kennet leaned into the door frame and crossed his arms. "Marta and I had a chat. Let's you and I go have one, too."

"What about your brothers?"

"They'll come later. Right now, I'm pulling rank as the oldest. Me first. With you. Alone."

It was Sunday and the bar was closed to the public. Kennet and Emil leaned elbows on the bar's shiny top. Only a few lights on, catching beams in the rows of bottles and the planes of ice cubes.

"I'm happy for you," Kennet said. "Honest. Once I got over the surprise, it made perfect sense."

"I don't know if I'm over the surprise yet," Emil said ruefully.

"Tell it to Sweeney. A dashing widower such as yourself. It was only a matter of time."

"I didn't want you kids to be hurt. Or think I forgot your mother."

"Of course not. And Ma's the last person who'd want you to be alone. You need a wife. You wouldn't know what day it was without one."

"You've gotten fresh in your old age."

"If I can go to war, I can listen to my father talk about being lonely."

Emil rolled his lips in and pressed them tight, nodding a little.

"I feel bad I never even thought to ask," Kennet said.

Emil waved a hand. "You have plenty else to worry about."

"And while I was worrying, I could've asked you how you were feeling. If you were lonesome. If you ever thought about getting married again."

"I wasn't entirely averse to the idea. But I never once thought that…" Shaking his head, Emil swirled the whiskey in his glass and took a pull. "Funny how it happens. Marta was always there. But one day…there she was."

"Like I said, it makes perfect sense."

"But it's more than my need for companionship. It's the future of this family. My three eldest boys going off to fight. Minor already having a close call and—"

"Don't. Come on, Paps, tonight's for celebrating."

"No, I need to talk to you about this. I know what war is. I know what's coming for my boys and you don't know how it…" He looked away abruptly and reached in his back pocket for his handkerchief. "Well, damn it all, look at me now. I swear to goodness, Kennet, I can't stop crying lately."

Kennet touched his shoulder. "You can tell me, Paps. I won't think less of you for letting your feelings show while you're telling. In fact, it only makes me admire you more."

See, Astrid taught me that.

Emil wiped his eyes. "Gullgosse, I worry so much about you, I think sometimes I'll go out of my mind."

"We'll be all right," Kennet said lamely.

"I don't mean all three of you. I mean, yes, all three of you. But I worry most about *you.*"

"Me?"

"You're not built for war. I don't say that as an insult. I know you're a fine soldier and you'll do what's expected of you. I mean your soul isn't made to process war. Nalle has his principles to sustain him. Minor will get by on sheer personality. But you? You were always the one who liked to sort and label and name everything. This was this. That followed this. If this, then that. You like rules to define the edges of your life. You like people to behave within those rules. And war blows all those things to shit. Absolute shit. You'll see people doing abhorrent, unspeakable things. You'll find yourself doing things that go against every rule, every standard, every ethic you ever held. War rubs against the very grain of who you are, and some men just can't..."

He pressed the back of his fist against his mouth a moment. "I saw it happen with my brother when we got home."

"I know, Paps."

"You don't. Nyck couldn't shake it off. Couldn't come back. Couldn't stop fighting. Couldn't reconcile who he'd been before the war with everything he did and saw in France. He couldn't process it. He had no construct between the soldier and the man. That's what worries me most about you."

"Look, I'm his namesake but I'm not him," Kennet said gently.

"I know, gullgosse. I won't ask you to promise to be careful. That's a given. I want you to promise to take care of yourself. To separate your *self* from the soldier. You like rules. Promise me you'll remember that war breaks all of them. That when you find yourself doing something that would be considered unforgivable in peacetime, you remember you're not living by those rules. And you forgive yourself."

He slumped a little on his stool, shaking his head. "Anyway, that's what your old man needs you to do. But we were talking about Marta and the future of this family, weren't we?"

"Right," Kennet said, more than a little bewildered.

"If I lose one of you boys… If I lose one, two or *all* of you, I still have to do right by Little and Trudy. And Kirsten, too, because Charlie Lund isn't coming back. His heart, mind and soul all left this earth when his wife died. His body has gone to war simply to finish the job. So Kirsten's one of the family, as far as I'm concerned. She and Trudy are becoming young women, but they need a mother. A woman's influence. Marta loves them like they were her own girls. She knows how to handle the house and the hotel. She knows I need a way to get through this war. The both of us are scared rotten and sick at heart for you and Minor and Nalle. We may as well be scared and sick together."

Now Kennet burst out laughing. "Look at you dancing around the subject, giving every explanation except the obvious."

"What?"

"She loves you."

Emil blew out a short, sheepish breath. "So she says."

"Do you love her?"

"For the life of me I don't know why she'd throw her lot in with a man old enough to be—"

"Oh, bullshit on white toast. Marta never settled for anything in her life. She doesn't own a lot, but what she owns is the best. And

I've never known you to celebrate mediocrity, so I know you're not just marrying her because it's convenient, or because it's best for Little and the girls. Cripes, I hope you love her. She's my friend and one of my favorite people, so I may just insist that you love her. Otherwise go be sick and scared with Major."

"I do love her," Emil said quietly. "It's a little embarrassing how much."

Kennet crossed his arms and affected a stern expression. "I am less than pleased with her unadorned fingers, Mr. Fiskare. Did you control your embarrassing emotions long enough to get her a ring?"

Emil laughed. "I did, sir. Well. Major helped. He insisted."

Their eyes screwed up as all the lights in the bar suddenly flicked on.

"Has the party started?" Minor called. "Are we late?"

"Yes," Kennet said. "And you're ruining the ambience. Kill the light."

"Minor mine," Emil called. "Make us a round?"

"Aye, skipper." Minor slid behind the bar and began setting up glasses with the swift, economical movements of the experienced bartender. "Old Fashioned for you, Paps? Kennet, what sourpuss soda are you drowning in?"

"Gin rickey. Two limes."

"What about you, Nalle-Bear?"

Nalle elbowed in between Emil and Kennet. "Surprise me."

"One Shirley Temple, coming up."

"Hardee har har." Nalle shook out a cigarette and tossed the pack on the bar. "Is Major coming?"

"Not tonight," Kennet said. He took a smoke and slid the ashtray closer. "Just us."

"What's the occasion?" Minor asked, slicing limes.

"It's a bachelor party."

Minor didn't miss a goddamn beat. "Who'd you knock up this time, Paps?"

"Watch your mouth," Emil said automatically.

"C'est la guerre," Nalle said, lighting his cigarette, then Kennet's. He moved the match toward Emil, who licked his thumb and forefinger and snuffed the flame out, scowling.

"Never three on a match," he said. "Have I taught you nothing?"

Nalle grinned and lit another. "Sorry. Kennet, turn on the radio."

"No news reports," Emil said.

Kennet twisted the dials until he found the *Champion Spark Plug Hour.*

"Here we go," Minor said, sliding glasses along the bar top. "What should we toast?"

"Me." Emil glanced at Kennet, then blew a smoke ring. "I'm getting married again," he said through it.

Minor lifted his glass. "To Paps getting— What?"

"Married?" Nalle said.

Emil half-lifted his drink. "Again."

"To whom?"

"Marta."

Minor blinked twice, then downed his entire drink and plonked the glass on the bar. "Well, holy shit, I believe I'll have another."

"In other words, congratulations," Kennet said.

"Bachelor party," Nalle said slowly.

"As it were," Emil said.

"Why didn't you tell us before?"

"I wanted to wait until you boys were home. Tell you in person."

"I didn't mean tell us you were getting married. I meant why didn't you...*tell* us?"

"Tell you what?"

"That you were sneaking up the attic stairs, so to speak," Minor said.

"Don't be crass," Nalle snapped. "Maybe your mind lives in the gutter, but you don't have to take every conversation there."

"Oh, but I do," Minor said coolly.

"Settle down, boys," Emil said. "Nalle's asking why I didn't mention this courtship. Am I right?"

Nalle shrugged, reached a leg back to hook a stool and draw it closer. He sat, hurt etched in every line of his body.

"It's a fair question," Emil said.

"It's also none of our business," Minor said.

"Oh, but it is," Nalle said.

"Touché, brother. You going to try your surprise?" Minor indicated the Horse's Neck he'd made for Nalle. It was a beautiful cocktail of rye, bitters and ginger ale, named for the long strip of lemon peel that coiled within the Collins glass, with the "head" dangling over the rim.

"One reason I didn't mention it," Emil said, "is it all happened rather suddenly. Or rather, I think it was happening slowly and gradually, but I realized it suddenly. Another reason, honestly, is I worried how you would feel about it." His words encompassed the group at the bar, but his eyes and his posture were focused on Nalle, the family barometer. The heart, soul and conscience of the Fiskares. And Ingrid's favorite.

Nalle glanced at Kennet. "Did you know?"

"I found out tonight, just the same as you."

"I told Kennet first because he's eldest," Emil said. "Which is how it's done. Now I'm telling you and Minor, which is proper. Then I will tell Little and Trudy."

"And Kirsten," Nalle said absently.

"Yes. And Kirsten, too."

"Well, Paps, I think it's great," Minor said. "A man like you isn't meant to go through life alone. Ma wouldn't want you to be alone. She had her ideas, but grudges and jealousy were never in her nature. Cripes, she was the most damn generous woman that lived. Hoboes chalked it on the sidewalk in front of our house, remember?"

"It's not the kind of thing you forget," Emil said. "Nalle, this doesn't mean I've forgotten your mother."

"I know," Nalle said, sitting still and tight behind his crossed arms.

Minor nibbled on an orange peel and chuckled. "You're a ridiculously lucky man, Paps. Some fishermen don't make one good catch. You made two."

"Ma would be happy," Kennet said. "Because I think if she were at all displeased, lightning would've struck the house by now."

Nalle made a small noise, which might have been a chuckle.

"Nalle-Bear?" Emil said quietly. "I'm going to marry Marta. We'd like your blessing. It's important to us."

Nalle shook his head a little and seemed to emerge from a dream. He smiled. "I'm sorry. I was just…being a dumb kid about it." He stood up, took his drink and put his other arm around Emil. "You're right. Minor's right, too."

"Gosh, do you mean it?" Minor said, touching his chest.

"Kennet's right and Marta is more than right. In fact, she's perfect."

Knowing his middle brother was an open window without shades or curtains, Kennet's ears strained for false cheerfulness. He detected none, and true to nature, Nalle's mixed emotions were evident in the way his eyes shone at the edges, and how his hand shook a little when he raised his glass high. "Skål."

"Skål," Minor said. "To twice-in-a-lifetime love."

"To kind ladies who live here," Kennet said. "Skål."

Emil glanced around the little group. "Till mina vackra söner," he said gruffly.

My beautiful sons.

The glasses clinked together.

"Skål…"

Good Enough

As the days of the leave turned over and fell away, Kennet tried to show his face in all the Clayton establishments that had been part of his life. Both to say goodbye aloud, and ask silently to be remembered.

If I don't come back, remember I was here.

The bait and tackle, the drugstore, the post office, the library. A special trip to the five-and-ten where he'd always bought penny candy from Mrs. Vetter, who'd been his beloved first grade teacher until she got married. You couldn't throw a stone in Clayton without hitting a fellow whose first crush was on Elizabeth Vetter. Close friends called her "Peach," and she was high on Major Fiskare's list of swell dames. Her late husband was a good egg who knew his onions, too.

"Brian Vetter couldn't do better," Major always said. After D-Day, he added with a sigh of genuine sadness, "Until he did worse."

"You be careful," Mrs. Vetter said, handing over a bag of assorted sweets and reaching to squeeze Kennet's free fingers.

"Yes, ma'am, I will. You keep an eye on my folks, please?"

She nodded and gave one last pump of their clenched hands. "Goodbye, Kennet."

"Goodbye, Mrs. Vetter."

Now she put her hand on her hip and tilted her chin. "Call me Peach."

Pleased from eyebrows to toenails, Kennet grinned back at her. "Goodbye, Peach."

Kennet went to the cemetery and put holly on the graves of Björn, Beatrice and Ingrid. At mealtimes, he and Minor and Nalle asked Emil for tales they'd heard a thousand times before. They listened as if recording every word for posterity. When the family gathered in front of the fire, Kennet took down the old book of Swedish folk tales and read out loud.

He walked along the river and took mental photographs of his favorite views. Memorizing the light. Preserving how the sun hit the frozen parts of the water and turned them to bars of solid gold. He tried not to put Astrid in each and every picture. But it was hard not to. She was everywhere. And right now, he was feeling everything. Beneath the river's icy surface, the normally mischievous Fossegrim was playing the most plaintive of laments on his fiddle, making Kennet's heart hurt and his teeth ache.

He let her memory slide arms around him from behind and bury its face in his neck. He let himself remember. He let himself feel. Soon, he knew, this depth of emotion would be a luxury. And a liability. It was a childish thing he'd need to put away, for it had no place in combat. But for now, alone on the riverbank, he let it fill him with all its terrible beauty.

I've had a good life.

I've had a life full of gold and light and terrible beauty.

It's just a little life, but it's mine.

And I don't want to die.

He found a place by the riverbank that wasn't iced in and threw a penny.

Nick! Nick! Needle in the water! Thou sink, I float!

As he packed on the last evening, Marta knocked softly on the jamb of his bedroom door. She came in and gave him the two photographs of Astrid, which she'd taken from their frames.

"If I'm out of line, just thump me in the nose," she said. "But before you met and fell in love, she was always your little faraway friend. A sort of guardian angel. Cripes, that sounds ridiculous when I say it out loud."

Kennet hesitated. Then he took them and carefully tucked them in the spine of a small notebook he was planning to use as a diary. He all at once wanted Astrid to follow him into war. There, more than ever, he'd need her behind him.

"Thank you," he said to Marta, as his heart thumped enormous in his stomach.

Gold and light and terrible beauty and I don't want to die.

On the last morning, the two soldiers and the sailor walked through the hotel, saying goodbye to staff. They left via the front veranda, each reaching up to touch the tail of the carved wooden fish and make a wish. Perhaps their last wish.

The goodbye at the station was horrible. Marta and the girls crying. Emil pale and grim. Major miserable. Little looking at his brothers with his heart on his face, but shoulders squared as he buttoned up the mantle of heir presumptive.

Kennet stuffed his eyes with them, inhaled and gobbled and tried to stay in the moment. But it was all like a dream, sliding through his fingers and memory at the first light of day.

The three fishes rode the train together as far as Santa Fe, where Nalle switched lines to head north to Colorado. On the bustling platform, swarmed with troops and civilians, Kennet had to reach up to hug the little bear, ruffle his hair and hold his jaw in the palm of a hand.

"You're the best brother a fellow could ask for," Nalle said. Then he glanced at Minor. "And you're good enough, I guess."

Minor laughed. "I'll do in a pinch."

"I'm kidding. I love you." Nalle put arms around Minor and held tight.

"I love you, kid," Minor said, rubbing his back. "No kidding." He stuck out an arm and pulled Kennet into the embrace. "You'll do, too."

They stood in a motionless triangle of arms and heads. A pyramid in the shifting humanity. Private, and yet somehow public, for strange men patted their backs in passing, mumbling, "Good luck, boys" before moving on. Women's hands caressed their shoulders, "God bless you, darlings. Be careful."

They were the hope of the world and they belonged to everyone.

Remember this, a desperate voice screamed in Kennet's bones. *Remember, remember, remember.*

But it all seemed a dream.

The rest of the journey to California, Kennet and Minor didn't say much, but barely a minute went by when their upper arms weren't smushed tight together, or one brother's head dozed on another's shoulder.

Remember, Kennet chanted in rhythm with the rumbling cars over the sleepers. *Remember, remember, remember.*

They parted ways in Los Angeles, repeating the farewell on the platform. Hugging, ruffling heads, cracking weak jokes as they held on tight.

"Try not to get yourself killed," Minor said.

"Don't do anything stupid."

"I won't if you won't."

"Minor mine, you are so fine."

"It ain't no trick to love my Nyck."

All over the country, brothers were bidding farewell, their hearts in their throats, their fear and anger on a tight leash. Mothers, fathers, sisters, wives, sweethearts, all saying *goodbye, I love you.* There was nothing special or unique about the misery twisting Kennet's chest right now. He was one lone cog in a massive machine of fear and sadness and death and grief and loss.

Yet at the moment, he felt he were the only one in the world being asked to feel all the emotion within it.

"I love you," he said, digging fingers into Minor's shoulders, trying to memorize him.

"We're gonna live through this, come home, have a beautiful life on the river and die in our beds. Understand? No alternatives. That's the plan."

"I'm in."

"Fish don't die in the earth. We die in the water. Or near it. We're coming home."

"I'll see you soon then."

More strangers, in and out of uniform, slapped Kennet's back when he climbed aboard and found his seat, offering a word of encouragement.

"I know how you feel, buddy."

"It's tough."

"Let's give 'em hell and get it over with."

Kennet imagined war couldn't be much worse than all these gut-shredding goodbyes.

He knew how wrong he was. But he hoped it wouldn't be much worse.

PART TWO:
The Fisherman at War

"But when it has been ordained that one shall live, one cannot think of one's funeral," said the old woman. "And so one has to take the world as it is, and still be satisfied."

"That may be," said the magic fish, "but if you do as I tell you, you shall have three wishes."

—*"The Old Woman and the Fish," Swedish folk tale*

DECEMBER
1944

Captain Who?

The long troop train trundled across America with its precious cargo. California to New Jersey, crossing deserts and mountains. Past plains of grass and cornfields. Hamlet villages and bustling cities. The country. The motherland.

Eight GIs were assigned to each sleeping compartment, bedding down in triple-berths against each wall. The bottom-most berth was wider than the top two—it doubled as a seat during the day, and two men shared it at night.

Excited at first, bored eventually, the soldiers called on other compartments, crammed in doorways, loitered to smoke and jaw in the narrow corridors and the coach cars. After twenty-four hours, the train was fetid with cigarette smoke, body odor, nervous sweat and stories.

There were the soldiers who talked incessantly. The soldiers who barely made a sound. Those who snored. Those who talked in their sleep. It took a long time for the compartments to settle down at night.

Hey, no whacking off.

Are you pissing out the window again?

No end of retorts to passed wind:

Who cut the cheese?

Who let go?

What crawled up your ass and died?
Captain Who?

They exhausted their dirty jokes. Their lurid tales, sexual conquests and family lore. Sometimes they sang—usually in a joking manner, but sometimes quite seriously. Like when the train passed an open field with a carnival at twilight, the Ferris wheel beautiful and jeweled against the sunset. People came down to the crossing to wave. Old men took off hats and put them on their hearts. Little boys stood stiff and saluted. The very young perched on a mother's hip or rode high on a father's shoulders, holding their cotton candy and toffee apples.

As they receded into the distance, a soldier said, "That's the most goddamn American thing I've ever seen."

And another soldier began to sing softly:

> *O beautiful for spacious skies,*
> *For amber waves of grain,*
> *For purple mountain majesties...*

They all joined him, in harmony and with feeling.

The train arrived at North Platte, Nebraska, a giant hub of the Union Pacific Railroad. Here, people from surrounding communities erected a massive, volunteer-based canteen, dedicated to the needs of the soldiers passing through. Not just the needs of the stomach, but needs of the soul. Brisk, efficient women posted at desks would place long-distance phone calls for you, not suffering inept operators gladly and either cajoling or bullying a free line. They would send telegrams and cables. Wire flowers to your wife or sweetheart. One booth had piles of postcards, paper and pencils. *Drop your folks a line, postage is on us!*

Steam trains pulled into North Platte long enough for crews to relubricate the wheels, top off water levels and perform other routine maintenance which could take anywhere from fifteen minutes to an hour. No matter—the canteen could pack a party into a stay of any length. If soldiers were ordered to stay aboard because the train was only there for five minutes, volunteers grabbed pre-made baskets of food, hit the cars like a swarm of reverse-engineered locusts, passed out goodies and wished the men well, with never a worker ending up a stowaway.

GIs with a longer break at the canteen were treated to the time and attention of dozens of women. Music came from an old piano in the corner, or record players. An area was cleared for dancing. And all around the perimeter of the cavernous station were booths with sandwiches, drinks, sweets, cigarettes, magazines, newspapers, even paperback books.

"Take it with you," the women said of the stoneware mugs filled with coffee and tea, the glass bottles filled with milk, the plates, the cutlery, the wicker baskets. "Just leave the dishes at the next station. We'll collect them tomorrow."

The single girls begged for the insignia badges of all the units. In return, they took soldiers' names and APO addresses, promising to write.

"Happy birthday," a woman said, putting a plate with an *entire cake* into Kennet Fiskare's hands.

"It's not my birthday," he said.

"It is now." She smooched his cheek and melted into the throng.

Kennet went to one of the mail booths, took a postcard and wrote a quick note to Marta: *I think even the Harvey Girls would say North Platte is the nicest place in America.*

The men climbed back aboard the cars, arms full of bounty, balancing dishes and cups. Cheeks sporting lipstick kisses and collars smelling of a half-dozen perfumes. Hands still feeling shakes, backs vibrating from many a slap. Flirted with, praised and thanked within an inch of their lives. As the train lurched and pulled away from North Platte, nobody in Kennet's compartment could speak. They clutched their baskets of sandwiches, coffee and treats and stared at the receding, magical city that had created a canteen out of nothing but kindness and goodwill. They broke open popcorn balls to find slips of paper with a woman's name and address:

Please write. I'll write you back. I'll be your friend from North Platte.

Even with the heightened emotions, nobody cried. Not until the train passed the little storybook depot at Kearney, Kansas. This was Corporal Jefferson's hometown, and his parents and sisters, alerted to the train passing through, were waiting on the platform. The train wouldn't stop, but that didn't mean Jefferson couldn't reach for one last touch. The conductor was a nervous wreck but the men ignored him as they got Jefferson situated on the steps leading down from the little, noisy vestibule between cars. They hung onto his belt, craning their necks as Jefferson leaned out far and reached one hand toward his father's rough fingers and the other to his mother's softer ones.

"Goodbye, darling!" she cried. "Be careful!"

The train listed as every man hung out the windows, their own fingers reaching, tingling in sympathy, longing for a whisper of skin and a taste of home. They yelled and whooped as if at a ball game. They reached to catch the sisters' blown kisses, clutch them, swallow them, light them up and smoke them.

Jefferson stayed on the step, anchored by his mates' hands, waving until the little depot disappeared. His jaw clenched like a dam against a raging river. The men averted their own brimming eyes and pounded Jefferson's shoulders and rubbed his back. They passed him chocolate and gum before letting him be.

Kennet divided up his birthday cake. He ate his way through a popcorn ball, finding a slip of paper at the center: *Mrs. Hilda Messer, RR2, North Platte, Nebr.*

When conversation began to flow again, the stories told were deeper, more personal. The men spoke about failures, disappointments, despicable behavior they regretted, heartbreaks and fear. Fear of death, pain, torture, dismemberment. Fear of shame. Fear of being left behind to rot in the hinterlands. Flesh and bones and ash, no gravestone, no remains, nothing to comfort loved ones at home.

Fear of being forgotten.

Photos of sweethearts, wives and children passed up and down and across, along with lit cigarettes. Chocolate was exchanged for gum, a ham sandwich swapped for an egg salad.

They unfolded the bunks and told ghost stories that night, huddled around a campfire of lit cigarette tips. The crackle of candy bar wrappers. The pop of gum between unbrushed teeth. The waft of someone cutting the cheese—"I knew I shouldn't have eaten the egg salad." And they tried to scare each other. Scare off the real fears with legendary ones.

"Your turn, Fish."

Kennet stubbed out his cigarette. "I don't know any ghost stories."

"Tell us a fish tale."

"Yeah, tell us about the one that got away."

Kennet thought a moment. "How about a woman who got away with murder?"

"As long as she has big tits."

Groans and whistles. Bodies shifting. Joints cracking. Zippos flicking. Chocolate unwrapped. Stale gum spit out the window and fresh sticks folded into dry mouths. Popcorn hulls littered the floor. Slips of paper with women's names buttoned safely into pockets. Opening lines of letters already being composed: *Dear Miss Wilson, what a swell place North Platte is…*

"Go ahead, Fish."

"Go, Fish."

"Got any threes? Go, Fish."

Kennet told a condensed version of Hildur, Queen of the Elves.

"So everyone lived happily ever after," someone said, when the story was finished. "That's not a ghost story."

"I told you it wasn't," Kennet said. "They lived happily ever after, but Hildur still got away with murder."

"Who cares?"

"I do. Especially now."

"Tell another," Richard Hook said. He and Kennet had been buddies since Camp Polk, and now they shared one of the bottom-most bunks. A potentially awkward situation, once upon a time, but after years of all-male communal living and next to no privacy, Kennet barely gave it a thought. He liked Hook. Cripes, with their last names, it was kind of impossible *not* to.

The military was a last-name world and nicknames doled out during basic training stuck around permanently. Sergeant Preist—"Preist rhymes with Jesus Christ, who has no authority here!"—had no patience with a name like Dziedzice. "You goddamn Poles are letter happy," he said. "From now on, you're Dizzy. Fall in."

Likewise Preist thought the surname Babbiolamente had four syllables too many, and shortened it to Baby. Fragiacomo became Jock, or if the sergeant was in a bad mood, Jockstrap. Losquadro was easy to say, but Sarge liked calling him Squad Car. Friefeld became Free Fall. Two guys in a barracks named Ellis? The shorter one got called Squirt.

"You like that nickname, Squirt?"

"Sir, no, sir."

"Appreciate the honesty, Squirt."

The platoon sergeant glanced at the next name on the roster, Fiskare, and barked for Private Fisher to fall in. Kennet didn't correct him. He was the last F surname on the list and there were none starting with G. Next to fall in was Private Richard Hook.

"Well, isn't this poetic," said Preist. "We got a Fish and a Hook. You guys lovers?"

"Sir, no, sir."

"That's right, because all the fags are in the Navy. Now listen up, you bunch of cocksucking pansies…"

Kennet's insignia patches arrived as *Fisher* and he quietly got them fixed while answering to the new name. Within three days, he was Fish to all. He and Hook stuck together, out of poetry at first, and little by little, out of genuine liking.

They were able to share the bottom berth with little problem. Hook took the space nearest the wall because he liked to turn away and tuck himself into the dark. Kennet gladly took the open side, because not being able to see everything made him uneasy.

Marco Malinda hung his head over the edge of the berth above. "Tell another fish tale, Fish."

Kennet waved him off. "Snip, snap, snout. My tale's worn out."

"Hey guys," Hook called. "You know there's a Swedish legend that if you catch a fish, you get three wishes?"

"You have to catch the magic fish," Kennet said.

"You'll do," Hook said. "And my wish is another story. Grant it or you get no sleep."

Now Malinda hung his ass over the berth's edge and let a ripe one cut the air. Everyone groaned, coughed, retched and cursed.

"Goddammit, Malinda, you've polluted the entire train. You wreck government property and they take it out of your pay, y'know."

"Light a match," someone yelled.

"Christ, no, you'll blow up the damn car."

"*That'll* take a hunk out of your paycheck."

"Shit, that's an instant court martial."

"Tell a fucking story, Fish," someone called. "Before we either asphyxiate or wind up in the clink."

I Might Kill Someone Tomorrow

US base camp, somewhere in England
15 Dec 1944

Dear Paps and all the Fish,

I'll start by apologizing for the vague address, but better get used to that. Little, I know you've become the Master of the Map, but I'm not allowed to tell you where I'm going, and I can only tell you where I've been after I've left.

Anywhere, we're "here" for the duration, however long that is. The brass is adamant we not become lazy. Physical conditioning is ten times what it was stateside, which I didn't think possible. We are run ragged all day in cold, damp winds and ankle-deep mud. Exercising, drilling, running, crawling, target practice, hand-to-hand combat. The nights are free, though, and most of us get a second wind and head into the village of XXXXXX. If we get a 48-hour pass, we can hop the train into London (I'm allowed to say that).

Things in the city are expensive, so we stick to free sight-see-ing. Some little establishments will give a guy in uniform a cup of tea. I think I'm the only one in my squad who actually drinks tea, so this works to my advantage. Although some Londoners are appalled at how dark I take it. "You can stand your spoon up in that," they say, just like Marta. So it's like being home.

The YMCA does a fine job billeting us, and I've told the canteen girls about Ma's days in France, handing out coffee, smokes and sweets. They really appreciate the part of the story when she meets Paps. The young women in London are lonely, which is more irony than a body can process. The city is over-flowing with young men while at the same time, it has a dearth of young men. Am I making sense? The men in London are only passing through. They are here, yet not here. They have no per-manence. They are dreams of men. Ideals of men.

I'm hopeless. Nalle could explain this better. I've yet to hear from him or Minor but if you have, let me know.

I'm all right, no need to send me anything but news. We boys are bored, beat and brooding (allow us all the alliteration). Lots of speculation on where we'll be heading from here, but no orders yet. I wish they'd just tell us. A fellow can tie himself in a million anxious knots, imagining what lies ahead. At least if you're certain, you can narrow it down to…maybe half a million knots? Still, I know it can only get worse from here, not better. So I'm trying to collect the fun moments of horsing around with my buddies, mud football, live music on Tuesday nights, a pass to London, the British museum, a pretty YMCA canteen girl… Carefully collect all those experiences and take them with me to wherever that might be.

I take you all with me, too. Miss you awful.

Love,
Kennet

Paps,

Just a private note to you alone. There's a fellow in my squad named Richard Hook and with a name like that, you might guess we've become rather close. He's a true orphan. He was born in Waco, Texas, his mother died when he was four and his father—often referred to as "that no-good, drunk son of a bitch"—put Richie into the Jewish Children's Home in New Orleans, with a promise he'd fetch Richie once he was back on his feet. Richie never saw him again.

So Hook is a river rat like me, but our lives are nothing the same. Once out of the children's home, he had a rough start. Fell in with the wrong sort of people and started dealing in petty crime. Right when Pearl Harbor happened, he was facing charges of forgery. He could go to jail or join the Army. He didn't think twice. He enlisted the next day and the military life has been nothing but good for him. Here's a fellow dying for discipline and structure, for rules to define the edges of his life (as you once said) and most of all, for father figures and surrogate brothers. He's found it all in the Army.

Anyway, all this to say that he's a good egg. For the first time in my life, I feel like I have a best friend who isn't a brother. Yet he feels like another brother and it bothers me that he's got nobody at home worrying about him. Which brings me around to the point and a favor I need to ask my old man. I need you to find a fish hook and… I don't know, keep it close? When you put the gold chain on first thing in the morning, put the hook in your pocket. When you take the chain off at night, put the hook with it. Adopt my friend Hook as a son for the duration and give him a little worry if you can. He deserves it.

Your gullgosse misses you.

Love,
Kennet

The 21st Armored Infantry Battalion crossed the English Channel on December 15th. That same day, Kennet began writing in his notebook. The Army officially frowned on soldiers keeping diaries, but many did. Kennet appreciated the disastrous consequences if a journal with future missions fell into enemy hands, but he wasn't an officer with knowledge of future missions anyway. Grunts didn't know where they were going until they got there.

He wrestled a bit with his patriotic duty, then decided if he kept his diary on the down-low and kept it to events well in the past, the Army could turn their frowns elsewhere. He told no one of the notebook's existence except Hook, because he told Hook everything.

"Anything happens to me, send it back to my folks," Kennet said.

Hook gave a single, solemn nod. "I'll bring it personally, but only if I get to read it."

"You can read it if I'm dead."

"Oh, I'm reading it while you're still kicking," Hook said. "You gotta hit the latrine at some point."

"When do you think I write in it?"

"Yeah, you seem like the type who does his best work on the crapper."

Kennet blew a smoke ring at his mate. "Tell it to Sweeney."

That night, he cracked the spine of his notebook, turned the flyleaf and pressed it flat with his palm. He set aside the photograph of eighteen-year-old Astrid, which he planned to use as a marker. Addressing the entries to her was no more a conscious decision than breathing.

15 December 1944
Cherbourg

Dear Astrid,

You can still see the beating Cherbourg took, but you can see signs of restoration, too. Cold and grey today, and very muddy in the fields where we've set up our tents.

After we set up camp, one of our half-track drivers came up to me and said, "I heard you speak French. Get in, let's go find some booze."

I grabbed Hook, we got in the track and drove into a local village. We found a shop and bartered cigarettes and C-rations for four bottles of cognac.

We went tent to tent, doling out good cheer to our mates. Except the very religious Pvt. Anderson, who doesn't drink, but isn't disapproving of those who do. The field where we're bivouacked is a sea of mud. The perimeter has become prime real estate, but Hook and I didn't hustle fast enough, so we're bedded down smack in the swamp. But we're snuggled up to our bottles and managing to keep warm.

On the move tomorrow. Don't know to where.

16 December 1944

Dear Astrid,

Battalion is now in camp at Barneville. So far, war is rain, mud and shivering cold.

I imagined this journal would be the definitive narrative of the American soldier's experience.

So far it seems to be a weather report.

19 December 1944

Dear Asta,

Yesterday we received orders and moved 120 miles to the south, near Rennes. Stayed in camp today, and supposedly we're moving to Saint-Nazaire on the coast, to clear out some lingering German resistance. The Krauts there are surrounded on three sides but managing to get supplied by submarine. I hear Saint-Nazaire is the training ground for new, inexperienced troops.

I might kill someone tomorrow. What a thought.

I hope I don't fuck this up. Pardon my language. We soldiers don't have much to do right now except smoke, sweat and swear.

Allow me all the alliteration, darling.

20 December 1944

Asta,

Saw no action at St. Nazaire. News from the southeast is bad. Nazis attacking on a 50-mile front in Belgium. Panzers overrunning 1st Army positions. We're heading there, still green.

24 December 1944

A,

God jul, Merry Christmas. 500 miles in two days. We march through towns that were battlefields not so long ago. A lot of us are passing places where our fathers fought a war that was supposed to end all wars. Sure gives a fellow something to think about.

Now we're quartered in French barracks near Sedan and officially part of Gen. Patton's 3rd Army.

Holiday season, but not much time to celebrate. The tank crews are frantic to install track extensions on the Shermans, so it's double-time work all day today. Tomorrow as well—we'll be on the move to Belgium, though we'll get a break for Christmas dinner and services.

I've been thinking a lot about my mother. I'm ashamed to say there are times when I'm glad she's gone. She doesn't have to—

...

...

...Got interrupted there by a burst of rifle fire. Whole camp jumped out of its boots but turns out it was the fellows in the 82nd Airborne, pissed at being ordered back to Belgium, where they've seen combat before. They know what to expect and are taking their aggression out on the sky. This display of frustrated dread puts a real kink in my stomach.

25 December 1944

A,

On the road toward Bastogne all day. The cooks did a fine job serving turkey dinner on the way. For now, this is home and these are my brothers.

Asta, I'm not saying so in these entries, but I think about you all the time. All the time. Wondering what you're doing. If you're wearing the little gold Hildur around your neck and if your fingertips reach to touch it during your days. My guess is not. You're a lady of your word, which includes wedding vows. You married him, for better or worse, and if that makes me into something kept secret in a drawer of a jewelry box, I have to respect it.

Still, I wonder desperately what you're thinking and feeling and is it ever of me. I know you can't flaunt me, but am I still part of you? Most of the time, I believe I am. But I have moments where I fear I've been forgotten. Or set aside as merely a fond memory and you have no need to visit the drawer where I live.

Please need it.

28 Dec 1944

A,

We've been told to be ready to move early tomorrow morning. Into Belgium, where there's heavy fighting.

This account may end here. In which case, I love you with all my heart and soul and I wish to goodness I had better words to say so.

28 Dec 1944—Postscript

Hook, if you're reading this, don't give it to anyone. I'm begging you. It's so boring. Keep it for toilet paper. Or go to Clayton and throw it in the river, where my soul plans on resting anyway.

And don't make fun of my maudlin crap or I'll haunt the hell out of you.

Civilian Terror

Company B pulled off the highway used by the Red Ball Express—
the convoy of trucks bringing supplies to the front, and ambulances bringing the wounded to the rear of the line. The men would
bivouac on the hillside that night, but before pitching their tents,
many went to get a look at the wreckage of a downed German
plane, and the two dead fighter pilots who lay in the snow.

"You don't want to look," Private O'Hara said to Private Martin.
"Take my word for it, kid."

Marty took umbrage at *kid*. At nineteen, he was the youngest
of Kennet's squad, and he possessed a dumb innocence that made
everyone want to protect him. Tired of being treated like a tyke
to be sheltered, he stomped toward the broken fuselage and stood,
hands on hips, looking down at the two corpses. Then he walked
off another six yards and puked.

"You want to take a gander?" Hook asked Kennet.

Kennet didn't, but, "Might as well get used to seeing it," he said.

It was a mistake. Both the looking and the theory he'd ever
get used to it. The corpses were horribly broken, arms and legs
thrust at unnatural angles, bone poking through clothing. Their
faces bloated, their eyes bulging in eternal horror. But hardest to
take in was the turned-out pockets, devoid of possessions. The
feet stripped of their boots and hands of gloves. One airman had

a missing finger—clearly he'd been wearing a ring that was now some American GI's booty.

To the victor go the spoils, Kennet thought, curling his own ring-less hands in his empty pockets, resolved not to carry anything into battle that some Nazi could show off to a family member or lover.

"Come on," Hook said lowly. Then louder, "Marty, come on. You got nothing left to bring up. You wanted to look and you looked. It's done. Now you know."

Thankfully, previous units had already dug in foxholes and gun positions, so setting up the outer defense went quickly. A couple of straw stacks kept the men from laying their bedrolls on the cold ground.

Kennet got a few hours sleep before it was his turn for guard duty. He rolled up his sleeping bag—nothing more than two Army-issue blankets sewed together—and stuffed it inside Hook's bag. Hook curled around the bedding, keeping it warm with his body heat, and Kennet piled more straw on top of him. They'd learned this trick from a guy in the 82nd Airborne. If a buddy gave you a field-tested tip to keep from freezing your ass off, you took it.

Kennet shared the shift with Ralph Ingle, and they hadn't been on watch an hour when a German reconnaissance plane swooped low over the camp. Lieutenant Jorgensson, the platoon leader, came to stand by the privates and regard the aircraft.

"Bed Check Charlie," he said. "Listen. He'll bank around and take another look."

Kennet squinted and turned his ear toward the sky. Sure enough, the plane came back around.

"He's flying low, sir."

Jorgy grunted.

"Will he shoot?" Ingle asked.

"Nah. If he fires, we'll take him out. And if we take him out, we give away our position and risk getting shelled. This flyby is nothing but a game. And it's already a draw."

"Hijo de puta," Ingle said to the sky. "Me cago en tus muertos."

Jorgy gave a terse chuckle. "I caught *whore* and *shit*," he said. "I can extrapolate the rest."

"Bravo, sir," said Ralph Ingle, who'd been born Rafael Íñiguez in Cuba.

All during the watch, American artillery occasionally fired on the enemy rear, shells lighting up the sky and making the ground rumble. When relieved, Kennet headed back to camp. It took a few tries to remember which heap of straw was Hook. He retrieved his bedding, which Hook had managed to keep toasty, and piled hay on himself as best he could. He didn't so much sleep as catch brief catnaps between shelling. As it neared dawn on the 30th of December, the frequency of the attack increased and no more sleep was to be had.

30 December began with a wrong turn, Kennet wrote. *Our B Company was supposed to follow the Baker of the 22nd Tank Battalion. But our platoon lost contact with the tank column. We asked the battalion commander which way they went. He pointed down a road. Confidently. He's the goddamn commander, right?*

It was the wrong road.

We ended up in no man's land with the German artillery laying down a bombardment. Lt. West was trying to make radio contact, meanwhile we're sitting on the road, asses exposed, and the shells are exploding in the distance but they sound right next to us and coming closer.

A farmhouse was on fire not ten yards away and shrapnel was making a high-pitched whine as it flew through the air. West went back to the crossroads to figure out where we were. We stayed in the track, huddled down below the line of the plate armor, trying to hide inside ourselves…

Boots came running along the side of the track and Lieutenant West flung himself into the passenger seat. "We're turning around, move it," he said to the driver. "Let's go, let's go, let's go."

It took an excruciating amount of time for every vehicle to three-point its nose in the other direction, but once the column was moving, everyone in the half-track exhaled at once and sat up a little.

"Man, that's the trick," Hook mumbled. "Don't sit still because then you start thinking. Just keep fucking doing someth—"

The sky ripped in two and an avalanche of dirt and metal dropped into the track. The road erupted in geysers of earth as shells fell along the column. Two to one side. Three on the other. Then a direct hit to the lead track.

It was a day of firsts, among them being the first time Kennet heard men involuntarily shriek in civilian terror, then bite down hard on their training, lock their jaws and become soldiers.

"Take cover, boys," West said, and in Kennet's ringing ears, it sounded almost conversational.

His teeth set, Kennet slammed the back of the vehicle open, hopped down and flipped his rifle into position on his shoulder, ready to lay down cover fire as the rest of the men jumped out and ran toward a sunken railroad track. All except Arnold Schmitt, who was the 50-caliber gunner and obligated to stay at his post at the pintle mount behind the front seats.

"Go, Fish," he yelled, swinging the sight around.

Kennet had never gone so fast in his life. He reached the railroad line which looked deserted in both directions. Then he saw Corporal Jefferson, one of the squad assistants. The Kansas fellow who'd hung out the side of a train to touch his parents' hands.

"Spread out, Fish," the corporal cried, pointing down the track. "Take up position but spread out."

Kennet started running again but stopped dead when something screamed over his head. He looked back to see Jefferson blown into pieces. Arms in the air, one tangled in the rifle strap. A leg tumbling down the embankment, the torso flying up like a rocket and Jefferson's head looking down at Kennet with a curious expression.

"Jesus Christ," Kennet whispered.

A shock wave of mud, snow and gravel knocked him on his butt. The shells were advancing toward the railroad tracks like a storm front, jackhammering into the frozen earth, turning it into shrapnel. Kennet scrambled to his feet, charged up the slope and into the woods.

He pressed his back against a pine tree, breathing hard. His heart in his stomach, his stomach in his boots, his boots frozen to the ground and far above it all, his head, swiveling, looking for someone. Anyone.

He was utterly alone.

Alone and directionless. Not knowing what to do and even if he did, not knowing which way to go to do it. The cacophony of whistling, blasting, booming and rattling made no distinction between American and German. No telling who else was taking cover in these woods.

His eyes swerved wildly among the trees before he squeezed them shut, following some instinctive impulse to look with his ears, not his eyes.

Listen.

Listen for your men.

Hold still and listen.

Listen below the noise. Between the noise. Wait for the war to take a breath, then listen.

There.

In the gasping lull between shells, a human noise. A whistle. The opening bar of the "Colonel Bogey March."

Kennet peered around his tree, following the sound. Toward a gigantic pine that had fainted on the forest floor, tugging up a massive root ball. Around its edge peeked a face. It was Ralph Ingle. He held up a flat palm, then leaned out more to scan the woods. He rolled to his belly, rifle to his shoulder. He held up one finger now. *On your mark.* Then another. *Get set.* Then three.

Go.

Kennet crouched and ran to Ingle. Hopped neatly over his prone body and rolled behind the root ball. Ingle pulled in and there they sat, smushed shoulder to shoulder, trembling all over.

"Jesus, Pescado, am I glad to see you," Ingle said.

"Shit on a fucking stick."

"Me cago en todo lo que se menea."

"Fan i helvetes jävla skit."

They sat a moment, exhausting every curse word in every language they knew. It seemed to clear their heads, as did the security of each other's company.

"We need to find the others," Kennet said.

"*Our* others," Ingle said. "Christ, don't let us find theirs."

The Eighty-Eight
That Kills You

Kennet and Ingle found and followed a dirt path, heading toward where the trees stood farther apart. Moving from trunk to trunk, pausing to scan, scout, look and listen, it felt to Kennet they were on a week-long journey, although it couldn't have been more than half an hour. They came across a group of soldiers and Kennet seized up all over as he squinted at their uniforms and weapons. Then his body melted into a gorgeous relief. These guys were *theirs*. Unknown to Kennet—not their platoon or battalion—but God, were they beautiful.

Soon Ingle and Kennet were back among familiar faces and their column was retreating to the nearby town of Jodenville.

That's it? Kennet thought. *No more action today?*

He blinked in disbelief at himself.

What the fuck, you want more?

> *I couldn't believe it,* he wrote. *I took one shot from the liquor that is combat. Became immediately drunk. Ugly drunk. Staggering, stinking and delusional, guaranteed to be puking on my shoes with a hangover that wouldn't quit. The horrible high wore off and for an insane moment, I wanted to belly-up to the*

*bar again. Because I'd never been so frightened in my life. And
I'd never felt more alive.*

That's a side of me I've never seen before.

I don't like it.

*The column drove into a deserted field outside of Jodenville.
This town was our spoils of war, all we had to show for the day's
efforts. The men were ordered to sit tight in the tracks while Lt.
West and Lt. Jorgensson went into town to meet up with other
COs. For some reason, Jorgy motioned for me to come along
with him.*

*These military nicknames fascinate me, Asta. Soldiers either
take long surnames and shave them down, or take short names
and extend them with a "Y." Some names get shaved AND
"Y'ed." Why is that? Why do some of us get a moniker and others
just get their last names? And why does every squad have one
guy who gets called by his first name? Like our Hank Berliner.
He's not Berliner or Berl or Berly. He's Hank. Nobody decides or
declares this. It just happens.*

*Even funnier are the differences between platoon command-
ers. Of course we grunts don't nickname an officer to his face,
but none of us call Lt. West "Westy" even when shooting the shit
among ourselves. He just doesn't invite that kind of familiarity.
Yet Lt. Jorgensson is always "Jorgy." He runs a tight ship and
suffers no bullshit, but he's approachable. And he's Swedish, so
naturally I feel a little smug kinship.*

While they were in town, the Germans started shelling again.
"Here comes the music," Jorgy said.

They hightailed it into a basement and waited out the concert.
West and Jorgy were stone-faced under the bombardment, and
Kennet tried hard to emulate their stoic demeanor. But with every

whistling advent of a shell, his eyes screwed shut of their own accord.

I should be home, he thought. *I don't belong here.*

Home seemed another world away.

"Easy, gullgosse," Emil said softly.

Kennet's eyes popped open.

Paps?

The endearment hadn't come from Emil's lips, of course, but Jorgensson's.

"Those are eighty-eight millimeter shells," Jorgy said in Swedish. "They fire so fast, you only hear them after they've passed by."

As if cued, another whistling scream seemed to slice the building apart.

"See," the lieutenant said. "That's the sound of leaving, not arriving. Believe me, gullgosse, you won't hear the eighty-eight that kills you."

> *You never know what little bit of something-or-other is going to shore up your courage,* Kennet wrote. *After Jorgy told me about the sound of 88-shells, I didn't exactly relax, but I didn't jump out of my skin at the noise every time. I came to be relieved to hear them, knowing it was the sound of leaving, not arriving.*
>
> *When the Germans let up a little, Jorgy sent me back to the field where the tracks were parked, so I could tell the boys to come into town and take shelter.*
>
> *My mates had flung themselves in ditches or behind hedgerows, stone walls and trees. Any place they could take cover. There wasn't a calm expression among them. Faces whiter than the snow, eyes halfway out of their heads. More than a couple had pissed themselves and I couldn't blame them one bit.*

I found Hook and he threw arms around me and pounded my back with his fists. His face was covered in blood but he said it was from a surface wound on his scalp. It bled like hell but no great damage done.

A bunch of men were badly wounded and many others dead, but none from my squad. I'll write "Thank God," but I won't feel good about it.

None dead today. But tomorrow is coming.

Tomorrow makes a sound when it arrives, not when it leaves.

One poor guy from our platoon snapped his cap. He was crying like a baby but Anderson had him in hand. He had the guy's rifle across his shoulder and was walking him along like you'd help old folks across the street. Talking low and soft about this and that. Two gentlemen out for a stroll instead of two soldiers limping out of battle.

The night of the 30th was a real bitch. The temperature dropped and the wind kicked up, bringing first sleet and then snow.

We were assigned a sector of the town to defend, and the entire platoon squeezed into one house, bedrolls crammed shoulder to shoulder and head to foot. Packs, weapons and equipment in big piles. Mud everywhere. Two toilets for fifty fellows with nervous stomachs.

All night long, men coming in and out, blasting cold air across the floor, the wind snatching the door right out of your hand and slamming it. The crying fellow wouldn't stop crying. Some of the wounded were moaning. Those who couldn't sleep lit up to pass the time, and the air was full of smoke and anxiety.

Hook kept my bedroll warm while I was on guard duty. Then I came back and we switched off, me snuggled up to his sleep-

ing bag, trying to ignore my frozen feet. God, my feet are so cold all the time. Working at Pine Camp in 1941 was nothing like this. You froze during the long, hard day but at least at night you could warm up.

I slept a little. Fitfully. Jolting awake out of mixed-up dreams, not knowing where I was. My feet hurt so bad and I couldn't nod off again. I lay awake, smoking, thinking about my brothers. Wondering if this war could go on long enough to suck Little in, then Paps would have four boys fighting. Four stars to hang in the window. A fourth charm to hang on his chain.

In every fairy and folk tale ever told, wishes are only granted in threes, not fours.

Little has to stay out of it. He just has to. If he's written into this story, it'll be the end of us all.

So here I am, Astrid. I am one sorry-ass, homesick gullgosse listening for the sound of tomorrow. It's no good pretending I feel one way when I feel another. I can be a good soldier and let my feelings show. If I do it here, no one will know. If I don't do it here, no one will know. And I want it to be known, so here goes, darling girl.

I want you so much and I need you right now.

I miss you. I think I will always miss you. Sometimes it's a freckle on my elbow. Other times, like tonight, it's a disease in my bones and my senses ache, ache, ache to drown in you again. To see and touch and hear and smell and taste you. I want to make love to you again. So badly.

So badly, Asta, I want you so badly.

I think I might be going crazy with it.

The desire waxes and wanes between lofty and obscene. One moment I'm staring at you all moon-eyed, quoting romantic poetry. The next moment I'm on my knees at your feet, unhooking your garters and begging to fuck you.

Is that shocking?

It shocks me. Look at how my handwriting jostles around the word 'fuck.' I winced writing it, but now it's settling on my eyes and the sound of it is getting comfortable in my brain. It's disengaging from the sordid and crass, and slowly turning divine. Intense. Even beautiful. I want to be your lover again and feel that sweet understanding between us when I'm fucking you into beautiful pieces... And don't think this can't go two ways, my darling, wonderful beauty. I know what strength is in your glorious body so climb up on top of me, hold me hard, pin me down. Make me beg and don't give a choice or chance, just take me for your own pleasure and obliterate me as an afterthought. Use me, command me, fuck me. I'm yours.

I am, honest to God, blushing right now.

Oh what the hell, I can write it here. I'm not long for this world so I can tell you everything in these pages. You'll never know.

But maybe you will. Maybe you, future Asta, is reading this last entry of my diary, because Hook sent it to you after I was killed tomorrow.

In which case I hope, honest to God, you are blushing too, as you read these words to the last and learn the truth: joining the Army helped put you behind me, but war has only confirmed that I will love you until I die. I'll die with no patriotic fervor, no idealistic notions of the good fight or freedom or the cause. I will die only wanting you to my bones. On the way to my death, I'll be lusting for you in the worst of ways, the best of ways, the most holy and tawdry of ways. Because I died loving you with every beat of my heart.

Holy Schmitt

By mid-morning on December 31st, the men of Company B were still standing around Jodenville, pent-up with nervous energy and uncertainty. Their temporary barracks had become such a fetid den of humanity, they congregated outside, despite the freezing temperatures.

> *War is indeed hell*, Kennet wrote. *But winter war has its own special, hellish delights. Take the Army-issue overcoats: they give an already overloaded soldier a few extra pounds to lug around. The length keeps your legs warm when you're standing still, but it trips you up when you're on the run. Still, the coat is a godsend when you fling yourself down in the snow to take cover or give hell. Or stand around on a street corner in Belgium to kill time.*

The moons of Kennet's fingernails were blue and he had no compunction about slipping his freezing digits into the armpits of anyone standing next to him.

"Buy me dinner first," Chris "Jock" Fragiacomo said, shoving Kennet away. "You slice of frozen fruitcake."

Soldiers clustered by the tanks' exhaust pipes, laying their gloves on the chugging machinery to warm before slipping them over chilblained fingers. More than a few pairs were lost when the tanks drove off, and then a fellow was really fucked.

Keeping hands warm enough to shoot was such a priority, even the principled Private Anderson wasn't averse to stripping the gloves off the fallen, whether friend or foe. Yesterday, Private Arnold Schmitt shot a German scout who wore a wool cap with earflaps beneath his helmet. It sat rather smugly on Schmitt's head this morning, and Ingle offered fifty dollars for it.

"Serious offers only," Schmitt said.

"I'll give you a hundred bucks and a hand job," Jock said.

Schmitt pulled the cap lower and chewed the air a moment.

"Holy Schmitt, he's considering this," Ingle said.

Schmitt shrugged. "I've resigned myself to the fact that I'm not getting laid before I die. A frig from Fragiacomo might be a satisfactory consolation prize."

"Fuck you, satisfactory," Jock said. "I'd ruin you for anyone else."

"He already ruined me," Boyd O'Hara said quietly.

"Damn right," Jock said. "I don't— Wait, what?"

O'Hara was walking away and the squad was doubled over laughing.

"Son of a bitch, O'Hara, fuck off," Jock shouted after.

O'Hara looked back and gave one of his rare smiles. He was the squad's enigma. Disturbingly devoid of personality, he barely said ten words in a day, barely registered an emotion above awake, barely registered a *pulse*. It was impossible to explain how or why he was close mates with Jock, one of the loudest and most vulgar of the squad's loudmouthed, vulgar jokers. No two fellows could have been less alike, and the pairing ought to have ended in murder. Yet one was rarely seen without the other. O'Hara was the only man who could get Jock to shut up, and Jock the only man who could get the corners of O'Hara's mouth to lift up.

The Army is full of such bizarre, improbable friendships, Kennet wrote. *And you can't explain them any more than you can explain love.*

It was noon when the battalion mounted up and took off, following the tanks through the valley they'd retreated from the day before. They bumped and battered down the crummy road, machine guns blazing from both tanks and tracks.

Too soon, the valiant advance got bogged down and came under enemy fire. The company dismounted and ran for cover behind an embankment, quickly setting up a skirmish line across the road. Private Dziedzice, known to all as Dizzy, was the last to get out of his half-track before a shell blew it to bits. He dove into the line with a hysterical bray of laughter, exhilarated by the near-miss.

Guy Babbiolamente, whom everyone called Baby, grabbed Dizzy by the belt of his greatcoat and hauled him into firing position. "You got a goddamn horseshoe up your ass, Diz."

"I better not shit my pants," Dizzy said. "I'll lose all my good luck."

The tanks pulled into a line behind the infantry, firing their machine guns.

"Put on the full armor of God," Anderson said. "So that you can take your stand against the devil's schemes."

"You stand up and I'll shoot you myself," Ingle said.

Word began to ripple down the line, like a spreading brush fire: *sniper.*

"Son of a bitch just took four men out," Lieutenant Jorgensson said. "Keep your heads down and your eyes up."

On the other side of the road, a row of large stone houses faced the line, all looking hollow and abandoned to Kennet's eyes.

O'Hara paused his pull on the BAR. "Schmitt," he said. "Corner house. Attic window is open."

"Move." Schmitt raised his bazooka to his shoulder.

The men flattened themselves against the snowy ground. The bazooka gave its signature belch and the projectile flew into the attic window. It was a gorgeous shot. Almost dainty. A split-second of decision, as if the house were chewing on the rocket, deciding if it liked the taste. Then the wall on the opposite side of the window burst open and a German soldier flew out, as if spit from a mouth.

"Holy *Schmitt*," the squad cried.

Even though the terror is all-consuming, Kennet wrote. *Even though it paralyzes your lungs, and chokes, smothers and unmans you, still there are moments when the fear relaxes just long enough to let you see something funny. Or something admirable. You get a second to catch your breath and think 'Great shot, buddy,' or even 'Man, that was hilarious!'*

You get little moments to be proud and human. I'll try to be grateful for them. Or siphon strength from them.

Grand and Casual

Major Tendry and Captain Patrick led Company B along the railroad tracks and across the countryside. Kennet's platoon was first to crest the hill above Chenogne, breaking through the knee-deep snow. They crawled through barbed wire and passed foxholes left by the 9th Armored, who had been driven out a few days before. Two American GIs were in one of the holes, slumped over and frozen. Dead.

Kennet and Private Marco Malinda—the famous farter—stopped to gawk at the corpses. A blanket of snow erased the dead men's facial features and obscured their wounds. Their pose was almost angelic. They could've been asleep.

"Keep going, Fish," Corporal Riley said. "Malinda, move it."

Malinda spit viciously at the snow. "Sons of bitches."

"That's why no prisoners," PFC Silver, the squad assistant said.

Malinda looked back. "No what?"

"You heard me. No prisoners. Remember the Germans slaughtered eighty-four of our boys at Malmedy. My brother was one of them."

"Fuck me," Malinda said slowly.

"Our boys surrendered and the fucking Krauts shot them all," Silver said through his teeth. "They want to play that game? We play. No prisoners."

Abruptly, Captain Patrick halted the line.

"Someone fire a few shots into that haystack," he said, pointing further down the hill.

Marco Malinda shouldered his rifle and picked off a few rounds.

Kennet stared. Not at the haystack but at the soldier. The blinding sun backlit Malinda, giving him a righteous halo. Then he leaned out of it, going from divine to human. He was chewing gum, and Kennet fixated on the rhythmic contract and release of a single, round muscle in Malinda's scruffy jaw. Minute twitches at the corners of his eyes. He looked grand and casual. He glanced sideways at Kennet and winked.

"You like that, sweetheart?"

At the precise moment Kennet went from smiling to laughing, a crackling rattle shot across the slope and Malinda's head was gone.

I don't remember diving for cover, Kennet wrote. *It's one of many moments lost to me. All at once my face was in the snow and when I picked it up, blood and gore were left behind. I thought I was hit, still I scrabbled like mad with my hands, looking for the closest foxhole the 9th had left. I couldn't find one. I was trying to dig myself straight into the hillside like a mole. I made myself flatter than a piece of paper, kept my head down and listened to the Germans' machine gun fire. Their guns are faster than ours. You can immediately distinguish them by the speed.*

The firing died down. I picked up my head and looked straight into what was left of Malinda's face. One eye, one cheek and the bridge of his nose. The rest was a shattered, bloody mess. Four feet away lay his body, whole and pristine and perfect.

Fucking Krauts literally shot his head off.

I yanked my gaze to my other side, trying to forget forever what I'd just seen, and PFC Silver stared back at me. His hands clutched a horrible belly wound, grey and pink loops falling between his fingers.

"Oh Christ, Silver," I said, knowing he was a goner.

"Malmedy, Fish," he whispered. "Okay? My brother at Malmedy. No prisoners."

And he died.

Kennet was penned in by death and suffering. Behind him, two men were moaning. Ahead of him, Baby was yelling he'd been hit. To his left, the gut-shot Silver. To his right, Malinda's head.

Oh my God his teeth that's a tooth right there on the snow like the Hun whose head exploded and his tooth went into my father's leg...

Kennet pushed his face into the snow and counted five freezing seconds.

Okay. You're done. That's all you get. Think about it later. Feel it later.

He looked up as a soldier and made a brutal triage of his three wounded comrades. Baby was closest to the machine gunner in the haystack, so Kennet crawled through the snow to him.

Baby had taken a shot in the arm but the wound looked clean. The rapid German fire kept rattling, but it became background noise in Kennet's ears as he fell into an odd trance of efficiency, remembering all his training, knowing what to do. Every soldier carried a first aid kit with a Carlisle dressing. Kennet took Baby's and bandaged the wound. He found the kit's sulfa tablets but the water in his canteen was frozen. He told Baby to swallow them with a handful of snow.

"Start crawling. Head toward the rear. Stay as low as you can."

"Take my clips," Baby said. "On my belt. Take them. There's a foxhole about twenty yards down the hill."

Kennet took the ammunition clips from Baby's belt. A beat when they looked hard at each other.

"Good luck, Fish," Baby said, his eyes glazed and voice tight. "Don't do anything stupid. Now go get in that hole and if I see you look back, I'll shoot you myself."

Kennet made a run for it. The foxhole was no pit. It was a shallow slit that he could not fit himself into. No matter how he turned and shifted, some part of him was always left out. A foot. His ass. Or his head. The machine guns continued to spray death across the snow and still no sign of Kennet's platoon coming over the hill.

For the second time in two days, Kennet found himself alone on the battlefield. If he'd been a fish out of water in the woods yesterday, right now he was a sitting duck.

Looking toward the crest, willing his comrades to come to him, he could make out Malinda's bloody head on the snow. Beyond it lay Silver's lifeless body and the shallow trench left by Baby as he crawled away.

He looked downhill. Frozen corpses. Abandoned tanks and guns. A large, stone house in the distance, Germans running all around it.

There was the enemy.

Where were his friends?

Kennet wet his lips and whistled the first line of "Colonel Bogey."

Nobody peeked out at him. Nobody was coming.

At that moment, he was sure the company had withdrawn, retreated, and left him to die here and become another lifeless body.

"I didn't think I'd die alone," he whispered. "Goddammit, Hook, I didn't even say goodbye. How'd you let me get away?"

A thread of panic wove over and under his ribs.

I am alone out here. This is where it ends.

The next unit to march over this hill would find him shot dead, frozen in the snow. Or maybe they wouldn't. More snow would fall and cover him and not until springtime would his bones be visible. And nobody would know whose bones they were.

"Easy, gullgosse," he said, pulling in deep breaths, trying to shake off the cords binding up his ribcage and making him stupid. Baby had specifically instructed him not to be stupid.

"I am a fisherman and a pirate," he heard himself say. "I was conceived in a casino in Aix-les-Bains. The gold in my veins is inherited from my father, who got it from a Hun's tooth. My namesake uncle is king of the river."

A few of his terrified bits and pieces pulled together. He found he fit better into the narrow slit in the ground when he calmed down. And talking to himself helped him stay calm.

"You are a fish with the power to grant wishes," he said. "These Jerries get no wishes if they don't catch you. Don't make it easy for them. Dizzy may have a horseshoe up his ass but you, gullgosse? You have gold in your blood, a gun in your hand and Baby's extra ammo. Three gifts you got right now. Do something with them."

The receiver of his M-1 had gotten clogged with dirt and snow, but he could still operate it by hand. He aimed downhill at the house swarming with German soldiers, and he opened fire. He was an army of one with nothing to lose. He doubted he was hitting anything at this distance. It didn't matter. The point was, he was doing something. He'd go down fighting. They might find him dead, but they'd find him with empty clips.

And then... the sweet sound of machine gun fire. Sweet because it was slower than German gunfire. Sweeter because it came from *behind* him.

He whirled around just as the red tracer bullets began arcing over the snow and the familiar roar and rumble of the American tanks began to shake the earth.

Kennet let out a yell as the fear drained from his body. A primal scream of triumph shot up from his boots and made his helmet lift an inch off his scalp. He was full of electric relief, alive from frozen toes to frozen fingers, and holy Hildur, was he actually sporting a goddamn *erection?* He was, and at that moment, he could've charged down the hill and taken the enemy alone.

The infantry was crawling down the slope now, moving in short, economic surges from bushes to rocks to snowdrifts. And then Hook—*Oh, my buddy, my mate, I knew you'd come*—was yanking Kennet out of his hole, yelling, "I'm swear to God, I'm going to *kill* you."

"Rain check," Kennet said.

"You owe me three wishes, don't you fucking dare die on me."

"Wish later, move your ass *now.*"

Gold pumped hard through his veins as he and Hook ran down the hill and took cover behind a wrecked German tank. They were joined by O'Hara with his BAR, Marty draped with bandoliers of ammunition, and Schmitt with his bazooka.

"You all right, Fish?" O'Hara said, setting up his gun.

"I will be when you start playing my favorite tune."

O'Hara gave a tight nod and then opened fire on the German positions. Sheltered behind the massive tank tread, Kennet quickly field stripped his rifle and got all the crap out of it.

Gradually the company built up enough strength to rush the house. Three Germans came out with their hands in the air. Machine gun fire cut them down in two seconds. Two more Jerries emerged from a dugout and Kennet saw Lieutenant Jorgensson shoot both with his pistol.

"No prisoners, Silver," Kennet whispered.

All the while, machine guns were chattering, grenades exploding, tanks rolling and sometimes knocking into each other. Men constantly yanking their mates out of the path of the treads, or clear of the blasts of the 75-guns.

As the column pushed toward Chenogne, the adrenaline of the day squeezed out of Kennet's bones. Time swelled out of meaning. It sped up and slowed down. The little bits of action that got him from here to there went fuzzy, or missing.

"You okay, Fish?" Hook said, hanging onto the strap of Kennet's rifle.

"I'm just tired."

"Stay on the Hook."

"I will," said the Fish. "I will…"

Extraordinary Soldiers

The company didn't get far into Chenogne. It was past sunset when the officers decided to dig in, with Company B on one side of the road, Company C on the other.

Kennet's squad did a quick huddle-up to count heads. To the outward eye, it seemed no different than the other times they'd gathered to talk. But they'd been different men then. Yesterday they were individuals. Today, they were a *unit*.

> *None of the men in my squad are extraordinary soldiers,* Kennet wrote. *But I'm learning that an army that relies solely on the extraordinary is an army that will soon fail.*
>
> *We train in strictly defined units of squad, platoon, company, battalion, and we expect to stay within those confines on the battlefield. Instead, we're gathered up like dice, shaken and thrown out in random combinations. I found myself fighting by men I've never said good morning to, following orders from a CO I've never seen before. And yet fighting and following seamlessly, because we've all been trained exactly, precisely the same way.*

The Army was a factory, churning out millions of generic parts that could function and cross-function in any unit. Across the country in hundreds of bases, every inductee looked the same, every barracks looked the same, every bed made the same and locker organized the same. You fucked up and everyone paid the price. You excelled not by being your best, but by making the unit its best. Excellence was measured by men trained to do rote, plain, dull and boring things under extraordinary circumstances. This was the basic fuel on which the complex military machine ran.

Run from here to there. Don't ask why. Don't question. Run from here to there, then stop and wait for the next direction.

Simple.

Now do it over. And over. And over. Until you can do it under gunfire. Do it under gunfire when you haven't eaten in three days. Do it on no sleep. Do it *in* your sleep. Do it while pissing down your leg in fright. Do it while mourning a mate who got his head blown off yesterday. Do it with blood in your eyes and a load of shrapnel in your leg. Do it with a shot-up buddy dying on your shoulders.

That's all battle was: men doing what they were told, no matter the emotion or circumstances. Some men had a talent for the telling, but most were simply good at the doing. Sure, there were the crack sharpshooters. The ingenious mechanics. The miracle-working medics. The artistic camoufleurs. The canny, iron-nerved sappers. The soft-stepped, eagle-eyed scouts. But most of the military force was made up of grunts, going where told, doing what told.

Standing with his buddies, listening more than talking, Kennet realized even the grunts had their hidden talents. The jokesters who could find humor in anything. The vulgates who could find the innuendo in anything. Or men like Alfred Martin who never got the jokes, never cursed, and blushed at anything the least bit suggestive. Marty's talent was his innocence. He was the unit's baby brother.

Nolen Anderson, a born-again Nebraskan, could drive you batshit crazy with his biblical recitations, but he had a preternatural ability to look over the platoon and find the soldier poised on the brink of his sanity, staring into the abyss. Anderson would put a hand on the tight shoulder, find the thousand-yard stare with his own and say, "You're going to be okay. I prayed for you this morning. God and I had a long talk, I told him about you and I know it's going to be all right."

And with that strong hand on their shoulder and Anderson's earnest gaze never wavering, men on the edge stepped back, believed Anderson, and lived to fight another day.

Anderson put that hand on Kennet's arm now. "Fish? You all right?"

"For sure," Kennet said, though his voice warbled a little.

"Man," Hook said, rubbing circles on his chest. "Even the time I got arrested, I never felt panic like that."

"I don't panic until O'Hara panics," Jock said.

And the unflappable, stoic O'Hara smiled, almost looking bashful.

The squad huddled closer and took inventory. Silver was dead. Hank Berliner and Corporal Riley wounded. Schmitt was in a state because his best buddy, Nichols, was missing, and nobody could say where he was or recall where they'd seen him last. Schmitt was beside himself, and for the first time, Kennet grasped how essential these wartime brother-bonds were, and just how much of a liability. The camaraderie was the glue holding the unit together. Not just spiritual glue but tactical: every soldier carried half a tent and half a sleeping bag. To make a whole shelter, you had to zip up with a friend.

The squad could feel the waves of anxiety radiating off Schmitt, and all of them realized they might have to unzip and unstick from a treasured partner, and do it *fast*.

"He's all right, Schmitty," Anderson said. "Just lost in the shuffle somewhere."

"I know," Schmitt said. "I'd feel it if he were dead."

The men could believe this. Schmitt and Nichols finished each other's sentences and walked in lockstep. One itched and the other scratched. They also bickered and argued nonstop, needling at each other, pushing, mocking, jeering.

"Would you two just get divorced already?" was a frequent platoon quip, made with the full knowledge that only death could part Schmitt and Nichols.

Possibly, it had.

No more time to fret, though. Lieutenant Jorgensson came by to break up the meeting and get them hustling to dig. "You can expect a counter attack after you take up positions. Which means, ladies, we got about forty-five minutes before the show begins."

Hook and Kennet scraped snow away from a rough square and began to hack at the frozen ground with their ridiculous little shovels.

Just keep digging, Kennet thought, quickly running out of gas. His toes were numb, his hands cramped and his lower back howling.

Dig for your life. Dig for gold. Dig for wishes.

He was so tired.

Ingle was singing the Brits' parody lyrics of "Colonel Bogey" as he dug. The talent Ralph Ingle brought to the squad was endurance. He was tireless. *Tireless.* His eyes would be ringed with sleepless shadows but he never gave up. He never gave in. Men siphoned stamina off Ingle like gasoline. If Ingle whistled as they marched, they worked up some spit and joined in. If Ingle sang, everyone sang.

Hitler has only got one ball
Göring has two but very small
Himmler is rather sim'lar
But poor old Goebbels has no balls at all

The shared song helped in the task, but it was the first rumble of artillery that put a little more spring in Kennet's step. His singing turned to cursing. Christ, if he lived through this war, he was going to have to re-train himself not to swear every other word.

If she were alive, Ma would have a field day washing the garbage out of my mouth.

By the time the barrage started in earnest, he and Hook could just cram themselves in their hole and sit on its ice-cold, rocky floor.

"Barely enough room to swing a shovel," Hook mumbled. They got on their knees and chiseled at the rough walls, elbowing and bashing each other, scraping dirt into their helmets and throwing it out the top. Frantically digging a little more width here for extra ammo, a tad more length there to pile grenades. A smidgen more leg room. It didn't have to be palatial. A few steps above wretched would do.

A shell exploded and the ground lurched around them like an earthquake. Kennet let out a yell and his mouth filled with dirt. He choked and the handle of his shovel hit Hook's head, a split second before the edge of Hook's shovel caught Kennet in the face. They grabbed onto each other, spitting mud, gravel and curses, shaking all over.

"Goddammit, where's my helmet?" Hook said.

"You just had it."

"I must've thrown it out."

"Stay down."

"I'm just gonna look for it quick. I can't sit out here bare-headed, darling. You know how easily I catch cold."

"Well don't lose your fucking head. I already looked at one shot-up face today and you know how it upsets me, sweetheart."

Maybe we can just joke and curse this whole goddamn war away, Kennet thought, as Hook raised his brow above the rim of the foxhole and crouched back down again, grim-faced.

"Fuck, that last shell took out Ellis."

"Squirt?"

"No, the other one. Tall Ellis. Guess he didn't dig deep enough, poor bastard."

"Fuck."

They grabbed each other again as another shell went off, raining down dirt, rocks, snow and, like an absurd punctuation mark, Hook's helmet.

"Ah, there you are," he said, putting it on. "Thanks, fuckers," he yelled up at the sky.

Kennet fell back against the wall, putting his face against his kneecaps and dissolving into a bizarre mix of laughter and despair.

"Happy New Year, Fish."

"Oh my God." Kennet picked up his head, tears making icy tracks on his face. "Did you bring the champagne?"

"I forgot."

"I can't rely on you for anything."

"Holy shit, I clocked you good with the shovel. Right on your cheekbone there, it's bleeding."

"Oh." Kennet swiped his wet face and his hand came away red. "I thought I was crying, not bleeding."

"Well, ain't that a fucking metaphor for war?"

They looked at each other. Two filthy, freezing and fatigued fellows. With only each other to rely on.

"If it's not an inopportune time, o magic fish," Hook said, "I'd like to call in my three wishes."

They flinched at the fall of another shell, slamming their hands over their ears, screwing up their faces and squeezing their eyes. They shook off the dirt, exhaled, smiled weakly at each other.

"You were saying?" Kennet said.

"My three wishes." Hook put up a finger at a time. "We see this through to the end. We go back home. We die in our sleep. What do you think, too unreasonable?"

"No. Good wishes. I'll see what I can do."

"I believe the words are, 'Your wish is my command.'"

"That's only for genies in bottles. Magic fish just do what they can."

Jokes and cursing are all you have left in a foxhole, Kennet wrote. *It beats thinking about every shell that missed you and wondering if the next one has your name on it. Wondering how long the barrage is going to last. Wondering if the German infantry is poised to attack. Wondering how long you'll last if they do.*

Amazing what a body can get used to. Even with all the wondering, all the booming and rattling and rubble pouring on us, I dozed off for a bit while Hook kept a lookout. Not a solid rest by any stretch of the imagination but for a few precious moments, I went. I was gone.

If a shell has my name on it, it'll find me. Whether I'm asleep or awake. Might as well grab what winks I can.

Our tanks and artillery laid down shells and machine gun fire in front of our positions. So that held off an attack and one by one, we could leave our foxholes and go up to the tracks which were parked on the hill, get our coats and some rations.

New Year's Eve supper was some frozen beef stew à la Uncle Sam, dug fresh out of the tin and elegantly served on the tip of a trench knife. If you nick your tongue, the blood adds to the flavor. Accompanying the main course was some lovely frozen condensed milk, which one chews rather than drinks.

The ambience was first rate. Instead of romantic candlelight, we were treated to a line of burning houses along the road. The flames lit up the sky, flickered on the dirty snow and lent an air of eerie mystery to the mealtime hour. Nothing like a roaring fire to warm the heart. And the hide, as Hook and I took a walk to the inferno to thaw out. Pete von Asselt came with us. He's a swell guy.

The intense heat sure felt good on my sore muscles. I was telling the boys about the Finnish institution of the sauna when two men came walking down the road.

When he had time to think about it, Kennet was astonished how quickly he went from storyteller to soldier. A sentence was still coming out of his mouth as he set his rifle to his shoulder and opened fire on the two figures in the road. They were silhouetted against the burning houses and Kennet didn't know how he knew they were Germans. Just that something about the way they moved wasn't right.

"Nicht schießen," a voice cried out of the smoke. "Genosse!"

Gullgosse? Kennet thought wildly, and for a sick moment he thought he'd shot Lieutenant Jorgensson.

"Kamerad!" the man yelled. "Freund!"

"Hände hoch," von Asselt shouted above his aimed rifle.

"Kumpel, Kamerad, Freund!"

Von Asselt went on shouting. "Beweg dich nicht. Don't take your eyes off them, Fish. Hände *hoch*. Leg die Hände dort hin, wo ich sie sehen kann, Arschloch."

"Rough translation?" Hook mumbled out the corner of his mouth.

"Hands up, asshole," von Asselt said.

So for dessert, Kennet wrote, *we were treated to two German prisoners.*

A little before midnight, we were ordered to evacuate our current positions, pull back to the hill and dig in there. Why? Ah. Grunts don't ask why. If you're told to pull back and scratch a hole in the frozen earth for the second time in six hours, you pull back and scratch.

So, in a weird circular coincidence to end this bizarre day, I ended up back on the hillside, right by that same goddamn haystack where all the trouble started this afternoon. But I wasn't alone this time, thank God. AND, a bit more luck was in the air: the 9th Armored had left their trenches behind, and Hook and I stumbled into the Taj Mahal of foxholes. I don't know how many men dug it, or if a shell created it, but it was so roomy that we waved down Ingle and Pete to come join us.

Pete von Asselt is such a swell guy. Did I say that already? He's just decent and level-headed. Of course, we all call him von Asshole. It's irresistible. But we do it in a friendly way and he takes it in stride. Says he's been called that since kindergarten.

So that was my New Year's Eve, celebrated in a little-known hole in the ground. Not much of a party. The food was terrible and the band only played one song. I didn't get kissed, but I snuggled up to Hook while he snored on the back of my neck.

Now if we, darling girl, were together tonight, I'd kiss you until you forgot your name. I'd take you to bed at midnight and wouldn't stop making love to you until 1946.

JANUARY
1945

To Kill For Friends

New Year's Day 1945

A holiday back in the States but here in Belgium, just another day in the salt mines. Breakfast of frozen C-rations pried out of the can. Wondering over terrible coffee and endless smokes what the day would bring.

We had orders to attack Chenogne again, and the crews were warming up the tanks. Our hillside swarmed with activity and I couldn't believe how many vehicles occupied the slope behind us. Half-tracks and tanks and tank destroyers. Ambulances and jeeps.

While we were assembling, Lieutenant Jorgensson called me over and said, "You stick by me today, gullgosse."

I turned about as dumb as a schoolgirl asked on her first date and stammered "Sir?" or something asinine.

"I'm about dead on my feet," he said, which didn't exactly explain why he wanted me, but I shut up and did what he asked. That whole hellish day, I saw few of the guys from my squad, but I was never more than two feet from Jorgy. I confess I sometimes pretended he was Paps.

Even the war heroes need their heroes.

It was a terrible day.

As soon as the American forces crested the hill above Chenogne, the German machine guns sprang to life in their lightning-fast cadence. Mortars rained down on the American tanks with horrifying accuracy, dropping into turrets like basketball shots. More artillery was called in.

"Move our assaults up the crest," Lieutenant West bawled over the radio, "Knock out those goddamn machine guns."

The receiver flew out of his hand and he dropped onto the snow, hit through the shoulder. Blood began to puddle. Crimson on white.

"Don't move," Jorgy yelled. "Fish, get a—"

The order was cut off by another explosion and then two more men were down.

"Get a goddamn medic," Jorgy cried.

Kennet looked around a helpless moment. The battalion was pinned on the ridge, the dead and wounded scattered everywhere. Medic jeeps were all over but every one of them seemed occupied, with countless calls of "Medic! Over here, medic! Medic, *hurry!*"

So I shanghaied a half-track, he wrote.

Desenrascanco, darling.

I drove it up the hill and put the wounded men on. I looked around for a buddy to come with and give me cover. I wanted Hook bad and had no idea where he was or if he was even alive. Then I saw Pete von Asselt a few yards away. Goddamn, he was something. Machine gun on his hip, four bandoliers across his chest. Just spraying the hell out of everything and looking like a war hero straight out of the movies. It was one of those slow-motion moments when the war takes a breath and you get to be human.

Von Asselt jumped in the track with me and we went like hell

*for Jodenville, where the battalion aid station was set up. We
dumped the wounded and headed back.*

*"Step on it, Fish," von Asselt said. "I'd sure hate to miss the
fun."*

*He was being sarcastic, of course, but when we got back, the
scales were just starting to tip in our favor and we were inching
down the hill into the town. Men along the sides of the road
started getting picked off by sniper fire and someone yelled at me
to take cover. A bullet hit my left hand and ricocheted off my
rifle's upper guard. Knocked the damn thing out of my hand,
spun me around and toppled me into the ditch, right on top of
Nathan Eisenstein.*

"Fancy meeting you here, sweetie," he said, shoving me off.

See what I mean about the jokes getting you through?

*The bullet grazed my wrist bone. It bled nine ways to Sunday
and hurt like a bitch but Eisenstein slapped my Carlisle dressing on it and did a neat job. At least it wasn't my trigger hand.*

*Eisenstein and I ran up the road to the corner where I'd seen
Jorgy. We passed a medic giving aid to Squirt (the short Ellis;
now the only Ellis) who'd been hit in both legs. I still didn't know
where any of my squad was. It's just a horrible feeling when you're
cut loose from that tight unit, and I wanted to get back within
two feet of Jorgy where I belonged.*

"Enemy fire's coming from that big house up ahead," Jorgy said.
"Tanks coming in to take it out."

The tanks fired from less than thirty yards away, putting gaping
holes into the thick stone walls of the house.

"Europe builds shit to last," Jorgy said. "You need a lot of fire
power to bring these buildings down. You two take your grenades
up there, throw 'em through the basement windows."

Kennet and Nate ran forward and crouched by the house.

"I'll throw first," Nate said, and before Kennet could stop him, he heaved his Mk 2 at an upstairs window.

"Not the up— Oh *shit*," Kennet yelled as the grenade bounced off the shutter and came back to earth. He flung himself down and covered his head as the pineapple exploded. He looked up, steeled to see another head like Malinda's, half torn up and staring back at him.

Nate was indeed staring. Then he blinked. Pushed up and patted his arms, torso and legs. He was all there.

"*Stay* there, you moron," Kennet cried. He pulled the pin on his grenade and lobbed it through a basement window, like Jorgy had said. Then he dove away and took cover, curling away from the blast.

When he looked back, Nate Eisenstein lay dead where Kennet told him to stay. All of him still there. The blast didn't get him. Just a neat bullet hole through his forehead.

"Oh, fuck *me*," Kennet muttered. He was pissed now. The same electric thrill he'd felt on the snowy slope above the town, but mean and nasty. A bear rudely woken from hibernation, wondering who he had to kill to get some goddamn sleep around here.

He pulled the pin on his second grenade and threw it through the next basement window. He grabbed Nate's second grenade and noticed Nate had a third pineapple on him, which was odd, but fortuitous—it was time to get the fucking job *done*. Kennet rolled down the line of the house's foundation, like some macabre version of a penny arcade game. Pull, throw, roll away and cover. Pull, throw, roll and cover. One window after another until he reached a hedge at the far side of the house, where Jorgy yelled at him to take cover because the tanks were going to shell again.

Kennet crawled to his commander, settled back into that two-foot safety zone where he could catch his breath.

Soon, all the windows in the house were erupting flames.

"They're coming out," someone yelled.

The cry went through the troops and every American rifle trained on the house. Kennet was on his feet, aimed, angry and itching to avenge.

Let's finish this, he thought. *Finish it all and let's go the fuck home.*

A man came out. Something white in his hand. It fluttered to the ground as the rifle fire cracked open. He spun, jerked, twisted and fell. Crawled a yard. Then died.

The house belched smoke. A wail of noise from within. Shouting and wailing. The sound of a terrible choice: die in the smoke, or face the guns.

"Come out," the soldiers screamed.

"Come out," Kennet cried, on fire as the world began to tear apart. "Come out, you sons of bitches."

Men came out. The Americans fired.

But then…

Listen.

Some tiny part of Kennet's awareness was tapping his shoulder. *Hear that? What was that?*

More Germans came out and were cut down.

Listen. Can you hear it?

The rifle fire was incessant. The bodies piled up outside the doorway and under the first-floor windows.

No, not the guns. The screaming. Listen to the screaming.

Kennet's finger came off the trigger. He closed his eyes.

What is that sound *in the screaming?*

His rifle came down. "Jorgy, there are *women* in there…"

He made a dash for one of the basement windows. "Hold your fire," Jorgy screamed behind him. "Hold your fire. *Women are in the house.*"

The word rippled through the ranks. *Women.* Soon joined by *children. Civilians. Hostages.*

Tiny, tear-streaked faces crowded the basement windows.

The same windows Kennet had thrown grenades through.

My God, I could've killed them.

He knelt in the broken glass and charred earth. A pair of arms locked around his neck. He pulled a little girl onto his chest, passed her to the guy behind him, then reached back in and pulled a woman free. Then another two kids. Another mother. An old man. A child. Mother. Grandmother. A bucket brigade of humanity.

Vaguely, in his periphery, Kennet saw his mates kicking aside dead bodies to stand beneath the first-floor windows and catch the tykes who were lowered down. The American men who had rushed forward to kill now staggered back with their arms full of women and children. These Belgian civilians were half-mad with relief and fright. Some rushed around, hugging and kissing each other, hugging and kissing the soldiers. Others, traumatized and not trusting the situation, snatched their loved ones and ran for the woods, ignoring the dire warnings that the woods weren't safe from artillery fire.

The next child passed out of the window into Kennet's hands was dead.

And the next.

And the next.

Followed by a hysterical, weeping woman, who lay down by the three small bodies and refused to move.

Then one last boy, no more than twelve, seized Kennet's wrists and scrambled through. "Tous les autres sont morts," he said. "All dead." He mimed pulling the pin on a grenade, then made big explosion noises. "Boom."

Kennet shoved him along. He grabbed the grieving woman, hauled her to her feet and all but flung her toward the moving crowd. "Jorgy, basement is clear," he yelled.

He ran to catch up to his squad, then stopped once to look back at the house.

Tous les autres sont morts.

Boom.

The war paused to catch its breath.

Jesus H, I killed three kids.

The war screamed again, demanding attention. Kennet forgot about it, turned back and ran.

The American forces moved methodically down the road through Chenogne, scanning every building, most of which were either shattered or burning, but still could be harboring last nests of resistance.

I killed three kids, Kennet thought between the intense bouts of fighting.

Random sniper fire erupted every few minutes and the men would dive for cover, yanking each other down, locating the source, pointing up at windows. Holy Schmitt got off another beautiful shot with his bazooka, knocking two more Germans out of an attic, where they were cut down by machine gun fire.

I killed three kids.

Resistance turned to surrender. German soldiers crept out of the rubble and ruin, waving white flags, hands in the air and faces screwed up, braced for the same rifle fire that had greeted their comrades. They lined up along the road and the American GIs who spoke German searched them for weapons and booty.

"Jesus Christ," Kennet said to Hook. "Some of them can't be more than sixteen, seventeen."

They're kids. I killed three kids.

"Hitler Youth," Hook said. "Arrogant little shits."

Indeed, while the older German troops looked weary, the youths were smirking and sneering. Their hands were in the air or laced on their heads, but their chins were high and chests out. Many wore American Army clothing, and Kennet saw von Asselt tear the name insignia off one boy's shirt before backhanding him to the ground. Von Asselt strode back to where Kennet stood. His breath made frozen puffs in the air. It looked like he was breathing smoke. His face was red and his jaw clenched as he showed Kennet the blood-stained insignia.

It read *MALINDA*.

"Oh, you little fucking punk," Kennet murmured, feeling the fury rise in him again. He was pure pirate right now. His blood was up. His *gold* was up.

> *I think it began then,* Kennet wrote. *If a man's life is a tapestry, then I think today was the first tiny thread that snapped free. Just one thread but enough, when you pulled it, to unravel the whole warp and weft.*
>
> *One little thread to unravel a man.*
>
> *I remember Ma teaching Trudy to knit. How to pick up the dropped stitches and make it look like nothing happened.*
>
> *This is a female skill.*
>
> *Women know how to pick up dropped things.*
>
> *Women know how to stitch and mend and fix what's broken.*
>
> *Women know how to endure the unendurable.*

Women don't lose themselves.

Women would never let a war like this happen in the first place.

But we are men.

War does things to men. It blows the old rules to shit and writes new ones, making men do things they never dreamed. Like killing three kids by accident and turning around to kill three dozen kids on purpose.

If the world is going to rely on ordinary men to right the wrongs, then those men have to rely on each other.

And what men do in war, they do only for each other.

Asta, it's so much easier to kill for friends than for a cause.

Causes are distanced, abstract things. Friends are in your face, in your bunk, in your foxhole. They trust you with their lives, they die in your arms with their blood and guts sprayed across your face and their teeth embedded in your flesh.

Family isn't only your blood. It's who you bleed for.

What I did today, I did not do for Malmedy.

I did it for Malinda.

Say His Name

"Line 'em up," Captain Patrick said.

He and a couple other officers started picking random American soldiers. Those soldiers moved forward with their rifles and machine guns.

"No," Anderson said. "No, this isn't right."

"An eye for an eye," Jock said. "Look it up in that good book of yours. It says, 'A time for war' and 'a time to kill.'"

"And a time to forgive and a time for peace. No man can pass judgment. That's up to God."

"If there's a God, he isn't on this goddamn battlefield," Jock said.

"*We* are God," Holy Schmitt said.

"We're doing exactly what *they* did at Malmedy," Anderson said. "What the Japs did at Bataan. Are we going to stoop to their level, or rise above?"

"We're already above Nazi scum," Jock said. "They started this shit. They made the rules of the game. We're just playing by them."

"I won't be part of this," Anderson said.

"You don't have to," O'Hara said quietly. "Take Marty. Don't make a show, just move back quietly, move behind the tanks and go invisible. No shame, Andy." O'Hara's gaze went around the squad. "No shame," he repeated. "Not if you stay, not if you go. Am I clear?"

"We do what we have to, Andy," von Asselt said. "I'm not you and you're not me. We're still brothers. I'll still fight for you."

"Go," O'Hara said. "Get out of sight. Just back away."

Tears brimmed Anderson's earnest eyes. "Guys, please. You can't..."

"Andy, if you don't want to be picked, move away," Hook said. "Do what you have to do. No shame."

"I don't run away."

"You're not running away," Schmitt said. "You're just moving a little bit backward."

"You look like you need to take a leak, Andy," Jock said. "Jesus H, you're hopping up and down on one foot like a kid. Go piss on a jeep or something."

"Anyone asks where you were, tell 'em nature called," von Asselt said. "Go on now."

The German prisoners were lined up on both sides of the road now. Twenty to thirty in each group.

"Fiskare," Lieutenant West called.

"Fish, wait," O'Hara said. "I'll go."

"No, I'll do it." Kennet half-turned and held out a hand to von Asselt, indicating he wanted that little strip of olive canvas, machine-stitched with a name. "For Malinda, I'll do it."

Von Asselt gave him the insignia. Kennet put it in his pocket.

He took his place.

I am forever changed now.

When the order came, Kennet aimed at the little Hitler Youth punk who dared to walk around with Malinda's name on his heart. He looked for the German's eyes and when he found them, all the sneering bravado was gone. He was just a boy, begging for mercy.

And a boy who helped imprison Belgian civilians in a fortified house.

A boy who herded children down basement steps, to huddle up against walls and beneath transom windows, where an American soldier would be sure to throw deadly pineapples.

It was *his* fault, this little Nazi prick.

And I bet you think I'm going to be decent and honorable and kind about it, Kennet thought. *Because I was raised to be a gentleman. And look what that got me. Jack shit. Look at what always happens to gentlemen raised to do the right thing when assholes like you couldn't care less.*

A corner of his upper lip went into a frenetic twitch as his finger curled on the trigger. *Well, fuck you. Fuck you and your country for starting this goddamn shit. Starting it* twice. *Dragging first my father and uncle, now me and my brothers into it. Making me have to follow orders to grenade three kids to death and change who I am.*

Fuck you and everyone who looks, acts and thinks like you.

The order came.

Kennet fired.

That's for Marco. Marco Malinda. Say his name now, you miserable piece of shit.

He kept firing.

For Corporal Jefferson blown apart on the railroad track. For Silver's last words spilling from his guts, *No prisoners.* For Baby crawling wounded through the snow. For Nichols, still missing. For tall Ellis, who didn't dig deep enough, fast enough. For Squirt Ellis, who took it in both legs.

Kennet fired for his hero, Lieutenant Jorgensson.

For von Asselt, looking like a Hollywood star on the field's banner.

He fired for O'Hara, Ingle, Nichols, Jock and Hook.

He fired for Anderson, still principled enough not to participate, and astute enough to keep Marty out of it, too.

Kennet fired for all of his mates, dead and alive.

He fired for Minor and Nalle. He fired to keep Little out of the war. He fired for Uncle Nyck, who was still in a war. And he fired for Emil, clinging to his gold charms.

On New Year's Day of 1945, in a little place called Chenogne, Kennet Fiskare took his place in line and fired on eighty German prisoners.

Then, very deliberately, he put his old self in that snowy field. His old self with all its decency, honor and kindness. He put that man, *that* Kennet Fiskare in the field and shot him, too.

I am sorry it came to this, he wrote. *I feel no pride in it.*

It's war. It's retribution for Malmedy. It's what happens.

So I've written it here. If I'm to go on fighting this war, then I have to leave it here.

Today I killed both the innocent and the guilty.

It's done, I admit I took part. And I will never be the same, I accept it.

If this is the act that strips the gold from my veins, so be it.

If I no longer have the power to grant wishes, that's fair.

It's done.

We mounted up and drove out of town, passing the fields where the bodies of the Germans lay, my old self among them.

We drove until we couldn't, then we marched. When shells landed nearby, we lay in the snow.

We marched until we couldn't. Or were advised to stop. I didn't know for sure, I'd stopped thinking. I just got on my Hook and followed him.

We halted on a slope. Von Asselt, Hook and I dug in together. Two worked while one watched. We settled down. One watched while two slept. Or tried to sleep. Or lay awake with painfully cold feet, just feeling shitty and sorry for themselves. At one point, I heard von Asselt crying a little. He was rolled away from me with his face under his arm, stifling it. I didn't want to embarrass him, but I felt bad. My feet hurt so much, I felt like crying myself.

You can't expect a man to be pushed to the limit of his strength, endurance and courage, then be disgusted if he breaks down afterward. We're men, not Gods.

We're just cats, birds and eggs. Ordinary grunts doing what we can.

Finally I put my hand on von Asselt's back, but kept quiet. Just letting him know I was there. I pressed my palm between his shoulder blades and tried to give him some of my gold.

We do what we have to do.

It was a terrible day and a miserable night.

I should just leave it here.

Strong Letter
to Follow

Rise and shine to the sound of mortars landing around our vehicles, Kennet wrote. *That'll wake a fellow up.*

Word came down from on high we were to withdraw. After all that fighting and blood and death to secure this position, we had to leave it. That'll kick a fellow in the balls.

A frantic hustle to gather up all the ammunition, equipment and weapons. Pile it up to load in the vehicles. Then another word from on high: so sorry, hold your position (except for the 'so sorry' part). Back into the holes we go. And that will make even a saint like Anderson into one surly son of a bitch.

(You probably noticed I've stopped apologizing for my language. Apologies come with an intent to change, and I have no intention, hell, I have no chance of cleaning up my mouth. This is it, darling girl. Cover your ears, avert your eyes or just close the book and read no more.)

We saw a bit of action that morning, but it came in bursts and always when I was on the verge of nodding off, so I have bizarre memories of things Hook swears didn't happen. I must've been dreaming some of it. It left me disturbed in a way I couldn't shake off. Seemed the whole rest of the day, I didn't know if I was awake or dreaming.

Toward the evening we got orders again: proceed to the southwest to take control of the highway between Bastogne and Neufchateau.

You should hear some of these officers butcher the names of French towns. Noofchatooey.

For the second time, we left our foxholes and assembled.

It was quiet. I mean, quiet for war. There was the usual buzz of conversation and the roar of the tank engines. But no sound from the enemy.

It was quiet. The sunset wasn't magnificent, but it made some pretty pink and orange streaks on the horizon, like it was trying its best to put some kind of beauty in this ugly landscape. I stood with Hook and von Asselt by a tank. Just us three. We were warming ourselves and talking about home.

The war paused to take a breath and it was a good moment.

It was quiet.

It was too quiet.

And...

"I'm hit," von Asselt cried. "Fish. Oh shit..."

Kennet had been thrown to the side by the shell blast. He picked his head up out of the dirty snow. Von Asselt lay face down by one of the tank treads.

"Oh God," Kennet whispered. "Pete." He crawled over, thick and clumsy in his greatcoat. "Pete, hang on."

Hook was crawling over, too. "Pete. Oh Christ... Oh fuck..."

They rolled von Asselt over. Blood spurted up from a horrendous hole in his chest.

"Pete," Kennet said, his voice cracking. He pushed his fist against the gaping wound but the blood kept erupting.

"You gotta stop it," Hook said, trying to get his hands in.

"Get a medic," Kennet cried. "Get a jeep. Hook, hurry. Jesus Christ, Pete."

Hook went charging off through the chaos.

"Fish." Von Asselt's voice was a tiny thread of sound. Blood slipped from his nose and one corner of his mouth.

"Hang on," Kennet said, as much to himself as the wounded man. "You hang onto me. Stay with me. Don't you even think about checking out."

A bloody smile. "Hate…to miss…the fun."

"That's right. The party's just getting started. Hook's gone for help. You stay with me. Hang on, Pete."

Kennet had both hands clamped on Pete's chest. Pressing. Pushing everything he had into his friend.

Pete gritted his teeth and with a moan of effort he lifted an arm and dropped his gloved hand onto the pile of Kennet's bloody fingers.

"Sorry, Fish," he whispered.

"No, don't tell me sorry. You hang onto me."

"You… Good ones. Buddy."

Kennet widened his eyes to keep the tears back. "No, buddy, you're the good one. The best one." He tried to laugh. "Jesus, von Asshole, even with a shot to the chest you look like a Hollywood actor."

A ragged exhale of breath which might have been an attempt to laugh along. "Take two…"

Hook came back with a medic jeep, Kennet wrote. *It was already crammed full of wounded guys, but Hook had convinced, bullied or threatened the medic to come get Pete. In the end, we put our Hollywood boy on the hood of the car and I got on top of him to keep him from rolling off.*

As I lay with one hand clinging to the windshield, the other arm and both legs wrapped around Pete, I kept talking to him, kept telling him to hang on and stay with me. Joking about the shitty quality of the roads. How I had a few goddamn words for the people in charge (strong letter to follow).

Pete had stopped talking, but every now and then he'd make a little sound against my neck, or squeeze his eyes open and closed very deliberately. He was going grey and his eyes stayed closed for longer and longer. When they opened, the gaze was far, far away.

When he said "Mom" softly, I knew I was losing him and it made me feel like dying, too. I grabbed onto him even tighter. I was babbling anything I could think of to keep him with me, keep him alive. I paused for breath and he opened his eyes and whispered something.

I think he said, "Love you, Fish."

I'm pretty sure it's what he said.

I want it to be what he said.

Please let that be what he said.

When we got to the battalion aid station, he was dead.

. . .

Fuck this fucking war.

. . .

Like I wrote before, Asta, you never know what little bit of something-or-other is going to get you through or comfort you. When I think that von Asselt didn't die in the battalion aid station, but died in my arms, smiling at a dumb joke I made, whispering "Love you," it comforts me. It got me through the day. Because it's war. You kill three kids and leave it behind. You murder German prisoners of war and move on. You deposit your friend's dead body, unzip from his tent, unstick from the bond and go back to fight.

You do what you have to do.

No shame.

No prisoners.

No rules.

I had to walk back to the unit unarmed—in all the commotion of getting Pete on the jeep, my rifle got left behind. When I got back to the place where the shell had exploded, I found my gun all smashed up and useless. But a little ways away, I found a carbine in the snow. It must have been Pete's. So I took it.

I fell in line behind Hook, with Malinda's name in my pocket and Pete's gun in my hand. We advanced to the next village. I had a hold of one of Hook's pack straps the whole time. I just stayed on him, stayed on the Hook. No shame. Lots of guys hang on their buddies while stumbling along, half-asleep and wretched.

It's funny, Asta, how in peacetime, physical contact between men is considered odd. Even suspect. Yet out here, between battles, we touch all the time. Unthinkingly. Desperately. It reminds me of when you talked about Brazilian men always being conscious, almost competitive with their masculinity. If I ever see you again, darling girl, I think we should have a drink and continue the conversation, because war is changing my idea about what it means to be a man.

The sun was down but the skies continued to have an odd, orange glow. As we reached the outskirts of the next town, we saw many of the buildings were on fire. Something about the lines of men moving in silhouette against the flames was both eerie and magnificent. If this were a movie, the orchestra would be all swelling violins and ominous kettle drums, banging out the beat of thousands of booted feet.

We searched house to house, but found no Krauts. And few civilians.

My platoon wasn't on guard duty, so we took possession of a house that had a paddock with an ancient-looking horse and a couple cows. All fifty-odd of us men crammed inside. It was still cold, but it was a roof over our head. The half-tracks came up and we got our gear and rations, started warming up a little supper on the Coleman stoves.

Hook and I had some chicken and beans. We made cocoa that wasn't very sweet, but it was hot. He asked if I was all right. If I wanted to talk. About Chenogne or Pete or any of it. I said no, I only wanted to sleep.

We had one cigarette left between us so we passed it back and forth and Hook let me kill it. I drank the rest of the cocoa, even the gritty sludge at the bottom. Then I lay down and pretended to sleep. My feet were throbbing. My throat and eyes hurt so bad from not crying. I rolled on my stomach and pushed my face in my arm, thinking to hell with it, just let rip and get it out. But nothing would come. No tears, not even a sniffle. Hook put his hand on my head but said nothing.

There was some shelling during the night. The house shook all around us. I remember looking up and the pictures on the wall were tilting this way and that. Then I heard a scream. It wasn't human. It was the worst sound I ever heard. Like a demon giving birth.

The only one who didn't jump out of his socks was O'Hara. He tilted his head a little, then said sadly, "That's a horse dying." Without another word, he took his rifle, went out and put the beast down. Came back in and went back to sleep, as if he'd merely stepped out to take a piss.

He was so deadpan, some of the boys cracked up laughing. Me, I just lay there while a wave of hellish nausea swept through me. I'd never felt lower in my life. I'd been detached for so long, now every feeling on earth, I had it to death. Sad to death. Tired to death. Angry to death.

Scared to death.

I started whispering "Love you, Fish" to myself. I imagined the lurching house was a jeep bumping along a road of frozen mud, and I was on the hood. Wounded. Hanging on. It was a movie. That's all. I was a hero in a Hollywood war thriller and the director would yell "Cut!" soon. Until he did, I just had to speak my one line.

"Love you, Fish." I said under my breath, over and over. "Love you, Fish."

Little by little, though, it was you I clung to, Asta. You who lay on top of me, strong and secure. So clean and sweet, pretty and pure and peaceful. Pinning me with elbows and knees, pulling me up into your body where all was safe and soft. Whispering into my mouth, "Jag älskar dig, Fisken. Älskar dig, Fisken. Älskar dig…"

I held onto you all night, Asta, my darling, darling girl.

It's war. You do what you have to.

Whatever little thing gets you through to morning.

Now

The morning of January 3rd dawned with a mix of rain and snow. Two cows waddled around the paddock next to the house where the soldiers had spent the night. The men had little to say. The miserable lowing of the cattle seemed to say everything.

After a week of tense fighting, Company B was half what it used to be, its men exhausted and chilled deeper than bone. They were chilled to the soul. Slumped on an overturned bucket, Kennet stared at the dead horse lying in the paddock and felt nothing. Only a dry observation that an eviscerated horse resembled an upright piano split in half.

They were waiting for the half-tracks to pick them up. Lieutenant Jorgensson said the company was to be relieved. Young Marty seemed to have trouble grasping the concept.

"I thought… I mean, it's war," he said. "I thought you kept fighting until nobody was left."

Schmitt put a hand out as if to jostle Marty's head, but he seemed to run out of gas and the hand dropped. "We're left," he said. "And we get a break."

Schmitt's head was turned toward the eastern horizon, his stare somewhere in Russia. All around Kennet, men looked at the cardinal points with flat, empty eyes. Only Anderson's gaze was down, in the pages of his pocket bible. He flipped this way and that, unable to find a passage that suited him.

"I'm so fucking tired," Jock said to no one. A cigarette dangled from his bottom lip but he hadn't lit it. O'Hara sat next to him, hands folded over his mouth and nose.

Little by little, new troops arrived in the village, insignia identifying them as the 17th Airborne Division. Lounging and strutting around, they looked fresh, sleek, well-rested and cocky. Grinning and calling to each other, making cracks, showing off.

If you only knew, Kennet thought. *What lies ahead. If you'd seen what I've seen, you'd wish you were leaving. You poor bastards, if you could only...*

A wave of sympathetic anxiety rose up in his chest. His fatigued body gave a minute twitch, wanting to do something to protect these new brothers. Then he softened and slumped into resignation again. Nothing could be done. There was nothing for it. Kennet's platoon had clocked out, now these fellows from the 17th were the next shift in the factory of war. Kennet couldn't warn them, couldn't protect them, couldn't save them. They had to go in blind and do the job on the fly. Physically trained but mentally unprepared. And at the end of their shift—a week, ten days, two weeks—they'd be relieved and they'd sit around, depleted and staring, pitying the incoming troops and trying to avoid looking at the gaps in their ranks.

Every squad was full of holes, but the battered platoon would rest, then go back into battle and more of them would die. Rest. Fight. Count the dead. Rest. Fight. Count the dead. Until, just as Marty said, "nobody was left."

Kennet followed Schmitt's gaze toward the east. Toward Russia, Siberia, China, Japan, across the Pacific to Canada. His vision threaded out long, making a transcontinental leap to the Great

Lakes. It wended the ancient waterway of Superior, Huron, Erie and Ontario, into the mouth of the St. Lawrence River and the tiny peninsula of Clayton. His eyes looked up at the Fisher Hotel, at the carved wooden fish hanging over the veranda stairs, and he knew he'd never see his home again. Just as every man around him knew, or was quickly coming to grips with it.

Few of them were getting out of here alive.

And, thought every man in uniform, *I doubt I'll be one of them.*

They stayed quiet and introspective as they assembled and trudged toward the waiting half-tracks. Thinking of all the things undone, words unspoken, dreams unfulfilled, knowledge unlearned, girls un-kissed.

After stretching out long to circumnavigate the globe, Kennet's vision now retracted and sharpened to a short, immediate radius. The fish became a hawk, scrutinizing the drab, pulverized landscape, the silvery mist of rain turning into hard sleet. He noted every droplet in every muddy puddle. The ridges of every footprint left by every boot. The curves and contours of the countryside, the myriad shades of brown and grey. Crisp details set against a watercolor wash.

This was the land of his death. Belgium. He envisioned it chiseled on a gravestone beneath a date in 1945. Imagined his relatives saying, "Your Uncle Kennet died in Belgium."

Kennet climbed into a half-track with Hook, Marty, Anderson, Jock and O'Hara. Gear lay in a jumbled explosion on the floor, but they eased around it and collapsed. Just six more pieces of equipment. And their deaths—their deaths came along for the ride, too.

This is where it ends, Kennet thought, as the vehicle lurched down the road. *This is where I end. Somewhere in Belgium. A fish out of water. I'll meet my end in the muddy earth, in the rain and snow, among the corpses and carcasses.*

He felt nothing. No fear, no anger or upset. He didn't want to die, but there was nothing for it. He was too tired to care. The rock and roll of the track was making his thoughts fray. Hook slumped on his shoulder. Anderson had his hands folded and his head bowed. Marty was thumbing through the little pocket bible. O'Hara's arms were crossed tight over his chest and his eyes were closed. Jock put a cigarette in his mouth, forgetting one was already there.

I'll die with you, Kennet thought one minute, then was asleep the next. When he woke, it was evening and the tracks had arrived at a village. Kennet learned later it was called Chêne but now, he wanted only sleep. Sleep. His mind choked and clogged, he couldn't link thoughts together, couldn't remember names or relationships. But someone was in charge. Someone had arranged things. Someone pointed and directed. You men, go there. You men, go there. Follow me. Follow him. Go.

Kennet went. He stumbled like a drunk. Someone put an arm around his shoulders. Someone else lurched into him, he put an arm around those shoulders. His squad was led to a farm, with a large outbuilding stuffed to the rafters with hay. There the troops dropped like felled trees, face first into the fodder, with their helmets and boots on, rifles in hand, out cold before the straw settled over them.

Kennet woke on the 4th of January only because Jock was shaking him.

"Fish… *Fish.*"

"Jockstrap, wouldja fuck off?"

"Wake up, Fish. There's two women here."

"Wha?"

"Two women are outside with food. They don't speak any English and you're the only one who speaks French. Get up."

The two sisters who owned the farm had come to the barn, bringing hot coffee, bread and boiled eggs. And a proposition, which Kennet translated: in return for rations, the women could perhaps wash some clothes?

The men ripped open their packs and handed over tins from their C-rations. Kennet explained the labels had all come off, but the tins would either be meat and beans, meat and potato hash, or meat and vegetable stew.

The women took the loot outside while the squad stripped off socks and long johns. Assessing the disgusting pile of unmentionables on the floor of the hay mow, the sisters wondered what these dirty but brave soldiers might offer in return for the use of the hot water in the house?

Hot water was a baby gazelle thrown into the lion's den. The packs opened again and the squad all but pelted their hosts with cigarettes, condensed milk, sugar cubes, instant coffee and chocolate. Then they nearly came to blows over who would get first turn in the bathroom. Amused, the sisters finally interceded and made the men draw straws.

With six in line to scrub, nobody could take a long soak. "This is a B.A.C.K. bath," Jock said. "Balls, armpits, crack and kisser. And step on it."

Rushed or not, having a proper wash was heaven. The water was scalding hot and the homemade soap studded with orange peel and lavender buds. Kennet almost ate it.

The farmhouse was cluttered and shabby, but it pulsed with a quiet, competent and feminine energy as Solange and Bernadine produced a simple feast. Everyone squeezed around the scrubbed kitchen table, sitting sideways on benches or sharing chairs. They dined on omelets, bread, farmer's cheese, honey and jugs of red wine. Afterward they passed chocolate and cigarettes and tiny cups of bitter coffee.

Starved for female company, each man outdid the other in compliments, anecdotes, jokes and flirtation. Kennet had to be both interpreter and censor—toning down Jock's filthy humor, paraphrasing Anderson's bible verses and beefing up Marty's paralyzing shyness.

The sisters toasted the Allies and the men taught them the "Colonel Bogey" parody:

> *Hitler has only got one ball*
> *Göring has two but very small*
> *Himmler is rather sim'lar*
> *But poor old Goebbels has no balls at all*

The sisters screamed laughing when the lyrics were translated. Solange collapsed against Kennet's side and beneath the table, her calf curled around his leg. He guessed she was in her late thirties. Her face was gaunt, her eyes shadowed, her dun-colored hair threaded with silver. But her eyes were an extraordinary grey-green. She'd been so kind and generous. Her pleasure in the tumult of young, male company was evident and her body felt luxurious pressed against Kennet's.

On the other side, Bernadine and Jock were sharing a cigarette and exchanging smoldering glances.

All at once, the war seemed a long way away.

When you cut ties with your past and sever your future, Kennet thought, *all you have is now.*

The next few days of rest might be his last.

Now was now. He was clean, full, a little drunk. Secure in the company of his mates. Handsome and dashing in the eyes of a young widow.

"What are you thinking about?" she asked.

"Now," he said, using the French word *maintenant*.

Main meaning hand. *Tenant* meaning holding.

Now was only what you could hold in your hand.

He wanted now. The muscles around his eyes tightened and his hands briefly went to fists, curling around the knowledge that he would fight for now. Fight harder than he did for a first turn at the hot water.

A telepathic understanding seemed to ripple along the chairs and benches. Everyone except Kennet and Jock shoved back and stood up. Exaggerated yawns and exuberant stretching. Thanks for the splendid meal were offered. Good nights and sweet dreams were wished. A few smirking glances from the threshold except for O'Hara—his look was a sniper rifle trained on Jock, who ignored him.

Then the kitchen door closed, leaving two men and two sisters.

In another minute, the kitchen was empty.

Goose Egg

"How was it?" Hook asked the next morning.

"Fish never tell tales out of school," Kennet said, sorting out and organizing his pack. He meant to be glib, but the words came out curt and dismissive.

"Well pardon fucking me," Hook said. "I didn't ask the color of her underwear, just wondering if you had a good time." He loped off, exhaling a plume of angry smoke over his shoulder.

Kennet stared after, pissed that his friend was pissed at him. And the piss appeared to be contagious: at the far end of the barnyard, Jock and O'Hara were having a heated discussion. Oddly, O'Hara seemed to be doing most of the talking while Jock stared at his boots, arms crossed tight over his chest and an unlit cigarette dangling from his bottom lip. O'Hara made a half-hearted motion, as if he were going to backhand his friend. Instead, he kicked a rock against a fence post and stormed off.

"What the hell crawled up everyone's ass this morning," Kennet muttered. He shoved things around, confused and out of sorts.

Something had gone wrong last night.

He'd followed Solange to her bed. They kissed and undressed and lay down but something was amiss. Kennet's French was good for conversation, but useless in the bedroom. He didn't know how to make love in this language. Clearly she wanted and he wanted but the want was lost in translation.

"So healthy," she murmured, caressing his arms and shoulders. She smiled as he dug the Army-issue prophylactic out of his wallet, but it was a sad smile, as if she'd remembered the object in a happier context. She watched as he put it on, which made his fingers clumsy. She remained composed and patient until he managed. Then she lay back and let him in.

"All right?" he whispered.

She drew a quick breath. Started to speak. Stopped. Then said, "It's been a long time."

"For me, too." He pushed her hair back from her face. "But it's right now."

"Yes."

He struggled to hold the moment in his hands. The chemical, rubbery smell of the condom was disconcerting. Her kisses were short and tentative, and he was conscious of all the cigarettes he'd smoked tonight. She kept dipping her head into the curve of his neck and shoulder. After a bit she gently pushed him off.

"What's wrong?" he said.

"Nothing." She rolled over on her stomach. "Comme çi. Vite." *Like this. Hurry.*

He knew you could take a woman this way. He'd seen pictures of it in Jock's raunchy comic books. It didn't seem a thing real people did.

On the other hand, he'd never be a real person again.

He moved on top of her carefully. She had to help him settle between her legs and she reached back to guide him inside. He felt inept and foolish for exactly two seconds. Then his body clicked into hers like a puzzle piece. He fell down on his elbows, his open mouth against the nape of her neck. Her fingers closed tight around his wrist and she turned her lips into his palm.

"Yes," she whispered. "Like that. Go. Just go. Right now. Now."

Now became *then* and tumbled from Kennet's hands so fast, he was embarrassed. Over the pounding of his heartbeat, he could hear from the other bedroom the rhythmic creak and groan of the bedstead against the wall. Jockstrap was barely warmed up. By comparison, Kennet was a terrible lover. But Solange shushed his apologies and rolled them onto their sides. She clasped his arms around her from behind and burrowed back into his chest as if to press clear through him. Her thin body trembled. After a beat, Kennet realized she was crying.

The room filled with her dead husband's presence and Kennet felt profoundly ashamed. He'd gotten it wrong. All wrong. Her "hurry" hadn't been out of dire need or desperate passion. It wasn't *hurry, I need you.* It was *hurry, get it done.* She needed it over with so they could get to *this.*

"I'm sorry," she said, wiping her eyes with a corner of the sheet.

"Do you want me to leave?" he whispered.

"No, no more leaving," she said. "No more going. Stay. Hold still. I just want things to stay still."

He buried his face in her lank hair and pulled her to his heart. He tucked her head in the crook of his elbow, wrapped a leg around hers.

"Stay," she said in a moan that was almost ecstatic.

"It's all right," he said in French. Then he began to murmur in English into her hair. "It's all right if you pretend I'm him. I'll do it, too. See, I lost someone. She left me forever. I'll never see her again. But it's all right. You and I, we're together tonight and we can forget the war a little while. I'll be him and you be her. We understand each other. It's all right…"

He was a fool. He and Solange could've gone to bed, stayed dressed and done only this. She wanted comfort and contact. Wanted the feel of a healthy man's body against hers, holding still and letting her pretend *he* was back at home and would stay forever. Prolonging *now* into something secure and immutable.

Now.

Now backward is won, Kennet thought.

Won and one.

To win the war and be one.

One language and one perspective and one want that couldn't be misinterpreted or misunderstood. One moment to hold in your hand.

This morning he awoke alone. Solange's side of the bed was smoothed and in the nest of her pillow lay an enormous, hard-boiled egg.

He stared, his brain still thick with sleep. For a moment he was sure he hadn't slept with a woman last night, but some enchanted princess. Woman by night. Chicken by day.

He shook his head hard and took up the egg, marveling at its size. It must've been from a goose. It filled his palm like a warm moment.

He dressed and ambled back to the hay mow, peeling the egg. The shell was powdery and the yolk an astonishing orange. It would've been delicious, if not for the aftertaste of misunderstanding. His stomach held a grudge against it and he hated now. Hated a war that made one and one into a goose egg.

Jock walked by Kennet, hands stuffed in his pockets. "Man, what's a guy gotta pay to have a little fun around here?"

"You're a noisy fuck, Jockstrap. You know that?"

"Bite my butt, Fish. You were done in six seconds. Was it your first time?"

"Was it your million seventh? Can you even keep track of who you fucked anymore?"

Jock's cheekbones winced. "Jesus Christ, put me back in combat where people are friendlier."

He walked off, kicking rocks. Kennet found his notebook and a pencil. He found a flat board to serve as a desk and a place to sit in the sun.

He began to write. He went all the way back to the 29th of December, their first day of combat in Belgium. He wrote and wrote, thinking at first he'd only record the salient points, but soon his hand could barely keep up, remembering things he didn't know he had forgotten. Page after page, until he reached today.

If only you knew how badly I want you to be every little thing in my life, Asta.

But it's war. We rose up at dawn and learned we were relieved. We came to this village of Chêne and it's now January 5, 1945, the morning after I slept with Solange for all the wrong reasons.

I lay down with a woman and woke up with a goose egg.

C'est la guerre.

God, I want you so badly.

I say this not as the Kennet you knew, the guy who knew the cardinal points of right and wrong. He's gone.

I'll never be him again.

The last bit of him left Clayton and went back to Brazil with you.

And then it died. Disintegrated into silver pieces and bled out of you. The best of me. Lost.

I want it back.

Asta, my love, I want to be buried in your body. I want to take you from behind, hold you down on your belly, knot my limbs around you and fill my mouth with your hair. Then roll you over to face me, put my heart on your heart, my mouth on your mouth. Fill up my lungs with your breath. Fill your belly with another baby and this time, fight to keep what's mine.

I feel strongly it was a girl.

It was a girl, wasn't it?

It had to have been. Fiskare daughters are a rare thing.

I'm being maudlin, aren't I?

I don't fucking care.

God damn me to hell, I never should've let you go.

I should've broken down the hotel room door where your mother was keeping you. I should've gone through the window. I should've run after the train. I should've gotten on a boat to Rio. I should have. I should have I should have.

But I was raised to be a gentleman, so I didn't.

But that Kennet is no more.

The Kennet of today wouldn't have let you go.

And if there's a Kennet of tomorrow…he might not have any damns to give for gentlemanly behavior or social niceties. He might just show up in Rio. He might tell your husband, "We can do this the easy way, or do it the hard way. But we're doing this." This future Kennet knows how to fight. He takes no prisoners. He can kill a child then forget about it. He's more pirate than fisherman.

Say the word, my treasure. I will come dig you up. I will sail away with you. I will open your locks, plunge my hands into all your precious gems and metals and let them rain down on my head. I will sew you under my skin, like a Hun's tooth blown there by a grenade, and for the rest of my days, it will be your golden atoms in my blood and your silver beauty in my hands.

And we will be rich, Asta.

Fabulously, filthy, stinking rich.

Close as Any Man
and Woman

Kennet closed the little notebook. He'd sharpened his pencil four times and it was down to about two inches in his cold, cramped fingers. He shook them out as he walked back to the hay mow.

He'd written all morning, looking up every now and again as half-tracks arrived, dropping off more soldiers to be billeted on the farm, wherever they could fit. Kennet guessed there'd be no more feasts around the sisters' kitchen table. No more B.A.C.K baths or offers of laundry. The bartering of C-rations for bread, milk and eggs continued, but the newly-arrived soldiers cooked and ate over Coleman stoves and gathered to smoke and drink around small campfires in the barnyard.

At one point in his writing, Kennet was interrupted by a blood-curdling yell. A war whoop that split the barnyard in half and made him drop his pencil. Schmitt was running across the muddy ground, yelling himself hoarse. Down from a half-track stepped Nichols, a bandage swathed around his head. He started running, too. A little slower and quieter, but no less intent. He jumped and wrapped arms and legs around Schmitt, who whirled him in two klutzy circles before they both toppled onto the ground.

"You sorry fucker," Schmitt cried. "You cocksucking son of a bitch don't you *ever* pull that shit on me again…"

Nichols just lay there in the dirt, laughing and pounding Schmitt's back.

The hay mow now looked like a mini-barracks, with bedrolls placed with their head ends against the wall, boots at the foot, packs to the right, rifles to the left. Nobody mandated or suggested this arrangement. The well-trained men just did it, and piled the hay into insulating walls, making little rooms. Within the improvised quarters, pairings were kept sacrosanct. O'Hara still wasn't speaking to Jock, but his bedroll was right next to Jock's and he showed no intention of moving it. Likewise the Fish was still on the Hook, their kits close together under a small, square window, its frame stuffed tight with rags and straw to keep the drafts out.

Kennet put his journal on Hook's empty bedroll. As apology and peace offering, and also because Kennet had a sudden and dire need for a second pair of eyes on his account, to make sure he remembered it all correctly. Because he didn't want to talk about it, but he wanted someone to *know*.

He took off his boots, crawled into his bag, spread his greatcoat for a second blanket and fell immediately to sleep. When he woke up, Hook was back. He sat on his bedroll, reading the journal with his flashlight tucked between shoulder and cheek.

Kennet watched him read, trying to judge by Hook's expression where he was in the narrative. The way he rolled his lips in, or pushed them out. A sudden, sharp breath through his nose. A long sighing exhale. Minute nods of his head. Every now and then a soft "Huh."

At last, Hook closed the journal. He ran a palm in a circle on the cover and sat still a long time before he glanced over at Kennet.

"Hey."

"Morning."

Hook smiled. "It's almost six at night."

"Is the war over?"

"Not yet, my friend. Not yet." He handed the notebook back to Kennet. "You did good."

"Did I get it all?"

"Yeah. It was good. I mean, you wrote it good. Your folks won't be embarrassed reading it. Except for the sexy parts."

Kennet threw a handful of straw at him. "Want to grab a smoke?"

They went into the chilly barnyard and coaxed one of the dead campfires back to life.

"So who is Astrid exactly?" Hook asked.

"Someone I loved. Still love."

"Is that her picture tucked in the pages?"

"Mm."

"She's married?"

"Yes."

"Well, fuck me."

"No thank you."

Then they lit up and squatted by the flames, turning themselves like spit roasts to stay warm. One side. Posterior. Front. Other side.

"I know you don't want to talk about it," Hook said, as if choosing his words carefully. "What happened at Chenogne, I mean. And I respect that. But if you ever do want to talk. About any of it. You got me."

"I know. Honestly, I'm not sure I'm going to write about it anymore."

"No?"

"I don't know. All that misery was just one week. We're barely in it. If I keep writing it all down, I think I'll lose my fucking mind."

"You tell a good story. You pinned down some things I was thinking and feeling, but shit, I couldn't put it into words. Not like that."

"Mm."

Hook's elbow jostled Kennet's arm, just the tiniest bit. "You do what you have to, Fish."

Kennet smiled. "Whatever gets you through."

Hook blew a few rings. He'd finally mastered the trick and was now working on his nonchalance while doing it. "Mind if I say something else about your journal?"

Kennet's privacy bristled a little. "What?"

"What you wrote about the war taking a minute to catch its breath, and that's when you see the funny things? Or the proud things? Keep writing that stuff down. The battles go in the newspapers. Or history books. If anyone gets mentioned by name, it'll be General So-and-So or Major Such-and-Such. Us grunts? We disappear. So who will know what a magnificent bazooka shot Holy Schmitt made into an attic window unless you write about it? How Malinda's jaw moved while he was chewing gum, making him look grand and casual. Shit, Fish, how'd you put two words like that together and paint a picture? Grand and casual. That's *crazy*."

"Shut up," Kennet said. Softly, because his throat was oddly tight.

"Keep writing the little things," Hook said. "That's just my opinion. It's the stuff you'll want to remember. Five, ten years from now, you'll skim over the logistics and slow down to read the good parts. Like getting a goddamn hard-on while under fire. Holy hell, I thought I was the only sick pervert popping a boner on the battlefield."

Kennet laughed. "I don't even know how to *begin* explaining that shit."

"See? It's funny now. So write it down. Write the relief in hearing someone whistle 'Colonel Bogey' from behind a tree. Or von Asselt with four bandoliers across his chest, looking like a movie star. Saying he loved you before he died."

"Shit."

"And on a selfish note…" Hook drew a tremendous breath. "I got nobody. It's the dice I rolled and the game I gotta play. But you including me in your journal? Well, I kind of feel like I'll be remembered somehow. Things I said and did. Us being buddies."

"Brothers," Kennet said. "You're in my father's pocket, remember?"

"Not many minutes go by when I forget."

They were quiet a while, watching the logs burn in square sections of rosy orange, outlined white. The pop and crackle and steam as trapped moisture in the wood found its way out to die.

"I've never been with a woman," Hook said, flicking his butt into the fire. "Didn't know your feelings got that much involved."

"You will," Kennet said. "And they do."

"Hope so. On both accounts."

Jock moved across the yard, his body dipping in and out of the clouds of smoke, making his way toward O'Hara, who sat on the top rail of the fence. Jock stood in front of his buddy a long moment, then gave a single jerk of his head toward the land beyond the farmstead. He walked off. After a beat, O'Hara slid down and followed.

"Now those poor bastards," Hook said. "No one's writing their story."

"What do you mean?"

"Isn't it obvious?"

Kennet squinted through the smoky yard but O'Hara and Jock had disappeared from view. "Isn't what obvious?"

Hook gave him a long, sad look. "They're in love."

Kennet sucked his teeth. "You know, just because two fellows are close, doesn't mean they're in love."

"Tell me something I don't know," Hook said calmly.

"You really think?"

"I know. I saw them together once. Middle of the night when I was on watch. They were hiding between the parked tracks and... I mean, they weren't fucking on the ground, but they weren't sharing a smoke, either." He glanced at Kennet. "You think I'm full of shit, right?"

Kennet stretched out one leg. "This limb feels pulled."

"That's fair, I guess. But you know me, Fish. Better than anyone else. I pull your leg about things. I bullshit about *stuff*. Not people. Definitely not my mates."

"This is true," Kennet said slowly. "You saw them? Honest?"

"Wrapped up tight in each other's arms. Close as any man and woman I ever saw. And they were kissing." He crossed his arms over his chest and shook his head. "It was weird. Not them being in a clinch, but my reaction. You'd think I'd be shocked and disgusted, right? No, I only felt sad. Kind of sick at the risk they were taking. Sicker when I thought what if someone else caught them. And then I had this weird thought: screw guarding the perimeter. I need to guard *them*." He gave a little shiver. "I've been feeling protective about them ever since. A little love affair in the midst of war is hopeful. It's unconventional, sure, but I'll take it."

Kennet's mouth fell open as he went over every Jock-and-O'Hara anecdote through this new lens. "Holy mackerel."

"You can say that again."

"Wait. If they're together, then what the hell was Jock doing last night?"

"Alleviating suspicions, I guess. Shoring up his public record."

"Cripes, no wonder O'Hara was pissed off."

Hook put two new cigarettes in his mouth, lit them, and passed one over. "So. Them being queer bother you?"

"Should it?"

"Depends where and how you were raised, I guess," Hook said. "Down south, people have extremely set ideas about men like them. Mostly what religion has bashed into their heads about it. But like you wrote in your notebook, it's the end of that life."

"It's war. All O'Hara and Jock have is now."

"It's war, and I don't give a shit who's fucking who." Hook flicked his ashes for emphasis. "That feeling I had of wanting to guard them? It was kind of a selfish feeling. If they were found out, they'd be…I don't know, taken away, kicked out, and then the squad would be *fucked*. O'Hara's the best goddamn BAR man in the platoon, but even if he were a lousy shot, he'd still take a bullet for any one of us. Jock walks with a swagger and talks a lot of bullshit, but look at how he crept around all day—he can't bear it if a buddy's put out with him. He'd rather die than disappoint one of us. He'd never leave a fellow in the lurch. Ever. He and O'Hara are the kind of guys you want on your side. Not just in war, but in life. If they're queer, who gives a shit? Not me. I'm fighting with them. Not kissing them. They want to go behind a tree and…do whatever they do, I'll fucking guard that tree."

Now the gaze he turned on Kennet was calculating and expectant.

And you, sir?

"This conversation's making me feel a hundred different ways," Kennet said slowly. "And all of them hit close to home. Because my brother is queer."

The words burned his mouth. It felt like a betrayal. It was definitely telling tales out of school.

"Which one?"

"Minor. He's gay. Which is the word he prefers over queer."

"Oh," Hook said, pulling the word out long and slow. "So you got two reasons to worry about him."

"Yeah. But talking to you about it… See, I never fooled myself there weren't other fellows like Minor who joined up, but it was always nameless, faceless guys. But now, knowing O'Hara and Jock are together, I can truly believe Minor isn't alone." He jostled Hook's side. "And maybe the Navy has decent, protective guys like you looking out for him."

Hook hummed in his chest. "Does your family know?"

"I can only guess they do. None of us talk about it."

"Hence…" Hook gestured around the barnyard. "Here we are. Fighting for freedom but making guys like Jock and O'Hara and your brother keep sneaking around. They could single-handedly take out Hitler or Hirohito, but the brass would still lock 'em up for kissing."

"I'm getting depressed."

"Well, on the bright side, our lovebirds haven't come back yet. So either they killed each other, or they're making up." Hook leaned his head back, surveying the landscape. "I'm probably a dumb virgin for asking, but who can fuck outdoors in this weather?"

"You do what you gotta do."

"I hope to God I find out before I die." He glanced at Kennet. "Want to take a walk?"

For the second time, Kennet picked up a handful of dirty straw and threw it at Hook. "*Not* funny."

"Oh come on, it was a little funny."

"Fuck off."

"Sorry," Hook said, chuckling. "Guess I need to work harder on being grand and casual."

Something to Someone

Kennet stopped writing blow-by-blow accounts of the battles. Hook's advice was only part of it. The bigger reason was he was shutting down. Every day, he sensed the functional parts of himself telling his emotional aspects to get lost. Vamoose. Scram. This wasn't the time or place. Days were running into one another, the grind of each day's terror, misery, cold and hunger exactly like the day before. It was boring, and like Hook said, the history books would do the job.

So Kennet wrote dates, places, and terse descriptions of the action, noting any buddies who were killed or wounded. Then he tried to find a human moment, no matter how small or banal, to tease out into something he'd like to read later.

14 Jan 1945

Past two days saw action in Bastogne, with Co. B attached to Task Force Blackjack. Attacked town of Cobru. Heavily fortified with Krauts. Clearing the town a bitch, had to search house to house, under heavy mortar and tank barrage, plus sniper fire.

Saw two men get killed. Didn't know their names. Town full of terrified and wounded civilians who needed to be moved so we could outpost for the night.

Pretty young woman pushing a barrow cart stopped, took my face in her hands and gave me one hell of a kiss. My knees buckled and the boys gave me hell from all sides. But goddamn, it was a kiss for the ages. She stepped back and with a quick movement of her hand, nicked my cigarettes right out of my pocket. Then she was off, moving down the road.

What a swell dame.

15 Jan 1945

Attacked cross-country, first south of Sankt-Vith highway— little resistance—then north of the road—heavy fire from 88s. Had to keep reminding myself what Jorgy said, "You won't hear the 88 that kills you."

Now dug in for the night. Half-tracks coming up bringing C-rations and blankets. I'm so cold and hungry, I can't think of anything good to write. Nothing memorable to report.

16 Jan 1945

B company was attached to the 41st Tank Battalion and we became a mounted unit. The thrill of hitching a ride on the "big boys" lasted five minutes. Riding that contraption over hills and through snowdrifts was like riding a bucking bronco. It lurched and rolled and swayed and jerked. Everybody frantically grabbed onto anything that lent a grip, then grabbed onto someone else to stay aboard. Many new curses invented along the way and I don't think my ass has hurt this much since Paps' last hiding. Then when the tanks began firing, I thought my skull would explode and my ears turn inside out.

On the other hand, I rode with my feet near the exhaust pipe, which kept them quite toasty.

Attacked the woods south of Houffalize. Gave them everything we had, every barrel blazing. No match for us. Cleared them out and dug in for the night. I slept strangely well, with Hook having to shake me awake for my guard shift. Maybe it was my warmed feet?

If I get through this, I can't imagine ever losing sleep about anything again.

17 Jan 1945

German rocket barrage this morning. We lost Marty.

Feels like the heart has been ripped clear out of the squad. Nobody has a damn thing to say. Not even a curse.

The 17th Airborne relieved us and we marched to the town of Champs. I walked next to Anderson, who wasn't openly crying, but his eyes were red and brimming. I wanted to do something so bad. If I had the strength or the means, I would've taken his pack for him, let him walk along just with the burden of grief to shoulder. I felt useless and used-up, but I stayed next to him. I could do that much.

We split up among empty barns and ramshackle houses and collapsed.

19 Jan 1945

Still in Champs, resting, cleaning our guns and organizing equipment. Writing "Don't worry I'm fine," to loved ones at home.

24 Jan 1945

The town is Massul, Belgium, but by war standards, we are in Heaven. The Quartermaster Corps set up shower units and we got our first head-to-toe scrubbing since leaving England. The best goddamn shower I had in my life.

Funny moment: we were sudsing up and out of nowhere, Jock started singing "O Sole Mio." And when I say singing, I mean SINGING. Clear, beautiful tenor to make the hair stand on the back of your neck. Everyone looked around, stunned. Our loudmouth vulgate can sing like an angel. He won't do it on command, though, which is strange, since he never hesitates to clown around or steal attention. I guess singing is for him and him alone.

Or maybe it's all for O'Hara.

Anyway, we are clean from the inside out. Every stitch of clothing we stripped off promptly disappeared. Whisked away by the laundry unit, I wouldn't be surprised if it was all burned. We came out to stacks of clean pressed uniforms, fresh skivvies and long johns, new wool socks, new gloves, the works. Everyone had to shave, and while we all looked rather handsome, it was quite a shock having a bare face out in the cold again. I miss the beard.

Which reminds me of something else funny: a lot of us grumbled that the new long johns weren't keeping us warm as the old ones. Then a laundry private explained that after a month in the same clothes, the oils from your unwashed body seep into the fabric, adding an extra, very thin, but very noticeable layer of insulation.

"Give it a week or two," he said. "They'll start keeping you warmer."

War is apparently a choice of being filthy or cold.

Ain't that a kick in the head.

We were able to find good living quarters in Massul, a town not so badly hit by the war. Most of us were able to find houses to stay in. The people were extremely kind, friendly and generous. A lot of spontaneous handshakes, hugs and kissing, the youngsters raiding our pockets for chocolate and gum. Fraternization with the civilians is frowned upon, but there are many empty bedrolls at night. Keep it on the QT seems to be the rule about the rule. Nobody says a thing during the night, but a lot of sideways glances, stifled laughter and winks. Hook finally—

Kennet stopped. He'd been about to write *popped his cherry.* Hook was reading these entries and might not appreciate his personal business so freely recounted. Then again, Hook had read all Kennet's intimate, racy thoughts about Astrid. And Hook had run quite a public gauntlet the morning after he was deflowered.

"My boy," Schmitt had cried, when Hook came back from his assignation. "Let me look at you. Look in my eyes, let me see… Yes, by golly, you're a *man* now."

"Shut up," Hook said, his ears reddening.

Jock clapped an arm around him. "How was it? Tell us everything."

Hook glanced at Kennet, then dug at the ground with his boot. "Fish don't tell tales out of school and neither do Hooks."

"Well said," Kennet said.

Jock gathered Hook's cheeks in a hand and squeezed his face. "So proud of you."

Nichols started singing Ella Fitzgerald.

Must I extend an invitation
To make love to me?
Make love to me, my darling,
Tonight will end so soon.

"Christ," Hook groaned, turning redder.

Schmitt had joined in now, circling Hook like a lecher, twirling an invisible mustache.

There are moments when my lips, my lips adore addressing you,
But tonight my lips are only for caressing you,
But how about you?

Then the whole gang joined in:

Don't let the mood I'm in change,
Make love to me!
Make love to me, my darling,
I'm so in love with you!

"Thank you, I'm mortified," Hook said.

"Make love to," Jock said. "That's the dumbest expression. It makes no sense. You can't make something *to* someone."

"That's what you think," Ingle said.

301

"It makes no sense. Grammatically speaking."

"It's an expression," Hook said. "Like *raining cats and dogs.*"

"That's an idiom," Kennet said.

"Well, pardon me, Shakespeare."

"Make something to someone," Schmitt said thoughtfully. "Put that way, it makes more sense."

"What do you mean?" Hook said.

"Make something to someone," he said again, then raised a finger in the air. "Make something equal to someone. Important to someone. Maybe that's it."

"What's it?" Jock said.

"Maybe the *to* means *important.* If you say you're going to make love to someone, you're going to make love important to them."

"Make *them* more important than love," Nichols said, his own finger in the air.

"Or you can bypass all the poetic nonsense and just use the word *fuck,*" Jock said.

"You know, Jock, sometimes you can just participate nicely in a conversation to pass the time."

"I'd rather fuck to pass the time."

"We know."

"It's a lot of context to pack into one little word," Nichols said.

"Maybe it's an infinitive," O'Hara said quietly.

A beat as everyone looked at the normally reticent man, remembering he was there.

"What do you mean?" Kennet said.

"An infinitive. To run. To walk. To shoot. To kill."

"To fuck," Jock said.

"To be or not to be," Anderson said.

"Pardon *you,* Shakespeare," Hook said.

"Those are infinitive verbs," Kennet said. "But you isn't a verb. There's no *to you*."

"There should be," O'Hara said.

"What would it mean?"

"How would you even conjugate it?" Schmitt said. "I you. You you. He yous. She yous."

"We you?"

"I'm youing?"

"I want to you you."

"Damn, I wish I'd youed that."

O'Hara smiled at the banter, but his arms were crossed over his chest and his chin tilted into his idea. "Joke all you want," he said. "I think it works. *To you* means to be yourself."

"I'm going to make love be yourself?" Kennet said.

"No." O'Hara's chin tilted the other way. "I mean, yeah. Kind of."

Schmitt laughed and jostled him. "You have no idea what you're talking about."

"I'm participating nicely in the conversation."

"Jesus Christ, this is stupid." Jock said to no one in particular.

"What's up your ass?" Nichols said.

"Nothing."

"Yeah. Like this whole war is 'nothing.'"

"Say what's on your mind, bud," O'Hara said. "Participate nicely."

"I didn't finish high school and when you guys talk all intellectual about infinite and conjugal verbs, I feel really stupid."

"You're smarter than all of us," Ingle said.

Jock sucked his teeth. "Go fuck to you."

Schmitt laughed. "See? That was a witty, clever comeback."

"Nicely done," Kennet said. "Touché."

FEBRUARY–
APRIL
1945

Nothing For It

February dragged by with an agonizing, mile-by-mile, battle-by-battle slowness. As well as becoming anesthetized to death and gore and dismemberment and misery, the men of Kennet's unit became immune to how they smelled after months of living, moving and fighting in the open. Body odor was the least of it.

"War smells like a million dirty diapers," Emil Fiskare had told his eldest and finest.

You were right, Paps, Kennet wrote home. *As usual.*

It was hilarious the first time Kennet saw a tank gunner clinging to the turret, pants around his shins, hanging on for dear life as he relieved himself on the run. But after watching a dozen such scatological feats, it became no more novel than the sunrise. You marched behind the tank treads, stepped over corpses, trudged through the shit and thought nothing of it.

> *Paps, the history books won't mention it,* Kennet wrote, *but man-to-man, the war does indeed smell like shit. And while I appreciate heck out of the care packages the girls send, if you, man-to-man, could go down to the corner drug and buy every can of Gold Bond Medicated Powder that will fit in a box and ship it to me, I guarantee more than a few fighting fellows would thank you from the bottom of their...bottoms. Ha ha.*

"It's too cold to wipe your ass," was a familiar Army refrain. Not that there was much to wipe with anyway. Some men used snow, not out of concern for hygiene, but because after months of C-rations, dubious water, crapping in absurd conditions without a square of toilet paper, and occasionally shitting your pants out of sheer fright, the crack of your goddamn ass was its own war zone. It itched and burned until you wanted to shoot yourself. Snow helped numb the torment. A little. You tried not to scratch, but sometimes it was scratch or go mad. Then you tried not to put your disgusting fingers anywhere near your mouth, but at the rate they were all chain-smoking, who the hell knew what ended up in their guts, leaving them squatting miserably on the trail and perpetuating the itchy cycle.

Since December, two guys in Kennet's company had been invalided out because of hemorrhoids. How the hell did you explain *that* to the folks back home with any dignity? It kind of made you grateful for mere burning itch. Sometimes. There was nothing for it anyway, except pray the next village had a chemist shop that sold any kind of magic relief and until you got there, fantasize about the day you returned to your own throne.

"When I get home," Jock said, as the squad gathered around a small fire, having their last smokes. "I'm spending a day in the bathroom. I mean it. I'll sit on the crapper until my legs fall asleep."

"I'm going to flush the toilet a hundred times," Ingle said dreamily.

"I'm taking a six-hour shower," Kennet said.

"I'm filling the tub to the brim with hot water," Schmitt said. "I'll use every goddamn bottle of bath junk my wife owns. Dump it all in there and soak all day. Occasionally I'll reach an arm out and flush the toilet. Just because I can."

"Get one of them beauty mud masks," Nichols said, delicately patting his cheekbones. "Two cucumber slices on your eyes."

"While your wife paints your toenails," Jock said.

"You better believe it," Schmitt said, stretching out his boots as if admiring a fresh pedicure. "I want 'em red, white and blue."

They laughed and elaborated their bathroom plans. But God, they stank. And there was nothing for it.

They left devastated Bastogne, crossed the Our River and finally, at last, their boots were on German soil.

"What, no trumpets?" Hook muttered.

Others also remarked about the anti-climactic feel of entering enemy territory, but not Kennet. He felt a shift as he left Belgium and entered Germany. Not in the land, but in himself. He was no longer liberator and lover, but an enemy conqueror.

I am a pirate prince of the golden blood.

I come on behalf of the River King.

I come to collect for Hildur, Queen of the Elves.

He wouldn't be lauded by the people here, but feared, targeted and hated. No more handshakes, hugs and hospitality. The women would rather kick than kiss him.

They arrived at Heckhuscheid, where they captured bunkers and took prisoners.

Lutzkampan, where they endured intense artillery and mortar fire, and Sergeant Montenegro was killed, leaving the squad leaderless until Heckhalenfeld, where Ingle was promoted.

Back to Luxembourg, to the town of Breidfield, where B company went into reserve and Lieutenant Jorgensson was promoted to captain.

To Lieler, on the banks of the Our, where they could see the enemy moving around their fortifications on the other side.

Back to Breidfield, where the weather at last broke. Winter let go its icy grip on the world and as the calendar turned to March, the days were soft with sunshine.

2 Mar 1945

Sellerich to Prum. Wet and muddy. Constant shelling. Walking the fine line between sanity and madness, looking over the edge and considering my options. Wondering if I should just completely lose my mind and let the chips fall.

Shell shock. I've heard the words before. I know that's what they called it with Uncle Nyck. Chaplains call it "combat fatigue," when a GI feels like he can't take anymore. In Uncle Nyck's time, they called you a coward and shot you. Today it seems the brass knows it's not something deliberate a fellow does. It's not really him making the decision. His body and mind just put up the white flag.

I never really understood shell shock or combat fatigue before. I did, but I didn't. How can anyone really grasp perpetual fear combined with the feeling that nobody can get you out of the situation, you are helpless and doomed. How could you know unless you live it?

Makes me think of when Paps said, "You don't know fear until you look into the eyes of a young, unmarried woman who's discovered she's going to have a baby."

I'd dismiss that as a load of hooey except I happen to trust my father on these things.

I wish I'd known, Asta. God, I wish you'd told me or that
you had time to tell me. You must've been so scared. Darling
girl, if I'd known, I would've come. I would have come to get
you. I swear I would've moved the earth...

Anyway, we're bivouacked on the high ground outside Prum.
It's cold. Jesus H, I'm so fucking cold all the goddamn time.

Kennet and Hook had their open-bivouac system honed to a science. First they zipped their bags together and laid them out for quick entry. They took the driest socks they had and tucked them inside their clothes. Then they did jumping jacks and pushups, getting their body heat to warm up the socks. They swung their legs in big pendulum arcs to get the blood to their feet. Then fast as possible, they kicked off boots, stripped off the dirty socks, pulled on the clean, warm ones and crawled into the double sleeping bag.

"Cover me," Hook said, and ducked his head inside the combined bedroll. He inhaled and exhaled enormous breaths, filling the bag with warm air. Then they switched and Kennet went under. It was ripe inside the bag—fetid with unwiped butts, unwashed hair, cigarette-smoked teeth, dirty clothes and grimy skin and nervous sweat. But if they wanted to be warm, this was the only way. There was nothing for it.

"Make three wishes," Kennet said, as he did every night.

"See this through," Hook said ceremoniously. "Go home. Die in our sleep."

"Remember, every night Hildur visits her elven kingdom at the cost of a human life."

"Not tonight, you bitch."

Both knew their friendship had no business lasting this long. Every day they survived was another day of daring Hildur to kill them. Every night they bedded down together was another night Hildur could spend angrily stewing. They were on her list. They were next. And there was nothing for it but superstition and ceremony, doing little mundane things exactly the same way every day and night, not missing a step or a word. Finding the good luck and the fortuitous signs. Playing their part in the game. If Kennet wanted to get through this, go home and die in his sleep, he had to stay on the Hook. And the Hook had to keep reeling in the Fish, if he wanted his wishes to come true.

They shared their solemn last smokes before battle, and the jubilant smokes after. They dressed in the same order, arranged their kits just so. Cleaned their guns in a choreographed ballet of pieces laid out on the ground and pieces reassembled. They told the stories and said the magic words. Nobody laughed at them. All the men of Company B were putting precious things in their pockets or taking precious things out of their pockets. If that dumb pebble you kicked down the long road from France was in your pocket the day you almost bought it, it had to go in your pocket every time after. If it was left behind with the chaplain the day you almost bought it, the pebble had to always be left behind with the chaplain.

The men went around giving secret handshakes, kissing each other's dog tags, reciting a canon of catch phrases, platitudes, dirty jokes. Every platoon had that one guy who could materialize out of nowhere to snuff your match if you dared try to light three cigarettes on it. And another guy who, if you threw your spent match on the ground, looked at you like you'd just shit on his shoes, then picked up the match and threw it over his left shoulder.

"That's for salt, you moron," someone always said.

"It's for matches, too."

"Bullshit."

And they'd argue for an hour about it, knowing it was all bull-shit. The superstitions and rituals, the matches, even the arguing—all bullshit. But they were unable not to cling to it. It was how the trust went on thriving. Trust in your buddy, trust in the squad leaders, trust in the platoon, the division, the mission, the cause, the war and above all, trust in their definitive stance on the right side of history.

Before battle, some went alone to take a last nervous piss. Others went together and crossed shaky streams. If they did it once and got lucky, they had to do it always. They prayed and davened and spit and swore and smoked and shook and touched. They filled and emptied their pockets, cast their spells and went off to fight. Some came back alive, and each mourned differently for the ones who died. There were soldiers who could cry in the open and sol-diers who crawled away to mourn. Soldiers who broke things in their grief, soldiers who consoled themselves by picking up tool kits or shovels and putting things together. And soldiers who did absolutely nothing at all.

At night, they bedded down and breathed hard to get warm. They ignored the stench and cuddled like brothers, spooned like lovers. One thrust his cold feet between his buddy's shins and there was nothing for it. Another slid his chilblained fingers into his mate's armpit because there was nothing for it. Two brothers in arms fell asleep in each other's arms and thought nothing of it, because there was nothing for it. Nothing except each other.

"What is it?" Kennet said. "Hook, tell me."

"It's stupid."

"Which is why you should tell me."

His hand clenched Kennet's sleeve. "I don't want to die."

"I know," Kennet said. "It's not stupid."

I don't want to die. I have gold in my blood, I can't die like this. Don't let me die like this and I'll be good forever. Good as gold. Don't let me die. Please don't let me die...

They hung on tight through the cold, terrifying nights. Woke up in the morning to go and fight another day.

Day after day after day after day...

Hungry

10 Mar 1945

Neider Oberweiler

Happy birthday to me. We reached the Rhine in a fast, furious and exhilarating drive. German resistance is almost laughable. Troops surrendering in the thousands, the roads clogged with POWs. We'll be here a few days for a maintenance break. The mail unit caught up to us with quite a backlog. Mrs. Messer (from North Platte) sent cookies and 4 pairs of socks.

Almost every soldier Kennet knew had a pen-pal in North Platte, Nebraska. The slips of paper with names and addresses, tucked inside popcorn balls handed out at the canteen, were not empty promises. Letters and treats arrived regularly and soldiers tried not to be remiss in replying.

Dear Mrs. Messer, Kennet wrote.

Thank you for the care package which, by miraculous timing, was delivered to me on March 10th, which is my birthday. Knowing all the miracles that come out of North Platte, I shouldn't be surprised you hit the proverbial target. Well done. I'm afraid the cookies arrived in crumbles, but I doled them out to my mates by the handful and every crumble was eaten. They were indeed fine as could be.

You were kind to think of both me and my buddy Hook,
and now we are the envy of the unit with our swell wool
socks. Two pairs each was so very generous, our poor feet
couldn't be happier…

In her latest letter, Mrs. Messer had let down her veneer of sweet formality, and wrote about her son, Ted, who was killed on D-Day. The grief was eating her alive. She couldn't bear the thought of him dying terrified and alone, wanting his mother in his last minutes.

Between the lines, Kennet could read a mother's plea for something comforting, straight from the horse's mouth.

Jesus, how many lies do men tell just to make mothers not worry?

He chewed on his pencil a bit, then tried to write honestly about fear. To describe to a grieving woman how fear was a skeleton for some soldiers, but for most, it was an exoskeleton. The fear within turned inside-out to something functional: black humor, superstition or detachment.

Yet things pull us back within and most times, that thing
is the memory of love and kindness, such as we saw in North
Platte. For your son to have grown up in such a generous and
loving community I'm sure left him with enough good memo-
ries to sustain him through anything. That's what we're fight-
ing for, ma'am. All the love and generosity and all the memories
not yet made.

I don't know if this will make you feel better, Mrs. Messer, but
more often than not, we soldiers are hungry, rather than scared.
And a gift of cookies makes us feel like we can do anything.

There, he thought, pleased. *Surely a woman can worry more con-*
structively about hunger than fear.

Kennet had never been a husky fellow to begin with. Now his belt was cinched three inches tighter than where it had been in England and when he wasn't thinking about death, he was thinking about food.

Dear God, food. Not the C-ration crap they were forced to choke down but real, honest-to-God, down-home and made with love *food*. Some soldiers couldn't bear to speak of it. Others spoke of nothing else. But they all thought about it.

Kennet thought food might succeed in making him go mad, where the horrors and trials of war failed. A soldier said *apple* in passing and Kennet's mouth flooded with saliva. He could see the crisp, tart word written out a page, all round looping letters ready to burst their juice. His teeth came together, tasting, crunching and chewing, and he nearly wept he was so hungry. Remembering the ham sandwich in North Platte, tangy with mustard and pickle on soft white bread buttered on both sides. The cold, thick milk in a little glass bottle. The fluffy angel cake that painted your tongue with sugar and left a citrus tang clinging to the ridges of your palate. A ball of salty-sweet popcorn to munch through the night. All those delicious, sticky bits to pick out of your teeth.

If the boys stood around and talked about baseball, Kennet could only think of a hot dog with relish. Or a bag of roasted peanuts. He longed for a cheeseburger, seared on the outside and pink within, piled high with lettuce and onion and ketchup. A mountain of crisp, shoestring fries on the side. All those warm, sloppy mouthfuls washed down with an ice-cold Coca-Cola. Rattling slurps through a straw to suck out every bubbly droplet clinging to the ice cubes.

He concocted elaborate restaurant fantasies, with Astrid in a waitress uniform, bringing him course after course of grilled fish, rare steak, roasted potatoes, string beans, candied carrots, cream of mushroom soup, oysters, applesauce and ice cream. She sidled past his chair, hips swinging. She leaned over him, fussing with the place settings, asking, "Good? Enough? More?"

Wonderful. No. Please.

She sat on his knee and fed him, the gravy and grease sliding down her forearms, which she then offered him to lick. "More?"

More.

Over his ravenous mouth Astrid dangled thin asparagus spears.

More. Hungry.

She unbuttoned her blouse and dribbled butter and honey on her breasts.

Me so hungry.

Kissed him with a mouth full of watermelon and cherries.

Feed me. Fuck me.

He arm-swept the loaded table and devoured his server. Stuffing his mouth as he ripped open his pants.

"More," she cried, wanton and greedy.

There was more than enough. There was plenty. In a marvelous, belly-gorging glut, Kennet slid his cock into the oven of the Astrid's bounty and came like a cornucopia. She came right back at him, gushing raspberries and cream, dark beer and champagne and cold, clear spring water.

A Different Breed
of Brothers

14 Mar 1945

We moved to the town of Glees, for no other reason than to let the 4th Armored take credit for securing the city of Worms. Obviously they have a better PR officer than the 11th.

By the way, not one single soldier says the name of the city the right way, which is with a V, Vorms. No, we are honor-bound as good Americans to delight in saying WORMS, goddammit.

We found an abandoned house with—holy shit!—an Opel Admiral convertible and a berry-red Opel Kapitan. You never saw such a reaction. Fellows stumbled toward the cars in a trance, staring and whistling as if they were a couple of naked women. Walking circles, admiring from all angles, popping the hood and talking shop about engines. Jock hotwired both cars and we all took them for a spin.

We also found an abandoned steam engine train. I don't know how the hell fellows managed to get it up and running, but we piled aboard to drive it back and forth along a stretch of track. I can't remember the last time I had so much fun or laughed so hard.

"Pescado," Ingle called from the side of the tracks. "*Fish.* Get down, come here."

"What?"

"Jorgy wants you."

"What for?"

"Come on."

Kennet surrendered his spot on the steam train's engine and hopped down. "Am I being promoted?"

Ingle didn't answer and Kennet felt a trickle of foreboding touch the back of his neck.

"Ralph, what's going on?"

"I don't know. But Jorgy told me to get you, and the chaplain was with him."

Kennet closed his eyes, now cold all over. "Shit."

"You know I won't ever lie to you, Pescado. It's not going to be good news."

"What, like, a death in the family?"

"Probably."

"It's my father. Shit, it's my father or my uncle."

Ingles eyes on him were soft, a little puzzled. But he only said, "Go on in. I'm gonna get Hook, and he and I will wait for you."

"Shit…"

"We'll wait outside the whole time. Whatever they tell you, it's our news, too. Go on. Get it over with."

Kennet walked in, the whole narrative framed out in his mind. *Paps. Aw, Paps, shit.* Shit. *I didn't even get to… Oh Christ on a cracker, Paps, I'm sorry.*

He saluted the officers. Jorgy told him at ease and motioned him to sit. The chaplain hitched his chair a quarter-inch closer to Kennet. He was a new and dearly welcome attachment to the battalion. Their last spiritual counselor had been a cadaverous square with the personality of an ironing board. This new guy, Patrick Scott, was young and personable. Comforting, but never a sap. Spiritual without the accompanying stick up his ass. He was "sir" or "chaplain" at first meeting, then nothing but "Chaps" or "Padre" or even "Scottie."

Jorgy cleared his throat. "Fish, I'm afraid I—"

"Is it my father, sir?" Kennet said.

Jorgy blinked. "Come again?"

"It's about my dad, right?" Kennet glanced at Scottie, then back at Jorgy. "Is that the news?"

"No," Jorgy said. "No, Fish. It's your brother."

The cold fingers at Kennet's neck became a choking vise. Mocking as they cut off the air to his lungs. *You thought it was Pappa? Aren't you precious. In the middle of this stinking, filthy war, you thought your old man was going to be a casualty. Not a thought for your brothers in arms. How droll.*

A buzzing in his ears. Jorgy was talking. Scottie, too, with a hand on Kennet's shoulder. Jorgy passed an envelope over the small table he used as a desk. It was a letter on Fisher Hotel stationery, addressed not to Kennet but to the captain. It was already opened, no doubt read by the censors, then by Jorgy and the chaplain, leaving Kennet the last to know.

He took it. His lips moved, shaping soundless words.

Minor or Nalle? It's Minor or Nalle, which one, which death am I holding, who is dead, which of my brothers is dead?

Tadpoles swam in Kennet's eyes as he pulled out a letter in Marta's handwriting, folded around the flimsy, yellow paper of Western Union.

31 GOVT
WASHINGTON D C 845 PM 2-28-45
MR EMIL FISKARE
HUGUNIN STREET CLAYTON N.Y.

THE SECRETARY OF WAR DESIRES ME TO EXPRESS
HIS DEEPEST REGRET THAT YOUR SON PRIVATE
BJÖRN K. FISKARE WAS KILLED IN ACTION ON
TWENTY-SECOND FEBRUARY IN ITALY. LETTER
FOLLOWS.

ULIO THE ADJUTANT GENERAL

"I'm so sorry," Jorgy said.

"Was this your only brother?" Scottie asked gently.

"No." Kennet pulled a deep breath through his nose. "I'm oldest. Then Minor, I mean, Erik. He's in the Navy. Then comes Nalle… Björn…" He gestured with the telegram. "He's with the 10th Mountain. Was. *Shit,* I can't fucking believe it. Sorry, Padre."

"Don't be."

A long moment stretched out. Kennet felt both officers were waiting for him to do or say something, but he had no idea what was expected of him right now.

"Do you want to talk about it?" the chaplain said. "Don't be bothered if the answer is 'no.' It takes time to sink in. You might even be feeling absolutely nothing. That's all right. I mean, it's normal."

"I think I… I can't take it in yet. I don't know what to say."

"I'm truly sorry," Jorgy said. He didn't add any canned phrases about honor and sacrifice and service, for which Kennet was intensely grateful.

"Why don't you go be with your men," Scottie said. "Nothing takes the place of a brother, but your men are a different breed of brothers. Your bad news is theirs, too."

He stood up and offered Kennet a handshake, and offered his time whenever Kennet did feel like talking. Jorgy shook his hand too and dismissed him.

The boys were waiting outside. Not just Ingle and Hook, but all of them.

"My brother's dead," Kennet said, holding out the telegram. "Killed in action. In Italy."

Anderson put a hand on his shoulder. O'Hara reached in his breast pocket for cigarettes. He gave the pack a shake and held it out to Kennet. It was the last smoke in the pack. Kennet took it. Hook lit it.

Nalle is dead. My little bear-brother is gone.

Kennet's mind wrestled with the idea, trying to pin it to the mat, line it up somewhere. He didn't know what to think, but a world of feeling gathered in his throat, impervious to the hard drags he was taking on the cigarette. It wasn't exactly grief. It didn't feel like grief. More like depletion. Surrender. He didn't have the strength or will to grieve, which felt shameful.

Nalle is dead. Do something.

He could only stand there and smoke.

"I'm sorry," Anderson said. His hand had moved from Kennet's shoulder to his nape, where it squeezed. "I'm real sorry, Fish."

As the bit of yellow paper passed from hand to hand, the circle chimed in softly, like notes building a chord.

"Rotten news."

"Aw, Fish, my heart's broke."

"I'm sorry."

"So sorry, Pescado."

Jock kicked his toe at the ground with a grunt. "This war's a real…"

"A real fucking cunt," Anderson said.

A shocked silence as everyone looked at Anderson as if he'd spouted fire. Then loud laughter, even from Kennet.

"I feel kind of useless," he said. "I mean, my poor dad… And my little brother and sisters."

"So hard that you can't be there," Anderson said. "I wish I could load you into a catapult and fling you over the ocean. You need to be home right now, comforting and taking care of things."

"Not a problem," Schmitt said, tapping the bazooka leaning against his hip. "Hop in here, Fish. I'll send you straight home."

Everyone laughed again and Kennet made a show of checking his watch. "Let's wait a few hours, the sun isn't up yet in New York."

"Tell us something about your brother," Anderson said. "One little thing."

"He was my Ma's favorite. She died in nineteen forty. I guess they're together now."

"No guessing," Anderson said. "They are."

"I bet she met his train," Jock said.

"What train?"

All eyes turned to Jock, and this boisterous clown, who loved nothing more than attention, took an uncustomary step backward. "Nothing."

O'Hara touched Jock's back and murmured, "Go ahead, bud. What train?"

Jock took a breath. "My grandpa always said you take a train to Heaven, and loved ones who have gone before meet you at the station."

The vision was immediate, as if a painting had been pushed in Kennet's face. Nalle stepping off a train, bouquet of flowers in hand. Seersucker jacket and straw hat. Bright, strapping and full of anticipation. Ingrid on the platform in hat and gloves, waving. Calling for her boy. Opening her arms. Nalle running down the platform, holding onto his hat. An exuberant, laughing embrace. An explosion of rose petals in all directions…

"I like that," Kennet said softly. He looked up, looked Jock dead in the eye. "I like that a lot, Chris. Thanks."

He didn't read Marta's letter until he was bedded down for the night, alone in the tent with Hook.

> *…Our hearts are broken to bits, but we're holding up as best we can. It's bizarre not having the closure of a funeral. No body, no wake, no service, no gathering… Makes it so difficult to take in and accept he's gone. We have nothing but a telegram's word. No tangible proof. Easy to ignore and pretend it never happened, say you'll think about it later. It leaves one feeling strangely detached and numb. We know he's gone, but it hasn't quite sunk in. Honestly, I don't think we're letting it sink in.*
>
> *Little is adamant about keeping Nalle's side of the room exactly as it was. He won't hear of moving the other bed out or touching any of Nalle's things. He's more obsessive than ever about tracking your and Minor's paths now. Every morning at the kitchen table, he diligently searches the newspaper for any mention of the 11th Armored or the Indianapolis, clips it out with scissors and then puts a pin in the map. I don't know if it eases his grief about Nalle, or only makes it worse. It's difficult to talk to him. Most days he's shut up tight within himself, but the other night I saw him and Major sitting down by the river.*

Major had his arm around Little and the way Little's shoulders were heaving and shaking, I knew he was crying. It broke my heart, of course, but at the same time I was relieved Little was letting it down.

Major does have that way about him—he's a haven for your worst feelings and fears. He knows how to rearrange worry into action. If I could arrange it, I'd send him out to you right away. He's a dose of everything you need right now.

Your father is… I won't lie. He's just devastated. I'm taking good care of him but promise me you'll write him soon. Like Little, he needs to know where you are.

I miss you more than ever, dear friend and darling fat-head. Be careful. You are so precious to us.

My love always,
Marta

Kennet put his back to Hook, curled in on himself and pressed his mouth hard into his wrist. Like carefully opening a pressure valve, he eased one long, stifled thread of a scream through his throat. A low, rushing hiss that could, he was sure, be mistaken for the sound of sleep.

"Come here, you damn fool," Hook said. His hands roughly rolled Kennet toward him. "That's no way to cry and it does nobody any good. Come here."

He pulled Kennet's head against his chest. Kennet half-protested, even as his hands closed in fists on Hook's sleeves.

"I don't know what to do," he said through chattering teeth.

"Let it out," Hook said. "No shame. You got to. You can't take it into the next battle with you, Fish. You got to let it all out here and leave it behind tomorrow. There's nothing for it. Do what I tell you and let it go now."

He rubbed Kennet's head. Roughly at first, like he was petting a dog. "Poor bastard," he mumbled.

Then his hand settled down, heavy and strong.

"I'm so sorry, Fish."

Nothing takes the place of a brother, but your men are a different breed of brothers.

Family isn't only blood. It's also who you bleed for.

Carefully, not quite trusting in the idea, Kennet let Nalle be Hook's brother, too.

He let Hook bleed for him.

And he let it out.

Everything a Father Could

Dear Paps,

I know what you're doing. You're looking down at the chain on your neck and thinking Nalle got killed because you didn't wear it right. You're thinking the charm didn't work because you didn't have all three golden fish on it. You're thinking about the mornings you put it on late. Or the prayers you forgot to say. Or the words you got out of order. You're thinking Nalle got killed because you didn't try hard enough to keep him alive. You're thinking you chanted, "I wish my sons to come home," instead of specifically declaring, "I wish my sons to come home alive."

I know you, Paps. I know you're doing it. Don't. Please don't. There was nothing for it. All these magic things we do to comfort ourselves and make ourselves believe we have control over the world, they have no power. There's nothing you could've done to stop this from happening. Nalle getting killed was nothing you could have prevented. Nothing you did or didn't do made him die. It's not your fault. It's nobody's fault except the man who shot him.

I want nothing more than to be home right now. I feel helpless. The only thing making me feel better is thinking about Ma. A buddy said you take a train to Heaven, and all your loved ones that have passed meet you at the station. I'm clinging to that image of Ma and Nalle at the station. With Marianne and the Old Bear. And little Beatrice, too. They're all together. Nothing can hurt Nalle ever ever again, and Ma's got her baby with her. I'm holding onto this as hard as I can. You hold on, too.

Paps, I love you. You did everything right. You did everything a father could. It's not your fault, I promise.

I'm doing everything I can to get home soon.

Love and courage from your gullgosse, who misses you awful,

Nyck

The Resurrection and the Life

19 Mar 1945

17 March—marched to Lausonhausen. 18 March we moved to the Moselle River.

Today we crossed the river, moving toward the town of Buchenbemen.

Ran into heavy German fire from a destroyed railroad bridge. We attempted to cross but the Krauts were using 20mm AA guns, which nobody in the unit ever encountered before.

Heavy casualties.

…

Fucking goddammit…

…

We lost Schmitt and Nichols.

We always joked that even death couldn't part those two bickering brats, and we were right. I saw it all. They were blown off the bridge together, they went flying through the air all tangled up. The medic found them together, still holding onto each other.

My heart is sick about it, but I think I'd feel even sicker if I had to see Schmitt mourning Nichols, or Nichols mourning Schmitt.

Both of them leave a wife and kids.

Poor bastards.

29 Mar 1945

Darmstadt.

We entered the city via a pontoon bridge over the Rhine. I'm not sure there's a military unit more trusted and admired than the corps of engineers. No way, you think, as your track starts to trundle across the bobbing span. No way that thing is going to hold up a tricycle, let alone a track. But it does. Even tanks cross them without a hitch. Unbelievable.

Or as you and I would call it, darling girl: desenrascanco.

Fold up this memory: as we were crossing I saw Captain Jorgensson throw a bullet casing into the Rhine. He saw me watching and kind of scowled, like he was embarrassed to be caught in a superstition. Smack in the middle of the most superstitious men on the planet.

So I shrugged and said, "Nick, Nick, needle in the water, thou sink, I float."

Jorgy's whole face changed. He flashed a grin that could only be described as boyish and smacked my back. "You make me feel like home, gullgosse," he said.

For a moment, I was home and if Jorgy asked, I would've dove into the river and gotten his bullet back. I would've killed for him.

I think we're all homesick and craving heroes out here. Not to be heroes but to revere them. When you think about it, we're none of us old fellows. Some of us are still in our goddamn teens. We're all of us far from home. We want father figures. When it gets shitty, we want to be told we're good boys, all of us eldest and finest and the best thing that happened to the unit.

(Oh, don't laugh at my maudlin crap, Hook. You know how sensitive I am.)

Anyway. Darmstadt was utter desolation. The bombing here was intense. I've never seen such destruction. Obliteration. We passed the train yard and gaped at the rails uprooted and twisted into ribbons. Not one whole building remained in the commercial district, just roughed-out remains of ground floors. Block after block of rubble and ruin, and not a soul anywhere. Were the residents long gone? Would they ever come back? How could people possibly rebuild from such annihilation? Is there enough desenrascanco in the world?

We kept pushing into Germany. Lots of fighting in little towns and villages. In a place called Cham, we encountered some of the worst house-to-house fighting I've yet experienced. It was mostly the Volkgrenadiers—very old men and very young boys, but desperation made them lethal with their rifles. They were ready to fight to the death, to the last man...

In Cham, Chris Fragiacomo took it in the neck from a sniper.

One minute he was pressed against a wall, rifle at the ready, eyes in all directions. Poised, alert, attentive, on his game.

Kennet saw him. Looked away a moment. Looked back.

Jock was down. Empty eyes looking at nothing, a stream of blood running from one ear and one nostril.

"Chris?" O'Hara crawled over and pulled the lifeless body into his arms, cradled it to his chest a moment, before tearing off his helmet, turning his mouth to the skies and howling. He *screamed* his buddy's name into the smoke, sounding like a demon giving birth, or a horse dying.

The squad stared, their bowels turning to acid, their hearts sinking through the soles of their shoes, their minds on the edge of the abyss. O'Hara was, at last, panicking, which meant they were all fucked.

"Don't you do this, Chris. Don't you fucking do this to me…"

As the iron constitution of the squad dissolved, nobody knew what to do. Nothing they'd experienced in combat had so instantly and thoroughly demoralized them. It was Anderson who finally managed to get close to the raving O'Hara and take the inconsolable madman's face in his hands.

"I am the resurrection and the life," he said. "Whoever believes in me, though he die— No, look at me. O'Hara, look me in the eye. Though he die, yet shall he live, and everyone who lives and believes in me shall never die. *Never,* O'Hara. Never die. He will never die. Look at me. Do you believe this?"

O'Hara pulled his face away, buried it in Fragiacomo's hair and cried like a child.

"Truly, *truly,* I say to you," Anderson said. "Look at me. Whoever hears my word and believes him who sent me has eternal life. He does not come into judgment, but has passed from death to life. Life, O'Hara. He lives. Now get up."

O'Hara didn't move.

"Get *up,* goddammit," Anderson shouted.

Every stomach in the unit spasmed. O'Hara was panicking and Anderson was blaspheming. Surely it was the end.

Through the choking smoke came Hildur, drooling with hunger, desperate to go home and reclaim her place as queen in the elvish lands, even if she had to kill every man here to do it. O'Hara was broken. He'd be easy pickings.

Not today, you bitch.

Kennet found himself moving. He shoved Anderson aside, pulled Jock out of O'Hara's arms and yanked the stricken soldier to his feet. "That's it," he said, jamming O'Hara's helmet back on. "That's all you get. You're done. Put it away. You think about it later. You feel it later. Understand?"

A ripple of purpose went through the rattled squad, shoulders squaring, expressions hardening, shit getting together. Rifles came up, eyes narrowed. Ingle barked strategy and the men swung back into action.

"Come on," Kennet said to O'Hara. "You stay with me. I want you two feet from my hip at all times."

"I don't think I can—"

Hating himself, Kennet cuffed O'Hara's jaw hard. "*Don't* think. Understand me? Don't think, don't feel, just do what I tell you. Stay with me. I don't want to hear a fucking word and when I look around, I better see you right there. *Move.*"

> *God, Asta,* Kennet wrote, *I felt like dogshit slugging O'Hara like that, but I had to do it. And I tried to get to him later, tried to say I was sorry, so fucking sorry and I was here for him, he could talk to me about it, I felt so goddamn bad...*
>
> *He looked right through me. He was just gone.*
>
> *Poor bastard.*
>
> *Christ, how much can a man take?*

As more and more Germans surrendered, Kennet could feel a shift in the American troops' dynamic. Men who'd only lived in the moment these past four months, were starting to talk about the future. To kick around the idea of what they might do with themselves when they got home, besides flush toilets all day long.

"You should come back to Clayton with me," Kennet said to Hook. "I might actually insist."

Hook grinned. "Mean it?"

"Mean it. We'll rest up at my home, then you can show me the Mississippi."

"You're on. One look at Old Man River and you'll forget Saint Larry."

"Bullshit. The Mississippi doesn't have an Old Nick or a Fossegrim."

"Of course it does," Hook said. "We just call him Huckleberry Finn."

Kennet opened his mouth to protest, then looked away, still open-mouthed. "Son of a bitch."

Hook blew a modest smoke ring.

"Hook, sometimes you are brilliant."

"Oh, it's just the company I keep. Hey, tell you what, we should *drive* from New York to New Orleans."

"Now you're talking."

"I mean let's really do it right. Get a goddamn DeSoto Airstream Convertible. Cream and black. Red hubs."

"Or a Maclaughlin-Buick Series Ninety Convertible Coupe," Kennet said dreamily.

"I'm getting a hard-on," Hook said.

"What do you think, O'Hara," Kennet said. "You in?"

O'Hara lifted one shoulder a quarter-inch. He was listening, but a blind man could see he didn't give a damn. He'd shut down completely since Jock died. He hadn't become a liability—his bravery was intact and he was deadly as ever with a rifle. But his already guarded soul had gone somewhere irretrievable. If you tried to talk to him about it, he simply tuned you out or walked away.

2 Apr 1945

Yesterday was Easter Sunday. Instead of collecting eggs, we collected Krauts. Thousands surrendered. It's almost becoming easy. We cleared two towns with training sites and barracks, then marched out again, toward a town called Oberhof. Once upon a time this place must've been a postcard-pretty alpine village. Now it looks like Darmstadt. Some of the houses were still burning.

My squad billeted in a house at the edge of town. Did a few hours guard duty, uneventful.

A boom like the end of the world woke the entire house up with a collective yell and a volley of cursing.

"Holy fucking shit."

"Fuck."

"Jesus fucking Christ."

"Who do I gotta fuck to get some *sleep* around here?"

Feet were crammed into boots, helmets jammed on, M1 rifles grabbed. The squad fell out of the house and crossed the road into the woods beyond.

Kennet's eyes bulged in the thick darkness. He couldn't see anything or anyone, only the muzzle flashes from enemy fire. He shook off the last of the shock, the last of the sleep fog, and sunk his teeth into his training. He fired, then quickly rolled away from where his own muzzle flash would've been, knowing the Germans would aim for it.

"They can't be more than twenty yards away," O'Hara said.

After a short, intense skirmish, Ingle started yelling from behind them. "Back across the road. Move it. Tanks are gonna lay down machine gun fire. Get back inside."

Blobs of yellow swam in Kennet's vision as he followed O'Hara across the road. Hook followed him, three crabs running in a crouch until they reached the door of the house.

"Life is full of rude awakenings," Hook mumbled.

"This is the worst hotel I've ever lodged at," Kennet said. "I demand to speak to the manager."

Hook guffawed and slapped Kennet's back. "Strong letter to follow."

Then the world exploded.

A crackling rattle and something hit Kennet in the face. Something big. Hard enough to spin him a full revolution. Then he was hit again, by what felt like a handful of red-hot coals.

"Fish?"

He was on fire.

"Fish?"

White-hot popping sizzles in his eyes, narrowing into a pinpoint as the walls of the world began to close.

So this is how it ends, Kennet thought.

Well, shit, this is easy. Dying is a fucking piece of cake. The hell was I worried about?

Then it hit him. Like a cauldron of molten lava thrown in his face, the delayed pain went tearing up his nose, into his brain and screamed behind his eyeballs and eardrums.

Actually, this is gonna be hard.

The last thing he heard was: "No, Fish, no don't you *fucking* do this to me."

Poor O'Hara. Everyone leaves him…

Fish Hook

7 Apr 1945

Dear Paps,

I'm all right. Hope the telegram didn't upset you too much. Doc says I was lucky. I ought to be in much worse shape after having a blast of broken glass and shrapnel in my head. Something about the angle at which I was hit. I don't know. I don't remember much. But I'm all right and it doesn't hurt too bad.

Yeah, I'm lying. It hurts bad enough to make me puke sometimes, but Doc says I will *be all right. So get your truth from him and the complaining from me.*

The bridge of my nose is broken and they took a bunch of metal bits out of my sinus. Feels like the worst hay fever you ever had. More pieces got pulled out of my cheek and temple, including a nasty one that came close to lacerating my eyeball. That side is all bandaged up and because they don't want infection spreading to the other eye, that's bandaged up too and I'll be blind for a few more days. My friend O'Hara is writing this letter. He got hit in the same blast and he's laid up here with me. My friend Hook…

Kennet stared into the dark, his last sentence hanging in the air. "Fish?"

My friend…

"You want to write more, bud? You tired?"

Kennet swallowed hard, tried to speak, but he was stuck. O'Hara's fingers closed around his wrist.

"I know you want to tell him," O'Hara said. "But it means saying it out loud. And if you don't say it out loud, then there's a chance it's not real. Right?"

Kennet knew the struggle of holding back tears. He didn't realize that when your tears were literally dammed up, they surged backward and tried to fight their way out of your body by any means possible, even if they had to kill you to do it. Gauze bandages blocked his eyes and nose, so the tears went crawling down his throat. Angry and thwarted, they tore up the whole length of his body, a marauding horde in his chest and stomach. Even his limbs ached.

Cause of death, he imagined a doctor writing on his chart, *inability to weep with ensuing complications from heartbreak arising from incalculable loss following…*

"Fish," O'Hara said. "I'll write it for you. Okay? I won't make you say it."

The weight on the mattress by Kennet's leg shifted, and then came the sound of pencil scratching on paper.

"I can't see," Kennet whispered.

"I know." A reassuring pat on the leg. "It's only for a few days more. Just to keep your other eye safe."

"Am I blind?"

"Nope. Doc promised. If he lied, he'll answer to me."

O'Hara's emotionless monotone was strangely comforting. He'd taken the brunt of the exploding window after the Germans machine-gunned it clear out of the wall. The frame bashed his head, resulting in a concussion that made O'Hara upchuck for two straight days. In addition to the egg on the noggin, he had a host of shrapnel wounds along the entire left side of his body.

"Fifty-four stitches total," he said. "Tell you, Fish, I look like a fucking needlepoint cushion."

Once he stopped heaving and could sit up without seeing double, O'Hara had never left Kennet's side. For all his aloof reticence, he made an astonishingly attentive nurse. Positioning a fork in Kennet's hand, he guided it from meal tray to mouth with deadpan delivery: "Meat's at two o'clock, mashed potatoes at six o'clock. Avoid ten o'clock, I don't know what the hell that green stuff is."

He didn't bother making idle conversation. Cracking jokes for his own amusement was never O'Hara's style. But he always made it known he was at hand. Kennet only had to shift or stir on his bed, and out of the dark came O'Hara's quiet, "Hey, bud. I'm over here."

The pencil stopped scratching.

"Did you write it?" Kennet said.

"It's done."

"Read it to me."

"Fish…"

"Just fucking read it."

A rustle of paper, then O'Hara spoke. "I wrote, *My friend Hook is dead. Machine gun fire got him right across the back of the head. My buddy's gone.*"

Kennet tilted his head back, trying to close eyes already shut. Trying to block out the world when he was already in the dark.

"Thanks," he whispered.

He imagined Emil reading the letter. Crumpling it into one sorrowful hand and with the other, reaching into his pocket for a fish hook. Regarding it in his palm, having long known such charms were powerless.

Kennet gazed into the black behind his bound eyelids, envisioning his father sitting at his desk, reaching for pen and paper. Rubbing the three charms at his neck. Reflecting a bit more on the fish hook. Then writing all the things Kennet needed to hear, but would never believe.

It was nothing you did or didn't do. You didn't get Hook killed by making future plans. You didn't sign his death warrant by talking about an adventure drive to New Orleans. Nothing you did or didn't do could have stopped this.

War blows the rules to shit, gullgosse.

Forgive yourself. Separate your self from the soldier. You promised me you would keep a construct between you and the war. I know war and I know promises are heavy things. And I know you so well. You are my eldest and finest. The best thing that ever happened to your Ma and me. And the best goddamn thing that ever happened to Richie Hook. You're a good solider, a good son, and you were a good brother to Richie. The best he could've hoped for. You loved and protected each other the best you could. He's gone and you're cut in two. Your heart's broken because you were mates. Nothing replaces it.

You're honorable and decent and kind. You'll never get over this, but you'll learn how to get next to it and bring it along.

And you'll come out the better man for it.

"Can I tell you something?" O'Hara said.

"Mm."

"The day they got Jock… You got me back on my feet. I'll never forget it."

"Probably because I slugged you."

"The slug isn't memorable, although I definitely needed it. It was when you said, 'I want you two feet from my hip at all times.' You bossed me around from hell to breakfast and I grabbed onto it like you wouldn't believe. It helped me get through the rest of the fight. I never said thank you."

"You'd do it for me," Kennet whispered, and touched his own hip. "See, you're doing it now."

"I'm so sorry, Fish."

Kennet turned up his palm. O'Hara put his on it and they folded fingers and thumbs down, gripping hard.

"I'm sorry, too," Kennet said. "About Chris."

O'Hara didn't answer but Kennet knew why. Some pain defied description to the point where describing it was unnecessary. Almost offensive. Talking about it only cheapened it, and O'Hara's grief was too dear.

Kennet and O'Hara returned to the platoon on April 22, both scarred men. Both changed men. Without discussion, they stayed together. Physically close—marching, guarding, eating and sleeping two feet from each other's hip—but at a deliberate emotional distance. The company they kept was largely silent. Each only wanted the other so neither would have to talk.

Kennet no longer wrote in his journal. Without Hook reading the entries, he saw no reason to keep recording them. And what was the point revealing your most secret thoughts and feelings to someone, anyway? They'd only leave you in the end, taking your heart and soul with them. Better you kept it to yourself, kept your head down and just did your damn job. The history books would tell the story. That was *their* damn job.

The 11th Armored crossed into Austria on the last day of April. As if to show what it thought of the invasion, the country's temperatures plummeted and it even snowed in the early days of May.

The unit slogged through Zwettel and onto Gallneukirchen. Their POW enclosure became so overrun with German surrendered troops, it became difficult to handle them all.

Rumors and intrigue rippled through the ranks. The war was over. No, it was almost over. The Germans had surrendered. No, they hadn't. Soon, though. Not yet. Move on. Keep going.

"Don't get arrogant," O'Hara said. "Relax now and you're a dead man."

Honest news came down the line: Hitler was dead. In Berlin. *Confirmed.* The son of a bitch shot himself in the head. The unit went mad, whooping and hollering and firing their rifles in the air. The soul had been ripped out of the Nazis. The brains of the operation splattered on a bunker wall.

Now, surely, they were close to the end. Close enough to taste.

Almost there, Kennet thought. *Almost done. Almost home.*

He almost relaxed.

But then, on the 6th of May, the half-tracks of B Company, 21st Armored Infantry Battalion, rolled into Mauthausen concentration camp.

PART THREE:
The Fisherman Adrift

"I find myself regarding existence as though from beyond the tomb, from another world; all is strange to me; I am, as it were, outside my own body and individuality; I am depersonalized, detached, cut adrift. Is this madness?"

—HENRI FRÉDÉRIC AMIEL in
The Journal Intime, July 8, 1880

"Where by the marishes boometh the bittern,
Nick the soulless one sits with his ghittern.
Sits inconsolable, friendless and foeless.
Waiting his destiny, – Nick the soulless."

—SEBASTIAN EVANS,
Brother Fabian's Manuscript

"The prisoner should compare themselves to a rock, one untouched by the filth and horrific events. He who has pity, will break. Look away when you see someone dying. Whatever you do, do not look back. If you cannot learn how to quickly forget, you will not survive the camp. You will be devoured by the events and lose your mind."

—RENATA LAQUEUR,
Diary from Bergen-Belsen

MAY
1945

True Hunger

If war smelled like a million dirty diapers, the hellscape of Mauthausen carried the stench of a million wars. It hit the American column like a shock blast of poison gas, assaulting noses, throats and lungs with a thick cloud of charnel, filth, blood, disease and despair. The pall of human excrement pressed down on all the available air until you could punch through it with your fists.

"What in the name of God..." Anderson whispered.

A collective gorge rose as every pair of eyes took the next barrage. Gazes ricocheted from one corpse sprawled on the ground, to another a few yards away. Then two more over there. A pile of four dead bodies. Ten. Two dozen. Eyes widened as incredulous gazes followed the gruesome carnage, bulging when they took in *piles* of the dead, stacked up like felled timber.

All around him, Kennet heard men whispering "Oh my God" beneath a humming din of moans and cries, in what seemed a hundred different languages. Some of the scattered corpses stirred and came to life. They tried to rise on legs no bigger than pipestems. Others could only reach an emaciated arm. All were half-naked and crazed.

The wind shifted. Now it was real smoke bearing down on the GIs, bringing with it the scent of burning flesh.

"Hildur, what have you done," Kennet said hoarsely.

He closed his eyes and vomited every meal he'd eaten in his life.

He'd never known such a violent, visceral reaction. Onto his shoes he upchucked every imagined feast. Into the dirt he heaved all the decadent banquets of his daydreams. Through the acidic waves, he heard hardened, battle-tested men scream in horror. More than a few keeled over. All up and down the column, soldiers were staggering off the tracks and staring open-mouthed, or falling to their knees, sobbing, banging their fists on the ground, puking right and left, ridding themselves of the notion they'd ever known fear, ever known misery or suffering, ever known true hunger.

I am not here, Kennet thought, retching the last of himself onto the ground. His past, forgotten. His future, canceled. In this raw, brutally present moment, every rule in the known world ceased to exist.

There is no more. There is nothing for it. Not now. Not ever.

He hurled his entire being inside out, bashing through the horror until it formed an exoskeleton, a protective and impermeable shell of armor.

He would never take it down.

No more.

Deep within his being, doors were slammed, switches thrown, wires ripped out, motors turned off, light chains pulled.

I am not.

I feel not.

This will not touch me.

Not this. Not anything.

Ever.

Again.

Shadows and Burrs

"Fisha," the boy said.

"Yes, I know," Kennet said. "Fish. That's me." He tapped the boy's chest. "What's your name?"

"Fisha."

"Not me. *You.*"

"Fisha."

"Goddammit. Where's Maslov?"

Maslov was one of many second-generation American soldiers who could speak Russian, German, Yiddish or any of the Slavic tongues. They were in high demand, and long hours of interpreting the atrocities of the camp left all of them stunned and glassy-eyed.

Maslov trudged over, exhausted and grey. He spoke to the tattered, scrappy boy who seemed to be the spokesperson of a band of emaciated, threadbare ruffians.

"His real name is Efim," Maslov said to Kennet. "The diminutive is Fisha." He spoke again to the boy in Russian, punctuating the words with an index finger on Kennet's insignia. "Fiskare. *Rybak,* da? My zovem yego 'Fish.'"

"Fisha," the boy cried, and wrapped arms around Kennet's legs.

"Good to meet you," Kennet said over his pounding heart and roiling stomach.

Fisha looked around eleven, although Kennet knew by now that conditions in Mauthausen had unnaturally aged the adults and stunted the children. Every reference point, along with every rule, was blown to shit. It was impossible to get your mind around the camp, let alone the arms of practicality to bring order out of this heinous chaos.

The lucid inmates reported that only the day before, most of the SS guards had fled the camp, leaving the prisoners guarded by unarmed Volkssturm soldiers and an absurd unit of retired police officers and firemen. The balance of power had just begun to tip in favor of the inmates when the American tanks rolled in, beneath a great stone gate emblazoned with a banner:

¡Los Espanoles Antifascistas Saludan a Las Fuerzes Liberado!

"Ralph, what's it mean?" Kennet said.

Ingle stopped swearing long enough to answer: "Anti-fascist Spaniards salute the liberation forces."

He resumed cursing under his breath. Florid combinations of *shit* and *whore* and *mother,* while Kennet stared stupidly at the flapping sign, unable to comprehend its existence. First the words being in Spanish baffled him, then he couldn't understand how the triumphant banner was made in the first place. Where? How? When?

Little by little, the GIs grasped how the camp's staggering mass of filthy humanity comprised an international crossroads of dissidents and unwanteds. Jews, of course—Polish, Czech, Hungarian, Balkan and Dutch. But there were large groups of Spanish Republicans. French political prisoners, too. Unwanted "-ists" of all kinds: socialists, communists, anarchists. Romani. Jehovah's Witnesses. Intelligentsia. Boy Scouts. (*Boy Scouts?!*) The ethnic undesirables: Poles, Slovenes, Slovaks and Serbs. Soviet prisoners of war.

From every corner of Europe they'd been crammed into this place, their sole purpose to be worked to death in the mines, quarries and munition factories. Killed by starvation, disease, exposure. Or killed for sport. Those too weak to work and too resilient to die were gassed and cremated.

No more, Kennet thought. *Not now. Not ever.*

No past. No future. No rules.

He walked around in a sort of functional fugue state, Fisha trailing behind him. Everything fragmented and surreal, mixed up with the past and present, reality and folk tale, life and death.

Hildur, what have you done? he wondered over and over, simultaneously horrified and detached. Even the murderous elven Queen knew she went too far with this glut of killing. Like a contrite child who'd lost utter control of a situation, she put bloody hands behind her back and hung her head, hoping someone else would clean up the mess.

Who would believe what happened here?

The quarry with its one hundred and eighty-six "stairs of death," up which prisoners carried blocks of granite from dawn to dark. Sometimes they were made to race each other up the flight. The winner got to live.

The quarry had a cliff edge known as "The Parachutist's Wall," where at gunpoint, prisoners had a choice of being shot or pushing one of their comrades over the precipice. A few of those pushed miraculously survived. Their reward: another turn at the edge.

Before deserting the camp, Nazi guards led a few hundred inmates to a cave rigged with dynamite. Trying to destroy the evidence. The dynamite didn't go off and the American soldiers rescued the prisoners.

The scene in the camp struck Kennet as an obscene, macabre reversal of the North Platte canteen: the soldiers were the ones attending to needs of the stomach and soul, while the prisoners swarmed them, hugging, weeping, patting. Blessing them, clutching them, kissing their hands, their boots, their guns.

"Fish," Fisha called, turning the short I to a long E. "Captain Feesh."

The boy was thin as water. Barefoot, scratched and bruised, his head sloppily shaved to the scalp. Yet his movements were spry, full of a hard, brutal confidence. Kennet soon learned the Russian communist prisoners were better organized than the Jews, and were able to take marginally better care of the children they had with them.

A margin you needed a microscope to view, but a margin all the same.

Fisha was a natural leader, although he seemed to belong to no one.

"Where is your mother?" Kennet said.

Fisha looked back, chin tilted. Smiling.

These children smiled. How could they?

"Mother," Kennet said. "Mommy. Mama."

Fisha exclaimed something in Russian.

Maslov translated: "She went up the chimney."

Fisha's finger made swirls in the air. His arms stretched wide and dropped on the shoulders of the boys nearest him. Dirty, ragged boys. Shaved heads, knobby knees, open sores. Motherless. Fatherless. All they knew of love went up in smoke.

And yet they were smiling. Chins and hands out, reaching for American breast pockets and the treats they now knew were within.

"Feed 'em *slow*." The harried medics begged, pleaded the distraught troops not to inundate the prisoners with food. Already dozens of starving people had gorged themselves on C-rations and died of shock.

Kennet broke his chocolate into small pieces and tried to pass them out, but Fisha shouldered in and exerted his authority. Kennet must hand the pieces to *him* and *he* would distribute to his mates.

All over the camp, boys attached themselves to GIs, appointing themselves sidekicks, aides-de-camp and lieutenants. Gleaning candy, cigarettes and words in English.

"Fuck Hitler," they quickly learned to say. Within hours, they all used it like a password, testing loyalty.

Stop. Are you one of us? Speak the code.

"Fuck Hitler."

You may enter.

You may live.

While the medics tried to keep soldiers from inadvertently killing prisoners with kindness, the officers desperately tried to keep the prisoners from killing the handful of SS guards left in the camp. The brass wanted these men alive, so they could be interrogated at least, prosecuted at most.

Some troops wanted to shoot them all and be done with it.

Others thought shooting too good for these sons of bitches.

"Calling these German fuckers *sons of bitches* is an insult to bitches," Ingle muttered.

"And fuckers," O'Hara said.

The Nazis were kept isolated and guarded, away from the now-liberated prisoners, who instead turned their vigilante justice on the kapos and the Volkssturm.

"They're hanging a guy in there," O'Hara said, jerking his head toward one of the barracks.

Such things would have shocked Kennet once. No more.

He followed O'Hara. Fisha followed Kennet.

Some boys were shadows—they followed their chosen GI at a distance.

Some boys were burrs. They stuck close. Devoted manservants.

Fisha was a burr.

In the barracks, Kennet watched murder disguised as assisted suicide. A kapo encouraged to push a table into place beneath a beam. Given a suggestion to tie a noose with the rope nobody else touched. Instructed to put his head through unaided. Nobody lifted a finger in complicity. Nobody would leave until the job was done properly. Judge, jury and executioner dressed in striped pajamas. They attended with narrow-eyed, dangerous patience until the kapo stepped off the table.

Kennet and O'Hara left, followed by Fisha.

The GIs sat in the foul sunshine, cleaned their guns and tried to talk about anything else.

The children conducted trade with chocolate and cigarettes. They pulled up their ragged clothes and compared scars. They laughed and snarled with a disturbing one-upmanship as they displayed infected wounds from accidents and fights and disease.

Many of their backs were striped with welts.

Maslov translated: the boys were made to flog each other.

"How do they act as if it all didn't happen?" Ingle said.

"They don't act," Kennet said.

"It's all they've known," Maslov said.

"Where are their mothers?"

Nobody answered. Stories coming out of the women's camp were too heinous to grasp. The minds and spirits of the soldiers were overloaded with the stench and the spectacles and the stripes. Taking in the horrors of sexual violence sent many into a frenzied rage.

When the wind shifted, Kennet didn't turn his face away. He couldn't smell anything. In a few days, it would occur to him he couldn't taste anything either, but in the nightmare of now, food was the farthest thing from his mind.

The whole world was far from his mind.

He felt nothing. And that was good. It meant his armor was holding.

Fisha thrust out a hungry hand. Kennet patted his pockets but he had no more candy. He gave Fisha his Zippo to examine. He'd had this lighter since 1942. Once shinier than a show girl, it was dull silver now, worn to brass at the seam from Kennet's thumb flipping it open countless times. One flat side was engraved with his name, *21st AIB* and the battalion's motto, *Tonitus Fulmen Secuti:* Thunder Follows Lightning.

Fisha flipped the cap open expertly and struck the wheel. The flame reflected in each of his eyes.

Watching the tiny fire, a tangible feeling settled into Kennet's heart, solemn and clean as a key fitting into a hotel room door: he was profoundly, purely grateful Hook was not here to see this.

Keeper of the Flame

"Sir, he won't stop calling me captain," Kennet said to Jorgy. "I keep telling him I'm just a—"

"I know, son," Jorgy said. He'd gone entirely grey. His incoming beard sparkled white and silver. "I know and it doesn't matter. We know who's who and it just doesn't fucking matter in this place. If it makes him happy, let him call you captain. If it makes him happy to call you shithead, just let him."

Kennet laughed. At least, he meant to laugh. It sounded shrill and maniacal in his ears.

"Take a walk, Fish," Jorgy said in Swedish. "Take a break, walk it off and come back."

"Take a walk in the woods," the soldiers were told when it got to be too much. The woods were cool and green. Kennet, unable to smell, imagined a scent of dirt and life and better times. Hope for the future in the leaves and sap.

No more. Not now. Not ever.

No past. No future. No rules.

"Take a walk with me, Fish," O'Hara said.

Kennet went. Fisha followed. And other boys, too. They smoked and ate chocolate and sang the "Colonel Bogey" parody lyrics, which Ingle taught them.

Anderson sat at the base of a tree, his little pocket bible clutched in both hands, shaking and sobbing.

"Another hanging," O'Hara said.

Kennet sat on a root and shook out a cigarette. His lighter was no longer in his possession: it was now Fisha's job and exclusive privilege to flick the Zippo for Kennet's smoke breaks.

The keeper of the flame, Kennet thought absently.

"My God," Anderson said through clenched teeth. "My God, why have you forsaken them… Why… My God, why…"

"O'Hara? Guys? Give us a minute alone," Kennet said. They all went, except Fisha, who couldn't be sent away. He lay down in the cool dirt and instantly fell asleep, his head tucked by Kennet's leg. One dirty hand holding the Zippo, the other on Kennet's service revolver.

Kennet put an arm around Anderson, rubbed his head. The scalp was hot and damp, as if he were running a fever. Kennet felt a dull concern. Along with lice and fleas, the camp was alive with dysentery, typhus, pneumonia and a host of other infections.

Oh well, it doesn't matter. Not now. Not ever.

He rubbed a couple circles on Anderson's tense back. "It's okay, bud."

Such lies were effortless when you had good armor.

"Let it out. Just let it go. Close your eyes, Andy. Go away from this place."

Anderson obeyed, and Kennet sat under his tree, smoking and guarding the two sleepers. He stared at the swath of skin between the torn hem of Fisha's striped shirt and the pleats of his trousers, belted tight with a piece of rope around bony hips. The skin was scarred horizontally, pink and wrinkled, as if the stripes of the shirt leached their pattern into the boy's skin.

Emil whipped Kennet when it was deserved. But never with emotion. Never for cruelty. Never, *never* delegating the task out to his other children.

And never to the point where he broke the skin.

Kennet couldn't stop staring at the welts, imagining each cruel blow into this little boy's tender body. No fat or muscle to cushion him. No mercy from the mate who held the whip, because a Nazi stood by to make sure every lash cut to the bone.

How do they all smile after such things?

He rubbed fingertips against his face, with its constellation of shrapnel scars. In his earlobe, he felt the little, hard lump. Just like the lump in Emil's bum leg.

I want my father.

I want to go home.

I want to be a child again. I want to go back to a time when getting my fish warm was my biggest fear.

He went on fingering the tiny bulge in his ear. No gold. Just ordinary, grunt metal.

Your golden time is gone, gullgosse, and it will never come again.

You're not him anymore.

You'll never be him again.

The tips of his fingers rubbed together, recalling the feel of a little burr. A sharp point on the hoop of the sugar barrel, where he bent over to collect his due, while his siblings waited in the kitchen and listened.

And counted.

Ordinary metal is good enough for Old Nick. He's got enough gold.

"You damn fool boy," he said softly.

Saudade sinks. Armor floats. And thunder follows lightning.

He wondered, dispassionately: *Am I going crazy?*

Fisha mumbled something behind closed eyes.

Kennet reached a finger, pushed the dirty fabric of Fisha's shirt up and began to count…

The Barrel

"You fool boy," Emil said hoarsely, one hand holding Kennet's head hard against his pounding heart. "You damn fool boy, don't you know what it would've done to me if you died?"

Kennet was sobbing now, his tears mixing with the rain that poured down over Clayton.

"Don't you know?" Emil said, rocking him. "You damn fool boy. If you die, I die."

"I'm sorry."

"Come inside. Your mother needs to see your face and you need to answer for what you did."

"I can't."

Emil's fingers turned him to face his deeds, moved him forward. "You can. And you will."

The four siblings were sitting in dry clothes around the kitchen table. Emil walked straight by them and into the pantry. Kennet followed. He'd go to meet this hiding. He welcomed it. He'd remember it. If it helped loosen the shameful fingers choking him, he'd even be grateful for it.

But then Minor got up from the table. "All of us," he said. "We all go."

Nalle got up. "It was all our idea."

Little got up. Even Trudy. Up until then, she had only taken her licks from Ingrid with a wooden spoon. Kennet's heart contracted at the sight of her now, chin up, shoulders squared. Marching with a soldier's deadpan resignation into the little store room with her brothers. All for one and one for all. Her little teeth clenched in her jaw and her slim fingers hooked on the rim of the sugar barrel as she took five from the strap. She backed to the wall by the jars of preserves, shook off Minor's encouraging pat and became a stone.

Up the chain in age order. Little took his five. Then Nalle. Then Minor, who, Kennet noticed, had changed out of his wet clothes into his thickest corduroys. Emil must've noticed too. His fifth stroke made Minor bark a startled *"Fuck,"* which got him a sixth.

Then it was Kennet's turn. He got five and was about to straighten up when Emil planted a hand in his back and held him down.

"All of you wait in the kitchen," he said to the others. "Shut the door."

He kept Kennet pushed down as footsteps shuffled out of the pantry and the door clicked closed.

"Drop your trousers."

Kennet swallowed hard. His face burned and his legs shook but he set his teeth, dropped his pants and took a fold of his shirt between his teeth. He bit the fabric hard as the belt crackled another five times across his bare butt. His skin was still wet and cold and it hurt like *fuck.*

"That's for Minor," Emil said. No emotion in his voice. He could've been observing the grass was green.

Kennet gripped the edge of the barrel harder, fingertips finding a little burr on one of the hoops. He understood now what was coming.

All your mother's children.

Another five on his ass, the last making him muffle a moan against his wrist. His other fingers pressed hard against the little burr on the hoop of the barrel, trying to make it more painful. No use. He wasn't going to make it.

You can. And you will.

"That's for Nalle."

This family tree sheared to the ground.

Five across the hamstrings for Little, and Kennet's head was buried under his forearms, spit and tears dripping off his mouth and chin. But it was better than sleeping in the graveyard.

He was on the plateau of pain now, and the five on his calves for Trudy were the worst. Each hard, stinging pop made Kennet see stars.

My only daughter.

Then it was over. Silence except for the sound of Kennet's quick, wet breathing.

"I don't ever want to whip you like this again," Emil said. "But if you break my rules again, you'll wish I had. What I'll do next time will make you remember tonight as something pleasant. Do you understand?"

"I understand."

"You're excused."

Kennet pulled up and buttoned, ran a forearm roughly across his face. His shirt was stuck to his back with sweat and he had to piss something awful. Following Emil out into the kitchen, he didn't look in any of his siblings' eyes.

"All of you go to your rooms," Emil said. "Minor, you sleep with Nalle and Little tonight. I want doors shut and lights out. I better not hear one footstep."

Thoughtfully, Minor sent Trudy up to Marta's bathroom to wash, and bossed his brothers in and out of the john quickly, leaving

Kennet time and privacy to run a cold bath and soak some of the sting out. And have the smallest and sorriest of manly cries in the thick, soft ear of a bath towel.

When he got to his room, he found Minor had left a glass of water and two aspirin on his nightstand. The night stretching before Kennet in hungry solitude, he skipped pajamas and lay down carefully on his stomach, exhaling the day away into his pillow.

Outside, the storm had passed. The sunset was all wide-eyed innocence, smoothing its pink and orange skirts. *Storm? What storm?* Kennet watched the trees drip as it slowly got dark, the enormity of his deeds heavy on his mind.

You could've killed all your mother's children.
I'd make you sleep among your dead siblings.
End of the family. End of our name. My only daughter.
You damn fool excuse of a…

His thoughts were interrupted by a scuttle outside his cracked bedroom window. A ghost-like figure in white was sliding its fingers beneath the sash. Quickly Kennet flicked the sheet, covering himself from the waist down. Even the soft, ironed linen on his skin made him wince. In another moment, a nightgowned Trudy was dropping into his room, having crawled across the gable between their windows.

"The heck are you doing?" Kennet murmured, his heart filled with affection. "If Paps catches you, don't come crying to me."

"He won't. They're eating dinner." She sat down on the edge of the bed, seemingly oblivious to his nakedness under the sheet. She had a handkerchief balled up in her hand which she now unfolded, revealing six sugar cubes. "It's all I could get," she said softly.

Catering to her solemnity, Kennet held out his palm to receive the gift. "Thank you," he said. "Exactly what I was wanting."

He popped one cube in his mouth and arranged the rest carefully on his nightstand. "You better scram now, kid. Give me some cash."

She pressed a kiss on his cheek and was out the window.

They all snuck in to visit him, bringing illegal gifts and tribute. Little brought lemon drops. Nalle dropped off half a chocolate bar. Minor risked his skin to swipe three apples from the foyer's fruit bowl.

"You're crazy," Kennet said, taking a bite of one. "You would've been over the barrel again."

Minor shrugged, taking his own bite. "Wasn't fair of him to make you take that many."

"What, you were counting?"

"It was hard not to. Goddamn, he didn't even give you a minute to put thick pants on."

"Wouldn't have mattered," Kennet said dully.

Minor almost choked. "Tell it to Sweeney. That hiding was em-bare-assed?"

"Mmhm."

"Cripes, man."

"I deserved it," Kennet said. "I'm the captain."

"And I'm first mate. I should've split it with you."

"Bare-assed?"

Minor's grin cut the dark. "Cheek by cheek, brother."

He ruffled Kennet's head and slipped out of the room. Sleep found Kennet eventually. A thin, glossy rest that merely took him out of his head and let him rise above the wincing burn of his butt and legs. Through it he was aware of the creak of his bedroom door and light footsteps. The waft of lemony sweetness that was Ingrid and her cool hand on the back of his neck.

You could've killed all your mother's children.

"I'm sorry," he whispered.

She kissed his head. "We all make mistakes."

"They could've drowned."

"Yes. But they didn't. And you'll remember they didn't every time you take to the river. From now on, you'll remember what almost happened and the price you paid. Isn't that right?"

He nodded into his pillow.

"Then the lesson was learned. I'm sorry it had to be this way, but…"

"I deserved it."

"That's how a man answers." Ingrid leaned and kissed him again. "Goodnight, love."

She refilled his water glass, then left. An interval of time later—minutes, hours—different footsteps came in. Heavier ones. And the smell this time of leather and machines and cigarette smoke and Bay Rum. The mattress sagged as Emil sat on its edge, elbows on knees. It was so quiet, Kennet could hear the little rasp of skin on skin as Emil rubbed his hands together. When he glanced through his cracked eyelids, he saw Emil was smiling, and he followed his father's gaze to the bedside table, where three apple cores were lined up by a stack of sugar cubes and crumpled candy wrappers.

"Will you remember now," Emil said, "that your brothers and sister will go anywhere and do anything for you? And that it carries a great responsibility?"

His voice was soft. As if he stood on the far side of a bridge. Kennet made the decision to cross. A boy would lie there in sullen, martyred silence. A man now, and a captain, he whispered back, "I will. I promise."

Emil's hand fell warm on Kennet's head.

"Godnatt, gullgosse."

"Förlåt mig?" Kennet said.

Emil leaned and brushed a rough buss above Kennet's ear. "Förlåten."

Forgiven.

Hangman's Coming

Kennet slowly came back to his soldier self, realizing he'd been telling his story aloud.

"What did I know of hunger?" he said. "I was a damn fool boy then. I'm just a damn fool punk now. I don't have an onion to know."

Fisha was awake, listening, attentive and solemn. Nodding as if he understood.

"Gullgosse," he said, moving the word around his mouth like a piece of the American confection he constantly craved. "Godnatt, gullgosse."

Kennet tugged the boy's dirty shirt down, hiding the scars.

He wished he could get back the way he cried, that night he tried to beat the storm home and lost. The way he opened his throat and sobbed from his guts while the rain beat down. What luxury. What indulgence. He'd never cry that way again. Not after today. What possible reason could there be?

The pain of his long-ago beating was nothing compared to the agony of this forsaken place, where hundreds of thousands of family trees were sheared to the ground. Lives ended. Names ended. Nobody left to tell.

The shame choking him that long-ago day was nothing to the shame of merely being alive right now. Being whole and fed and clothed and shod and inoculated. He was a grunt, a cog in the Army's labor force, but he had *value*. His body was the currency of war but Jesus H, it was sold dearly.

Nothing he ever suffered meant anything. Even losing Astrid. What a goddamn fuss over nothing. The loss of her didn't *starve* him. He lived to see another day and even fuck some other girls.

"Damn fool boy..."

He half turned to look through the trees toward the camp. Over there were men who had to answer for this world where mothers went up the chimney in smoke and young boys were worked to skin and bones and made to flog each other. They followed the GIs around, these flea-bitten ragged boys. Blackened teeth in their sardonic grins. How was it possible they *grinned*? They smiled and shouted and conducted trade with the chocolate and cigarettes the GIs carried in their breast pockets.

Shadows and burrs.

Fisha moved closer to Kennet's leg and closed his eyes. He wasn't smiling.

Kennet put a hand on the boy's head. The shaved, scraped head, rigorously deloused. Now sprouting a crop of gold hairs. This extraordinary boy was a gullgosse—a golden, blond boy. Like Kennet. Like all his brothers, save Nalle.

He's with Ma. She met his train.

He thought about Fisha's mother.

Who met her at the station when there's no one left?

He stared at the sun through the trees, his mind loosening.

Up in smoke.

Hitler has only got one ball.

Shadows and burrs.

A metal burr to dig your fingers against while your father gave the well-deserved hiding of your life.

A living burr who clung to you for life.

Stairs of death. The edge of a choice.

They're hanging a guy in there.

Take a walk in the woods.

The clouds parting over Wolfe Island.

Chocolate and cigarettes.

The river has enough gold.

And Hook isn't here to see this.

"Okay, Captain Feesh?" Fisha said, sitting up and smiling.

"Okay," Kennet said, trying to make the corners of his mouth lift.

There were accidental deaths.

The dynamite, still live in the caves.

The parachute cliff by the infamous stairs of death—its edge unattended.

A section of fence, unknown to still be wired and live until someone stumbled against it.

Lethal mishaps when boys tried to clean the guns of the soldiers they idolized.

Other children found live grenades and dumped the powder out to light it, often with deadly results.

Typhus. Dysentery. Cholera. The effects of starvation. The shock of too much to eat. The final breaking of a heart.

The inability to go on.

The bodies kept piling up.

Fisha's fingers kept reaching for Kennet's buttoned breast pocket for chocolate. Or into his own pocket for the Zippo lighter, for the keeper of the flame had somehow procured proper trousers, which had pockets where he could stash the first personal possessions he'd known in years.

"Keneet Feeskar," he said slowly, reading the engraving on the lighter. "Twenny-wun-ay-eye-bee."

"Molodets," Kennet praised, for he was now the keeper of a few Russian words. "Molodets, well done."

Something like a smile made the corners of his mouth twitch. What was that funny, awful, untranslatable word Astrid taught him? A word that meant a buddy you brought on a prison break so you could eat him?

You are losing your marbles, Fish.

Fisha looked around conspiratorially, inching closer to Kennet, turning his back to create privacy. His hand came out of his pocket and the fingers uncurled.

Kennet's blood went cold for an instant, then he burned hot all over.

In the boy's palm were three teeth capped with gold.

"Where did you get those?" Kennet whispered automatically. He already knew. He'd toured the camp's warehouses and workshops and seen the evil hoards of extracted gold teeth. Bins of them alongside piles of spectacles, heaps of jewelry, watches and other confiscated wealth. A special guard was posted around this grotesque booty and the officers were in a quandary about to whom it should be turned over.

And yet Fisha—clever, cunning, wily Fisha, managed to get past the guard and get a piece of the treasure.

"You little pirate," Kennet said, now in a quandary of his own. Maybe if the teeth came from the jaw of a Nazi, he could justify them as trophies of war. But they came from prisoners. Fisha's comrades. It was entirely disrespectful, almost sacrilegious to pilfer such things.

But was it? Really?

I'll be leaving here soon. Where will Fisha go? Where will he be sent? What will become of him? He has no family. He has no money. He owns nothing. How much is the gold in these teeth worth? A couple bucks? Couple hundred bucks? It'll be more than others have. It'll give him a head start others don't.

Let him keep it. Otherwise, the gold just ends up God knows where. In a government's treasury. Or the pocket of some corrupt punk. Or a collector with obscene taste.

War blows the rules to shit.

To the victor go the spoils.

Let him.

He crouched down and closed the boy's fingers over the three gold teeth, then shut that loaded fist up tight between his hands.

"Molodets," he said, looking in Fisha's eyes. "Good boy. You keep them. Keep them safe." He wished he knew the word for *secret.* He freed a hand and drew pinched fingers across his lips, pressed a palm over his mouth and shook his head firmly.

No tell. Silence. You can count on me.

Fisha's eyes narrowed above a tight smile. "Fuck Hitler."

"Fuck Hitler. And fuck Hildur. This is the golden proof that breaks the curse of the elven queen. This will show where you've been."

Commotion and chaos from within one of the barracks.

"Hangman's coming," O'Hara said.

Ingle closed his eyes and his forehead briefly touched Kennet's shoulder. "Pescado, I can't take this anymore."

But something was different about this chaos. Kennet turned his head toward it. He saw Fisha and his gang running toward the building. Not in glee or triumph. They were distressed. An upset anthill. Something was different. Something was wrong.

As Kennet walked toward the hive, a voice rose above the humming din.

"Captain Feesh."

Kennet's pace quickened.

"Captain Feesh!"

Kennet broke into a run. Fisha was calling to him from inside. Kennet fought through the throng, tossing boys and men aside, elbowing and shoving.

Anderson hung from a rafter.

This wasn't a mob, this was a rescue.

Two men were under Anderson's feet, pushing his weight up against the noose. Anderson kicked away their help, fighting to die.

Fisha stood on the tabletop, reaching up to the rope. Yelling in Russian, he tore at the noose with dirty, ragged fingers, trying to pull up against the force of the soldier's weight.

Kennet leapt onto the table, yanking his bowie knife from its holster at its hip. He frantically sawed against the rope until it broke. Anderson crashed to the floor, scattering small, stunted boys like bowling pins. Now O'Hara was there. And Ingle and Dizzy and Baby. A dozen other soldiers coming to the rescue.

Kennet sank to his knees on the tabletop, a hysterical Fisha cradled in his arms.

Korova, he remembered. The word for the buddy who was both friend and food was *korova.*

I think I'm going crazy.

"Thank you," he heard himself say, rocking the child. "You saved him. Molodets. Good boy. You're the best boy. The best that ever lived. Shh…" He held Fisha tight. "It's okay. I know. You'll never get over this, but you'll learn how to get next to it and bring it along…"

The day the battalion left Mauthausen, two Red Cross volunteers had to forcibly peel Fisha's fingers off Kennet's body.

"It's all right," Kennet said. "You're going to be all right. Here. Look…" He put his Zippo lighter into the boy's hand. "You keep it. Yours. Forever. Okay?"

Fisha hugged him again, crying, babbling things that required no translation.

Don't leave me. Take me with you. Let me belong to you.

"It's okay," Kennet said. "Fuck Hitler."

"Okay." Fisha squeezed harder. "Fuck Hitler."

"Molodets. Good boy."

As he removed the little arms from around his neck, he felt shittier than when he'd punched O'Hara over Jock's dead body.

"Okay," Fisha said between gulping sobs. "Okay, Captain Feesh."

Kennet took Fisha's face in his hands and kissed the knobby, scratched forehead. "You're a good boy. You're the best and bravest. I have to go now. All right? I have to. Goodbye, Fisha."

As Kennet stood up, the Russian boy grabbed his hand and slapped something into the palm, crunched the fingers closed and kissed them.

"Goodbye, Keneet Feeskar."

Then he ran away, darting through the shifting crowds.

Kennet opened his fist to find a gold tooth. He looked up quickly, but Fisha had disappeared.

PART FOUR:
The Fisherman
Back Home

"Prominent among Babylonian deities was Enki, called Deity of the Abyss, who had temples in Ur and other maritime cities. Sennacherib, when about to undertake a maritime expedition down the Tigris, offered to Enki a golden boat, a golden fish, and a golden coffin."

—FLETCHER S. BASSETT,
*Legends and Superstitions of the Sea and of Sailors
in All Lands and at All Times*

"We come back from war changed."

—JOSEPH BIANCO

AUGUST
1945

The Monastery

AX380CJ NEW YORK 35/34 4 1519
8-12-45
KENNET FISKARE=
32897544 AMMERU =

MINOR MISSING IN ACTION SINCE 30 JUL 1945
STOP WILL WRITE SOON
PAPS EE FISKARE

Stars and Stripes, 16 August 1945

CRUISER TORPEDOED, 883 DIE

PELELIU, Palan Is., Aug. 5 (Delayed) (ANS)—The 10,000-ton cruiser Indianapolis *was sunk in less than 15 minutes, presumably by a Japanese submarine, shortly after midnight July 30 and 883 crew members lost their lives in one of the Navy's worst disasters.*

The vessel went down in the Philippines Sea within 450 miles of Leyte. She was on the second leg of an unescorted highspeed run from San Francisco, during which she had delivered to Guam essential material for the first atomic bomb attack on Japan.

The fatal torpedo attack came without a second's warning.

Two explosions flashed out of her bow and she quivered while flames streaked through her passageways and slim hull.

In less than a quarter of an hour the Indianapolis *plunged head first below the surface of the sea. Nobody outside the oil-covered circle of men and debris in the water knew her fate until a Peleliu search plane led the way to the rescue of the 315 men who managed to survive five days afloat.*

Survivors believe two underwater torpedoes smashed into the starboard side near the bow of the 14-year-old cruiser, setting off one of the eight-inch magazines. The Navy gave no details, however.

Traditional flagship of the U.S. Fifth Fleet, the Indianapolis *was the tenth cruiser and 435th U.S. Naval vessel lost during the war.*

YA16GTG
BRA699 FT230=FM FTDRUM NY=
KENNET FISKARE=
32897544 AMMERU =

WONDERFUL NEWS MINOR SURVIVED INDIA-
NAPOLIS SINKING STOP 5 DAYS ADRIFT STOP
BURNS AND EXHAUSTION FROM OVEREXPO-
SURE PROGNOSIS GOOD STOP WRITE HIM CARE
US BASE HOSPITAL #18 NAVY #926 FPO SAN FRAN-
CISCO CALIF STOP
PAPS EE FISKARE

"Christ, O'Hara, I might start believing in happy endings again," Kennet said.

O'Hara scanned the newspaper article and gave a low whistle. "Lucky bastard. Five days in open water. Eight hundred and eighty-three dead. Jesus H." He slapped Kennet's back. "Glad it was good news for once."

They started walking back to the barracks. Troops serving in the Army of Occupation were housed at a monastery in Kremsmunster, forty miles south of Linz. German troops had been staying there, along with a number of Czechoslovakian collaborators and government officials. So esteemed were these "quislings," the Nazis had made an entire freight train available to ship their possessions to the monastery for hiding. When American forces took the Germans and Czechs into custody, they discovered the main hallway of the abbey—twenty feet wide and nearly the length of a football field—was crammed with personal wealth. Dishes, silverware, rugs, paintings, furniture, lamps, books, and all manner of knick-knacks. Stacks of boxes piled deep and high, leaving just a five-foot corridor to traverse.

An outdoor enclosure on the grounds was filled with the Czechs' automobiles, and there wasn't an American GI who hadn't taken one for a spin. Many soldiers did a little discreet "shopping" in the long hallway, appropriating gifts to send home to family, or keep tucked in a pocket or pack as a trophy.

So far, Kennet had taken nothing except a handsome cigarette lighter, to replace the Zippo he'd given to Fisha. O'Hara had never been a man attached to possessions, yet he seemed fascinated by the fabulous hoard. Kennet often saw him poking around the boxes and piles, taking a strange, obsessive inventory.

"Find anything you like?" Kennet asked.

"I don't like any of it," O'Hara said.

Kennet let it go. For all their time spent together, he still didn't know O'Hara any better, didn't know bushwa about the guy's family, or if he even had one. Or if he had one and they'd cast him out for being queer, and no way Kennet was going to bring *that* up. A mere mention of Jock and O'Hara's demeanor slammed shut like a door. Kennet respected his friend's pain and did not knock or ring the bell.

He went into the room he shared with O'Hara, Ingle and Maslov. Its proper term was probably "cell," but a private room, even shared, was such a novelty in a barracks setting, the fellows referred to them as suites.

Kennet sat on his bed, re-reading the article from *Stars and Stripes*. Trying to imagine five days afloat in open, shark-infested water. How badly burned was Minor? Where on his body? Jesus, the thought of burned flesh exposed to pounding sunshine and salt water, for five goddamn days…

"Minor mine, you are so fine," Kennet said. He reached for his pack and went digging for paper and pencil. He had to write his brother immediately. Or should he go back to HQ and telegram the hospital? He'd do both. Letter first.

"Hey, Fish," O'Hara called. He shuffled backward into the room, pulling a large box by one flap. "Look what I found."

He dragged the box close to Kennet's bed. Kennet reached to open the other flaps. The box was full of silverware, some of it brand new, still in its original packing. O'Hara took out an unwrapped fork and displayed it with the biggest smile Kennet had even seen him wear. "Look at that."

The fork's handle was shaped like a fish. The tail was situated at the top, the body curving out and in, to fit comfortably in the eater's hand and provide resting places for index finger and thumb. At the bottom of the utensil, the fish's mouth opened to hold a perfect scallop shell, tiny balls like pearls set delicately between each ridge.

"Look at that," O'Hara said again. "Silver fit for a family of fishermen. Waiting right here for you."

The fork felt beautiful in Kennet's hand. Sleek and expensive. Luxury and security radiated through the soft, strong silver. He wanted to hold it forever. Still clutching it, his free hand rifled in the box, finding more forks—dinner and luncheon, plus knives, spoons of all sizes, serving pieces, all with that gorgeous fish handle and the scallop shell at their ends.

"Take it," O'Hara said.

Kennet glanced at this enigmatic man who attached himself to nothing. A man who never opened a pack of gum or M&Ms without offering it around. O'Hara would give you the gloves off his hands or the socks off his feet. When he was down to the last cigarette in the pack, he shook it out for you and went without. It wasn't performance generosity. He wasn't looking to earn points or admiration or respect or even a payback. O'Hara simply didn't need or want anything. Now a possessive gleam lit up his dark blue eyes. He didn't covet the silver outright—he wanted it for Kennet. But he *wanted.*

"The spoils of war," O'Hara said. "What, is it supposed to end up on some German family's table? If you don't take it, some major or general will bring it home to his wife. Fuck that. You take it. You earned it. Bring it home to your father. Did you ever get a wedding gift for him and Marta?"

"No."

"This is it, then. Or hell, gift it to your bride on your wedding day and then hand it down to your kids."

"How would I get it home?"

"Mail it. You just need signed permission from an officer to send a package, but he doesn't have to know what's in it. If he asks, say it's a gift for your father."

Kennet's greedy fingers stroked the body of the fish, traced the open mouth holding the seashell.

I want it.

I deserve it.

Gift it to my bride on my wedding day. Bequeath it to my children. The spoils of war.

"You sort that out," O'Hara said. "I'll find something you can wrap it up in."

Kennet emptied the box and divided the cutlery into a dozen dinner-sized place settings, six lunch-sized, plus the serving pieces.

"Hey, look at these," O'Hara said. He brought in a smaller box filled with silver napkin rings, each festooned with the same scallop shell as the cutlery. "The Fiskares will have the best-set table on Thanksgiving."

He was absurdly enthusiastic about the project. With some found cloth remnants, he and Kennet wrapped up each individual setting as if swaddling a baby. One section of the crowded hall had entire bolts of cloth, as if the stockroom of a textile factory had been raided. The men used a blue-on-blue damask to wrap all the littler packages together. Then they wrapped the bundle in a piece of thick, sturdy tweed.

"You'll need a box to pack it in," O'Hara said. "Wood, not cardboard, so it doesn't fall apart on the trip. I bet someone in town could find one. Or make one."

Kennet was apprehensive when it came time to ask Jorgy to approve the shipment of the small but heavy crate. The captain, looking a decade older, smiled as he signed the chit. "Do a little shopping upstairs, Fish?"

"Just a little, sir," Kennet said. "Bought something nice for my father."

"Well, whatever it is, it'll have a better home than where it came from."

Kennet wrote a quick letter to Emil and Marta, saying a box would be arriving in a month or so. *Christmas present. Put it in the attic. No peeking.*

Angels of the River

During the nights, the contemplative majesty of Kremsmunster Abbey was frequently disturbed by men crying out in their dreams. On any given night in any given cell, a GI was talking in his sleep, confessing and reliving his most despicable or most terrifying moments. Thrashing in the sheets, yelling for dead buddies to take cover this time, trying to change the inevitable outcome. They worked themselves up until they rolled off the narrow cots, often striking out at the friends who tried to help them wake up.

"There ought to be a purple heart for a slug from a buddy," Ingle said, gingerly touching a bruised, swollen lip.

"I *said* I was sorry," Maslov mumbled.

Kennet found it odd that only one man in his cell fought nightmares at a time. It was never two guys experiencing bad dreams simultaneously. Never all four of them at once. As if a schedule had been agreed upon beforehand.

Some men experienced a variety of night terrors. Others were plagued by one horrific dream over and over. Kennet experienced the latter. In his recurring dream, he was being chased down by a mob of angry Belgian civilians and German mothers, all demanding retribution for the deaths at Chenogne. Over time, the pursuing riot expanded to include inmates from Mauthausen, even more terrifying in their near-death state of desperate starvation.

All of them coming after Kennet. After his survival. After his gold. After his soul.

He still hadn't regained his sense of smell or taste. That and the lack of sleep had him walking around in a robotic daze of mild confusion. The war was over, yet he remained constantly braced for something to happen, bewildered that nothing was happening.

Holy shit, I'm bored, he thought. And if that wasn't the definition of a royal SNAFU, someone would have to tell him what was.

The day a letter arrived for him, postmarked from St. Petersburg, Florida, with *A. V. Davis-Reyes* in the return address, he stared at it dispassionately, for a good minute, before making the connection and realizing it was from Astrid. Even then, he went on staring as if the letter were the electric bill. But finally, he opened it.

Dear Kennet,

I hope this letter finds you whole and well and unharmed. I expect it will find you changed. I know it will find you grieving. Marta wrote to tell me about Nalle. My heart hurts. I'm so sorry. That dear boy. I'll always remember him best from the day we made a fika on Tre-O. He was seventeen then? He seemed so much older. All of you Fiskare boys were mature, but Nalle especially so. He had a serenity. As if he viewed the world from some higher place.

I remember when he sat on the rocks, singing "South American Way" as he gutted and fileted the fish we caught, while a cloud of gulls wheeled around him. Like he was being visited by angels of the river.

I remember when he dove over the side of the boat to fetch my hat when the wind blew it off. Holding the brim in his teeth as he climbed back aboard, grinning around the straw, as if it were a cutlass. Another pirate of the river.

I remember when he told me to move into the shade because my shoulders were getting red. And I remember how he'd always look up and around, making sure your sisters were safe. Making sure others were content. The host of the river.

I remember the night we toasted marshmallows, and how Nalle looked standing beneath the portrait of your grandfather, the Old Bear and the Teddy Bear. How serious he was, reciting your funny masterpiece of alliteration. The poet of the river.

He was a real prince.

I feel badly for not writing sooner. I despaired it would only hurt you. I didn't know what to do. I didn't know how you felt. I still don't. I feel like I don't know anything anymore.

But I remember Nalle. I've never forgotten anything of that summer with all of you dear Fiskares.

It isn't easy to find joy right now, but whatever I can find, I share with you in your time of sadness.

Yours,

Astrid

"Bad news?" O'Hara said.

Kennet wasn't sure why he handed the letter over. Maybe he needed O'Hara's help figuring out how to feel about it. Perhaps some small part of Kennet was thawing out, enough to want to share something personal.

Or, most likely, he missed Hook badly and just fucking wanted him back. Hook, who'd always been around to read his life and letters.

"Who's Astrid?" O'Hara asked.

"Long story short, she's the love of my life," Kennet said. "Or at least, my old life."

"I figured."

"You did?"

O'Hara shrugged and read the letter again, cigarette clamped in a corner of his mouth, his dark brows pulled into a single straight line. "This is sweet."

"What do you mean?"

"I wouldn't know your brother if I passed him on the street, but these little memories she writes make me see him. Make me feel like I know him."

"She pinned down all his best qualities."

"It's obvious you two have a romantic history and she still cares about you, but—"

"You think so?"

"Oh, don't be dumb. It's *there* even if she doesn't explicitly talk about it. And that's the point: she keeps it about you and your grief. She just tries to comfort. It's sweet." He folded the paper and handed it back. "Hell, I'd love a letter like that."

O'Hara never got mail, but he didn't talk about who *might've* been writing him any more than he disclosed what kind of nightmares made him cry out at night.

Still, nobody had written to extend condolences about Jock. And that seemed a fucking shame.

"Dear O'Hara," Kennet said. "I remember when the Quartermasters set up hot showers at Massul, and Jock started singing 'O Sole Mio.' I mean *singing*, like goddamn Caruso. He knocked us all on our asses."

"Yeah, he had some set of pipes."

"I remember his response to anyone farting was, 'Captain Who?'"

O'Hara gave a tight little laugh. Kennet sensed he was inching too close to O'Hara's pain, and he wrapped it up.

"These moments I will fold into memory. I remain, sir, your humble, obedient servant, K. E. Fiskare."

O'Hara got up and left the cell, shaking his head. "You're way too easy to like, Fish."

Kennet folded the letter up without reading it again, and slipped it into the pages of his old notebook.

He forgot about it for a week, and then another letter came.

Dear Kennet,

Never a dull moment around here. Emil slipped on the dock yesterday and broke his ankle. It's his bad leg to begin with and a nasty fracture. He's fine, just annoyed with himself and offended by the inconvenience. Crutches for six weeks, and Doc Tomlinson feels Emil will probably need a cane afterward. But we'll cross that bridge, etc.

Of more concern is Minor coming home. He's been very ill as a result of the ordeal at sea. "Exhaustion" sounds like something you can fix with rest, and you'd think the cure for "overexposure" is shelter. It's more complicated than that. His body has been weakened and fatigued in every conceivable way, and it's constantly fighting to keep the burned parts of his arm from being infected. Navy doctors say it will be a long recovery and he'll need a lot of care. Fortunately, there's an excellent burn specialist at Strong Hospital in Rochester. If he can't manage the trip alone, Little will go with him. Or Major. We'll sort it. But with Nalle gone, you still abroad, your father laid up and me... Well, no use being coy about it: I'm expecting a baby next year and not too proud to admit I could use another pair of able hands.

So all this to say that I've written Astrid and asked her to come. Hear me out before you give me a row. I know from even an inch away, it looks like meddling and matchmaking and making amends that aren't mine to make. But it goes deeper than that. She's still my cousin and we've remained close all these years. Now that she's widowed, she's divorced herself, as it were, from her mother. She wants a new start for herself and her son. And if I may be frank, your father's a real pill right now and I know a guest in the house will put a civil tongue back in his head.

Kennet blinked. Read the paragraph again. Then once more.

Now that she's widowed…a new start for herself and her son.

Zé was dead?

Astrid had a son?

He read it again. The words bounced off his brain. He understood, but he wasn't *getting* it.

So for now, the plan is Astrid will be coming to stay. At the same time, I'm not ignorant or insensitive to your feelings. You're still my darling lump of a friend, so when you get home, if the arrangements need to be changed, we'll sort it without fuss. I promise.

So that's that. I will put Astrid and Xandro in the attic, it makes the most sense. I don't want to disturb Little and I really have no idea how you and Minor feel about continuing to share a room. I could move one of you into the spare room, but I'll wait to hear if you want to stay together or if it's time you had separate digs.

What is taking them so long to demob you? Ridiculous. Miss you terribly. Can't wait to see your fat head, fat-head.

Love,

Marta

Kennet went digging in his pack for his diary, and withdrew the picture of Astrid from its pages. He propped it on the little standing locker next to his bed. Elbows on knees, fingers twined, he stared her down. He had the room to himself, so he could talk out loud and reply in his head.

"So you're widowed," he said to the photograph.

Brilliant observation. If you glance out the window, you'll also see the sky is blue.

"And you have a son," he said. "Zé's son."

Did you think they were married in name only? You dumb punk.

"You didn't mention either thing in your letter."

Because, you ignoramus, she was keeping it about you and your grief. It's called kindness.

The windows in this wing of the abbey were high and narrow. Only blue sky showed through the diamond panes. Like the blue sky that shone through the windows of Marianne's bedroom on Tre-O.

"Did Zé fall asleep, too? Leave the incriminating evidence behind?"

You cannot be this dumb and be related to Minor. Since it's clear now you can divorce a family member, he's going to serve you papers when you get home.

"And now you're coming back to Clayton."

Aren't you happy?

He felt cold and tight within his skin, but nothing stirred in his heart that he could label.

Don't you get it? It's your golden time. It could come back. This is your second chance. This is what you wanted.

"But I didn't think I'd get it," he whispered. "I put her behind me. Over my shoulder. I wrote to a fantasy, not to *her*. It was just my little, dumb story in my big, fat head again."

You must be crazy. This is what you would've killed for four years ago.

"But I'm not him anymore. I kill for other things."

He sighed. It was no use pretending you felt one way when you felt another. But what use were you when you felt nothing at all?

Well, you managed to cook up a little stupid jealousy just now, he reminded himself. *A few weeks ago, you did a great job feeling greedy about the fish silverware. You're not that far gone. Pull your shit together and look at the facts. Are you mad at Marta? Did she step on your little toes?*

He wasn't. She didn't.

Did you catch that she's having a baby?

He had. And holy shit. The idea of a half-sibling twenty-six years his junior was slightly absurd, but kind of neat. He'd get O'Hara to have another poke around in the hallway, see if they could find a silver cup or rattle, maybe some baby spoons.

See, there's some genuine enthusiasm. You can feel things just fine. So how do you feel about seeing Astrid again? You'll be the one stepping off the train in Clayton and she'll be on the platform waiting.

"With her son."

We're back to this?

Kennet raked hands across his scalp. Regulation haircuts were de rigueur again and he didn't have much to yank on. He tried instead to scratch some clarity into his thick skull.

"Christ, Hook, I wish you were here…"

He heard echoing laughter and footsteps coming down the corridor. He needed to stop muttering. He leaned to stuff the notebook back in his pack and slide it under the bed. He sat back up, then slowly turned his head over his shoulder to find Astrid's gaze.

"What do you think?" he asked under his breath. "Have I built you up into another kind of dream?"

Her smile retained its ebullient joy but her silver gaze seemed flat and troubled.

I don't know, she said. *I don't know you anymore.*

Kennet put light fingertips on Marta's letter. He looked at Astrid, thought a moment, then went to find O'Hara.

I Had a Lover

"So," O'Hara said, after reading the letter.

"So?"

"Astrid's coming back."

"So it seems."

"And she's not married anymore."

"I can read."

"So what are you going to do?"

"I don't know."

"Bullshit on white toast."

"I don't," Kennet said. "Once upon a time, the me of yesterday thought the me of tomorrow, if he survived the war, would catch the next boat to Rio and show up at her house. Tell her husband, 'We can do this the easy way, or do it the hard way, but we're doing this.' Now tomorrow is today, but I'm not who I was and I don't know who I am. I can't smell. I can't taste. I sleepwalk around with a sheet of dirty glass between me and the world and I'm not sure I want to break it."

"You talk to someone about that?" O'Hara said. "The not smelling and tasting thing, I mean."

"Yeah, I told one of the docs. He didn't seem surprised or alarmed. Said everyone deals with shock and stress differently. It might be my body's way of keeping sensory stimulation to a minimum. Put that way, I guess it's better than being blind. I've been temporarily blind and it sucked."

"What, you didn't enjoy me coaching you at mealtimes?"

"Boyd, if you keep making jokes, I'm gonna start to think you have a personality."

O'Hara looked away with his bashful smile. He and Kennet sat on a high, stone balustrade of the abbey, enjoying both a smoke and the sunset over Kremsmunster.

"Who are you, anyway?" Kennet said. "I know you come from Cheyenne but that's all I know. You got a family?"

"I got one but they don't got me."

"So will you go back to Wyoming? When we're discharged?"

"I don't think so."

"Got a plan?"

"A few sketches and a list or two."

"You're a guarded man, my friend."

"Tell me something I don't know."

"I miss Hook," Kennet said. "You already know it, but… I never had a friend like him in my life. Growing up, my best friend was Minor. Sure, I had a circle of pals but Minor was my main buddy. I didn't need anyone else. Then I met Hook. At first it was just funny, because of our names. Next thing I knew, we were partners. Where he went, I followed, and vice versa. Zipping our half-tents and half-sleeping bags together to make one shelter. We had eight thousand little rituals getting us through every day. I'd write a diary entry, then show it to him. Everything I hid behind the mask of the soldier, Hook knew it all. Every word. It became *our* record. Our story. I still wake up and forget he's gone. I'm so sad and angry and torn up about him dying, it makes me want to break things. Or kill more people."

The unexpected lament left him tired. He slumped and gave a low chuckle. "But I gather you already knew that."

O'Hara was stiller than a painting. Finally, he drew in a long breath. "I miss Jock so much, it makes me wish I'd gotten killed. I never forget he's gone. I wish I could. Sometimes I wish I never met him at all."

His voice hovered anxiously above the words, which hung like knives in the air, ready to slash down judgment.

Kennet tried to make his own voice easy and open. "Did you two ever talk about what you might do after the war?"

"Do?"

"Together." Kennet reached with the foot of his outstretched leg and pushed O'Hara's side. "I'm not blind, I'm not dumb and I'm not an asshole."

O'Hara drew another tremendous breath, exhaling ferociously. His body caving, crumpling, almost pouring out of the shell of his clothes.

"It's all right," Kennet said softly. "I've known a long time and I don't care. You're my buddy and you won't lose my respect or my friendship. I promise."

O'Hara's entire face squeezed tight. "Jesus Christ, Fish."

Kennet put two cigarettes in his mouth, lit them and passed one over.

O'Hara took an enormous drag and blew a plume of smoke that nearly reached the border of France. "It was the one good thing about the war," he said hoarsely. "The only good thing about this entire fucking business."

"Tell me."

"I could get through every day of fighting and killing, terror, cold, hunger and misery, because every night, I lay down next to

Chris. Or I dug a hole and sat shivering in it with him. It didn't matter how or where. In the mud, the rain or the snow. In barns or basements, stables or attics. Whether I fell asleep out of sheer exhaustion or lay awake out of sheer terror, I was next to Chris. I had something getting me through the nights that nobody else in the platoon did. Everyone had their buddy, but I had a lover. We hid it during the day. Same way we hid it for all our lives. But at night... We had each other. We held onto each other. All night. And nobody knew." He glanced at Kennet. "But I guess you did."

"Hook figured it out first. I'm a little slower. Not sure who else knew, but..."

"Hook didn't care?"

"No. Neither did I. I guess that's the one good thing I got out of the war—figuring out what matters and what doesn't. What's worth fighting about and what isn't."

In the twilight he could see O'Hara was trembling, hands clenched in fists.

"You all right?"

"I've never had a conversation like this in my life," O'Hara said tightly. "I thought about it. Imagined it, I mean. Thinking it would be a wonderful thing. Now that it's happening, I feel like I'm gonna puke."

"Because you don't trust it."

"No." Half a chuckle through his nose. "No offense, Fish."

"Can't say I blame you. I'll shut up now."

Kennet took his own deep breath and rubbed his tongue on the roof of his mouth. He chewed on the bland, empty air, weighed the options and the consequences.

"Hey, Boyd?"

"I thought you were shutting up."

"How would you feel about coming home with me?"

O'Hara looked at him fast and sharp.

"Just while you figure out what you're going to do," Kennet said. "Come home with me, meet my family. Stay a while at our hotel. We're easy people. If you don't want company, you can be alone. Go off fishing. Or go explore Canada. You ever been?"

"No."

"It's right across the river. You can putter all day between two countries." His foot bumped O'Hara's hip again. "At the very least, I'd love if you sat for one dinner at my family's table, set with that fish-handled silver."

"I... I don't know. Thank you, I mean. But..."

"Think about it, all right? It'll be a place to rest and look over your sketches and lists. I can teach you how to pilot a boat if you want."

Now O'Hara smiled. "I lived in Carson City, Nevada for a year. I kept a boat on Lake Tahoe."

"Then you won't need me for anything." Kennet said. "I won't needle you anymore. Just know the offer's open."

They sank into their easy, comfortable silence. Kennet rubbed circles on his chest, where a strange feeling was thrumming. Not the tight, chilly waves of anxiety but a low little rumble, like the purr of a kitten.

He felt...good.

"Heading back," he said, getting up. "Gonna write some letters."

"Tell Astrid I said hello."

"Hardee har har."

Dear Asta,

It's good to hear from you.

Kennet's train of thought didn't get far out of the station. He brooded a long time over the first sentence, bopping the pencil against the pad, until Ingle told him to knock it off

It's good to hear from you, he thought. *So what now? Do we pick up where we left off? Do you even want to?*

He sighed. *Do I?*

"Sigh one more time, Pescado," Ingle mumbled. "Go ahead. I dare you."

"What crawled up your ass and died?"

"Your attitude."

"And you loved it."

Ingle threw a pillow at his head. "One of these days, your smart mouth is gonna get your pretty face in trouble."

Kennet threw it back. "Promise?"

Quit fucking around and just write what you feel.

> *Marta told me about your husband. I'm sorry. And she told me you're coming to Clayton with your boy. That's good. I'd like to be able to talk to you again.*
>
> *It's hard to explain how I've been feeling lately. Or not feeling, rather.*
>
> *A lot's changed. I've changed.*

He squeezed his eyes, imagining the long bridges of his life. All the ravines of tough growing-up he'd deliberately crossed because he was born with gold in his veins and raised to be decent, honorable and kind. The span he'd fled across from Chenogne crossed an entirely different kind of chasm. After Mauthausen, he'd turned a flame thrower on the structure and settled down in the scentless, tasteless, emotionless land of his post-war self.

Is this really where you want to be?

He thought about the pontoon bridge the Army Corps of Engineers had built across the Rhine. It defied credulity that a jeep could safely cross those bobbing spans, let alone a tank. And yet the armored leviathans crossed without a hitch, followed by all the other vehicles and the men, into the desolated, destroyed city of Darmstadt.

They will rebuild. All those cities in Europe in rubble and ruin… The people will build them back. It's happening already.

Desenrascanco, darling. Slap a solution together with whatever's at hand.

No corps of engineers is coming to do it for you.

He lifted his head and looked back over his shoulder. Seeing not a monastic cell occupied by Army-issue cots, but an abyss. And Astrid on the other side. Looking back at him.

I don't know anything anymore, she said. *You have to tell me or I'll never know. You look so troubled, darling. Come here and tell me. It doesn't have to be everything.*

Just something.

One thing.

Making an effort not to sigh, Kennet picked up his pencil again. He began to write. Slowly at first. One careful word at a time. Soon, his hand could barely keep up with the things he wanted to say.

Thank you for writing those memories about Nalle. It made him feel alive. Or rather, eternal? They were something I could fold up and carry along.

To survive war, you have to look for those little moments. Wait for the war to stop and catch its breath and then you can see something funny, or wonderful, or pure, before the madness starts again. I wrote a lot about such moments these past months, folding them into the pages of a little notebook.

Truth be told, I don't know if I'll ever feel like unfolding and revisiting them. But they're there.

I remember.

Don't feel badly about not writing me. You're writing now. All we have is now, and now backward is won. (That's just something silly I thought up.)

I'm all right. Mostly. Nalle's gone and I lost a real good buddy back in April. I saw a lot of friends get killed but this guy was… close. It's hard. I'm changed and I've seen things and done things I never thought I would. The world feels the same when it should feel completely different.

Saudade. The longing for things lost.

I'm longing for my old self, but I think he's long gone.

See, I did things…and I'm afraid my golden time won't come again.

I'm sorry this is such a jumble of thoughts. I feel like I'm emerging from a long nightmare and it's hard to think in a straight line sometimes. I don't trust the peace. I think all us boys are still braced for the madness to begin again. Bewildered that it doesn't. Our brains don't know what to do.

I don't know what to do now either. I'll just be glad to go home. I don't know anything anymore, either, but I do know I'll be happy to see you again.

I'm all right and I'm glad you wrote. We'll see each other soon. We'll talk and we'll see.

Write again. If I'm demobbed ahead of your letter, well, it will just have to follow me home. But write again and tell me about your boy. If you have any new, funny, untranslatable words, tell me those too.

Always,
Nyck

SEPTEMBER
1945

Trade Secrets

AX380CJ NEW YORK 35/34 4 1519
KENNET FISKARE=
32897544 AMMERU =

WHAT IN THE NAME OF HILDURS BRASSIERE IS
IN THIS BOX STOP TOOK ME AND 2 FRIENDS TO
LIFT UPSTAIRS STOP PAPS ASKS IS IT GOLD STOP
SAY YES
YR BROTHER EE FISKARE JR

Kennet and O'Hara arrived in New York City on the *Queen Mary*. The gangplanks lowered, and nearly fifteen thousand troops swarmed Manhattan. After the long slog from Austria to France and the crowded, noisy, raucous and sleepless voyage, Kennet wanted nothing more than to escape the throng and hop the next train to Clayton. But O'Hara coolly took in the teeming streets, the skyscrapers, the ebullient energy and crackling current of action, and said he'd be sticking around. He wanted to visit Jock's family in Brooklyn and return one or two personal effects he'd been holding since Cham. Tell them about the day Jock died. Give what comfort he could. And then explore the city a little.

"Be careful," Kennet said.

A wry grin lifted a corner of O'Hara's mouth. "Jesus, Fish, I'm not going to knock on the Fragiacomos' door, introduce myself and say their son was a hell of a foxhole fuck."

Kennet laughed. "Wouldn't that be something."

"A fellow can dream."

"Anyway, I meant be careful in the city."

"I know what you meant. I'm a big boy and not much scares me anymore."

"Sorry."

O'Hara shrugged. "It's not like I do this on purpose. If there was a button to press to make me like girls, I'd smash that thing with my fist yesterday."

Kennet hesitated. "Have you ever been with a girl?"

"Yeah."

"And?"

"It was nice. That's all. Just nice." He exhaled. "But I get with guys and it's like that bomb they dropped on the Japs. So…"

"Right."

"Anyway." O'Hara gestured vaguely around. "Wherever your train departs from, I'll see you off?"

Kennet hadn't a clue what station, but a puzzled-looking GI on a city street wasn't puzzled for long these days. Strangers swooped in to offer directions and advice, getting into heated debates with other strangers about the best route to Grand Central Terminal, the nearest YMCA, the not-to-be-missed attractions or the best goddamn cheesecake you had in your life. And by the way, could they buy Kennet or O'Hara a hot dog? A pretzel? A Coca-Cola? Something to thank them for their service? It was good to have them home. God bless.

The open generosity of the Manhattan populace was unabashed and shameless. It practically crawled inside your clothes. Kennet shied from the ebullience, but oddly, O'Hara seemed to enjoy it. As he and Kennet made their way uptown, his expression was expansive, his stride confident. He looked like he owned the place.

He's on the prowl, Kennet realized.

At Grand Central, Kennet bought his ticket while O'Hara found a bit of free space. The terminal was a continuation of the mob scene at the piers. The crush of humanity made Kennet dizzy, so he kept his gaze on one short wall of the enormous, vaulted space, where a war bond mural was installed. A tableau of tanks, battleships and aircraft beneath the arch of the ceiling. A giant soldier and sailor standing at parade rest, rifle butt against a foot. A center panel depicted a woman with a baby in her arms, standing high above a gaggle of adorable tykes. The caption read, "That these may face a future unafraid."

These, Kennet thought. *Only these? Or Jewish children, too? What about communist children? Slavs? Poles? Roma? What if one of those youngsters is queer? Do they get a future unafraid?*

Good lord, if one more person bumped into him, he was going to blow his stack.

He made his way to the corner where O'Hara was guarding their packs. O'Hara sat on the stack, elbows on knees, his eyes volleying back and forth. Jaw thoughtfully working around a hunk of gum.

He looked grand and casual, Kennet thought, folding the moment into memory.

"You need me, you phone the Fisher Hotel in Clayton," he said aloud.

"I *know.* You've told me about eight times now."

"I just don't want to lose any more buddies."

Without taking his eyes off the crowd, O'Hara elbowed Kennet's side. "I'm not averse to being worried about. To be honest, it feels nice."

"Nice like being with a girl, nice? Or nice like an atom bomb?"

Now O'Hara gave him a long, slow look. "Keep flirting with me and you'll find out."

His unwavering gaze was thrilling, no, *enthralling* in its intensity. A cobra soothing its prey before the killing strike. Centered in a handsome devil's crosshairs, Kennet was both repelled and fascinated by this strange fire. The hair stood at attention on his forearms as he thought, *And whose little boy are you?*

Then all at once, the flame snuffed out, the devil vanished and only Boyd O'Hara was left, blushing a little as he looked away. "Sorry," he muttered. "I was just wondering if I had any chops left."

Kennet gave an involuntary shiver. "I don't know much about chops, but you definitely have something left."

"Too bad you're not my type."

"What's your ty— Actually, never mind."

"Never you mind."

Kennet lit a cigarette. "Are you looking for love?"

"Love?"

"Yeah."

"To be perfectly honest, at the moment I am only looking to get laid."

"That's fair. And say you get your fill of those moments. Then what?"

O'Hara's eyes narrowed just the tiniest bit.

"This isn't meant to be the third degree," Kennet said quickly. "I'm just trying to participate nicely in a conversation."

O'Hara looked away, shaking his head a little. "You're way too easy to like, Fish."

"So what are you looking for in the long run?"

"I don't know, bud. I don't know what kind of run I get. I don't know what's possible for guys like me, I don't know what's allowed.

I don't know if this damn war changed the rules, or if the general public prefers I were locked up in a shithole like Mauthausen with a pink triangle on my chest. I don't know what I can get away with. I don't know what I deserve. All I know right now is that I'd like contact with something that isn't my hand, and I know a little about where to find it. I'd tell you more, but these are carefully-guarded trade secrets."

"Then I will mind my own worried business."

A few beats of silence.

"I will say," O'Hara said slowly. "I like the idea of coming home at the end of a long working day. To a little place I own. And meeting up with someone who's also at the end of a long working day, and going home to the same place. And we have a drink. We have dinner. We talk about our days. We play cards while listening to the radio. Maybe our song comes on and we dance. We walk the dog, put the milk bottles out and go to bed. Then go to sleep an hour later. All those things people do in their little someplaces with the someones they love. It's just my someone is a man. And I don't know jack shit about where to find that kind of contact, but a fellow can dream."

Home

When Kennet stepped off the train at Clayton and a long-legged creature hurled into his arms like a bazooka shell, it took a few shocked seconds to realize it was Little. This baby brother, always full of surprises, had beaten everyone to the punch and now he was wound like a vine around Kennet, who nearly staggered from the unexpected reception.

"Hey," he said, laughing as he regained balance. "Hey, kiddo. Look at you."

Little didn't speak, didn't cry, didn't make a noise. He just *clung*.

"Hey, bud," Kennet said over and over, a hand at the back of Little's head. "How's my buddy? Goddamn, you got so tall on me. You grew a *yard*. Who gave you permission?"

Over Little's shoulder he could see Marta and Emil wiping their eyes, Trudy and Kirsten chomping at the bit, and standing apart, Major and Johnny. Older and greyer, but all smiles.

But no Minor.

Little let go and Trudy and Kirsten, with those impossibly thick braids of hair, were in Kennet's hungry arms, kissing his face, squeezing him and crying on his collar.

"Cripes, I got lipstick on your uniform," Kirsten said.

Lipstick?

Trudy kissed him, then wound arms around his neck again. Kennet picked her up in a twirling hug, but it wasn't as easy as it used to be. And something about his little sister was suspiciously different...

Holy shit, she has boobs.

The girls finally let go, and Emil handed his cane to Marta and opened his arms.

"Gullgosse." His broad palms rubbed and patted Kennet's back. "Min älskade gullgosse."

"So good," Kennet said against his neck. "So good to be home."

Marta flung plump arms around him and kissed him silly. Major, in one of his rare, speechless moments, held Kennet tight a long time. Johnny offered a slightly bashful handshake, which Kennet batted aside for another hug instead.

"So good to be home," he said, right and left, to everyone and anyone. And then...

There. Standing in the shadows, his sailor hat cocked back on his blond head.

Oh, Minor mine, you are so fine.

"Jesus Christ," Minor said as Kennet lunged at him, grabbing, trying to be careful but unable to keep his embrace on a leash. Minor's hat fell off as a little grunt of pure relief squeezed out of his chest.

"You made it," he said.

"I made it."

Minor couldn't hug with both arms. The wounded one stayed at his side while the other clamped around his brother's shoulders like a trap.

"You son of a bitch," he said thickly.

"Don't talk about Ma that way." Kennet hugged and hugged, lifting Minor clear off his feet. It was easier than picking up Trudy.

Minor was alarmingly thin. Whittled down to ropy muscle and bone. His complexion a little sallow and the blue of his eyes diminished. But it was Minor and he was alive.

"Missed you," Kennet whispered. "Missed you bad."

"I'm so glad you're home."

"Me too."

"So much to tell you."

Kennet nodded, mute and helpless. "I know," he managed. "I know."

Minor pushed away a little, swiping his face on his shoulder. "Let's see what you did to yourself..." His finger traced the constellation of tiny shrapnel scars on the side of Kennet's face, lingering on the one near his eye with a low whistle. "Whoa, that was close. Another quarter-inch and you wouldn't have been able to see my ugly mug."

Minor mine, right now you are the most beautiful thing I've ever seen.

"You make me bawl and I will fucking kill you," Minor said. "Now before you ask, Astrid's back at the house. Her boy was waking up from a nap and she didn't want to take away from the family scene."

"All right."

"Are you?"

"I don't fucking know."

"Me neither. Goddamn, I thought you'd never get here."

They hugged again. The rest of the family drifted closer and Kennet held out an arm, gathering them in, kissing heads, squeezing hands.

Home.

In the abstract, at least. It took him nearly an hour to get to the house. Every other step, he was stopped by friends and greeted by neighbors. The crush wasn't as intense as the New York City scene, but it had the same dizzying effect. It quickly became too much, and it was Little who came to the rescue, deftly and graciously extricating the soldier from all the welcome and well-wishing. Yet as soon as he and Kennet were alone, walking through the hotel gardens toward the Fiskare home, all that smooth, practiced patter disappeared. Little only looked up at him, tongue-tied and over-whelmed. A half-dozen times he looked like he was going to say something, but didn't.

Kennet slung an arm around the boy's shoulders. "Kind of feels like you want to say everything, huh?"

"Yeah."

"We got lots of time now. All right? I'm not going anywhere. Not for a long, long while. Maybe not ever."

Little stopped walking and hugged him again.

"You took care of everything so good," Kennet whispered. "I knew you would. Ma knew it too. I didn't worry about a thing at home, knowing you were here. So proud of you."

Little sniffed and shook off the moment, managed a wobbly smile. "Astrid's here."

"I know."

"No, I mean..." Little pointed toward the house. "She's there."

Kennet looked up at the small back porch.

Behind the railing, Astrid walked slowly back and forth, holding her son. She was barefoot in shorts and a blouse. Her hair was longer—not bobbed around her ears but caught in a clip at the back of her neck, loose strands falling around her face. Her arms gently chugged the little boy.

Little touched Kennet's back and walked away.

Kennet reached the bottom of the stairs. He put a hand on the banister but went no further.

He and Astrid stared a long time at each other.

Funny I envisioned a bridge, he thought. *All this time, it's been a flight of stairs.*

He put a foot on a tread. "Hallå."

Astrid rolled her lips in and blinked rapidly. She drew a breath and her mouth formed "Hej," but no sound came out.

Kennet came up another step.

The child in Astrid's arms lifted his head. He had a short crop of dark blond hair, tousled in places, damp along his brow and ears. A little fist knuckled one eye, then he lay his cheek on Astrid's shoulder again, looking at Kennet. His eyes were deep brown. A little bleary with sleep, but the gaze was direct and unblinking.

And whose little boy are you?

Kennet took one more step. Then another. He was in front of her now, just as he'd been that day in 1941. Time stretched out in places, stuck together in others. A book opened. A page turned.

He put out his hand. Astrid regarded it a bewildered moment, then she shifted the baby and freed an arm. Her palm slid against Kennet's and they shook. She laughed, or maybe she was crying. He bent and carefully put his cheek against hers.

He held still.

"I'm Kennet Fiskare," he said.

She trembled, and the place where their skin met grew warm and wet.

"I know," she whispered.

"Does our returning hero wish grand dinner," Marta asked that night, "or nursery supper?"

"Nursery supper," Kennet said, which meant they'd eat simple food in the kitchen. It was a squash, because Major and Johnny came, and the baby's high chair was pulled up by Astrid's seat. But they all turned a little sideways and managed. Kennet sat by Emil, who kept patting him all through the meal. Astrid leaned over Kennet's shoulder and spooned roasted potatoes onto his plate. She'd changed into a navy blue dress with white polka dots. Her hair shone smooth and straight, and her red lipstick smile was warm on Kennet's face.

He watched the tines of his fork poke through the golden crust of a potato wedge, letting out three miniscule tendrils of steam. He could see the sheen of butter, the little crystals of salt and flecks of pepper. He put it in his mouth.

"Good?" Marta said. "I know they're your favorite."

"Perfect," he said, lying around the tasteless mass in his teeth. "Just what I wanted."

Across the table, Minor ate slowly and methodically, still learning how to manage fork and knife with his non-dominant hand. Johnny MacIntyre sat next to him, and Minor occasionally glanced in his direction as if dropping a cue. Johnny, who'd gone through life with a crippled arm, offered casual and discreet assistance with cutting meat or buttering bread, never breaking conversation or drawing attention. Keeping Minor's pride intact.

Family isn't blood. It's who you bleed for.

Emil patted Kennet's back. Trudy put her head on his shoulder. Little peppered him with questions, wanting anecdotes and first-hand accounts of battles. Kennet tried, but he was rapidly running out of gas.

"Hey, that's enough for tonight, buddy," Minor said to Little. "Kennet's getting tired. Remember when I came home and couldn't talk for long?"

"Sorry," Little mumbled, his ears red.

"He's just excited to have his brother back," Emil said.

Kennet smiled. "For sure. We got lots of time, Little."

Astrid excused herself and took Xandro upstairs for a bath. When she was gone, the light in the kitchen seemed dimmer. The hum of family chatter swelled and diminished in Kennet's ears. He stared through his people, feeling neither bad nor good. He was just here.

He was home.

"You poor thing," Marta said, taking his plate. "Go put your head down. Sleep the day away tomorrow. We won't bother you."

Kennet trudged upstairs, intent on bed, but the door to the attic stairs was tantalizingly ajar. He moved closer and heard splashing sounds. Astrid's voice echoing off tile.

He went up. Time doubled back on itself and for a moment he was twelve, bringing towels to Marta. A boy who'd gone nowhere and done nothing yet. No pins for him in the big world map on the wall.

"Asta?" he called, emerging into the sloping space of the attic.

"In here."

She sat on the bathroom floor, a forearm resting on the tub's ledge, the other hand drawing circles in the soapy water. Xandro sat in a nest of rolled-up towels, chubby and slick, batting and splashing with both palms.

"Hello, you," Astrid said.

"Hello, you." Kennet slid his back down the wall and sat.

"Good to be home?"

"It's all kinds of things."

"Mm." She put her cheek on her outstretched arm.

"How are you holding up?"

"Better now that I'm here."

"Marta said you divorced your mother, so to speak."

"I did. It was long overdue. It had never gotten any better between us."

"Not even after you married Zé?"

"No. Nor when Xandro was born. If a grandchild didn't make her happy, then what would? When Zé was killed, we found out his will included an annuity for Mother. Enough to keep her in comfort the rest of her life. And I left."

"And here you are."

Her gaze bore down on him. "Are you all right with it? Tell the truth."

"The truth is I don't know how I am." He ran fingers through his hair, weary and empty. "The truth is it's so goddamn lovely to see you. Honest. Right now I'm only looking at you. I don't know where to go from there."

"Then let's just sit and look."

So they did, for a long quiet time. Kennet inched slowly closer to the tub, until he had an arm on the ledge, too, making the herd of small rubber toys gallop around Xandro's fat legs.

"He's a nice little fellow," he said.

"Yes, he's good-natured. A sweet companion for anyone who wants to take him. Lucky for me." She twirled a bit of Xandro's hair around her finger, pulling it up into a comical cowlick.

"Did Zé ever meet him?"

"No."

"I'm sorry."

She smiled but it didn't reach her eyes. They went quiet again, sitting and looking.

"Did you know," Astrid finally said, "That the Brazilian Expeditionary Force and the 10th Mountain fought together in Italy?"

"They did? Wait, did I know that?" He squeezed his eyes, trying to conjure up memories of Nalle's letters. Surely a mention of any Brazilian troops would've caught his attention and stayed in his mind. "No. I don't think Nalle ever mentioned it."

She nodded. "This might sound strange, but I like to think Zé and Nalle met. I'm not sure why, but it comforts me. I daydreamed a whole scenario. After the battle, Brazilian and American troops mingling and trying to get to know each other." She looked at him sheepishly. "I know, I'm describing it like a cocktail party and I'm sure the aftermath of a battle was nothing of the kind."

"I like your version better," Kennet said. "Go on. What happens next?"

"Just one of those wonderful, serendipitous encounters. Zé spoke English so he'd be acting as interpreter for a group of fellows. Questions. Answers. One thing leads to another, and an American mentions upstate New York and the Thousand Islands. 'Oh,' Zé says. 'My wife's cousin lives in that area.'

"'Really?' the American says. 'Whereabouts?'

"'I think it's called Clayton?'

"'That's my hometown. What's the cousin's name?'"

Astrid's hand made circles in the air. "And so on. The pieces romantically fall into place. The violins swell. Two ends of a circle join. If it were any American but Nalle, the next line would be, 'Ah-hah, so *you're* the one who caused all the trouble. *You're* to blame for my brother's broken heart. Unmannered cur. I demand satisfaction.' Then a slap across Zé's face with a glove. Or is that too dramatic?"

Kennet laughed. "It's a little Napoleonic. But I get the idea. Let's step outside and settle this like men."

"But not Nalle."

"No. He'd be a gentleman about it. He'd even think it was wonderful. Because if war does anything, it makes you appreciate little, wonderful, serendipitous moments."

"So you wrote in your last letter."

A damp strand of hair had come loose from behind her ear. Kennet reached and tucked it back.

"Did you ever get your boat?" he asked softly.

She looked at him as if he were witless. "Of course."

"Do you still have it? Not that I thought you'd be wearing it, but I wondered if you kept it."

Now Astrid's incredulous gaze grew bright and damp at the edges. "Oh you big, dumb, darling fat-head," she whispered.

Her hand went to the neckline of her dress. She grasped a bit of fabric between her fingers and turned it out. Pinned inside the bodice was the golden *Hildur*. Like a piece of shrapnel Astrid wore on the inside.

The moment shimmered between them like a single soap bubble.

Kennet sat and looked at it.

And looked.

And just sat and looked some more.

Minor Mine

During Astrid's magical visit in 1941, Kennet had stayed on the sidelines, waiting for everyone else to have their turn with the alluring guest. Frustrated and impatient, catching Astrid's eye and thinking, *I need to talk to you.*

Now Kennet was the one in constant demand and Astrid who kept herself apart. She had a child to raise, a house to keep, two invalids to tend and, with the three youngsters back in school, a hotel to run. She rushed about, here, there and everywhere, but her gaze on Kennet was serene and gentle. Sometimes, when their eyes caught and held, she touched the neckline of her blouse or dress, reminding him what was pinned there.

When we have the time, the gesture said, *we'll talk. No rush. I'm just sitting and looking.*

September was typically the month the Thousand Islands shut down for the season. Not this year. The weather was gorgeous, gas rationing was over and everyone was keeping their boats on the river. The hotel marina was clogged with craft and Emil's workshop inundated with orders. Not only engine tune-ups and routine repairs, but inquiries about restoring old boats. The lucrative offers backlogged after Emil broke his ankle, and the old man was increasingly anxious about losing the business.

Thus Kennet had barely unpacked before he took over the marina. Minor worked with him. He moved slow and tired easily, but insisted the mechanical tinkering was good therapy for his wounded arm. When Kennet suggested they go out on the river during their lunch hour, Minor shook his head. "The noontime sun on my scars hurts like hell." He hesitated, then went on, "I find intense sun makes everything hurt like hell. Know what I mean?"

Kennet did. He had his own painful run-ins with banal things. Celebratory fireworks bloomed over the St. Lawrence nearly every night. Such pyrotechnic displays had never been anything but pure pleasure for him. But now…

"I'm not enjoying this," he said to Minor, as they stood looking up at the smoky, colorful skies. Both had their arms crossed tight, jumping in their shoes at every boom and blast, no matter how anticipated.

"Me neither," Minor said. "Let's beat it."

So the two river rats took the car and drove inland, finding quiet places away from the crowds and noise.

And they talked.

"The last letter you wrote me," Minor said. "When you talked about Mauthausen… It kind of broke me up. Because I saw something like it, but it was on our side. An ugly little secret nobody talks about."

"What's that?"

"Every so often the military goes on a witch hunt, rounding up known or suspected homosexuals. They lock them up in psychiatric wards. Or queer stockades. That's what they call them. Queer stockade, queer brig or pink cell. The ones stateside are bad enough. Overseas, in Australia and the southwest Pacific, these places are fucking concentration camps. Crappy conditions, physical abuse, mental abuse. Interrogations where they don't stop until they get a name out of you. If they can't get names, they'll settle for sordid details. Christ, the way they dig into the history of your pants, you'd think they were whacking off under the table. Buddy of mine who was in one of these places, he ran out of damns to give and told his interrogators in no uncertain terms how much cock he sucked." Minor gave a wry chuckle. "Kind of made me wish I'd been there."

"This was a buddy?" Kennet said slowly.

Minor drew a slow breath. "Maybe something closer to a Johnny MacIntyre."

"You were together."

"Yeah." Minor closed his eyes. "Telling you, Nyck, if you asked me which is worse: having two ships torpedoed out from under you, or having to spend your days terrified that you and your lover will be found out? I'd say I'd need to think about it. Hard. Because being sunk at sea is no fika, but on the *Lex,* when I was as close to being in love as I'd ever come, I'd never been so afraid in my life."

"What happened to him? Your guy? Where was he locked up?"

"Some shithole in New Caledonia. Interrogated from hell to Hildur, but he didn't name me..." Minor's voice frayed at the edges, and he shied away when Kennet reached a hand toward him. "Don't. Just let me finish."

"What was his name?"

"Daniel. It was the only name he gave them. He wouldn't finger anyone else. Wouldn't name me. He got a blue discharge. You know what that means, right?"

"It means you're out to the point you were never in. No pension. No benefits. No nothing."

"Right. Doesn't matter how hard you worked, how much you gave, how brave you were in combat. Dan was one of best pilots out there. The Navy was fucking lucky to have him, but sorry, old boy, queers are undesirable. That sounds a whole fucking lot like Hitler, if you ask me."

"Paps said war blows all the rules to shit. I guess not all the rules."

"They shipped Dan back to San Francisco and dumped him onto the street. Where was he supposed to go? He'd been on his own since he was a teenager. His family didn't want him. All his friends were at sea. I was laid up in Honolulu, still seeing double. I wired him some money and told him to get on a train to New York. I told him to come *here*. I wrote Paps and Marta, said a buddy needed a base. Just someplace safe to stay so he could figure out what to do. They were going to let him stay on Tre-O. Pay him to care-take and do some boat repairs." He rubbed his face wearily. "That was the plan. Danny had another one. Cops found him dead in a hotel room in the Castro. I got to San Fran just in time to iden-tify him in the morgue."

"Suicide?"

Minor nodded into his palms, then picked up his face and looked at Kennet. "What do you do with that? Huh? In the great filing cabinet of life, what folder does that go into? Who the hell is this country to say out one side of its mouth that it's a champion for freedom, and out the other side tell its best men they're undesir-able? To the point that none of their service is allowed on the record anymore. The time served, the battles fought, the risks taken, the injuries suffered…all of it expunged. Your pension revoked. Were you thinking about college? Not anymore. Thought you'd get a loan and build a house or a business? Think again. No blacks, Jews or cocksuckers need apply. You are not *desired*."

"Jesus, Mine, I'm sorry."

"Yeah. Well. That's my story of the Johnny MacIntyre that almost was. Never again. When I went back to sea, I just kept my fucking self to myself. If people knew or even suspected I was gay, I'd give them nothing to work with. But still…I had my buddies. Old ones from the *Lex*. New ones from *Indy*. God, the bond that happens between fellows in combat. You think you know, but you don't know until you're in it."

"It's like the military's greatest strength and its greatest vulnerability," Kennet said. "You can't get through it alone, so you pair your existence and survival with another guy's. You eat, sleep, shit, shower and suffer together. You see each other bleed, cry, scream, break down, choke up, fuck up or save the day. Then you watch him die. And you're just supposed to disengage from him and move on. Find someone else. Then watch him die, too."

Minor was nodding, the muscles in his jaw tight. His hand ran lightly up and down the opposite arm, with its shiny, puckered scar tissue.

"Does it hurt bad?" Kennet asked.

"Parts of it hurt. Some of it's completely numb. The nerves are shot." He gave Kennet a sideways smile. "But enough about me, let's talk about my arm."

"I don't know how you survived those five days."

"I don't know, either. We hit the water and cripes, it was just a slab of fuel oil. We were *basted* in it, head to toe, and we could barely find each other in the dark. And we laughed. In the beginning we were miserable but optimistic. We'd be found in a couple hours. Then the sun came up and we waited. And waited. And waited…"

The sun was merciless and the sailors had no way to escape the strong rays that tortured their oil-slicked skin, screwed up their eyes and parched their tongues. Hour after hour they watched the sun overhead, cursing her, unable to wait until she went down and they got some relief. As she slipped over the horizon, the air turned cool. Then it got cold. And colder. Until the men's bodies were numb and their teeth were chattering and they watched the night skies, begging that solar bitch to rise again.

Minor and eight other mates were clutching a cargo net, kept afloat by Styrofoam buoys. As ship debris floated by, they scanned and scrabbled through it frantically, looking for any scrap of food. If found, they put it in the center of the net with the intent of sharing evenly if the situation continued. Surely it couldn't go on much longer. No doubt they'd be rescued soon.

It went on. More sailors began to die. The seriously wounded first. Then the ones who succumbed to dehydration.

"You can't even imagine," Minor said. "It's like eating salt. Handfuls of salt all day long. I have nightmares about it. Dreams where I sit down to dinner and my plate has nothing but a mound of salt on it. I eat it and I wake up heaving. I can't shake the taste off. It's in my mouth all the time…"

The sailors' lips split and cracked. Their tongues swelled until they could barely speak. The sun dried their wet faces, leaving salt caked in their eyes and making their skin peel off in flakes. Crazed with thirst, men drank the ocean water and became first delirious, then psychotic. Knives were drawn, fights broke out over the scrounged rations and more bodies sank to the bottom of the ocean. Sometimes fights broke out over things that didn't exist— one sailor insisted a ship was on the horizon bringing food, water and girls, while his buddy insisted the *Indy* was down below, perfectly fine and intact and serving chow right *now*. They killed each other over hallucinations.

"And we just watched," Minor said. "About the third day, nobody had anything for anyone but themselves. A buddy slipped under the surface and you thought, *Well, there he goes. So long.* But the worst was the sharks. They came on the first day and never let up."

"Jesus Christ."

"You'd watch them swimming around below you. Waiting. Planning. A buddy would get separated from his group, you'd hear a scream, he'd go under and a few seconds later, his empty life jacket would pop up. The rest of us would paddle over together and retrieve it because… Well, he didn't need it anymore and it was useful.

"There was another cargo net like ours, maybe fifteen men clinging to it. One minute just floating along and the next, at least ten sharks were attacking. The water was a bloody froth. Hands and limbs getting tossed up and about. It happened so quick. Those men barely let out a yell. Some of them didn't even put up a fight. And the rest of us watching…we just watched. These were buddies. Good buddies. And we just stared like it was no big deal. *Well, there they go. So long.*

"By the last day, our little oil slick was more dead than living. Finally a search plane flew over, and we all started yelling and splashing and slapping the water with whatever object we could find. All that weird apathy disappeared in a flash. We were screaming and crying our lungs out. If the plane missed us, I swore I was calling it a day. Lovely party, but it's time to go. I was done.

"The rescuers started dropping survival craft. The dead were like fucking shoals, you had to barrel your way through corpses to get to the craft. More fights as everyone tried to pile on at once. Then the surface ships showed up and things moved faster. I helped this one sub-lieutenant get in a lifeboat. He'd been hanging next to me the whole ordeal. We kind of pooled our mental resources but by the end, he was in real bad shape, I honestly didn't think he'd make it. But he did and when he saw me later in the hospital, he said…"

Minor had been dry-eyed and stoic through the account, but now his face spasmed in some un-nameable emotion. Kennet was reminded of how Minor used to look when he was in Major's dog-house. Like the world was iodine and Minor an open wound.

"Tell me," Kennet said softly. "What did he say?"

"Something like, 'Thanks for getting me through. You're a decent guy for a faggot.'"

If the sub-lieutenant were standing by and Kennet had a machine gun, he would've mowed him down without his pulse rising.

"The fucking look on his face," Minor said. "You could tell he'd been crafting that line a long time. Couldn't wait to try it out."

"If I ever meet that son of a bitch, he's dead."

"He pounded my back with a big guffaw. 'Ahh, I'm just kidding. Really. I'm kidding. Thanks for being there. Want to suck my cock? Heyyyyy, just kidding…'"

"Did you punch him out?"

"I'm wild enough to entertain the idea of slugging a commis-sioned officer but not dumb enough to do it. I'd be in a psych ward or a pink cell fast enough to make my head spin, then tossed into the street with a blue discharge. Fuck that."

"Fuck all of it." Kennet got up and moved over to Minor's unwounded side. He put arms around his brother and pulled him in tight. "And fuck Sub-Lieutenant Cocksucker, too. Bet he's never been laid in his pathetic life. He's got such bad taste, not even the sharks want him."

Minor laughed, and then he was crying.

Kennet held his head, rubbing a cheek on Minor's crown. "It's all right. A blind man can see who the better man is. He's shit and you're gold."

"I feel so bad."

"I know."

"I either feel so fucking bad or I don't fucking feel anything. I can't find the place in the middle. I can't find me."

"I know. I know exactly what you feel, Mine. I know. It's the same with me."

"I can't tell you how happy I am you're home. The fucking relief. I've been waiting. I needed you back so much and… This is stupid."

"Tell me."

"It finally hit me Nalle was dead. I mean, it really sunk in. And then I got crazy scared that something outrageous would happen to keep you from coming home. My overactive imagination was having a field day with the possibilities. An attack from some last pocket of resistance. Some unexploded ordnance going off while you were on duty. A building collapse. A freak accident on the street. A repeat of the nineteen eighteen influenza. Your ship going down. Your train derailing. Telling you, Nyck—you need a ridiculous way to die? I'm your man. I bumped you off nine ways to Sunday."

Kennet squeezed him harder. "Tell your imagination to piss off because I'm home."

"I had no one else to talk to. No one who would understand."

"You do now. I'm home. You go ahead and talk your face off. Wake me up in the middle of the night if you need to tell me something. Tell me everything." He gave Minor a little shake. "I'll beat you up if you don't."

"No you won't."

"You're right. I'll just borrow your best duds and not return them."

Minor lifted his head. "Now them's fighting words. Keep your fingers out of my drawers."

"Bet you say that to all the boys."

"Oh, you little fucker," Minor said wearily, laying his head back down on Kennet's shoulder. "God, I missed your stupid face…"

Our Greatest Weapon

In all his twenty-six years, Kennet had never appropriated one of the rooms at the Fisher Hotel for his own use. But upon his return home, he lifted a key and let himself into #21, putting out the *Do Not Disturb* sign.

He filled the tub to the brim and lowered himself in. He had no bath junk, no beauty masks or cucumber slices. But he had a champagne bucket of beers, the radio on the closed lid of the commode, two packs of smokes and a stack of *Saturday Evening Post*s. He lolled in the tub until he was pickled, raising the occasional toast to Schmitt and Nichols, wondering how their widows were coping. He mused sadly that a certain crapper in Brooklyn would never again feel the touch of Jock's butt.

He worried about O'Hara, praying the visit to the Fragiacomos had gone well.

Nice to meet you. My condolences. Your son was a hell of a foxhole fuck…

Sighing, he reached out and flushed the toilet. Just because he could.

He spent another day suffering delayed bewilderment about the family's new living arrangements. When he exhausted being confused, he got pissy about it. Nobody in this goddamn house was sleeping where they were supposed to. Kennet had his bedroom to himself because Minor was in the old guest room. That was weird enough, but Marta, for crying out loud, was in his parents' bedroom, which was nuts. What had happened to his world? It was one thing to congratulate your father on his engagement before you left for war. Quite another to come home ten months later and find Marta sleeping in the master bedroom—as was her right, but *still*, no woman but Ingrid had ever been in that bed.

Of course Kennet knew all these changes had come to pass and hadn't forgotten them… He'd just never lived with them. Likewise, he knew Nalle was dead, but it took walking into the bedroom Nalle once shared with Little for the idea to sink a little further into Kennet's heart. He stood a long time before the maps pinned on the wall. Just as Marta had said, Little had been a meticulous field general. Lines of blue tacks connected by string traced Kennet's path across Belgium, Luxembourg, Germany and Austria. A similar green line traced Nalle's route up the boot of Italy, stopping abruptly in the Apennines, at Monte Castello. Minor's tours were tracked with red tacks in the Pacific.

Kennet sat on Nalle's pristine bed. Untouched since the fall of 1944, when they'd last been together. Nalle's old, battered teddy bear propped against the pillows. The picture of Ingrid on his bureau. All the personal possessions exactly where they'd been left. Lovingly dusted and undisturbed.

Kennet picked up another framed photograph: all four Fiskare sons on the dock, each holding up their catch. Nalle's handwritten caption: *Fiskare boys, 1938.* He'd written each of their names beneath their bare feet. *Kennet. Erik. Björn. Emil.*

How like Nalle to use their real, proper names. He was the best of the catch.

And the one that got away.

Looking at the photograph, Kennet got a little teary, but it felt gratuitous. Almost phony. Nothing made sense in this house. Nalle was gone but his things seemed to be waiting for him. Marta was kissing Emil good morning and Emil was rubbing Marta's belly, his eyes soft with happiness. Some strange, deep-voiced man was constantly walking around the place and then rudely revealing himself to be Little. Trudy had *boobs* and holy mackerel, Kirsten Lund was rather lovely.

What the hell happened while I was gone?

How *dare* things change like this?

It frustrated him that he had trouble speaking. More specifically, he struggled with civilized speech. Participating nicely in polite conversation. He'd grown appallingly used to cursing every other word, in between drags on a cigarette. Plus he was a little horrified to discover just how much he smoked. How much he relied on the habit to pass the time, occupy his hands and soothe his nerves. His fingers fidgeted constantly, looking for a cigarette, a trigger or a task.

He weirdly missed someone telling him what to do every minute of every day, and wasn't that a kick in the head? The kind of thing he and Hook could have a big laugh over, but Hook was gone. His talisman was in Kennet's pocket now, the fish hook solemnly transferred from Emil's pocket. At night, Kennet put it on his bedside table, next to two flattened copper pennies—one from the day Astrid arrived in Clayton, the other from the day she left.

But now she was back.

Aren't you happy? It's what you would have killed for, years ago.

On nights he couldn't sleep, Kennet stood at the foot of the attic steps and contemplated going up. Slipping into Astrid's room. Into her bed. Into her body.

But he couldn't, because her baby was sleeping up there with her.

And I've killed too many mothers' children already.

When Xandro was passed around the family, Kennet's hands itched for a turn. The little boy was bursting with life and health and innocence and unadulterated joy. Kennet wanted to clasp it into his arms, bounce it, ruffle it, cuddle it and believe in the future.

But then he'd remember Chenogne and the things he did.

He remembered Fisha and the things people got away with.

And when Xandro was passed to him, he quickly found a reason to pass him on.

This isn't for you.

Everything was different.

I'm different.

I'm forever changed.

He smoked too much during the day, and at night he thought about Fisha choosing a friend to be his flogger. Of other inmates choosing a friend to jump from the edge.

Of pushing tables under beams.

Of chocolate and cigarettes and dead people's smiles filled with gold teeth.

Asleep, he dreamed of running through smoke, a mob of vengeful victims pursuing him.

Hangman's coming.

Asleep or awake, his eyes couldn't unsee. His ears couldn't unhear. He couldn't smell or taste and his mouth couldn't speak nice things.

When Astrid touched her neckline, he wondered if she merely pitied him. That her gentle patience was how she'd treat a demented grandparent or slightly backward child.

Did I go insane and not realize it?

"Hello, Kennet," said Elizabeth Vetter, shaking hands across the counter of her five-and-dime store. "I'm so glad to see you."

"Nice to see you, too, Mrs. Vetter."

Her grip tightened sternly. "Call me Peach."

He laughed. "I forgot you gave me permission."

Now her other hand dropped on top of their grip and she peered at him. "You look like you haven't gotten a lick of sleep in a month."

"Let's say the sleep hasn't been sound." A weird embarrassment made Kennet's neck burn, as if he'd screwed up a ridiculously simple task.

"Bad dreams?" Peach's eyes were soft and full of concern. No longer a tired widow, but the best, sweetest, kindest first grade teacher a boy could wish for. Before Kennet knew what was happening, he blurted out the recurring nightmare of being chased down by a mob. He skipped the detail of the Belgian civilians, and spared Peach the horrors of Mauthausen, but he conveyed the abject terror within the dream and how it woke him up in a yelling sweat.

"They're chasing you," Peach said. "And they're armed? With what?"

"Guns?" he said, his tone lifting because all at once he wasn't exactly sure. Everyone in the incensed crowd was brandishing something as they pursued him. He assumed it was some kind of weapon.

"And they're angry with you?"

"I think so." It was odd to dig into a dream like this. Your awake self couldn't quite put a finger on what had seemed so immediate and real to your sleeping self.

"Goodness," Peach said. "As if you haven't been through enough."

"The war is over. But in my head, it doesn't quite feel over."

She nodded, her face far away and thoughtful. "My dad used to tell me something about bad dreams. Especially the ones where something was coming after me. Wolves or bears or monsters. He told me I should stop running, turn around and say, 'Well, what do you *want*, for crying out loud?'"

Kennet laughed. "Turn the tables."

"Exactly." She shrugged. "I have to say it worked. I'd either wake up, or the dream would go somewhere else."

"Well, maybe I'll give your dad's technique a try."

"You have nothing to lose. But enough of me gabbling away. What can I get for you, dear?"

Two nights later, no more than three, the dream came for him. This time it wasn't just the Chenogne residents or the inmates of Mauthausen. Jock was in the mob. And the headless Marco Malinda. Pete von Asselt. Marty, Schmitt and Nichols. And leading them all: Hook.

Perhaps it was the sight of his bosom buddy in the vanguard that made dream-Kennet turn tail and run twice as fast. He ran over snowy fields and through barnyards filled with dead horses, where his boots crunched over the shells of broken goose eggs. The mob pursued him into a forest where he dodged through trees and followed tank-treads across a bobbing pontoon bridge. They chased him over a golden river and through a desolated city of rubble and ruin, and finally up one hundred and eighty-six granite steps to a sheer drop-off littered with dire choices: pick a friend to push, or jump.

Kennet was here alone. He had no friend to pick or push.

He had to jump.

Then he remembered. Like a fragment of a dream within a dream, the alternative came back to him: *stop running, turn around and ask.*

He was already halted. Shaking inside his clothes, he turned to face the crowd.

Well, he cried out loud. *What the hell do you* want, *for crying out loud?*

The horde had been surging up the steps like a wave. They ceased as if hitting an invisible wall.

And he saw what they'd been brandishing all this time.

Not guns. Not sticks or staves or torches or knives.

They held notebooks.

Cardboard, canvas, leather, in all colors, brand new or worn to smoothness. Pages tight and trim, or loose and falling out.

They waved the books over their heads and roared at Kennet to behold them.

I got nobody, Hook yelled. *You were all I had and you* quit *on me.*

The crowd resumed the march up the steps but slower now. As they proffered millions of little diaries and journals, they spoke in one mighty voice:

These are our weapons. Our stories are all we have. And you. We have you. Our greatest weapon. The storyteller.

You were there.

Prove you were there.

Tell this fish tale out of school.

"Nyck."

Hook threw his notebook at Kennet's feet, backing him to the edge. *Tell it. That's your choice, Fish. Pick me and tell it, or jump.*

"Nyck."

Tell it or jump…

"Nyck, darling, wake up."

With a strangled cry, Kennet threw himself over the edge and out of the dream so violently, so thoroughly, he tumbled off the mattress, right against the legs of someone standing next to his bed. Like two bowling pins, they sprawled in a pile at Emil's feet, who was in pajamas and robe, leaning on his cane. Minor crouched nearby and in the doorway crowded Marta, Little, Trudy and Kirsten.

"Oh my God," Kennet said hoarsely, sucking air around his hammering heart. It was Astrid he'd knocked over, and he clutched at her.

"Easy, easy," Minor said. "You're okay."

"Oh my God, I'm sorry," Kennet said.

"It's all right," Astrid said, sitting up and taking his head. "You're awake. Look at me. You're awake now. You're home."

"I'm sorry," Kennet said, scrambling back on his butt to lean against the side of the bed. "It was a dream."

"Just a bad dream," Astrid said, her voice pitched low and smooth. "You're home. You're safe."

"You're awake," Minor said. "It's done. All over."

Kennet pulled his hands through his hair and then managed a wobbly smile for his family. "Holy mackerel, I woke up the house."

"I think you woke up the unborn," Marta said, a hand on her belly.

"He's all right," Minor said. "Bad dream. Happens to me all the time."

"Let's everyone go back to bed," Emil said. He planted his cane close to Kennet's foot and held a hand down. "Up you go now."

Rattled and embarrassed, Kennet didn't need the help, but he humored the old man and got up. He apologized again for the rude awakening, then went in the bathroom to splash cold water on his head and down two glasses. And shake hard enough to make his teeth chatter.

A tentative knock on the bathroom door. "You all right?" Little called.

"I'm fine, bud, just taking a leak. Go back to sleep."

Kennet flushed the toilet for appearances' sake, then stared at his pale reflection a long time, waiting for the last bedroom door to close and the house to go quiet.

We have you. Our greatest weapon. The storyteller.

Pale grey light was seeping through his bedroom windows. Dawn was coming, but Kennet was wide awake. He went digging in a drawer for the notebook he'd carried across Europe. The entries stopped after April 2, 1945, at Oberhof, where Hook was killed. Hook, who was leading the mob this time. Throwing his life story at Kennet's feet.

You're all I had and you quit on me.

Kennet sat down at his desk and switched on the lamp.

"All right, Richie," he said under his breath. "Jesus H, you do know how to get a fucking point across."

He found a pencil, turned to the page he left off, and began to write.

Bra Som Guld

Kennet wrote all morning, prying everything he could from the folds of memory and throwing it down on the page. It was fragmented and out of order, the narrative jumping ahead and doubling back like an untrained puppy. But he paid no mind, just writing what came to him as it came. Already he envisioned a brand-new notebook, into he which he would transcribe this haphazard mess.

It rained fish hooks and hammer handles, which lent him more time. He brought a sandwich and a beer up to his room and kept scribbling until his fingers were howling and he was yawning big enough to make his jaw crack. He toppled back into bed and slept the afternoon away, waking up groggy and disoriented. The house seemed oddly empty, which lent a dream-like unease to his walk downstairs, looking for his people. He felt tense and hyper-alert, as if about to head into battle.

He found Emil in the kitchen, reading the paper over coffee and the remains of last night's dessert.

"Here you are," he said. "Rip van Winkle."

"Is it today?" Kennet said, a little stupidly.

"Still. Get a cup and sit down."

Kennet sat and yawned against the back of a fist. He was absurdly divided: his body anxious and ready to fight or flee, his mind full of quicksand. "Sorry about last night," he said. "Or this morning, rather."

"Bushwa. I did my share of yelling when I got home from France. Scared your mother right out of the bed. I bet I woke you up in her belly, too."

"Were you married yet?"

"Watch your mouth." Emil smiled as he passed a plate with a slice of cake. "Tell you something. I loved my father, but he was a man of his time and he never once sat down with me and your Uncle Nyck and asked, 'How are you feeling, boys?' To him, the war was over and that was that. But you and I know it's not so simple. So it seems a good time to ask…how are you feeling?" He raised a single finger. "And if you lie and say 'fine,' you'll get your fish warm." The finger pointed toward the pantry. "Don't think I can't still do it."

Kennet's laugh was a little shrill. His heart kicked up as he rubbed his sandy eyes. "Not fine," he said. "And I appreciate you asking. Because a lot of the ways I've been feeling make me think I'm going a little crazy."

Emil's big hand fell on Kennet's forearm and squeezed. "The world went crazy, gullgosse. You, your brothers and all the boys like you were innocent bystanders."

"I changed," Kennet said, his voice raising, taking an edge of panic.

"Of course."

"I'm so different from who I used to be. I don't even know who…or what…"

"Take a breath now." The weight of Emil's hand grew heavier, pressing Kennet into place. "Remember who you're talking to, hm? It's not easy being back at home. You don't just turn off war like a light switch. You don't see your brother die, see your best buddies killed, see God knows what else, then shrug and say, 'Oh well, c'est la guerre.' Whoever does is lying. Or they're truly crazy."

Kennet cut off a bit of cake with the side of his fork and put it in his mouth. It was Marta's walnut cake—light spongy vanilla with a vein of chopped nuts and spices running through it. Kennet's favorite. But it tasted like nothing, as did the cup of coffee.

He felt like turning the table over. All the joy had been sucked out of the world. All his favorite foods reduced to tasteless bread and water.

Was he being punished?

"Paps, can I ask you something?"

"Of course."

"You don't have to answer."

"Go ahead. Everything's all right."

"Did anything happen in the war that still haunts you?"

Emil closed his eyes and his head tilted. "Did something happen *to* me? Or did I *do* something that haunts me?"

"Did you do something?" Kennet whispered. He was trembling in his clothes.

Emil's eyes were still closed. He took two careful breaths before speaking again. "Kennet, I think you'll understand when I say I only want to tell this story once. Förstår du?"

"Yes."

"At the battle of Soissons, I shot and killed my best friend."

"By accident?"

"No."

The whole kitchen had gone rigid, aghast. Kennet was ice cold, teeth clattering in his jaw. "What happened? What was his name?"

Emil opened his eyes now. "Matthew Lauren. But for some reason, we all called him Birdie. I can't even remember why. He had both legs and an arm blown off. He knew he was a goner. I knew it. Everyone knew it. We thought it would be a matter of seconds. No longer than minutes. But he died slow. And the sound of him suffering was giving our position away. He was screaming to die. It's branded on my memory. I remember every word. He said if I loved him, I'd put him down. For the sake of the other boys, I'd send him home. He begged me. He cursed me. He dared me. And everyone was looking at me, because he was my buddy. My best pal. My mate. I knew what to do. We all knew what to do. We'd been shown."

"Oh Christ," Kennet whispered.

"So the others moved away from us. Not far, but they made some distance and turned their backs. So later they could say they'd seen nothing. I sat down in the mud, pulled Birdie back against my chest, put an arm around him. I cried in a way I didn't know was possible. Birdie turned his face up into my neck and told *me* it was all right. He thanked me. Over and over. He thanked me as I put my service revolver against his temple. I told him how much I loved him, how he'd be home in just a minute and nothing would ever hurt him again. And I shot him in the head."

"Paps…"

"I wrote his family, saying he died instantly from his wounds. He knew no pain. He didn't suffer. I lied to the people who loved him. The others in my unit and your mother are the only ones who know the truth. When Doc Tomlinson said Ingrid was having twins, we decided if one was a girl, we'd name her Lauren, but call her Birdie." Emil turned a hand over in the air. "One was a girl. And she flew away from us."

"Oh my God." Kennet's mouth moved around the words without making a sound.

"I thought it was punishment. I felt like I didn't even deserve to grieve about it. You wonder why there's no stone in the cemetery? Why not even Minor knows what her name was supposed to be? It's because of me. It was all my doing. I don't think your mother ever forgave me. And I know for a fact Major never forgave me."

Kennet sank his head into his hands, pulling back his hair until his scalp protested.

"I still have nightmares about it," Emil said. "Not as much as I used to, but they come around occasionally. Most of the time, I've made peace with it. Gotten right with it. Other times I think there must be a table waiting for me in hell. Or I think about whoever fired the gun that killed Nalle, and I feel Matthew Lauren was guiding his aim."

Emil exhaled heavily, then hitched his chair up a little and slid his hand onto the back of Kennet's neck. "All of which means you can tell me what you did, or not tell me. But I forgive you either way."

"I killed three kids."

Emil didn't move a muscle. "Tell me more. All of it, Nyck. Tell me exactly what happened."

It came spilling out of Kennet like an evil syrup, puddling on the table and dripping off the sides, pooling around their ankles. All the unforgivable things he'd done mixed with the unforgivable things he'd seen. The grenades he threw into the basement of the house at Chenogne. The three dead bodies handed out to him later. Lining up the German troops with Marco Malinda's insignia in Kennet's pocket—Marco who had his head blown off, his teeth scattered into the snow, and his tunic pilfered by a Hitler Youth pissant with a cocky grin on his face. How Kennet looked the young German boy in his eyes and saw bravado turn to terror, right before Kennet killed him. How Kennet then put himself, his old self, his best self, into that field and shot him, too.

"You said war doesn't turn off like a light switch," he said. "But I walked into Mauthausen and within minutes I was *off*, Paps. A dead bulb."

"Tell me."

Kennet tried, but no words could wrap around the sheer obscenity of that forsaken place and do it justice. He talked about the filth, the corpses, the conditions. The extrajudicial hangings. He told how Anderson's faith was shaken to the point he couldn't find a reason to go on. He spoke of a boy named Fisha, robbed of every reason to go on, yet he went on anyway. Smiling.

At last, exhausted, Kennet told about the warehouses full of confiscated wealth. He reached in his pocket and put the gold tooth by Emil's plate.

"I shouldn't have kept it," he said. "It was all right for Fisha to have. He could use them, he deserved them. I should've put this back in the pile. Put it back with its fellows. That bin of gold teeth was a monument. Or like the famous Egyptian tomb that was opened back in the twenties, all full of treasure untouched but now men were digging through it and taking ownership. All the treasure stripped away from those camp prisoners, it belongs together. I should've left this tooth in peace, but I know why I took it. Because I wanted to be like you."

He took his father's hand and had him feel where a bit of shrapnel made a lump in Kennet's earlobe. "Just like your leg. But I wanted gold. Like yours."

Emil patted Kennet's ear. Then he clasped his fingers on the table top and looked at the tooth a long time. "Here's how I see it," he finally said. "You took this tooth. You stole it. It wasn't right, but now you have it and it troubles you. I could tell you to throw it in the river, sacrifice it to Old Nick, but somehow I don't think it'll be enough. You'll still feel its memory in your pocket. So you need to turn its meaning around. You're thinking it's a constant reminder of bad things you did in the past. I say, it needs to be a reminder of what to do in the future."

"What do I do?"

"Good things," Emil said. "That's all. Do good things. You can't just have gold in your pocket and expect it makes you good. You need to be the gold. Be golden. Do golden things. Simple, kind, decent things that make the world better."

With a fingertip, he delicately slid the tooth back toward Kennet. "Keep this in your pocket and when you're faced with a tough choice, rub it in your fingers and ask, 'What's the golden thing to do?' All right?"

"All right."

Emil reached behind and unclasped the square-linked chain around his neck. "I've been waiting for the right moment to do this. Seems the moment is here." He slipped off one of the gold fish and slid it aside. "This is Major's and was only on loan. The rest, however…" He held out each end of the chain, now with just the one fish and the St. Birgitta medal. His hands reached toward Kennet. "Come here."

"Paps, no. It's yours."

"It was mine and it served its purpose. The war is over and I'm giving it to you. Don't argue with your old man. Give me your goddamn head."

Kennet leaned, feeling rather like a man about to knighted. The chain was clasped around his neck. It was still warm from Emil's skin.

"There now." Emil patted the charms hanging between Kennet's collarbones. "You're my eldest and finest, and you wear this gold because you're good." He pointed to the tooth on the table. "You carry that gold so you remember to stay good. Bra som guld, hm? Good as gold."

"Excuse me?"

Both men turned to see Astrid at the kitchen door.

"Sorry to interrupt," she said.

"Not at all, my dear," Emil said. "Come in."

"Kennet, there's a phone call for you. At the hotel. Someone named O'Hara?"

Kennet pushed back from the table so quick, his chair nearly fell over. He righted it and headed for the door.

"Wait," Emil called. "You forgot something." He picked up the gold tooth and deposited it carefully in Kennet's palm. "Keep it close."

Kennet kissed his father's crown, then sprinted between the raindrops to the hotel. He slipped behind the front desk and into the little telephone nook, where the receiver lay on the table.

"O'Hara, how's the chops?" he called.

A fuzzy beat of silence.

Kennet frowned. "You there?"

"Yeah. Um…"

"Bud, what's the matter?"

"I fucked up."

"What happened?"

"I… Well…"

"Where are you?"

Another long beat. "I'm in jail."

"Oh shit."

"*Language,*" Little hissed from the front. "This isn't a barracks."

"Sorry," Kennet hissed back.

"No, I'm sorry," O'Hara said.

"What? No, no, no. It's all right."

"They gave me one phone call. You're the only number I had."

"It's all right. What do you need? Bail? A lawyer?"

"Bail. I'll pay you b—"

"Never mind that. Can I wire the money?"

A bit of muffled conversation, then O'Hara came back. "They want cash," he said miserably.

"Oh fu—fudge. Okay. Let me think. Will they give you another phone call or is this it?"

"This is it."

"Hold on." Kennet leaned out of the nook. "Little, is Major in the bar?"

"Yeah."

"Tell him I need him. Quick."

His brother gave him a cool look. "*Please,* Little?"

"Please, pretty please. And thank you, Little." Kennet spoke back into the phone, "Hang on, I'm getting my uncle. He'll know what to do."

"Fish, I'm sorry."

"Did you kill someone?"

A bark of startled laughter. "No."

"Then save your sorry."

Major came into the nook, wiping his hands on a bar towel. "I understand you need a body buried?"

"I got a friend in jail. You know anyone in New York City who can bail him out?"

Major swatted him with the towel. "Are you the new guy? Have we met?"

Kennet surrendered his chair. "O'Hara, I'm giving you to my uncle. He's the brains of the operation. You do whatever he says." He put a hand over the receiver. "Whatever you do, I need him on a train to Clayton afterward."

His uncle shook his head, expression puzzled, but he took the phone, sat down and cleared his throat. "This is Major Fiskare, with whom am I speaking? Hello, Boyd O'Hara, what seems to be the trouble?"

Thrumming all over, Kennet leaned against the wall, hands in his pockets. Fingers rubbing the little nugget of gold and feeling he was doing something good right now.

Erik

O'Hara stepped off the train at Clayton sporting a black eye and a sheepish expression. "I should've stayed two feet from your hip," he said as Kennet ruffled his head.

"Then we wouldn't have a funny story to tell."

"Well, I live but to amuse you."

"Come on. You must be worn out. When did you eat last?"

"I'm all right. I could use a wash."

Knowing O'Hara would balk and protest at a suite, Kennet had secured him the finest of the standard rooms at the Fisher. Small, but it had river views both north and east and on a clear day, you could see the Thousand Islands Bridge.

"Take your time getting settled," Kennet said, setting the key on the dresser. "How about we meet in the bar and have a drink?"

"I'd like to meet your uncle," O'Hara said.

"The bar is where he'll be." With a half-ass salute, Kennet left and went downstairs, whistling "Colonel Bogey."

The bar was in the lull between lunch and cocktail hour. A few salty dogs were bellied up to the bar, jawing with Major. A single couple occupied the window table that Kennet had always thought of as his and Astrid's. Astrid herself sat at the far end of the bar, folding napkins while listening to the radio.

"Where's your friend?" she asked.

"Unpacking," Kennet said, sliding onto a stool. "He'll come down for a drink."

"Oh, good. He's from your unit?"

"Mm. One of the few left from my squad."

She nodded with a smiling glance, and then gave Kennet a longer look. "Hello, you."

"Hello, you." He put elbows on the bar and his chin on his fists and stared back. Letting the moment yawn and stretch between them.

"You look pleased with yourself," Astrid said.

"I do?"

"You have a smug, accomplished air right now. What are you up to?"

"Nothing." He put his foot on the rail of Astrid's stool and made her swivel a bit. "Used to be whenever I was feeling smug and accomplished, I'd go look at your picture and ask what you thought of me."

"What would I say?"

"That you knew I could do it. You knew me."

She smiled up to her eyes, rivaling the sun. He pretended a strand of her hair had come untucked, and drew a fingertip along her cheek, into the secret place behind her ear. "All my life," he said softly. "I'll never get tired of looking at you."

She drew a deep breath. "Nyck, I was wondering if we could— Goodness, is that your friend looking like Cary Grant?"

Kennet turned on his stool. O'Hara was surveying the room with a bottle in his hands. He looked combed and neat and yes, a bit like Cary Grant, minus the cleft chin, and the black eye adding an air of insouciant danger. Kennet waved him over with one hand, beckoned to his uncle with the other.

O'Hara's bottle was Armagnac de Montal, a token of appreciation for Major.

"Well now, Boyd O'Hara," Major said, examining the label. "You didn't need to do that."

"Oh, but I did, sir."

"I see New York City gave you a souvenir." Major tapped under his eye, indicating O'Hara's impressive shiner. "Hope you got a swing in."

"I held my own until the cops came."

"Good boy. Sit down, let's crack the seal and have a drink. Have you met our cousin yet? Astrid Virtanen."

"Not in person, but I've heard much."

Astrid raised eyebrows at Kennet as she shook hands. "Much?"

Kennet glared at O'Hara. "Don't make me regret this invitation."

"Too late."

"Ignore him. We're so glad you came," Astrid said. She bade him to pull up a stool and they chatted easily. Soon O'Hara's hands reached for a napkin and started folding too, as if perfectly used to pitching in with little tasks and chores around here.

Marta came in, with Xandro perched on her hip.

"Is this the new hotel manager?" O'Hara said, getting to his feet.

"I'm the old manager," Marta said. "This is my trainee."

"Come here, mitt lilla odjur," Astrid said, reaching for the child. "This slobbering beast is mine."

Marta and O'Hara shook hands. "Thank you so much for having me," he said.

"We're nothing but delighted," she said. "Kennet wrote so much in his letters, I feel like I already know you."

O'Hara glanced at Kennet. "Don't make me regret accepting this invitation."

"Too late."

Xandro pushed the top of his head into Astrid's neck, a wet fist in his mouth. He was cutting a tooth, and his cheeks flamed red beneath the gaze he leveled at O'Hara.

"He's looking at you like you owe him money," Kennet said.

O'Hara raised an eyebrow, then put out hands to Xandro. Astrid passed him over and O'Hara tucked the boy easily in his arm, giving him a few bounces. "Hey, kiddo. Aren't you something?"

"Do you have children?" Marta asked, folding a napkin.

"No, ma'am. I'm not the marrying type."

"Good. The world needs more honorary uncles. You're hired."

"What, is this a party?" Minor called from the door of the bar. "Am I not invited to anything anymore?"

"It's not a party until you crash it," Major said. "About time you showed up."

"Mine, come here," Kennet called. "Someone I want you to meet."

O'Hara passed Xandro to Astrid and stood up. As Minor walked over, hands in his pockets, his eyes went from Kennet to the stranger and again to Kennet.

Then back to O'Hara.

Please let this be a good idea, Kennet thought. *At least not a terrible one.*

"Hi," Minor said. Cautiously. Almost questioning.

Kennet felt the air in the bar thin out as O'Hara took a deep breath. "Hi," he said, like an answer.

"This is my brother, Minor," Kennet said.

Minor glanced over. "I have a first name, you know."

"You do?"

Minor flicked his eyes to the ceiling then extended a hand to O'Hara. "I'm Erik Fiskare."

"Boyd O'Hara. Nice to meet you."

"Nice to be met."

They kept shaking hands.

"A bit of what you need, nephew?" Major said, sliding a snifter across the bar. "Our guest brought it. He's a man of good taste."

Minor took the glass, raised it and drank, without a word.

"We got an hour or two before dinner," Kennet said to O'Hara, "so how about we go out on the boat? Do the basic grand tour."

"Take some cold beers," Major said. "Have a floating cocktail hour. It's the best kind."

"Sounds terrific," O'Hara said.

"Minor, you in?" Kennet said, feeling even more smug and accomplished by his brother's blank, somewhat dazed expression.

"Sure," he said, blinking. "Sure, I'm in."

"Astrid?"

"Well…" she said slowly.

"Oh go on," Marta said, reaching for Xandro. "It's a beautiful day and we have company. Enjoy yourself."

"Avanti," Major said. "Go forth and revel."

O'Hara shook out a cigarette. His hands patted shirt and trouser pockets and came up empty. "Erik, you got a light?"

The name was extraordinary in his voice. Soft, but sturdy. Like a well-worn leather jacket that hugged your back and draped your arms, but kept out the wind and cold.

Kennet barely breathed as Minor flicked his Zippo and held the flame out. The fine, golden hairs on his forearm were raised and trembling. The bar's lamplight shone on the downy blond nape of his neck, every tiny filament sitting up and listening.

If he called me by name… If it sounded good in my ears and made the hair on my arms and neck stand up… He could be the one.

They took the *Hildur* and Kennet piloted the old sightseeing route, but left the narrative patter to Minor, who sat in the back with O'Hara. Astrid often turned back from the passenger seat to interject her own knowledge of the river and the islands.

"I taught her everything she knows," Minor said.

"That's why he has so little left," Kennet said over his shoulder, and got promptly slugged.

"Take us by Tre Fiskar," Astrid said, so they tied up at the dock on Grennell Island and took O'Hara to see the two family cottages. They stayed together, not pairing up in any deliberate fashion, until they reached the campsite on Tre-O. Astrid stood with her hands on her hips, her face far away while Minor explained the institution of fiskfika and the gatherings that had taken place here. O'Hara listened politely, then started kicking along the rocky shore, picking up flat stones and skimming them along the water's surface. He had a good arm and a natural, athletic ease. Minor picked up rocks, too, but his dominant arm could no longer throw or skim. He piled them into little cairns instead.

"I'd like to see the house now," Astrid said to Kennet, as though he were a realtor and she had an appointment. He hesitated, tilting his head questioningly toward the two men, but Astrid turned on her heel and started on the path toward the cottage.

"Mine, I'm just going to see the house a minute," Kennet called.

"Sure," Minor said, weirdly engrossed with his stones. Boyd had moved further on down the shore, almost out of sight, as if he couldn't get far enough from present company.

This was a bad idea, Kennet thought.

When he reached the cottage, Astrid stood on the small porch, her forehead and fists pressed to the door, beseeching the place. Her shoulders rose and fell rapidly. She'd run here so fast, she was winded. Or else she was crying.

"Asta," he said.

"I've wanted to come back here," she said, sobbing. "Every day since I got to Clayton. I didn't know who to ask to bring me out. I didn't want to explain why. I guess I could have asked Major, but..." She dissolved again into tears, her clenched fingers tightening. "I wanted to come back here. It's all I wanted. All these years."

"I know. Me, too."

She turned around and roughly ran her wrist across her face. "Did you come here?" she asked. "After I left? Ever?"

"Once," he said. "The day I found out you were married. I came and smashed a few things."

"You must've thought me the weakest woman on the face of the earth."

"I figured you didn't think much of my strength, either."

"What do you mean?"

"I let you go."

"I let you let me go."

He wasn't quite sure why he did what he did next. Perhaps some deeper wisdom realized this self-incriminating exchange was glossing over the real matter. He found himself coming up the last step, sinking to his knees at her feet and putting his hands on her stomach.

"You lost the baby," he said. "It was ours, wasn't it?"

"Yes."

He didn't put arms around her, only gathered two handfuls of her skirt. "I wish I'd known. If I'd known, I would've come after you. Why didn't you tell me?" The pain of the past reared up on him like a spooked horse, and he resisted the impulse to shake Astrid by putting his forehead against her belly. "I wish you'd told me."

"I'm so sorry. By the time I found out—"

456

"I know. I know why you couldn't tell me. I know you must've been out of your mind, terrified, caught in a situation with so fucking few options. I know now, Asta, but back then, I was just…"

"I'm sorry," she whispered, crying again. "Nobody gave you a chance and I was no help. I didn't fight. I should've fought."

Her knees bent and she came down to him. They didn't kiss. They didn't even hug. Only their foreheads pressed tight.

Finally, he dried her face with the tails of his shirt. "Did Zé know about us?"

"Yes."

"He knew the baby was mine?"

"He knew everything. I couldn't lie to him. On top of everything. And I thought…or hoped…"

"Telling him absolutely everything would make him not want you."

She nodded. "It was a wretched time. I despised myself. Every day I wanted to write you and tell you everything, but each time I started, I couldn't think of a thing to put on paper. I was sure you hated me and anything and everything I said would only make it worse. I had only two ways to interact with you: totally in love, or totally estranged. Then your last letter came, with the *Hildur*."

He slid his palm from her shoulder, across her collarbone and to the little lump of gold pinned inside her blouse. A bit of shrapnel from when their love affair had been hit by a grenade.

"I'm sorry," she said.

"I told you once," he said softly, "that being a lady of your word is nothing to be sorry for."

"What about the word I gave you?"

"There was none. We were ripped apart so fast, we didn't have time to make promises." He smiled and pushed a strand of hair behind her ear. "If I recall correctly, we barely had time to put our clothes on."

Her hands came up to her face, but he couldn't tell if she was laughing or crying.

"You have no idea how the memory of the day we spent here sustained me through everything," he said. "I thought about it all the time."

"I thought losing the baby was punishment for not fighting. I still feel it."

He folded over his knees and picked up the hem of her skirt again. He held it to his face, thinking of all the world's lost children and all the parents who treated their deaths as a punishment for some unrelated but despicable moment of human frailty. He thought of all the soldiers, himself among them, who inadvertently caused the death of children and wore the act like a hairshirt. All because they'd simply done their job. First lesson rammed into a grunt's thick skull was paying attention to detail and following orders to the letter. Dumb Nate Eisenstein threw his grenade through an upstairs window. Kennet listened to instructions and threw his pineapples into the basement. He killed three Belgian children. Three that he knew of—no telling how many were left behind when the house was evacuated.

Tous les autres sont morts. Boom.

Who was at fault? Jorgy for giving the order? Kennet for following it? The Germans for having the Belgian civilians trapped in the house in the first place? The gordian, unfathomable rules of war? Hitler for starting the whole goddamn business? *Someone* was at fault for the grieving woman lying in the snowy ground by the corpses. The rest of her days, she would be cataloging her words and deeds, searching for the thing she was being punished for.

She had her sentence and would forever search for the crime to fit it.

Kennet already had the crime. What would be his fitting punishment? Which of his loved ones would pay the price for Chenogne?

Love or estrangement, he thought. *Won backward is now.*

His hands slid up to cup Astrid's breasts. He'd done this before: the day they declared themselves and flopped exhausted in a field of flowers, he'd curved his hand around her breast but not with passion or ardor or even intention. Merely to hold her, feel the beat of her living heart and let the moment be lagom—not too much, not too little but just enough.

"I'm so sorry," she said, covering his hands with her own.

They looked long and hard into each other's eyes. Then Kennet pulled Astrid against him and dug his fingers into her sun-heated hair.

"I'm sorry," he said. To her, to himself, to the mothers, to the world.

To the future loved ones who might have to suffer for what he did.

A Bit of an All Right

Nobody talked much on the ride back to Clayton. Astrid had her eyes closed although the trip was too short for even the thought of a snooze. Minor and O'Hara sat in the back again, arms crossed tight over chests, each staring out their side.

I tried, Kennet thought. *Not every good, golden thing is a success. I can do no more.*

Nobody had thrown a penny in the water on this jaunt. Kennet glanced overboard at the churning water and his eyes narrowed at Old Nick's eternal greed.

You have enough, old man. Lagom. Count it and be happy for once.

When they docked at the marina, Minor needed a hand out of the boat. His cheeks were flushed red, while the rest of his face look pale and drawn. Astrid shook off her lethargy and became brisk. She pressed the inside of her wrist to Minor's forehead and gave a knowing nod.

"You have one of your evening fevers going," she said. Then to Kennet, "It happens. The proverbial tank is empty so his body has to fight harder. He needs to put his feet up and eat something."

"Go ahead and take him home."

"He's standing right here," Minor mumbled, leaning back against one of the posts.

"Come on, sailor," Astrid said, hooking her arm through Minor's. "See you at dinner, Boyd?"

O'Hara made a polite, but ambiguous noise, reaching in a pocket for his smokes.

Kennet went into the boathouse, more than certain he was about to be chewed out from hell to breakfast. He counted exactly five seconds before the door slammed closed.

"So what is this," O'Hara said. "You invited me home for my company, or so you could play matchmaker?"

"Both," Kennet said calmly. "And both—"

"I can take care of myself."

"—because I give a damn."

"I don't need you for a pimp."

Kennet winced. "What the fuck are you talking about?"

"I don't need you giving a damn about my sex life. I can get laid on my own."

"No shit you can. *And* wind up in jail for it."

"Fuck you."

"No thanks."

"Goddamn smart mouth." O'Hara threw aside his still-unlit cigarette and seized two handfuls of Kennet's shirt. "If we weren't buddies I'd knock your block off."

"If we're buddies, start acting like it." Temper flaring behind his eyes, Kennet shoved him off. "Cripes, Boyd, are you the new guy here? Have we met? You were my goddamn *eyes* for two weeks, think I'm going to screw around with your heart? You're one of the best guys I know. My brother means the fucking world to me and I want the best kind of life he can possibly have. So yeah, I thought you two would like to meet."

"So you could watch the freak show?"

"Holy hell, no."

"Get your jollies from the fags wooing each other?"

"Knock it off," Kennet said in a sharp bark. "I didn't want *anything* out of this. I don't even figure into the equation. You want a fight, go box your shadow. You want a conversation, then participate nicely."

"Fine." Glowering, O'Hara turned a hand over in the air. "Go ahead."

"I wanted you to meet," Kennet said. "Full stop. I figured worst case, nothing happens, but you'd still have a pleasant vacation with my family. Best case…something happens. You and Minor hit it off. Or become friends. And you have an even more pleasant vacation with my family. Most of all, I wanted you to meet because I trust you. Minor is someone I love more than myself. If I'm going to introduce him to *anyone*, it's you."

O'Hara stared, lips pressed tight.

"Look, Boyd, if I fucked this up or overstepped my place or offended you, then I'm sorry. Truly sorry. I didn't mean any harm. I swear I did it from the heart. I did it with best intentions."

"I know you did."

"Did I do wrong?"

"No." Bit by bit, O'Hara's face relaxed. His crossed arms dropped and his hands went to his hips, then to his sides. He exhaled. "Minor is… I wasn't expecting…"

Kennet smiled. "He's a bit of an all right."

"Yeah."

"Am I forgiven then?"

O'Hara nodded. "I wasn't offended, I was just… I'm not used to people knowing I'm queer. Much less being all right with it. Or making well-intentioned introductions."

Kennet nodded. "I can see how it comes across as a little sneaky. I didn't think that part through too good."

"Thank you," O'Hara said. "For inviting me here for a vacation, which I'm sure will be a good time. And for the sneaky introduction, which I don't know what to do with." He rubbed the back of his head. "I seem to have trouble trusting good times. So when people care about me enough to orchestrate good times, I attack those people. I'm sorry."

"Don't be. Just enjoy yourself. My home is your home."

"Christ on a cracker, Fish, you're way too easy to like."

"I wish I were your type."

O'Hara put up his palms. "My chops are rusty. One beautiful Fiskare brother at a time, please."

Kennet waved him off. "You don't have to call me beautiful."

O'Hara leveled that enthralling cobra gaze at him. "Oh, but I do."

"Don't friggin' *look* at me like— Get out of here."

"Can I come in?" Kennet said through the crack of Astrid's bedroom door.

She sat in the easy chair in the corner, reading. She shut the book around her finger and beckoned with the other hand.

Kennet moved on soft feet. Xandro slept on one side of the big bed, a wall of pillows keeping him contained. He had both arms thrown over his head, thumbs tucked beneath curled fingers.

"Whenever my grandmother said goodnight," Kennet said, "instead of *sweet dreams* she'd say, *aux poings fermés*. With closed fists. Like a baby sleeps."

Children's books were stacked on the nightstand, along with a few small toys and a framed picture of Zé Davis-Reyes in uniform. Kennet picked it up, studying the soldier.

"What does Reyes mean?"

"Kings," she said. "Why?"

"Just wondering. Davis is his mother's name?"

"Yes. It's typical in Brazil to combine your parents' names."

"I see."

Astrid's nightstand had a stack of books as well, the tome of Lord Byron poems on top. Plus her clock, a water glass, and a large mussel shell. Nestled in its opalescent blue cup was the little *Hildur*.

"I wanted to show you something," Kennet said.

"What?"

"Treasure."

She said nothing, but her eyes glittered above a smile that was positively mercenary. He took her hand, pulled her out of the chair and led her to the storage area of the attic. A single bulb on a pull chain illuminated the accumulation of clutter and boxes. It took a few minutes to locate the wooden crate Kennet had shipped from Austria. Then he had to run back downstairs and get a hammer and the scissors.

Astrid sat on the dusty floor, nightgown tucked around her knees, patient and curious as he pried the crate open and carefully cut the cords around the cloth-wrapped bundles.

"Oh my goodness," she breathed as he revealed the first set of fish-handled silverware. "It's gorgeous. Where did you get it?"

Her hands reached to help unwrap more little bundles as Kennet told about the monastery in Kremsmunster, with its great hall of Nazi wealth. Soon he and Astrid had cleared a rough rectangle on the attic floor and set an imaginary table. Kennet set the large serving pieces in the center while Astrid pulled the smaller pieces of cloth through the napkin rings.

"It's magnificent," she said, stepping back with hands on hips.

"It's stolen," he said. "Never stole anything in my life until I became a soldier."

"To the victor go the spoils." She picked up the piece of blue damask and began to wind it around herself, draping it like a Roman toga. "You could have a lovely tablecloth and napkins made from this."

"Or a gown."

"It drapes beautifully." She turned a slow circle. "What do you think?"

"You're a queen," he said.

"And you're a pirate." Their gazes held a long moment and Kennet felt his chest loosen just the tiniest bit.

"So, pirate, will you allow the treasure to grace your table?"

"I'm not sure."

"It's less cumbersome than a severed head."

"What?"

She smiled at him. "The queen does not begrudge trophies of war. On the table or not, I declare it yours."

She picked up a serving spoon in each hand and stood for a moment with them crossed over her chest. Then she stepped to him and touched him lightly on each shoulder. "I dub thee Lord High Fisherman of Silver and Gold. If you're ever broke, you can sell it. Or if you're flush but you can't stand the sight of it, sell it and throw the money in the river."

He laughed then, and slid down the wall to sit, arms wrapped around his knees.

Still clad in her blue robes, Astrid picked up the length of tweed and her tone turned shrewd and expert. "Now *this* is quality. You'd be a fool not to use it. So well-made. Thick and warm. You should make it into a winter coat."

"You take it."

She shook her head, but her arms held the tweed a little closer, her hand stroking its weave.

"I insist," Kennet said. "To the victor go the spoils and to the queen goes her tribute."

"Well…"

"I have a winter coat. I have two, for crying out loud. My Army-issue monster, and the one I bought before I left for boot camp. I'll be warm forever. You take the cloth. Make a coat and line it with the blue damask if you want. Take it or I'll throw it all in the river."

"You would, too." She folded the tweed carefully. "Thank you."

The harsh light of the single bulb threw a halo around her head. Her nightgown moved like liquid around her body. It made him remember their first boat ride in 1941, with the family on the *Marianne III*. How they'd stood together and the wind off the river made the hem of Astrid's dress ripple and flap against Kennet's leg.

"Do I scare you?" he heard himself ask.

If the question startled her, she didn't show it. "No."

"Then please hold me."

She knelt between his feet and took him in her arms, rocking him against her for a long time.

"You don't scare me," she said, stroking his head.

Jacques' Trap

The Fiskares made a grand dinner with the new fish-handled silverware, which was spectacular when laid next to Ingrid's plain, bone-white china.

"Credit goes to Boyd," Kennet said. "He found it."

"Did you keep any for yourself?" Major asked.

O'Hara laughed. "I'm only an expert finder of things."

"Now where have I heard that before?" Kennet mumbled to Minor.

"Shut up," Minor muttered back.

"I think it's great," Little said. Since O'Hara's arrival, Little had been looking at him with circumspect fascination. As if O'Hara were a circus lion that had strolled into the house. Trained, but unpredictable.

"Boyd, sit here," Little said, indicating the chair next to his, eliciting some discreet raised eyebrows. This had always been Nalle's place and kept deliberately vacant.

Unaware of the honor, O'Hara sat. He had Johnny MacIntyre on his other side and Major directly across. This meant an unavoidable third degree and Kennet was interested to see how O'Hara would handle it.

What followed was a performance worthy of a tennis pro. O'Hara was a master at the graceful, bare minimum return to a served question. He offered that he was from Wyoming—born in Laramie and raised in Cheyenne. His family were all ranchers, except those who were livestock veterinarians. He was the middle of seven kids, but hadn't been back home since enlisting in 1941 and was in no particular rush, for no particular reason. After a polite volley, he effortlessly lobbed the ball into someone else's court. Usually Major's, having grasped that Major was a superb raconteur.

As dessert was served, Minor caught Kennet's eye and shook his head the tiniest bit. "I like my still waters a little less deep," he said quietly in Swedish.

Kennet gave a humble, conciliatory smile. "Tall, dark hair, blue eyes, et cetera. It was worth a shot."

Minor patted the back of Kennet's chair. "You're a good egg."

Well, that's that, Kennet thought, and something in him relaxed. He rubbed the hard lump in his earlobe, smiling a little.

You can't wish grunt metal into gold.

"Boyd, how long are you staying?" Little asked.

"Long enough to make a few lists and sketches."

"Be careful," Trudy said. "Marta came to us when I was a baby and stayed forever. Astrid came four years ago, tried to leave, but then *she* came back, too. People who come to visit Clayton once always come back forever."

O'Hara's expression was serious. "Always? Forever?"

Trudy blushed under his intense gaze. "Most of the time."

Now O'Hara smiled, breaking his cobra spell. "Thanks for the warning, kiddo. I'll try to resist your town's charms."

"Don't try too hard," Little said. "If it feels good here, then stay a while."

"It's an open-ended invitation," Marta said. "Make Clayton a base and venture around. See if New York fits you. If not, we'll be happy to see you off to your next destination."

"That's nice of you, ma'am. Thank you." The words were courteous, but Kennet could see the old defenses making O'Hara's muscles twitch. The distrust of good intentions, the fierce and justifiably fearful guarding of his private life. The pervasive thought that nobody *really* wanted him, a man who loved men. A distasteful mess people preferred were swept under the carpet and ignored. *Happy to see you off* might just as well mean a mob to run him out of town.

Not from Marta it doesn't, Kennet thought. *Nor from any of us. We're in the business of hospitality, and kind ladies have always lived in this house. My grandmother took in Johnny, who was crippled. My mother took in Kirsten, who was orphaned. When Fiskare women extend an invitation, they mean it. Not carved in stone, but chalked on the sidewalk.*

"Kennet, love, please eat," Marta said softly.

O'Hara gave a sympathetic smile as Kennet picked up his heavy, fish-handled fork and took a tasteless bite of his grand dinner.

The idea of creating a base, rather than being an extended guest, seemed to appeal to O'Hara. He knew his way around Clayton in an hour, and just as easily navigated the Fiskares' stretch of the river. He used one of the hotel's guest boats, and when Little suggested O'Hara take ownership of the *Melissa*, Nalle's old craft, O'Hara adamantly refused.

"I'm no river rat, and that boat is irreplaceable. If I fucked it up or sank it, I'd never forgive myself." He put a light punch into Little's shoulder. "You're real swell to offer, though. I'm touched."

He was just as adamant when he moved out of the hotel and into a cheap, rented room over Clark's General Store. Exactly where his funding for food, rent and essentials came from was a mystery. O'Hara insisted he'd had nothing to spend his Army pay on all these years, and *this*, right here and right now, was the rainy day he'd saved up a few pennies for.

"Quite a stash of pennies," Minor said.

"I guess it's the upside of not being interested in possessions," Kennet said.

"I was more than happy for him to stay in the hotel," Emil said. "That room over Clark's doesn't even have hot water."

"Leave him be, Paps," Minor said. "He's proud, he's private and he's used to being on his own. *And* washing in cold water."

Eventually O'Hara bought a used Chris-Craft, which Kennet and Minor gave a good going-over and a thorough tune-up, threatening to throw O'Hara in the river if he tried to pay them.

"You have to name her," Minor said, thumping the stern where the boat's former name had been scraped and sanded away.

"I have to?"

"Bad luck if you don't."

O'Hara sighed, then looked at Kennet. "I suppose calling it—"

"Her," Minor said. "A boat is always her."

"I suppose calling her the *Jockstrap* would be frowned upon?"

Kennet laughed and so did O'Hara. *Really* laughed. A guffaw from the belly that Kennet had never heard before. Minor looked puzzled and O'Hara kept chuckling as Kennet explained the evolution of Chris Fragiacomo's name.

"Disguise it then," Minor said. "Hide it behind French."

He stepped to the boathouse window and with a fingertip, wrote in the dusty pane: *Jacques' Trap.*

"He did have a famous trap," Kennet said.

O'Hara nodded, tongue pushed into his cheek. "You're a clever guy, Erik."

"So I'm told."

"Except someone will figure it out eventually."

"Fuck 'em," Minor said. "Play dumb. Be offended that their mind is in the gutter. How dare they besmirch the memory of your buddy. Pistols at dawn."

"Reel it back a little," Kennet said.

"Sorry. I have an inherited flair for the dramatic."

"All right then," O'Hara said softly. Then again, with more conviction. "All right. *Jacques' Trap*. I like it. He'd like it. Her. It."

"Don't hurt yourself," Minor said.

A week later, O'Hara fired a small split of champagne at the hull of his boat, then puttered out from the hotel marina, heading east. The Fiskares cut bait and with a few worried, wistful glances, they let their catch swim away.

"Just sit and look," Astrid said, coming to be by Kennet at the dock, waving as O'Hara adventured off.

Kennet didn't answer. He felt intensely bereft and his thoughts had gone back to the farmhouse in Chêne, and the misunderstood night he'd spent in Solange's bed. He'd asked if she wanted him to leave.

"No, no more leaving," she'd said. "No more going. Stay. Hold still. I just want things to stay still…"

Exploring the border between two countries, O'Hara would go off for two, three days at a time. But he always came back, tapping on the Fiskares' kitchen door. The family learned to expect him when they saw him, and not to ask how long he'd be staying.

O'Hara seemed to thrive on benign neglect. Too much attention and he vanished. But just the right amount of disregard, and he sidled up, casually looking for company, wondering if he could help out with anything. It wasn't unusual to find him drying dishes while Marta washed up after dinner. Once Kennet came up the back porch steps and, through the window, saw the two of them in deep conversation. Marta had taken her hands out of the suds and stood with crossed arms, listening to O'Hara, who held a towel and plate. His expression was so open and earnest, and Marta's so rapt, Kennet backed down the steps, retreating as quickly as if he'd interrupted a church service.

If you didn't actively look for O'Hara, you'd eventually find him tending bar with Major or playing cards with Emil. He'd be topping and tailing string beans with Kirsten, puzzling over math problems with Trudy, or washing the hotel windows with Little.

It was O'Hara who started calling Little "Emilio."

"It suits him better," O'Hara said. "He's not a kid and he's nothing close to little. Why keep saddling him with a nickname he never liked in the first place?"

Addressed as Emilio, the already sunny disposition of the youngest Fiskare son turned dazzling. The moniker stuck (*Like a burr*, Kennet thought) and soon, "Little" was used only in the most intimate and teasing of family moments.

"Have you noticed how Emilio looks at Kirsten?" O'Hara said one night, when he, Kennet and Minor were having a beer.

"Only an idiot wouldn't have noticed," Minor said.

"Noticed what?" Kennet said.

Minor sighed. "Like I said."

"Do you think she knows?" O'Hara said.

"She's a *kid*," Kennet said. "What are you talking about?"

"Nothing gets past Kirsten," Minor said. "And Emilio's barely being subtle about it."

"Well, he's young," O'Hara said. "And he was cruelly robbed of your expert guidance during a critical time in his life."

"Obviously in my absence, he attended the Kennet Fiskare School of Maudlin Crap."

O'Hara sucked his tongue with a pitying air. "Shame. It'll take years to unlearn those bad habits."

"At least Emilio knows how to dress himself."

Kennet got up. "Jesus, put me back in combat where people are friendlier."

He walked out of the bar in a half-ass huff, secretly pleased for the excuse to leave O'Hara and Minor alone. They'd eased into a comfortable, un-fraught companionship grounded in a shared enjoyment of picking on Kennet. The two of them could be lethal, but Kennet decided it was worth the merciless ribbing to see the friendship blossom.

Boyd wants a home, Kennet thought. *A little place to go at the end of the day, where he can do all the normal, boring things of everyday life. With someone special who lives there, too.*

He's not ashamed of who he is. He's just realistic. And maybe he's content with a good buddy who lives close by. Someone who speaks his language and knows which way the wind is blowing. An ally.

Maybe this is enough right now for Boyd. Not too much and not too little.

Minor's not a lover, but he's lagom.

Following Kennet into the attic one day, to retrieve something or other, O'Hara took a look around the cluttered space with a disgusted expression. "How can you *find* anything in here?"

"It looks a mess but it's actually extremely organized."

"Bullshit."

"Yeah, I know, it's a disaster area."

"You should clear some of it out for Xandro," O'Hara said. "Growing boy needs a place to play. And look at all the junk blocking that great window with the built-in seat. It's a crime."

"You going to help me? Or just drop the suggestion and disappear down the river again?"

O'Hara snorted. "Like you even care when I'm gone."

"Oh, but I do," Kennet said blithely, though he was a little hurt by the remark.

"Mm."

"Minor says you leave just to see if anyone misses you."

Kennet expected another snorted dismissal, but O'Hara stuffed hands in his pockets and kicked at the dusty floor. "He does?"

"Yeah."

"Huh." O'Hara looked up and his expression was sheepish. "And I thought I was being so clever about it."

"You're saying you've been testing him?"

"I test everyone, Fish."

And Kennet couldn't think of a thing to reply.

Still a Sort of Fisherman

"Can I come in?" Kennet asked at Astrid's bedroom door.

"Of course. Hello, you."

"Hello, you."

She sat on the floor, watching as Xandro discovered his legs. He was hanging on the edge of the bed, clutching the spread in fists and teeth. He gave a few vigorous bounces, pleased as punch, then let go the bedding and toppled back onto his butt. He pushed his bottom lip out, looking at his mother, who pushed hers out too. Finding no sympathy, Xandro dug fists in his eyes and yawned. Then looked at Kennet and held up his arms.

Kennet swung him onto a shoulder. It was becoming easier. Kennet was able to hold and play and roughhouse with the boy without feeling he was taunting fate.

"So I had an idea," he said. "Actually O'Hara had the idea, I'm just the executioner."

She drew back from him a little, expression wary. "Indeed?"

"I mean executor," he said, laughing. "The corps of engineers."

"So it doesn't involve a dead body?"

"No. Just hammer and nails. Come out here."

He walked her through his idea to build a room where Xandro could sleep and play.

"Oh, you don't have to," Astrid said.

"I want to."

"It's so much work."

"That's why I want to," he said. "The season is over and there won't be much boat work. I need something to do with my hands. Building something or making something. It helps me."

"Well," she said slowly. "I'll want to contribute. For the materials and such. It will need to be painted."

"For sure. And a rug of some kind."

She looked up at him. "You really want to do this?"

"I do."

She stared at him another beat. "O que vou fazer com você, pescador?"

"Translation?"

"What am I going to do with you?"

"I don't know." He couldn't tell if she were being provocative, or just lamenting. "Sit and look?"

Smiling, she closed her eyes a moment. Then opened them. "He's asleep."

They went back in the bedroom and Kennet carefully lay Xandro down on his side of the bed, pulling the pillows between him and the edge. Astrid was unlooping the drapes, pulling them closed.

"All my life," Kennet said, "I'll never get tired of looking at you."

She smiled over her shoulder, but it didn't reach her eyes.

She was tired. Not physically tired. Just tired of *him*.

What am I going to do with you?

"Can I show you something?" he said.

"More treasure?"

"No. No, it's...the opposite of treasure."

"All right."

He headed toward the door but was compelled to look back. "Don't go away?"

She pointed. "I'll wait out there for you. In case it's noisy."

When he came back, she was sitting on a box, waiting patiently among the clobber and clutter. She gave a little laugh when Kennet handed her his war notebook. The second version, with all the new entries carefully transcribed in order. In pen and ink. A permanent record.

"This time I really was expecting a severed head," Astrid said, fanning the pages with her thumb. Almost immediately her photograph dislodged and wafted to the floor. "And here it is." She held the picture out with a critical expression. "Shoddy sword work, Private Fiskare. Aim for the neck next time."

"No next time," he said. "There better not be."

"I'm sorry," she said quietly. "I'm afraid I picked up Minor's habit of making jokes when I'm nervous."

"Am I making you nervous?"

She held up the notebook. "This is."

"It ought to. The only other person who read it got killed."

"Who?"

"My buddy, Hook. I let him read every word. All my fears and doubts and less than noble thoughts. I feel like it cursed him."

"You don't have that kind of power," she said. "Magic books are only in stories. Curses aren't real. Words have magic—they can transport you to different places, they can inspire or educate, but they can't bless or curse. Your friend died because he was in war, not because reading your diary brought him bad luck."

"Sounds so simple when you say it. I don't know why it's hard to believe."

"Maybe…when you're in a situation where so much is beyond your control, you compensate by giving yourself power. Even if it's silly things. It comforts you." She pointed toward the chain around his neck. "Like how your father gathered and wore his little fish."

"And it didn't make a damn bit of difference."

"Right up until he found out Nalle died, it did make a difference. It got him through the days. It did its true job."

"I guess."

"He wore it with the best of intentions. Just like you invited Hook into your thoughts with good intentions. And invited O'Hara to Clayton with the same."

They looked at each other a long time in the weak light of a single bulb.

"Are you inviting me to read this?" she said, holding the notebook as if giving him a chance to take it back.

"I am," Kennet said slowly. "But some things I wrote may shock you. Horrify you. I need you to know about them. It's… It's like how you told Zé about us."

"You're trying to make me not want you."

"I'm trying to make sure you do. I need you to know how war changed me. I need you to know the things that made me put up a wall between myself and the world. I'm not being poetic when I say that, Asta. I haven't been able to smell or taste anything in months. You and Marta and everyone pushing me to eat more and I swear I'm hungry but eating is just such a goddamn joyless *chore.*"

Beneath wide eyes, Astrid's mouth formed soundless words, "Oh darling…"

"But I did things too. Things that broke the rules of war and put me on a level with Nazis and Japs."

"Nyck, no."

"Yes. And I want you to know. I want you to be sure. You don't begrudge my spoils of war, but you need to know what happened."

"All right," she said quietly.

Kennet slumped a little, rubbing the back of his neck. "Don't start reading it tonight. Don't lie awake in the dark with my thoughts in your head. Read it by sunlight."

"I will read it by the brightest lamp I can find. I'll come talk to you about it at high noon. I won't secretly decide you're an abhorrent human being, leave in the middle of the night and disappear forever. I think you've had quite enough of people you love vanishing."

"That's true," he said, his voice thinner than smoke.

No more leaving. No more going. Stay still.

Astrid stood up decisively and reached for the chain that led to the light socket. She couldn't quite reach, so Kennet pulled it and plunged the space into darkness.

They stood there, with the dark pressing them from all directions and Astrid's cheek against Kennet's pounding heart.

"A fisherman he had been in his youth," she whispered. "And still a sort of fisherman was he."

"Still."

Her arms tightened about him. "Still, Nyck. I believe this. Still."

No more leaving, he thought. *Stay still.*

Guarding the
Perimeter

Kennet left the attic and went downstairs, feeling thirsty. He thought he heard voices from the kitchen, but all was dark within, shadowy and sleeping. The back porch light was on, though, and through the kitchen door's window Kennet saw O'Hara and Minor sitting on the back steps. Both zipped into jackets, each with a cluster of empty beer bottles by his hip. The night was cold, and their breath made little puffs in the air.

Some irresistible compulsion took hold of Kennet, knocking aside any semblance of decent behavior. He shrank into the shadows, pulled himself small and silent. His ears bulged against the night, but he couldn't discern words. Only the slow, slurring ups and downs of two deep voices. Two feet of space separated Minor's right shoulder from O'Hara's left, making a third entity that shimmered and stretched.

It almost seemed to yearn.

Slowly, Kennet became that space, condensed into the essence of patience.

He waited.

And watched.

O'Hara's head dropped, his fingers laced at his nape.

Minor drained the last of his beer, then set the bottle down. He slid closer.

O'Hara moved over a little, head still bowed.

They sat still a long time.

Kennet barely breathed.

Minor put his hand between O'Hara's shoulder blades. Above it, O'Hara's head was shaking. *No. I can't.*

Minor's hand made a few easy circles before gliding up to rest at the back of O'Hara's head, on top of O'Hara's twined fingers. His torso expanded and contracted in a big sigh that materialized as steam, then dissolved.

O'Hara seemed to shrink, down and to his left. His dark head now lolling on Minor's shoulder. Nodding. *Yes. I can.*

Minor set his chin on O'Hara's crown. They held still. Breathing.

Kennet swore he could feel their combined heartbeats through his feet. Minor's face was in profile, showing his guarded, brooding, scarred side.

His twin's side.

Lauren, Kennet thought. *Say her name. Lauren. Birdie. Don't fly away this time. No more leaving. Stay. Stay with him. Let him feel this moment with his entire, twinned soul. Stay, little bird. It's safe here...*

Minor turned his mouth down into O'Hara's hair. His eyes closed and his hand caressed O'Hara's head. He and O'Hara were rocking a little. Leaning on each other. Testing the tenacity of the night. Following where it led.

Little by little, Minor's fingers, soft and easy on O'Hara's head, began to stretch out wide. Taking hold. Taking ownership. They dug furrows into O'Hara's hair and slowly pulled.

O'Hara's chin came up. His head dropped into the cradle of Minor's forearm, face to the sky. A cloud of his breath rose as Minor pressed his mouth into O'Hara's throat.

Stay, Kennet thought. Without him being aware, his palm had lifted, as if making a place where a bird could perch. *Stay, please stay.*

A ripple went down the back of O'Hara's jacket. Now his head canted toward Minor. His hand slid along Minor's jaw.

They kissed each other.

Slow and cautious at first. Drawing back to look nervously around the gardens, then back at each other, wide-eyed and trembling. Minor's hand came out of O'Hara's hair, moving to the side of his face, thumb stroking a cheekbone. His other arm, the wounded one, started to come up. A flicker of pain crossed his face.

O'Hara smiled then, and in perhaps the most tender gesture Kennet ever saw between two human beings, O'Hara picked up Minor's weak left arm and gently helped it onto his shoulder. As he pressed his mouth against Minor's scarred wrist, another rippling shiver went through him.

Then they were kissing again, this time as though the world could end and they'd take no notice.

Now it was Kennet who peered into the night. Empty palm still in the air, he stared straight through the two men, his gaze boring into the dark beyond. This, he knew, was how Hook felt when he first glimpsed O'Hara and Jock stealing a furtive, secret moment that could quite literally get them thrown in jail.

Screw guarding the perimeter, Hook had said. *I just wanted to guard* them.

As he kept watch, Kennet imagined a little bird flying circles around Minor and O'Hara, too. Singing as they kissed. As they became Erik and Boyd, each hearing his name, feeling the hair stand up on arms and napes in response.

It was a golden, gargantuan moment. Fierce and fragile. Too immediate and *now* to be folded into memory and become *won.*

Kennet would destroy anyone and anything that dared disturb it.

OCTOBER
1945

Juicy Fruit

The construction of the new attic room soothed Kennet's soul more than boatbuilding. When immersed in the precision of measuring and marking, the hands-on creation, the purpose, the *job*, he thought of little else.

Sometimes his brothers or O'Hara came up to lend a hand. Kennet enjoyed side-by-side laboring, but found he especially liked working alone.

Well, not entirely alone. Occasionally he was joined by a short, rather useless apprentice.

"Good thing you work for free, kid," Kennet said.

"Nee," Xandro said.

"Nyck."

"Nee."

"Close enough."

Kennet carefully sanded odds and ends of wood smooth, and gave them to Xandro to bang together, stack and chew on. Remembering how Ingrid used to keep Trudy contained, Kennet lined an orange crate with a blanket and popped the boy inside with his blocks, his tin measuring cups and clothes pegs. These simple toys, the radio and Kennet's company were all Xandro needed. Plus a bit of whatever Kennet was having for lunch.

"You're a lousy assistant," Kennet said over a couple cookies and a glass of milk. "But you're nice company for a working man."

After lunch, he zipped Xandro into his jacket and carried him down to the river to wave at the boats. A sleepy Sunday afternoon. A crisp chill was in the air, and the green of the archipelago was slowly transforming to yellow, red and orange. Xandro's cheeks turned rosy. His hair had grown in enough to lift and ripple in the cool breeze. His solid weight felt good in the crook of Kennet's elbow, little butt perched on his forearm and one fat fist holding onto Kennet's collar. The other hand reached for the gold chain on Kennet's neck. The boy had recently discovered wonderful shiny things hung from it.

"Fee," he said, pulling the chain.

"Fish," Kennet said. "That's right. Hey, not for eating." He hooked the charms out of Xandro's mouth. A futile task—the tyke was cutting more teeth and chewed on anything. Not a minute went by and he was gnawing on the Saint Birgitta medal again.

"You want some gold inside," Kennet said. "Don't we all? Look at me, I carry it everywhere. I'm becoming just like Old Nick." He hitched Xandro to his other arm and dug in his trouser pocket, fingers sifting through loose change and a fish hook, looking for the gold tooth. "See?"

He held it up for Xandro to see. The boy stared, expression solemn, then he leaned toward Kennet's pinched fingers, mouth open.

"No," Kennet said, laughing. "You definitely don't eat this. It belongs to another little Fish in the world."

Not for the first time, his thoughts wandered to Fisha. Where was he? Was he alive? Safe? Sheltered? Did the gold teeth give him any kind of advantage? Did he find a pair of parental arms—blood or surrogate—to hold him?

Family isn't blood, it's who you bleed for.

Kennet thought about the Zippo lighter and prayed it and Fisha hadn't been separated.

May you still keep the flame. May you be safe, fed and clothed. May your trousers have pockets and those pockets not have holes. Keep me within that pocket. Fish to fish. Flame to flame. Guard your gold but spend it to stay alive. Survive. You're a fisherman and a pirate.

"Fee," Xandro said.

"Yes," Kennet said. He put the tooth in his pocket and came up with a penny. "Ready? Say *Nick, Nick, needle in the water! Thou sink! I float!*"

"Nee," Xandro shrieked as Kennet made a pendulum of their clumped hands and flung the coin into the river.

"Molodets," Kennet said. "Now say *fuck Hitler.* No, no, don't. Cripes, your mother will kill me."

I bet your father would laugh, though.

The thought of Zé was unexpectedly smooth in Kennet's mind as he walked back to the house. Xandro was asleep on his shoulder by the time he reached the attic stairs. He emerged into the new, renovated space. Painted fresh and white and fitted with a blue carpet and pale green curtains at the window seat. Astrid had procured another easy chair and lamp at an estate sale. They were tucked in a corner beneath the sloping eaves, next to a bookshelf stacked with every Fiskare's favorite stories.

Kennet put Xandro down in his crib and went to the window to pull the curtains shut. He paused, squinting over the roof of the hotel and beyond to the marina, where he could just make out the *Jacques' Trap* at the dock. O'Hara was already in the boat, holding her steady, a hand on Minor's back as he came down the ladder. Holding him steady.

Kennet peeked in the bedroom. Astrid lay against a stack of pillows, asleep with Kennet's journal face down on her chest, her hands crossed on the spine.

He moved to the other side of the bed. Xandro's old side. He sat on the floor, back against the mattress, on an eye level with the photograph of Zé Davis-Reyes.

Zé was in uniform: wool fatigues bunched around boots, combat shirt and an officer's overcoat. A light scarf around his neck. One hand in a pocket, the other holding a cigarette. A handsome fellow, dark hair parted on the side and combed back. A cleft chin. He looked at the camera, smiling, squinting a little, as if the sun were in his eyes.

Kennet leaned to one side, then the other.

Zé's gaze followed.

I wonder if you met Nalle, Kennet thought. *I hope you did. I hope it was one of those weird, wonderful, serendipitous moments when the war catches its breath and you and a stranger realize you have something in common.*

Someone in common.

Like you and me.

So, about Xandro.

He's a swell little kid and I wonder if you'd mind if I taught him how to say "fuck Hitler."

He imagined the photograph coming to life. Zé throwing back his head and laughing. Taking a drag on the cigarette while the other hand came out of his pocket and playfully socked Kennet's shoulder.

I'll make sure he knows your story, Kennet thought, wrapping his arms around his kneecaps. *I'll find out everything I can about the Brazilian Expeditionary Force. We'll put pins in the map of Italy. I'll tell Xandro his father and my brother fought together. I know it might not be true, but every fish tale is embellished in some way.*

I'll take care of him. The Fiskares are in the business of hospitality, but this house has always been a haven. Kind ladies live here. And decent, honorable men. When Fiskares extend an invitation, we mean it. Our word is good as gold.

I give you my word, Xandro will know his name is Virtanen-Reyes. Reyes means kings. And...

Kennet sat up a little. He twisted, looking back to Astrid, still asleep beneath his diary.

And Virtanen means river, he thought slowly.

"Holy Schmitt," he whispered.

The hair stood up on his forearms as he got up. He tiptoed to Astrid's side of the bed. On her nightstand, the little gold *Hildur* was resting inside the mussel shell. Astrid didn't wear it pinned inside her dress anymore. Perhaps it hurt too much there. Perhaps it made her tired, so she put it in the shell, where it could sit still and just look.

Kennet picked it up, held it in a carefully cupped hand as he went out the door and over to Xandro's crib. As usual, the boy slept with both arms thrown over his head. His little mouth pursed, as if he were chewing on deep thoughts.

Or counting gold.

Slowly, gently, not wanting to wake him, Kennet pinned the *Hildur* on the river king's sweater.

My word is good as gold

He went to his work table in the boathouse to putter around. The temperature had dropped a little more, so he switched on his little electric fire, pointing it toward his poor feet which had never recovered from the winter of 1941 and the subsequent tramping across Europe.

"Shit on a stick," he muttered, patting his pockets. He'd forgotten his cigarettes. Oh well, he smoked too goddamn much anyway. Gum would have to hold the habit today. He reached up high for an old cigar box on a shelf. Good old Minor—almost thirty years old but still stashing candy.

An hour slipped away as he tinkered with a dodgy engine. An hour measured in songs on the radio and a trail of gum wads pressed under the edge of the workbench. The Wrigley Company was slacking off, in Kennet's opinion. The flavor in a goddamn stick of Juicy Fruit didn't last for shit anymore.

He folded another piece in his mouth, crumpled the wrapper, picked up a wrench.

He stopped. Froze mid-turn of a nut, backtracking his last thought.

The flavor in a what?

He chewed slowly, pressing the rubbery wad against the roof of his mouth.

It had taste.

Faint, but there. A fruity whisper back behind his molars. A tiny bubble of sweetness in the well beneath his tongue.

He swallowed and swallowed, one hand still clenching the wrench. Was his sense of taste back, or was this just a trick of the mind? Was he only remembering the flavor of Juicy Fruit? He spit the gum into a far corner and went scrabbling into the cigar box. His fingers shook as he unwrapped a Tootsie Roll. He held it to his nose first. Nothing. No. Wait. A low fudgy note, here and gone, like a flirtatious tap on the shoulder. He bit off one end, closed his eyes and chewed.

Yes. No... Yes.

Like the scent, the chocolate taste came and went. Shyly touched his tongue and ran away.

It wasn't back.

But it was *coming* back.

He opened his eyes and the room blurred hot and wet. He picked up an oily rag nearby and sniffed it. Nothing. He dug into a coffee can of washers and held the handful to his nose. A little puff of metallic rust. He trawled the workbench, loopy with the need to put anything and everything to the smell test. He needed to get the world back into his mouth.

That was when a blast of cold air swirled behind him. He turned to see Astrid slip inside the boathouse, close the door and lean back against it. Windblown. No coat. She held his journal to her chest.

The Way He Wrote It

They stared.

Faintly, across the space between them, a clean, bright scent beckoned. Tantalizing and elusive. Kennet took a step, wanting it.

Then it was gone. But Astrid was here.

He breathed in and swallowed. "Whose little girl are you?"

Her returned gaze made him feel hot all over.

"So, Captain Fish," she said, "are we doing this the hard way or the easy way?"

In one dizzying swoop, the blood drained from his head and pooled below his belt. Harder than he'd been on the battlefield, harder than he'd ever been in his life, he answered, "Easy."

She opened the notebook to a page marked by her finger. She walked toward him, reading aloud:

> *I am, honest to God, blushing right now.*
>
> *Oh what the hell, I can write it here. I'm not long for this world so I can tell you everything in these pages. You'll never know.*
>
> *But maybe you will. Maybe you, future Asta, is reading this last entry of my diary, because Hook sent it to you after I was killed tomorrow.*

In which case I hope, honest to God, you are blushing too, as you read these words to the last and learn the truth: joining the Army helped put you behind me, but war has only confirmed that I will love—

The notebook fell to the floor as Kennet devoured the rest of the sentence, sliding his hands into Astrid's hair and crushing her lips with his. Their feet trampled pages as they stumbled backward, kissing open-eyed and ravenous. Kennet got his palm behind her head just in time to keep it from banging hard against the wall. Her arms wrapped tight around his neck, her knees climbing his hips as if he were a tree. Her tongue was in his mouth and her skin in his hands and all of her was dancing up into his nose and down the back of his throat, catching hands with chocolate and fruit and all of it was close enough to taste.

"Leave now or I'm taking you right here," he said, his hands full of her breasts.

"No more leaving. Stay *still*..." Her hands were burrowing underneath his sweater, simultaneously pushing it up and pulling it off. She said something else but he was stuck in the neck hole, ears folded forward.

He popped himself free, crazed. "What?"

"Lås dörrjäveln."

Lock the fucking door.

The time it took to turn the lock and switch off the lights was entirely too long. In only the glow of the radio's luminescent dial, Kennet and Astrid flung themselves at each other, cracking and coiling like two whips. Out of patience, his hands ripped the front of her dress open, buttons spattering like water in oil. They reached up her skirt and tore the underwear clear off her legs. She laughed and laughed as he swept an arm across his workbench and laid her out before him like a project.

"Come get your treasure, pirate," she said, reaching.

But Kennet had left piracy and was approaching something closer to a Cossack, or a Vandal. He scarcely recognized himself, holding Astrid down with one hand, spitting in the other palm and slicking himself up. He slid deep into her body, palms now braced on the rough tabletop. Tongue swirling luxurious circles on her breasts before gathering a nipple in his mouth and sucking hard. Her skin filled his head like a forgotten dream. Soap and powder and perfume and *Astrid*.

"I never stopped wanting you," he said hoarsely.

"Don't stop."

She squirmed this way and that. He could hear minute ripping sounds as the rough wood of the bench laddered her stockings to shreds. He withdrew and reached to set her heels on the table top. Winding her garters around his fingers, he bent to drag his tongue against her wet heat. Over and over, lost in the taste that came and went and came again. As Astrid came and went and came again, just the way he wrote it. Gushing raspberries and cream, dark beer and champagne and cold, clear spring water.

"God, I can taste you," he gasped.

"Kiss me."

He pushed into her body again and fell into her mouth. "Sweetheart," he whispered, lost in this foreign, delicious desire. "Älskling... Sweet little... So sweet when I fuck you..."

They snarled and snagged and clutched and tore at each other, the air hissing with filth, obscenities whispered like secrets and dares. Turning the windows of the boathouse opaque with steam.

"Jag älskar dig, Fisken," Astrid said, over and over. "Älskar dig, Fisken. Älskar dig..."

Love you, Fish.

"Christ, woman," Kennet said through a heaving chest. His rough touch went soft. His dirty mouth turned clean and tender, kissing Astrid's eyelids, her sweaty temples, her damp, hot nape, the palms of her hands. "Asta…"

She held his head against her pounding heart, legs still wrapped around his waist. "I love you," she whispered.

"Do you?"

"Yes."

"Even now?"

"Especially now." She picked up his head and looked in his eyes. "You pinned the *Hildur* on Xandro."

"Yes. We'll go to Montreal soon. The deWrennes will make him a chain."

"You want him to have it?"

"Yes." Kennet took her hands and kissed each of her fingers. "Clayton can be your home. I can be your man." He put her palms back on his face. "And Xandro can be our boy."

She wrapped arms around his neck, pulled him against her. He closed his eyes tight, falling into the gold behind his lids.

The evening went from ardent to absurd as they skulked around in the dark, searching for tossed and torn clothing. Stifled giggles and hissed whispers, as if there were any point to being stealthy now. Astrid had to secure her dress back together with a fish hook—"Desenrascanco, darling," then purloin an old corduroy work jacket to cover her handiwork.

Once they were decent, Kennet flicked on the lights. He collected loose buttons while Astrid stuffed her torn underwear in the bottom of the wastebasket.

"Like you'd never know," she said.

"Minor will figure it out in six seconds."

He switched off the electric fire and took Astrid in his arms for one more long, scorching kiss before locking up. He took her hand and they started toward home.

"Wait," Kennet said. "Come here a minute." He wheeled them around to walk toward the river instead, to the very edge of the dock. He fished in his pocket and came out with the gold tooth, hefting it a few times on his palm.

"We got our golden time back," he said. "So many millions won't."

"Remember objects don't have magic. Or power or charm. They have a job." She put her hand over the tooth. "You don't need this as a reminder of the things you saw. You won't ever forget. You don't need it as a reminder to be good. You've never been anything but. So now what's its job? What's its purpose?"

"To belong to everyone?"

"I think you want it to prove where you were and break the curse. It can't. And even in the story, after the curse was ended, Hildur still got away with murder." She lifted her hand and lightly touched the gold with a fingertip. "Some of the people responsible for this will get away with it, too. But you did your job. You gave everything you could. Your strength, your hunger, your terror, your sleep. You gave your taste and smell. You gave your sanity. You gave friends. You gave a brother."

She moved behind him, wrapped arms around his waist. "It was enough. But if you're not convinced, then give the gold and *let* it be enough. Lagom. Not too much, not too little."

Kennet cupped the tooth, glancing toward Grennell Island and Tre Önskningar, where Erik and Boyd were saying each other's names.

I did a good thing for them.

Not too much and not too little.

496

Kennet squeezed his fist, wished for the lovers everything they deserved, and lobbed the tooth into the St. Lawrence River. Then he twisted in the circle of Astrid's arms to look back at her.

She gazed up at him, golden hair tousled and silver eyes shining. Eyes filled with love. Maybe something growing within, right here, right now.

Now backward is won.

"I'm Kennet Fiskare," he said. "Fisherman and pirate. I was conceived in a casino in Aix-les-Bains. My namesake uncle is king of the river. The gold in my veins is inherited from my father, who got it from a Hun's tooth. My table is set with Czechoslovakian silver. My flame is kept in the pocket of a Russian boy."

He turned all the way around and took Astrid's face in his hands. "I don't need any more gold or spoils of war. You're my greatest treasure and it's lagom."

"I know." She held his head and kissed him. "I know who you are."

Taking hands, they walked away from the river. Past the train station and across the main thoroughfare of Clayton. Up the wide front stairs of the small hotel where they reached to touch the tail of the carved wooden fish.

The doors closed behind them.

The fish swung on its chains, contemplating wishes.

The river flowed on while Fossegrim played his music and Hildur got away with murder.

Old Nick counted a new gold tooth among his immeasurable wealth.

And the Fiskares, fishermen and pirates alike, went on telling their tales.

JUNE
1947

All Here

Spring had been reluctant to show her face this year, but now, at last, the sun shone warm over Clayton Village Cemetery. The surrounding fields exploded with ox-eye daisies, cornflowers and poppies, inviting a multitude of bees and butterflies. Songbirds competed for attention, swooping among the trees, landing on stones and markers to call for a mate or mark their territory.

On this afternoon, the school of Fiskares had gathered at the family plot for a small ceremony and a grand unveiling. The top of the Old Bear's marble obelisk was shrouded in canvas. Ropes were attached to two corners, the ends held by Major and Emil.

Kennet and Minor stood close together, hands shading their eyes as they gazed up.

Please let this be a good idea, Kennet thought. *At least not a terrible one.*

"Ready, Minor?" Emil said.

Minor gave a tight nod.

The old brothers pulled slowly, drawing the canvas off and revealing the tip of the obelisk. Perched on its ball filial was a stone bird. Her outstretched wings gleamed fresh, pure white against the rest of the weathered marble.

"Voilà," Major said. "Now we're all here."

Minor gave a little laugh as his hands went to his hips.

"You like it?" Kennet asked, his heart thumping beneath his ribs.

Minor just stared up, mouth poised in an open smile.

Emil dropped his end of the rope and came limping over. "It's long overdue."

"It's right on time," Minor said softly. His elbow touched Kennet's side. "This was your idea?"

"I'm entirely to blame."

"It's beautiful."

"Come around to this side. You can see *Lauren* is carved into one of the wings."

Minor's eyes blinked rapidly. "Look at that."

"It was Paps's idea."

"And also long overdue," Emil said.

Minor looked over at his uncle. "And what did you bring to the table?"

"Absolutely nothing," Major said gruffly, looking up at the bird.

"I disagree." Minor moved closer to his namesake, and each Erik put an arm around the other.

Emil cleared his throat. "Förlåt mig?" he asked his brother and son.

Forgive me?

Minor reached out his free arm, the wounded one. As Emil came close, Minor needed no help putting that arm on his father's shoulders. Healed and whole, he leaned and brushed a rough buss above Emil's ear. "Förlåten."

"Förlåten," Major echoed.

Kennet moved back toward the family, giving the three men their time. Marta and Trudy stood together, looking at the new bronze military marker at the base of Nalle's gravestone. Marta fussed with the flower arrangement while Trudy held her half-sister, Elsa, now a year old.

Our third surviving daughter, Kennet thought. *And you better stay, young lady. No leaving.*

Emilio and Kirsten were trimming the grass around Ingrid's stone. Lately they were doing everything together and looking at each other in a way that seemed, to Kennet, far beyond their years. Emilio was eighteen, Kirsten sixteen, but their combined presence pulsed with an affinity that felt ancient.

Ma told me Little would surprise us all. I guess I should stop being surprised by it.

Xandro's laughter pealed like a bell. He was walking along the top of the cemetery's stone wall. On one side, he held hands with Johnny MacIntyre. On the other, with Boyd O'Hara. For reasons known only to himself, Xandro addressed Johnny with the Swedish *onkel,* but used the Portuguese *tio* for Boyd.

What are uncles for?

"You look rather smug and accomplished," Astrid said behind Kennet.

"Because I'm both." He looked over his shoulder and smiled at his wife. "What do you think?"

"I knew you could do it."

She held their three-month-old son, who was asleep under the sunshine, his thumbs tucked tight beneath his fingers—aux poings fermés. The decision to name him Byron Erik had taken all of five seconds. Another gullgosse, the fine hair on his head was growing dark blond. When open, his eyes were an otherworldly shade of blue, flecked with gold. Like a river filled with sugar, treasure and stories.

He was conceived in a small hotel in New Orleans, Kennet mused, *along the mighty Mississippi where his own onkel-tio, Richard Hook, reigns as the river king.*

"Kom hit, lite fisk," Kennet said.

Come here, little fish.

He tucked Byron in the crook of one arm, and drew Astrid close with the other. He pressed his mouth against the crown of her head and stood still, a fisherman and pirate at the crossroads of the past and the future. Not all his wars were won, but he had gold around his neck, a Hook in his pocket, and the world in his grasp. He had everything right now.

And now backward is won.

Won and one.

One language and one perspective and one want that couldn't be misinterpreted or misunderstood.

One moment to hold in your hand and fold into memory.

"When the steeple bell says,
'Good night, sleep well,'
We'll thank the small hotel together.
We'll creep into our little shell
And we will thank the small hotel together."

—RODGERS & HART

Acknowledgments

Typically, during a book's early drafts, I rely on my twin towers Camille and Rach. Camille requested to be left completely in the dark so she could read this book the way she read *The Man I Love*— knowing absolutely nothing. So the role of author therapist (and poser of that horrible question, "Why do we care?") fell to Rach Lawrence, whom I thank with all my heart and soul. Darling golden girl, my treasured friend, I honestly don't know what I'd do without you.

I thank Julie and AJ, my oldest, youngest and finest. The best things that happened to me and JP, who I will never tire of looking at.

I thank my design team: Colleen who makes beautiful interiors and Tracy who makes beautiful covers. I also thank Katerina who generously donates her extraordinary jewelry collection for promotional graphics.

Thank you to the linguistic integrity team: Jenny and Emmy (Swedish), Francesca (Portuguese), Katerina (German) and a delightful Facebook crowdsource (Russian).

Kennet Fiskare's booty of silverware was taken from a story told by J. Ted Hartman, who served in combat with the 11th Armored Division from January 1944 to May of 1945. You can read Hartman's entire memoir in *Tank Driver: With the 11th Armored from the Battle of the Bulge to VE Day,* Indiana University Press, 2014.

Kennet's extraordinary fifteen minutes in the North Platte Canteen was inspired by Bob Greene's book, *Once Upon a Town: The Miracle of the North Platte Canteen,* Harper Collins, 2002. It was Pvt. Jack Manion who stood on the platform between cars and leaned out to touch his parents' hands as the troop train passed the little depot at Kearney, Nebraska.

The exceptional bravery, along with the tragic prosecution and incarceration of American homosexual troops in World War II is recounted in stark detail in *Coming Out Under Fire* by Allan Bérubé, University of North Carolina Press, 2010.

I had no idea of the legend of Napoleon's gold being lost in the St. Lawrence River until I read Thomas Pullyblank's *Napoleon's Gold: A Legend of the St. Lawrence River.* As well as giving me a golden idea, the book was full of real-life details that give a book authenticity. I read it just once, committed as much as possible to memory, and then didn't trust myself to look at it again. He's too good a writer, too much of an expert, and I'd either despair or plagiarize if I read it again.

In addition to the above books, online research was the life's blood of this novel. I really don't know how people wrote books before the Internet and it's hard to know who to thank for the almost magical amount of information available if you're willing to hunt for it. So…thank you, Internet?

All the Swedish folk and fairy tales were found in first editions of beautiful, old books scanned to and available from the Internet Archive website.

The story of the Fiskare brothers delivering a case of bootlegged whiskey to Irving Berlin and Bing Crosby was a real-life event experienced by Dan and Rolland Garnsey, who, according to their grandson Jeff, were "two of the most well-known, if not the most notorious bootleggers" in Clayton.

Ingrid Fiskare's experience as a YMCA volunteer during World War I was taken from the accounts of Marion Baldwin and Ethel Ash, both who ran YMCA canteens in France. You can read more about Baldwin in her book *Canteening Overseas 1917-1919*, and read more about Ash in the article "In Her Words: Women's Duty and Service in World War I," at the Smithsonian National Postal Service's website.

I could write an entire story about Marta's experience as a Harvey Girl. Maybe I will. But a really terrific book on the subject is *The Harvey Girls: Women Who Opened the West* by Lesley Poling-Kempes, Da Capo Press, 1994.

I am deeply indebted to the men who not only served valiantly with the 21st Armored Infantry Battalion, but wrote down their memories to preserve on the 11th Armored Division's website. Generous poetic license was taken as I pieced together various soldiers' testimonials, drawing in particular from the accounts of Ray Johnson and John Fague. Any resulting historical, logistical or military inaccuracies are purely mine.

Confession: I've never been to Clayton. I *planned* to, but then 2020 happened. So I owe tremendous gratitude to Thomas LaClair, the historian of the Village of Clayton, and his community Facebook page that is a treasure trove of photographs, scrapbooks, memorabilia and historical details. Also the Facebook page "1000 Island River Rats: Then and Now," which has amazing stories and pictures of the river, both modern and historical. I'm sure I didn't come close to portraying the true beauty and uniqueness of the Thousand Islands. In fact I'm confident I'll have disappointed several locals. But as with all my novels, I feel there's always a lot more I can get wrong than right. All I can do is give a book my respect, my curiosity, my love, my soul, my best intentions.

It is my sincere, golden hope I got it right.

—SLQR
Somers, New York
July 7, 2021

In Tribute

Members of B Company
21st Armored Infantry Battalion
Killed in Action

1st Lt.Wilbur F. Jones

1st Lt. Adolph V. Karkula

2nd Lt. Vincent M. Mulvaney

Pfc. Wallace G. Adkins Jr.

Pfc. James M. Lang

Pfc. John C. Allen

Pfc. Felix O. Lujan

Pvt. Ansel D. Bailey

Pvt. Anthony Mattozzi

S Sgt. Karl H. Bauder Jr.

Sgt. Robert McDaniel

Pfc. Kenneth R. Brust

Sgt. James C. McGriff

T Sgt. John O. Clark

Pfc. Richard G. Niklas

Pvt. George O. Cozad

Pfc. Mack C. Pardue Jr.

Pfc. Thomas P. Crider

Pvt. Steve Peigowski

Pfc. James O. Cust

S Sgt. Carl E. Petersen

T/3. Thomas G. Dierenger

Sgt. Hubert D. Reed

Pfc. Lyman B. Duke

Sgt. Thomas Rignola

Pfc. Wayne H. East

Pfc. Everett J. Riley

Pfc. Jack R. Elliott

Pvt. Murry Schneiweiss

Pfc. Robert A. Fordyce

S Sgt. Vernon W. Schultz

Sgt. Edwin J. Fraley

Pvt Stanley Smolak

Pfc. Paul L. Gentile

Pfc. Henry C. Stascsyk

Pfc. Louis A. Grossen

Pfc. Roy E. Stout

Pvt. Frank W. Harris

S Sgt. Ralph Swenson

Pfc. Benjamin J. Hewit

Pfc. Harold M. Veal

Pfc. Frederick J. Huddleston

Pvt. Earl J. White

Pfc. Benjamin Berkstra

Pfc. Hoyt T. Willard

Pfc. William D. Kidney Jr.

Pfc. Arthur L. Wright Jr.

T/4. Ezra L. Vaughn

In Imagination:
Kennet's Unit

1st Lt. George West, Platoon Commander
2nd Lt. Peter Jorgensson, Platoon Leader

Squad 1

Able
†Sgt. Thomas "Monty" Montenegro, Squad Leader and Scout Rifleman
†Pfc. Jacob Silver, Squad Assistant and Scout Rifleman
†Pvt. Michael Nichols, Scout Rifleman

Baker
Pfc. Boyd O'Hara, Senior BAR
†Pvt. Arnold Schmitt, Senior BAR
Pvt. Nolen Anderson, Assistant BAR
†Pvt. Alfred "Marty" Martin, Ammunition Bearer

Charlie
Cpl. Charles Riley, Squad Assistant and Scout Rifleman
Pvt. Ralph Ingle, Rifleman
Pvt. Henry "Hank" Berliner, Rifleman
Pvt. Kennet "Fish" Fiskare, Rifleman
†Pvt. Christopher "Jock" Fragiacomo, Rifleman
†Pvt. Richard Hook, Rifleman

Squad 2

Able

Sgt. James Hoffman, Squad Leader and Scout Rifleman

Pvt. Wojtek "Dizzy" Dziedzice, Scout Rifleman

Pvt. Guy "Baby" Babbiolamente, Scout Rifleman

Baker

†Cpl. John Ellis, Senior BAR

Pfc. Warren "Squirt" Ellis, Senior BAR

Pvt. Anthony "Squad Car" Losquadro, Assistant BAR

Pvt. Benjamin "Free Fall" Friefeld, Ammunition Bearer

Charlie

†Cpl. Peter von Asselt, Squad Assistant, Rifleman

Pfc. Nicholas Maslov, Rifleman

†Pfc. Marco Malinda, Rifleman

†Pvt. Nathan Eisenstein, Rifleman

About the Author

A former professional dancer and teacher, Suanne Laqueur went from choreographing music to choreographing words, writing stories that appeal to the passions of all readers, crossing gender, age and genre. As a devoted mental health advocate, her novels focus on both romantic and familial relationships, as well as psychology, PTSD and generational trauma.

Laqueur's novel *An Exaltation of Larks* was the grand prize winner in the 2017 Writer's Digest Book Awards and took first place in the 2019 North Street Book Prize. Her debut novel *The Man I Love* won a gold medal in the 2015 Readers' Favorite Book Awards and was named Best Debut in the Feathered Quill Book Awards. Her follow-up novel, *Give Me Your Answer True*, was also a gold medal winner at the 2016 RFBA.

Laqueur graduated from Alfred University with a double major in dance and theater. She taught at the Carol Bierman School of Ballet Arts in Croton-on-Hudson for ten years. An avid reader, cook and gardener, she started her blog EatsReadsThinks in 2010.

Suanne lives in Westchester County, New York with her husband and two children.

Also by Suanne Laqueur

A Small Hotel

THE FISH TALES

The Man I Love
Give Me Your Answer True
Here to Stay
The Ones That Got Away
Daisy, Daisy

VENERY

An Exaltation of Larks
A Charm of Finches
A Scarcity of Condors
The Voyages of Trueblood Cay
Tales from Cushman Row
A Plump of Woodcocks

SHORTS

Love & Bravery: Sixteen Stories
An Evening at the Hotel

ANTHOLOGIES

Flesh Fiction